ABOUT THE AUTHOR

Daniel James is a London born writer residing in Toronto at the release of his debut novel.

THE SAME LEDGE

DANIEL JAMES

Copyright © 2020 Daniel James.

All rights reserved. No part of this book may be reproduced, stored, or transmitted by any means—whether auditory, graphic, mechanical, or electronic—without written permission of the author, except in the case of brief excerpts used in critical articles and reviews. Unauthorized reproduction of any part of this work is illegal and is punishable by law.

This is a work of fiction. All of the characters, names, incidents, organizations, and dialogue in this novel are either the products of the author's imagination or are used fictitiously.

ISBN: 978-1-71694-271-6 (sc)
ISBN: 978-1-71694-270-9 (e)

Library of Congress Control Number: 2020907604

Because of the dynamic nature of the Internet, any web addresses or links contained in this book may have changed since publication and may no longer be valid. The views expressed in this work are solely those of the author and do not necessarily reflect the views of the publisher, and the publisher hereby disclaims any responsibility for them.

Any people depicted in stock imagery provided by Getty Images are models, and such images are being used for illustrative purposes only.
Certain stock imagery © Getty Images.

Lulu Publishing Services rev. date: 05/14\/2020

ACKNOWLEDGEMENT

For my family; it isn't worth it without you.
For my siblings; thank you for protecting me.

It always seems to start with a question: what are you doing here? Not in a meaningful existential way at first but questioning what you are doing, right this second what's the point, why even bother? The existential meaning of life comes after, when you are so far down you no longer see the light.

1

He sat on the bed, his back leaning against the headboard, two misshapen pillows stuffed against his body. His legs stretched out and feet crossed over like hands giving themselves up for arrest. The duvet lay unkempt on the other half of the bed, a body of colours and feathers. He stared blankly at the wall opposite, listening to the gentle hum of traffic; the car starts in the far corner of the room and works its way past his right ear, disappearing into the night as if it never existed at all.

He thinks of being a kid again; he thinks of Cameron. He thinks of what he should be and what he is not. He wants to know where he lost his way and why he cared so much. The past becomes a ghost that talks to him in his sleep. Sleep becomes harder to find; it's a dream to dream but one turns two and the bed felt like fire. The pillow becomes a body; heavy and hot, the dreams move slowly towards the open window. Tonight is different. Tonight, he wants to sleep and not wake up.

The thought of Cameron conjures the ghosts that haunt his dreams. Steven is always there – a child lost in the darkness reaching for his hand as he turns away. Steven calling his name. Not in an angry or desperate way, not asking for help, but his name simply stated as a fact without any question mark.

"Michael."

"Sorry Steven, you're not a winner."

He uncrossed his legs and swivelled on the white hotel sheets, planting both feet into the green carpet. He rose and walked towards the bathroom. Fragments of the past crashed against the inside of his skull like waves on a pier. Aiming through habit more than concentration, the splatter of urine flicked against the white surface of the bowl, delicately flicking the rim enough for him to feel the gentle splash on his feet.

He moved to the window overlooking the crowded street below. Sao Paulo was a city of different faces – the streetlamps were attached to wires that hung menacingly over badly kept streets raining light down onto the rich and the poor.

He wondered what it would be like to fall to the pavement ten storeys below, what he would feel as he fell through the air. Fear? Regret? He thought of Steven again, desperate to know his last thoughts as he became drowsy from the pills.

MICHAEL

2

It was September first. They had spent much of the day putting things into boxes. The room he had spent his childhood in was desolate; just walls and a carpet. They had outgrown the two-storey terrace house, lost in a network of streets behind the main jugular of Battersea. The street was quiet as it always was on a weekend, its smattering of low-income families muted somehow, its portion of the south London aged shuffling between their smoky homes and the corner shop. London was divided between the rich and the poor and what started as a means to reduce the number of slums in London became a means to fortify them with bricks. Streets of poorly kept and poorly maintained houses slept in the back streets of the country's capital, out of sight and out of mind. The estates of terrace houses or large ugly tower blocks boasted their own facilities, almost as if there was a need to reduce the risk of the residents slipping out of the shadow of their homes and wandering into the streets of London proper. The spaces were equipped with schools, grocery shops and laundrettes; critical organs to the heartbeat of the estate. Communication posts for the elderly and life buoys for the families that found navigating through London almost as expensive as living there.

In the estate, a small parade of shops sat back from the pavement containing a newsagent, the laundrette and a bakery. The newsagent's carpets were black with age and the strain of shuffling slippers but, for the kids here, it was a paradise. The shop counter was stacked high with penny sweets brightly shimmering. He would run side by side with his brother from their house two streets over. Their sweaty fists grasped twenty or fifty pence coins, money from the tooth fairy or a birthday exchanged for a set of stickers, a fluorescent toy or a handful of sweets wrapped snugly in their paper bag with the top rolled over.

Now he stood in a new room in a new house no more than ten minutes driving from the old. These houses were managed by a trust that was responsible for the maintenance. It had been almost eight years since his sister was born and five years since their mum had applied for a bigger home for the six of them. He would still share his life and room with his older brother.

The house stood on a cul-de-sac under the shadow of a tower block in the council estate. Council estates seemed to be darker places than housing estates. The parade of shops was buried under the mass of the tower block with a web of underground passages that fell completely dark at night. A home to the poorest, those most in need and those willing to take everything from you at knifepoint. This place was different. Opposite there was a patch of grass almost the size of a football pitch. The edges were lined with tall trees; from the highest windows of the house you could imagine you were looking over a park. There was a sign with 'NO BALL GAMES' clipped to the lamp posts and below that a black-and-white image of a dog squatting down with the words 'NO FOULING' written beneath him. Despite this there was usually a group of kids kicking a ball between each other, no more than ten years old. 'NO FOULING' would become an ongoing joke as they played. The edge of the green was home to a small playground, fenced with black iron bars, a ramshackle collection of bushes squeezed between even more iron bars. Balconies overlooked the grass with washing hanging to dry. It gave the impression of a community. Here, at least, was the illusion of safety.

The house itself was painted white with sash windows. Behind, the tower block loomed; brown brick and greying plastic window frames. In some ways, the new house was little different to the one they'd left behind, except the windows were bigger and the rooms seemed brighter. Maybe that was just how he felt. The darkness had yet to descend on this house. Hope was still alive.

His brother came up behind him with a handful of small fluorescent toys that they had collected together from cereal boxes or bought at the corner shop. His hair, a dark brown, flopped around his ears, a striking contrast to his blue eyes. Physically they were of a similar height and build. If anything, William was slightly shorter despite being eighteen months older.

"Look what I got out of the boxes," he said gleefully, holding out his hands showing the fluorescent toys. "Shall we play something?"

"Like what?"

"Like Penny-up-the-wall."

They spent the next two hours standing in the doorway throwing the toys against the opposite wall. It was a game that they had seen the older boys play at school, betting to see who could get closest to the wall with the winner taking all the coins.

3

As September came drifting to a close there were spaces all over the house as their belongings stretched to fill the rooms. Michael started school. The building was a grotesque square structure that had more in common with a factory. It had large windows framed in white plastic and a ventilation tube exiting from the roof like an industrial chimney. It was one of the lowest ranked in London. Those that could afford to, sent their children to other schools by means fair or foul. The families with no money or kids that punched the shit out of other kids ended up here. London, like many heavily populated cities, was a place where money talked, and only money meant choices.

His home and school were within touching distance of the main street which cut through Battersea, starting from Wandsworth and forming a direct route to Vauxhall; four miles of heavy traffic and black air. Less than half a mile apart, the entrance of the school cowered from tower blocks of council flats. The playground sat on the main street where it was possible to see through the black diamond wire mesh fence that stood twelve feet in the air. Enclosed inside, on the grey concrete with faded games painted into the cracking canvas, boys played with footballs using a crooked white frame cemented into the ground as a goal and girls clustered in groups near the fence.

He had met Steven on the first day, a blur of new classes and new rooms, corridors swarming with older kids in blazers rolled up to the elbow. Each change in lesson was an experience of navigating his way through the corridors desperate not to be trampled and desperate not to be noticed. Michael was a small studious boy, so slight in frame his bones stood out on his flat chest and ribs. He was under average height for his age, though he would explode in height before his sixteenth birthday, which would leave him with stretch marks on his hips and aching pains in his knees. His hair was a mop of thick red, unkempt and forgotten on top of his head, and freckles dotted across his small button nose and cheeks. The corridors and rooms were decked with students in brand new uniforms that seemed to effortlessly fit their bodies. He compared this to his own uniform; the trousers crumpled in rolls at his new black boots his mum had bought on offer from Clarkes, his blazer finished only slightly above his knees and the sleeves left only his thin pale fingers poking out like worms. He went to school that first day with Stephen King's *It* stuffed in the pocket of his blazer, the pages ruffled and curling. He read it in the corridors, trying to focus on the words as he was bumped from side to side like a pinball off the shoulders of taller kids.

In amongst the chaos, he had found Steven, a chubby kid with a round face and short shaven dark hair. Running late, after losing track of the door numbers, he ran into the science lab and slumped quickly into an empty chair near the front of the class, swinging his oversized backpack onto the desk. He looked at the boy next to him, blue eyes staring absently at the whiteboard. They sat this way for most of the class, quietly watching the black pen squeak notes onto a greying board. Mrs. Canterbury swiped at the words on the board with an eraser almost as quickly as she wrote them.

He turned to Steven, studied his face for a few seconds, watching as he quickly and expertly captured the last of the notes before they disappeared. "Can I look at your notes?" MIchael whispered.

Steven turned to him. Michael waited. Finally, he turned the book at an angle so that Michael could see, noting "X-men" scribbled in the corner of the pad in thick patterned letters.

"You like X-men?"

Steven studied his face again, as if waiting for the joke. Michael held his stare, waiting patiently for a response.

"Yeah," he said softly.

"Cool. I really like Cyclops."

They whispered quietly to one another, stopping regularly when the teacher's eyes followed the sound, sharing their favourite X-men and recounting storylines. When the bell chimed to signal the end of the class, they continued to talk whilst packing their books into their backpacks and walking to their next class.

They passed the year in each other's company, enduring the few lessons they didn't have together. Weekends meant a trip to the comic store, its aging blue exterior and large windows filled with colourful editions of Spider-Man, Superman and X-men. The comics stacked and lined deep shelves, where they would both, mostly in silence, flick through the books, rolling their fingers across the smooth plastic cases. After they had made their purchases, they would sit together on a park bench, their eyes flicking through the colourful artwork, absorbing the action-packed storylines. They would swap over the comics when they had finished and read each other's.

In the evenings they sat on Steven's single bed playing on a Sega Megadrive that was wedged under the mountain of games underneath an old box colour television. The room filled with the clacking buttons of the controllers and the gentle music of Alex the Kid, like a song made with a single finger on a keyboard. Some evenings he would stay for dinner, eating on a small table with Steven and his dad, their elbows almost touching.

One evening when Michael had asked about the collection of wigs glimpsed through the open door of Steven's dad's bedroom, Steven told him his mum had died the previous year. Cancer. Michael had read about cancer in the news but never known anyone that had it. People died from it, he knew that much. The look on Steven's face as he turned back to the computer game told him how raw it was.

Their friendship was built around the quiet moments. They would never discuss emotions or ask each other for profound advice; rules that they had mutually agreed to without ever discussing them. Later, as an adult, he would recognise that the thing that they shared most was their level on a social structure. Like London, divided between the rich, the poor and those desperate to be rich; school was divided into groups. It wasn't as cliché as an American teen movie but there were the kids that studied hard enough and confined themselves to the library, there were the boys that played a lot of sport and those that spent most of their times with groups of girls. There were layers and layers of groups and cliques and there were kids that were in none of these groups. That was his place. He would ghost through hallways, unrecognised, unaware. He liked it this way for a while, it allowed him to get through the first year without attracting too much attention, but it was a lonely existence. Steven kept him company but sometimes that wasn't enough. It was fine to spend the days with a quiet, unassuming boy that would agree with everything he said but sometimes he wanted someone different to notice him.

It was inevitable they would get bullied. His name was James Burrell. It started with swiping a Spider-Man comic from Steven's hands as he sat cross legged on the floor, his back pressed against the wire fence. Michael watched his face crinkle and his eyes observe the empty space between his hands where Spider-Man had been swinging from the buildings only seconds before.

"Give it back," he heard Steven say softly. Burrell was pretending to read the comic, his friends gathered behind him craning to see the pictures, laughing. They were all laughing. The boys gathered around the comic book, the girls leaning against the fence with their ties so short they barely fell lower than their flat chests.

"What was that, Uncle Festa?"

More laughing, rapturous back slapping. The girls now showing more interest in the comedy show, forming a semi-circle at Steven's side.

"Give it back," he almost whimpered, slowly getting to his feet. Michael watched, still sat on the floor, his pale face flicking between Steven and Burrell.

"Or what?" Burrell offered, staring intently at Steven, stepping forward with the comic curled up in his hand. Michael could feel Steven squirming at the sight of the comic book. It was sacrilege to roll it so roughly. Something seemed to sweep across his face as if he thought for an instant of laying the gap-toothed kid flat but then thought better of it, shrinking back against the fence as Burrell stepped further forward. His shadow loomed over the pair of them.

"I heard yor mum's got cancer, can you catch it?" Burrell looked at the comic book in his hand. "Can I catch it from this?" he said, his face screwing up with disgust.

Steven looked down at his feet, tears pricking the corner of his eyes as the growing crowd screamed with laughter. Burrell tore the comic in half, throwing it to the floor before wiping his hands on Steven's sweater. Steven stayed still and let him finish before Burrell turned and chased his friends with his hands out in front of him. The crowd dispersed, screaming and laughing, threatening to give each other cancer, passing it around like a game of *tag*. Steven quietly picked up the shredded comic book and sat down again next to Michael.

"You ok?" Michael whispered.

Wasn't long before Burrell was returning regularly to get his fix of humiliation. One day, Michael saw him, striding towards them, his gapped-tooth grin spread across his face, his eyes narrowed and focussed on Steven. Michael nudged Steven in the ribs. He raised his round head and followed Michael's gaze. They slid their comics into their backpacks, shrugging the shoulder straps on and made to leave. Burrell reached Michael first, grabbing his backpack and almost yanking him off his feet before kicking away his legs. He planted a kick in his stomach. The air escaped his lungs, releasing a breathless *oof* sound. He crouched over, his mouth dry and gasping for breath. Tears pricked the corners of his eyes, he focussed on holding them in. He couldn't show them that he wanted to cry no matter how hard he was hit, a trick he learnt courtesy of his stepdad's hands and stick. He steadied his breathing and slowly clambered to his feet. Steven watched him; his fingers wrapped around the straps of his backpack. His beady blue eyes caught Michael's. *He does look like Uncle Festa*, Michael thought. He turned and looked Burrell in the eyes, his face expressionless and unmoved. He dropped his hands from his stomach and let them hang loosely at his side.

"Didn't hurt," he said.

"He's like the Terminator," the kid almost screamed, pointing at Michael. He stepped forward and punched him firmly on the upper arm. Michael flinched, reeling back. He rubbed his arm once, feeling the muscle burn as it went numb, before letting his hands drop again. He glared again at the bigger boy; his face motionless.

"You see?" Burrell turned to the other boys, searching for approval.

They sniggered like jackals. One of them stepped forward and thumped a fist into Michael's chest. A crowd had gathered, baying for violence. Steven looked at his shoes, unsure what to do. The three boys shared a look and a wicked smile spread across their faces. They had a crowd to please. The punches came quickly, thumping into his chest and arms like stones. He dropped to the floor, his hands protecting his face, another trick he learnt at home. The boys grunted, raining punches until eventually they got tired and the crowd got bored. Michael lay curled up on the concrete as the crowd dispersed. He felt Steven's shadow loom over him, his thumbs still clipped into his backpack.

"You ok?"

"Yeah," he said as he dusted the dirt from his trousers and sweater.

The beatings continued throughout the winter and deep into the spring. He wore long-sleeve shirts even on the warm days to disguise the red knuckle marks on his chest and arms. When they turned purple and yellow, he covered them up with a dusting of his mum's makeup. The punches became harder and more frequent. More boys joined in desperate to make him cry, laughing and screaming in a frenzied mob and still he choked back the tears. He turned the pain inwards and it became frustration and the frustration turned to anger, which grew in him like a tumour.

At school, his mind sought a distraction, itching for chaos. Steven watched with his sunken eyes as Michael threw balled-up bits of paper at Mrs Canterbury's turned back. He shook his head in disappointment as Michael soaked up the laughter in class and he stayed quiet when Michael spent late afternoons in detention, waiting for him quietly outside the door like an obedient dog.

Michael became accustomed to the lectures in quiet classrooms from angry teachers, his mum sat in silence next to him, hands folded in her lap. She watched him as he was given a stern talking to, her lips so tight together that her mouth was no more than a line on her face. He mimicked her stance, his head lowered and nodding at the right moments. They would drive home in silence afterwards and each time she seemed hunched further over the wheel as if the weight of the air lay thick on her back.

It was after the fifth trip back from the school, when his mum followed him up the stairs. She sat him down on the lower bunk in their room, her neck arched to keep from banging her head on the wooden base of the bed above. She looked at him intently for a moment, studying his face.

"Do you want to change schools?" she said finally.

He looked at his hands, the words slowly shifting around his head like a washing machine. He studied the lines of his knuckles and his smooth rounded fingernails.

"Well?" she pushed softly.

He agreed because he was tired. The bruises no longer had the time to heal before red marks were punched over them, doubling their size. The crowds that laughed with him as he mocked the teachers were the same crowds that gathered to see if someone could make him cry. He was so tired of trying to please them. He was relieved to be able to leave it all behind. The fear of starting again was overshadowed by the burnout he felt in the back of his mind and the desire to sleep without rolling over and awakening an angry bruise.

Steven stared at the remaining half a sandwich in his lunchbox. They continued to eat in silence before Steven spoke again. "Don't you like it here?" His voice was gruff, his tone downbeat.

"No. Do you?" The question was rhetorical. He couldn't imagine Steven enjoyed coming to school here every day.

"It's ok."

More silence.

"Did I piss you off?" He still didn't look up from his sandwich.

"No, why do you think that?"

"Dunno."

"No. It's a chance to get out of here."

"Not for me." He started to nibble on the edges of the sandwich.

They spent the first few weeks of the summer together. The days spent walking through department stores and the evenings sitting cross-legged on Steven's bed playing computer games talking about everything and nothing. Steven's dad had won free tickets to Alton Towers with work and offered them to Steven to share with all his friends. In the absence of friends, they had ended up taking the journey to Derby together in the back of his dad's Ford Escort. The day was spent queuing hours for short and fast rides and eating hamburgers, doughnuts and slurping on slushies to cool off in the hot June sun. It was a day that would live long in his memory and one he would relive as an adult, looking for signs and clues that the boy laughing beside him that day was the same boy he would next see in a coffin.

4

He often thought that changing school was a crossroad in his life that would ensure his destiny would intertwine with Cameron's. Their past became the stone that kept them anchored together, a quiet desperate need to find a companion amongst the chaos. He remembered as a kid that there was always a moment before his mum left the house, a moment where they would all wait in hope that she would take them with her. He would cry deep drawn-out sobs as the door clicked shut with the beady eyes of his stepdad watching over him, like a shark waiting for its moment. Terry had a short fuse and a quick hand. It didn't take much to trigger him, but they knew it was worse when the house emptied of an audience.

Once the door clicked shut, a tense shadow descended over the house. The click was the signal to scatter like cockroaches into the safety of their rooms where they held their breath, fearful that even the sound of moving air would bring him to them. He always came. Opening the door with a firm shove, letting it swing open and crash into the wall behind. A dramatic entrance for the small man with the wispy goatee, his hair pulled back in a ponytail, his shape in the doorway seeming to block out the light in the hall. The first strike would be quick and painful. The whistle and crack of his walking stick and a streak of pain coursing up the thigh. In the early days, they would cry. *I'll give you something to cry about.* Eyes firmly fixed on theirs, waiting to strike again.

For fifteen years, the man that they had come to know as a father served out helpings of wrath from his stick or fist. The mark stayed with each of them far longer, an unwanted guest that would make victims of them all, slowly chipping away until it was big enough to destroy them from the inside.

For Terry, the beginning of the end came on the night Ben was born. It was August; almost a year since they had moved to the new house. Ben was born in a hospital further south of Battersea, near Tooting. The day clear and bright, the contractions started intensifying as the afternoon settled in. As his mum sat on the sofa, eyes closed and both palms flat against her rounded stomach, beads of sweat broke out on her forehead; her hair was tied neatly away from her face. His stepdad was limping up the stairs without a stick in a frantic side-to-side motion. Michael sat quietly on the floor, watching whilst Terry wore an anxious, almost hopeless expression, managing to manoeuvre the stairs with surprising agility. He soon emerged with a dark blue holdall, overflowing with white baby clothes and muslin cloths. He helped her off the sofa, pulling firmly on her hand whilst keeping one arm pressed against his lower back. They left the house, a supportive arm curled around her back, moving slowly towards the large blue Nissan that waited outside with the passenger door open. Michael watched from the doorway as the car accelerated down the cul-de-sac, the noise of the engine slowly fading as it approached the end of the road and turned left before disappearing from sight.

Much later, Terry returned alone. They heard the rumble of the car, the grinding of gears as he threw the car into reverse and the hum of the engine as he slowly backed it into the empty space outside the house. There was a flutter of activity as the three of them shuffled quickly through the living-room space gathering stray toys and collapsing quietly, cross-legged and upright, on the jaded carpet in front of the television. Their eyes were trained on the glowing colours that flashed across the dimming room. They watched Tom chasing Jerry without watching at all, listening for the key in the lock and the gentle rhythmic thud of the walking stick on the floor. As the door opened, they felt the gust of air sweep through the room. He looked tired and his face was long and pale, but his eyes scanned the room looking for something out of place, a broken ornament or a smashed mirror.

"What you doing?" He spoke gruffly, staring intently at all of them.

"Watching TV." William spoke first, not breaking his gaze.

The soft glow of the television continued to dance and change shape, casting shadows on the wall like laughing demons.

"We're going to the hospital," he spat.

"Now?" William offered, his face innocent and eyes wide.

Terry looked back, gripping the top of his walking stick tightly enough to turn his knuckles white. "Yes. Now."

With army-like precision, they jumped to their feet and, single file, bound up the stairs to tug on battered trainers and hand-me-down jackets.

The hospital room was a large square with pale blue floors, white walls and ceilings. It was divided into eight cubicles separated by white plastic curtains that rattled on railings as they swished open and closed. Two of the cubicles were empty; curtains pulled back revealing tall single beds supported with wheels. Metal levers with white globes for handles hung from the sides. The rest of the rooms remained hidden by the plastic curtains. Terry walked to the third on the right and pulled the curtain back with a soft swish. Inside, their mum lay asleep, her head turned to one side and her hazel brown hair covering two thirds of her face. Only her eye and nose were visible. In her arms was a blue hospital blanket wrapped tightly around a small bright pink face.

Michael watched the small face twitch, marvelling at the thousands of small dots that spread across his nose and cheeks and the folds of skin that wrinkled his hands, at the long -like fingers opened and closed intermittently. Michael placed a finger in the wrinkly palm and smiled as it closed like a Venus flytrap. They spent an hour taking turns to hold the baby, softly whispering so as not to wake him, stroking his soft hands, feet and face. When it was time to leave, their mother kissed them all individually and they left the way they had come. The beautiful happy moments were over. Their time had passed, and they were punching the button of the lift, taking in the chemical smell that drifted from room to room in the hospital and watching, longingly, as the plastic curtain of their mum's room disappeared down the bright hospital corridor.

The journey home was quiet; a subdued atmosphere filled the car, each of them sat silently, lost in their own thoughts, their faces turned towards the window. It was late and the yellow glow of the streetlamps ran across their faces in rhythmic pulses as the Nissan made its way through the London streets.

"Teeth. Bed," Terry growled as he flicked the lights on in the hallway.

The light ushered away the shadows but still the darkness loomed. They all took the stairs slowly, heads lowered, relieved to be heading towards a sleep that kept them away from him. The boys were quickly changed into pyjamas and heading towards the bathroom to brush their teeth. William plucked a water gun from the bathtub. The yellow handle attached to the fluorescent green barrel still contained water. Smiling to himself, he crept behind Michael. Michael was staring at the mirror, his teeth clenched, and his mouth filled with white foam. A cold jet of water filled his ear. He screamed out loud with surprise but couldn't move in time to avoid the second shot that hit him in the cheek. "DON'T!" he cried out, a smile spread over his face. The fourth and fifth burst of water hit his face as he tried to turn away. Their shrill laughter filled the room.

He looked at his reflection in the hotel window. He could make out the globe light dangled above his darkened self like a halo, hovering above the dark street below. The memory drew a frown across his face. *Just boys*, he thought. *Boys being boys. Why did he get so angry?*

The thud of the walking stick on the first stair was enough to make them both spin and stare anxiously at the bathroom door. William leant over and quickly returned the gun back to the bathtub, desperate not to make any noise. The head of their stepdad appeared through the bannisters.

"What the fuck are you doing?" he shouted, turning the corner of the staircase.

His face was taut as if his skull was pulling itself out of skin and his eyes wide, his glasses balanced delicately on the tip of his nose. He held his walking stick loosely by the handle with a firm grip around the bannister.

"Nothing." Michael spoke first, his voice meek.

The question was rhetorical; he was moving fast towards them and showed no signs of slowing. His face was red, and his lips pulled back revealed his clenched teeth. They started to back away towards the wall until they felt the solid brick against their backs. William stood in front of his younger brother, his arm stretched out to keep Michael behind him. Michael cowered until his backside touched the wall and he slid down into the corner. There was a whistle through the air and the walking stick came crashing down on his brother's right arm. Turning his face away and clenching his fist, William took the first blow on the bicep. He stumbled backwards, tripping over Michael, and fell on top of him. The second strike caught William on the thigh. He raised his arms to protect his face, adopting the foetal position with Michael stuck beneath him, shielded from the blows. A third and fourth blow rained down, hitting him in the ribs and his back between the shoulder blades as he tried to turn away from the frenzied attack. Underneath him, Michael was screaming.

"Shut up. Shut… the… fuck… up!" Terry swung the stick between words as if banging a drum, his breath was short. He was tiring; sweat had broken out on his forehead in clear bubbles.

"STOP! DON'T TOUCH MY FUCKING BROTHERS!"

The scream came from behind them, piercing the house and freezing the scene in front as if it had the ability to stop time. The stick paused in the air above Terry's head; slowly he rotated to look at Sarah. The stick stayed in the air, his eyes bulged in their sockets and his teeth were still clenched. The sentiment of her words was not lost in that moment. He was not their father, that was clear, and these boys were not his sons.

"What did you say?" He was panting hard; he lowered the stick and placed the black rubber tip onto the tiled bathroom floor.

"Don't touch my fucking brothers," she repeated. Her finger still pointed at him.

He rotated his body fully and took a step towards her. She stood her ground, hand raised, finger pointed. He stood one foot in front of the other, stick firmly planted in the ground. They stood this way for a second or two like a paused scene in a movie before he moved forward. Her confidence faltered. She lowered her hand, took a long look into his eyes and turned to run. Taking the stairs at speed, she spun the corner using her hand as a pivot on the rail of the bannister. She stopped, looking through the gaps in the bannister at his fierce face and the small bodies crumpled in the corner, peering through hands held up for protection.

"Don't you touch them!" she shouted again through the bannisters.

The tears stung her eyes, making them seem bright and lucid before they broke free and rolled down her cheeks. Her red hair was pulled back in a bun at the back of her head, the sweat visible on her forehead. The sound of her voice broke his trance. He thundered forward like a three-legged machine, the walking stick used to propel the rest of his frame forward with pace. He was less than 5"8', broad around the shoulders and lean for his age. At the sight of him moving towards her, she ran. Darting down the stairs two at a time and jumping the last four, she opened the front door and slammed it shut behind her. The thud boomed through the house, shaking the frame. Michael heard the metal gate crash shut as Terry's head disappeared from view. He stumbled down the stairs after her.

The two boys heard the front door open again, slowly, letting the cold air drift up the stairs. It blew softly against their bare feet before the click of lock broke the strange moment of calm.

5

Michael lay on the bedroom floor, absently rotating a toy in his hand. The morning had been filled with banging doors, raised voices and then deathly anxious quiet. He stayed quiet, letting the morning pass by, slowly feeling the glossed plastic of the toy. He became absorbed into its colours and texture. The Nissan had set off early that morning to pick his mum up from the hospital. She had arrived home with the small baby wrapped in a blanket swinging in the car seat she gripped firmly by the handle. The baby's black eyes stared blankly at the room around him. The moment should have been filled with joy, a homecoming for mother and new-born; instead, he was transferred from car seat to cot and left alone to watch an animal mobile spin gently above his head as the remainder of the family became wrought with worry for Sarah. The early morning became late morning, late morning slipped into midday. It was almost one in the afternoon when the doorbell shrilled. Michael sat up, watching his mum move uncomfortably towards the door. When it opened, she let out a gasp. It was doused in relief. There was loud talking and crying. He pulled himself on his backside and swung his feet out from underneath him, perching in the doorway, his arms wrapped around his legs and his chin resting on his forearms. He could just make out the figures stood in the doorway; two broad-shouldered police officers, their hands hooked onto their belts like modern-day sheriffs, one of them talking to his mum in a soft tone. His mum stood in front of them with an arm hooked around Sarah's shoulders. Sarah's head was lowered, her red hair still tied back in a bun, but loose strands now covered her face. The sound of the police voices drifted up the stairs as they said their goodbyes, then he followed the sound of the footsteps and the soft clink of the gate as one of the officers pulled it closed behind him. As the door shut, his mum and Sarah moved towards the living room. Terry stood in the corridor, silently watching the scene. Michael had become a voyeur, watching the characters perform in front of him as the plot took shape.

Five minutes later, Sarah walked out of the living room, glancing at Terry before she moved up the stairs. He stood motionless, his eyes scanning her face. She passed Michael as he sat at the open door. He tried to catch her eye, to give her a smile as a sign of gratitude, but her eyes were trained on the faded carpet of the stairs, her face sad and exhausted. Michael waited for her to pass. He glanced down at the space where Terry had stood moments before. It was empty. His shadow passed through the doorway to the living room. Michael felt safer. He followed Sarah; he wanted to be near her to make sure she was safe like she had done for them. When he arrived at her bedroom, she was sat in bed, the covers pulled over her knees. He let himself in without asking and sat quietly at the foot of the bed.

"You ok?" he started, unsure how to fill the silence. She nodded, her eyes never leaving her hands which sat limply in her lap. "Where did you go?"

She looked up at him, her eyes flooding with tears. Michael stared wordlessly, feeling powerless and wishing he hadn't followed her to the room. "I dunno," she said finally. The tears spilled over and left glistening snail tracks down her cheeks. "Mum's gonna be so angry."

"Why?" He felt like he was falling into a rabbit hole, but he needed to know what she was hiding.

"Some guy. He made me go back to his place. He had a knife." Her words trailed off, she resumed staring at her open hands.

Michael watched his mum expertly remove the nappy from the baby's hips, keeping the feet in the air between her fingers as she reached towards the wet wipes with her free hand. He sat quietly, squeezing the tip of his thumb.

"You ok?" She looked down at him. He looked at her, nodded slowly and gazed at his feet.

"You sure?" she persisted. His green eyes met hers.

"Sarah told me not to tell you."

She stopped cold, letting go of the baby's legs. They came to a rest on the soft towel. Michael watched his legs kick slowly at the air. "What is it? You can tell me." She looked at him and through him. Almost as if she were looking deep into his mind, picking away at the thoughts buried inside. He felt the pressure of her gaze, the secret bubbled in him, forming in his stomach until he felt he could do no more than vomit it out.

As he spoke, he watched the colour drain for her face, her hand raised, shaking and covered her open mouth. He felt a knot in his stomach, unsure if he was doing the right thing or making everything worse. The baby's naked legs continued to ride its imaginary bicycle.

"Watch him," she said when he had finally relayed Sarah's story. He watched her stride up the stairs two at a time. Michael stood up slowly, his eyes trained on the baby. He ran the back of his hand softly down the infant's face.

Pushing through the bathroom door, she found her daughter sat upright in the bathtub. The water splashed around her mid-section as she scrubbed frantically at her body with a sponge. She was sobbing; her red eyes met her mum's and there were no words to share.

"Mum," she cried softly.

His mum knelt at the bathtub, her knees thumping on the soft rug, she leant forward and threw her arms around her daughter, squeezing her body close to her chest. The water soaked through her t-shirt as she held her head tight into the nook of her shoulder. She, too, started to cry.

6

It was a few years before he would cross paths with Cameron. Terry had been gone more than a year. The beatings had stopped but his ghost haunted the house like a dark cloud that refused to shift. His eyes peered from every shadow and every open cupboard. Michael was taller, lean and pale, his face no longer carrying the rubbery quality of youth.

He left the train station into a dark passage that led towards the main road. He smelt the cooking from the African Kenkey shop before he turned the corner. The smell of cooking fish made his eyes water and caught at the back of his throat. He kept his eyes trained on the small wooden bench, pushed sadly against the wall of the church, its wood dark with damp and tinged with green moss creeping up the legs and arms. He would meet Cameron at this same bench ten years later, when both of their lives had changed beyond recognition.

As he turned into his street, the rain had left the streets dark, but the lamps allowed him to see into the playground. There were a handful of kids in there, all around his age. It was too dark to see how many. He kept his head lowered as he approached. On each swing there were two boys. One was thin, pale in the face with dark hair that fell across his forehead. His eyes were big, almost swollen, and the pupils were a light colour; later he would realise that they were a deep blue. He wore a black jacket with a white Adidas logo on the right breast. The tracksuit bottoms he wore were also Adidas with the trademark strips the full length of both legs ending at his white Reebok trainers.

"Eh," he called. "Oo are you, bruv?"

Michael stopped and looked at him, his heart pounding. "Nobody," was all he could manage. It was the truth.

"I ain't seen you before, where you live?"

He pointed down the street where his house sat at the end of the cul-de-sac visible from the full length of the street, even now in the dark.

"A'ight, you must've moved 'ere recently? What's your name?"

"Michael, I moved a couple of years ago, but I changed schools."

"I know where you go. We kick the shit out of your school, bruv." He smirked as he said this, the smile curling each end of his mouth with his beak-like lips pointing downwards. He pointed towards the crest on Michael's chest.

There was no reply. He was not sure if one was expected.

"Listen, come rown, man, if you want. We're just chatting shit, this is Chris." He gestured towards the lad sitting next to him on the swing, his hair blonde and pushed away from his forehead in sharp spikes. "He's Mark, that's Wayne and I'm Cameron."

He gestured to the other boys standing next to the climbing frame. One was black and wearing all black, almost invisible in the dark. The other was another pale faced boy, bigger and broader than the rest with dark hair. They both nodded their heads in a gesture of greeting; subtle and nonchalant.

"I need to go in and have dinner, my mum's waiting for me…" The sentence trailed off as he realised how pathetic it sounded.

"Come out after, innit."

Later that evening, he sat in front of the TV with a warm plate on his lap. The cheese was melting softly under the beans on his baked potato. His family stared quietly at the TV, spooning food into their mouths. Forks clinked like chains against the plates and the gentle hum of the TV filled the remaining holes of sound. He ate slowly and methodically. When he had finished, he put the dirty plate into the sink before throwing on his jacket. He mumbled in his mum's direction about meeting friends and being back before ten, then disappeared out of the room. The rules had relaxed since Terry had left, though the atmosphere felt the same. Sometimes Michael imagined that the demons that they had left in the old house had finally come home and were roosting in the walls and the floorboards. It was better to say nothing at all. Better if he disappeared.

He wandered out into the brisk night, pulling his jacket tight to his slim body. Cameron was now standing on the swing, lazily rocking back and forth. The other two boys by the climbing frame had moved to the wooden benches, sat on the back of the bench with their feet on the seat. They were sipping from cans of Heineken as the two boys on the swing argued about football. The conversation was aggressive; they shouted their opinions back and forth drowning each other out, flinging insults amongst the tangle of words; "you're a dickhead, bruv, you don't know what you're talking about," but the smiles spread on the boys' faces told a story of friends who understood the tradition of this back and forth. It was these smiles that made him feel at ease when he walked into the playground. The gate, supported by a spring, swung shut behind him crashing metal against metal in a familiar clang. The boys on the bench looked around. They nodded, cool and nonchalant. Now, with the green cans in their hands, they seemed older.

"Yes, Mike, what you saying, bruv? Do you like football?"

He spent the next hour and a half listening to the boys talk; their favourite players, their favourite games. It was a chaotic game of point scoring where victories were defined by well-established arguments often rounded off with an insult. He didn't follow football but knew he would now.

CAMERON

7

Cameron walked home from the estate in Battersea. The fifteen-minute walk took him through the underbelly of the larger estates encircling the council estate that he spent so much time in. The towers were hoisted up on great pillars, allowing car parks and walkways to stretch solemnly in the shadows like the unused space under a fridge. He would leave the estate through the narrow alleyway that led round the back of the house that Michael lived in, pass under the railway bridge stemming from the main station in Clapham. Eventually the streets would open out into the large blocks. It was difficult not to feel afraid of the territorial eyes watching from dark windows and protruding balconies. He understood what it meant to feel like a cockroach, fearing light and fearing others.

He clambered the stairs to the small block of his flat and made his way across the corridor. Pushing the key in the lock, he heard shouting from the other side of the door. He sighed as he turned the key and heard the latch fold back into the door. He swung open the door to see his brother crying. His hands were raised up and his palms pressed against his jet-black hair. Cameron's stepdad was leant over him, his open hand raised above his head, his eyes were scanning for gaps to land another blow.

"What did I tell you, ya stupid cunt?" Veins stuck out from his neck like gas pipes and the spit was forming on his lips, some settling on the cotton tracksuit bottoms of Cameron's eight-year-old brother. Although big for his age, he was a quiet boy and was never any trouble at school or at home. Cameron, on the contrary, was no stranger to trouble.

"What the fuck you doing?" he said calmly to his stepdad's back as he closed the door behind him.

"What'd you say?" His stepdad turned towards him, eyes still wide with fury, gums pulled back into thick white lines over his teeth.

"Just fucking leave 'im alone, man." Cameron placed his keys on the hook. He saw a flash of movement from the corner of his eye, then the punch landed square on his cheek and nose. He staggered back and thumped his back against the door. There was a warm sensation on his lips as the blood flooded from his nose and poured down onto his lap. He looked up, dazed. His eyes were full of water and the image of his stepdad was blurred but he could just make out the shouting over the ringing in his ears. He raised his hand to his nose and felt the blood drip quickly onto his hand and fill his palm. The outline of his stepdad came into focus as did the words, "fuckin' talk to me like that."

His mum appeared in the doorway, her hand wrapped around a tea towel. She watched in silence as he leant over Cameron's dazed body, screaming until his face was bloated and red. Cameron looked up at his mum, his eyes scanning her face, begging her to say something. The rage raised up inside him from the pit of his stomach to the space between his eyes. Pushing with his legs underneath him, he sprung up from the floor and started swinging punches in front of him. The first one connected with his stepdad's forehead, the second with the side of his neck just below the ear. Cameron started to swing again, but his stepdad had come to his senses and managed to rotate him using his own momentum against him. In an instant, Cameron was moving through the air and came down hard onto the sofa, the air forced from his lungs, his stepdad's broad shoulders pushing into his chest. The room started to fade, spots exploded into his vision and the world started to drift away.

He pressed the button at the pedestrian crossing and waited for the light to turn. He touched the swelling on his face and winced. Across the street was a red phone box, each side sprayed with thick black ink. It was only nine in the evening. He crossed the street towards the phone box; pressing the grotty buttons, spelling out the number he had scrawled on a scrap of paper.

"Hello, hi, it's Cameron. Sorry it's late, is Michael there please?"

8

By December, Cameron knocked on Michael's door every evening and throughout the day on the weekends. Chris would stand, solemnly, by his side, watching the kids in the playground swing so high that only the tops of their heads and dangling feet were visible. Unlike Cameron, Chris wasn't accepting of another face in the group – especially a scrawny bottom-feeder like Michael.

But Cameron saw something in Michael that he didn't see in the others. He had liked him the moment he had watched the uncomfortable fear spread across his face the first time they spoke. He liked his courage to swallow that fear and meet them in the playground. Like Cameron, Michael was an outsider. For even amongst those that weren't rich enough to live in the beautiful whitewashed buildings of Kensington or the old brick mansions that lined the park in Battersea, there was a hierarchy. The working class had their own system, like rats looking down on cockroaches. His parents were poor; the others had parents with jobs and mortgaged properties. Cameron's mum worked part-time in the pub, being paid in cash so she could continue to claim benefits. He lived in a council house with subsidised rent. Every afternoon, his scruffy flop of hair would match his faded unwashed clothes. He wore a black Adidas tracksuit, the knees fading from black to grey. The socks pulled up over the bottom of his tracksuit were fading from white to grey. His cool blue eyes and turtle-like smile covered a fire that burned beneath the surface. He had fought his whole life for attention, and he wouldn't be trodden on.

They passed the winter in the playground or playing football. Michael saddled up to Cameron like a pilot fish, following him around the littered ocean, desperately avoiding being devoured. He was his protection from others and from home. Instead of going home after football, they would spend hours walking along the intricate pathways through the council estate together; sometimes climbing into the apartment blocks, past the stairs that reeked of bleach and urine until they reached the top floor. They would push through the fire-exit door that opened out to the gravelled roof and sit with their legs dangling over the ledge, looking down at the street below that ran along the back of the estate. It was always quiet; the black roofs of the terraced houses looking up at them with their collection of skylights and chimneys. The occasional car would pass by gently rumbling in the quiet of the back streets and they would fall silent, letting it pass.

Cameron gathered spit in his mouth, leaning over the edge of the building. It dropped slowly from his lips like a tear and plunged to the pavement below, exploding into a small dark circle. Sometimes, when they came to the roof as a group, they would throw eggs at passing cars but not when the two of them were alone. The silence wrapped its warm arms over them as they watched the London horizon; the ledge their tree-top house. It was the only place he would talk about his life at home. He lived in a different estate, further up the main street towards the station. A small two-bed flat located in a brown brick council block with piss-stained stairs and rows of flats that all looked the same. He shared the flat with his mother, a small Scottish woman who worked in the local pub and smelt of alcohol at every hour of the day. His stepfather was a tall broad Englishman, who spent the evenings sat across from his wife whilst she worked. His broad back slumped over the bar and his big shovel-like hands tenderly holding a pint glass filled with beer. They had two kids that were six and nine years younger than Cameron. They would sleep in one of the two rooms whilst his mother and stepfather would stay in the other. Cameron's bed was a mass of blankets and a yellow stained pillow on the couch, shovelled away in the mornings when the house came alive. He talked about a mum who drank too much, a stepfather that spoke with his fists and two young children that looked up to Cameron for protection. He felt powerless. He was homeless and alone even when he was at home.

"What 'bout you?" he said once, looking across at Michael. His blue eyes narrowed as he studied Michael's face.

"What 'bout me?" Michael watched another car slowly rumble past below their feet.

"You never told me why your stepdad left."

Michael shrugged.

"I get it." Cameron returned to watching the pavement below. "You think it's your fault. I know, bruv, bin there, innit."

Michael lowered his head and squeezed the top his thumbs. Cameron reached across and tucked his hand in the crook between Michael's neck and shoulders. He squeezed his shoulder and patted him once on the back, without taking his eyes from the London skyline.

"The thing 'bout you and me, bruv, is we're always on the same ledge. No matter what 'appens, I'll keep you from falling. Don't worry 'bout that." He looked across to Michael and nodded, as if agreeing with himself. Michael smiled back nervously and returned to the rooftops below.

MICHAEL

9

Summer. It was stifling hot. The hot days gave way to warm evenings. The divorce finally went through and his mum spent long afternoons sitting glazy-eyed, staring out of the window as the net curtains billowed into the room like ghosts on a string. Every floor panel, crack in the wall and empty room whispered stories. Truth resonated off the walls, only now they were slowing falling around her. The statement to the police had been enough for her to understand that this wasn't isolated. She had picked away at the wallpaper that covered the cracks and the pinholes became a theatre, with years of physical and mental abuse on stage. She had bought the tickets, unsure whether it was a performance she wanted to see and watched with horror as the truth that had been hidden from her untangled in front of her. The final scene saw her daughter's childhood abruptly ended. She was forced to start her life as an adult prematurely by two men; one a stranger, the other a man she was supposed to trust and who was supposed to love them all unconditionally. Guilt tugged at her mind and pushed her further from reality. She became a ghost in her own home.

Michael stretched out on the hotel bed and closed his eyes. Sleep still evaded him and the memories were painful. Her face was gaunt in his mind, her eyes hollow and face unsmiling. It hadn't been the failure of the marriage that had destroyed her. Failure as a mother had been the stone that sank her. They had sat on the small roof garden, that summer, watching the sun set over the rooftops in silence. He had turned and looked at her small round face, the orange in the sky reflecting in her glasses and her hair, now showing strands of grey, falling over her shoulders and around her face. She must have seen that he watched her, but she pretended not to.

"It wasn't your fault. You weren't to know," he had said.

She looked at him then. Her eyes still glazed behind the windows of her glasses. Her lips pulled tight to form a small line across her face. She nodded once. "I know," she said and turned back to the horizon. He didn't mention it again, but he knew that she was lying. Instead, he had drifted further away in the hope of escaping the weight that hung over them. Cameron became his life buoy. The evenings they shared became his haven.

That summer, he learnt that alcohol had the ability to freeze reality if you drank enough that consequences became an afterthought. They had started with the dust-laden bottles in the kitchen cupboard and topped up with beer stolen from the off-license. It had been petrifying at first, nerves shredded as shaking hands fingered the plastic holders and their legs shook as they took the beers towards the counter. Instead of paying, they ran. It took almost an hour before his heartbeat returned to normal, a cold shiver shooting down his back and his stomach. By the third time, they laughed so hard as they ran that they got a stitch and were on the verge of giving up running. The shop owner gave chase but only managed one length of the road before pulling up, breathing hard and hands holding his hips. Their laughter echoed behind them like an engine as they disappeared into the network of streets.

The fourth time it was a different shop and a different owner. Michael broke free of the door and started running, his head up and an arm looped around four cans. Cameron was waiting for him and was running as soon as he saw Michael spring from the door, like a relay runner. An Asian man followed him; he was younger than the rest, less than thirty and clad in a tracksuit, glistening Reebok trainers on his feet. They turned into the side street. Michael's feet pounded the concrete; he could hear the slapping of his soles on the tarmac as the man followed them. He could see Cameron ahead, head back, legs pumping, drawing further away from him. Fear pulsed through his chest. The sound of trainers hitting the floor was closing in and showed no signs of slowing. Michael risked a look over his shoulder. The face was less than two meters behind him, teeth clenched, brown eyes fixed on Michael's. His heart pounded in his chest. He pushed harder, his legs throbbing, streaks of pain coursed through his thighs and ribs. Something touched the back of his t-shirt. He dared not look but he knew it was the fingertips of an angry shop owner. He closed his eyes and pushed as hard as he could with his feet, but he was tired. His breath was coming out in short bursts and his chest heaved with the effort. Then he stopped. He felt his t-shirt choke his throat, making him gag. The ground disappeared from underneath and his feet were swinging uselessly in front of him. He landed on his backside; a fresh streak of pain ran up his back.

The man grabbed his throat and pushed him onto his back, laying him in the middle of the road. Some people had stopped to watch the young Asian man shout at the scrawny red-haired boy in the middle of the road.

"Ya 'fivving ginger cunt, you come to my shop again…" He grabbed the beer from Michael's arms. *Don't open them*, he thought idiotically, *they'll go everywhere.* He wasn't scared of taking a beating. He was worried the man would call the police. He raised his hands to protect his face as the man swung a slap at him. The shopkeeper had raised his hand again, searching out a gap between Michael's skinny arms when Cameron landed a kick, firmly, into the small of his back. He lurched forward, catching his feet with Michael's. His face slapped against the black tarmac, the beer falling from his arms and rolling back towards Michael. He watched him roll over and sit up. His eyes looked cloudy as he raised a hand to his face. Michael watched him, stunned by his own fortune until he felt Cameron tugging his arm.

One of the passers-by was shouting something at them but they didn't wait to find out what. Michael grabbed the pack of beer and they were running with a fresh energy. Cameron had come back for him. As they ran, he looked over at the face of the boy running beside him. His blue eyes were focussed ahead, his face distorted with effort as their arms pumped like pistons. He had come back for him. As they ran, Michael's face burst into a smile. He burst into a manic laughter. Cameron look across at him, his legs and arms slowing their motion and a grin spread across his face. His eyes lit up and he, too, brayed with laughter. They ran a few more metres before pulling up in fits of laughter, leant over, holding their sides. The road behind was empty.

The sun swept away from the bright blue sky, descending behind the tall buildings that littered the skyline projecting oranges, yellows and reds through the gaps in the buildings. The clouds remained stretched out like purple tears in the wallpaper. They sat on the ledge of the council block, both pairs of legs hooked over the lip of the building. They had taken the long way back after running from the shop to be sure that they weren't seen. They had taken large swigs of the aged vodka stolen from underneath the sink in his mum's kitchen and chased it down with beer. The vodka burnt on the way down and sat in the stomach like hot lava. The beer had started to become warm and the taste stale. Michael felt the sensation of spinning in his head; the skyline felt like it was winding down for the night by rotating quickly into the ground. He looked down at the pavement below to help steady himself. The sensation passed, leaving a giddiness within that felt empowering and good.

"I'll get him," Cameron said quietly, staring across the horizon.

"Who? The shop guy?"

Cameron smiled. "Na, he ain't worth it. My stepdad."

The swelling on his face had long past, but his nose was still crooked. A yellow and purple bruising under his left eye was a sign that it hadn't been the last time he had taken a beating.

"Why don't you tell the police?"

Cameron snorted. "They ain't gonna do fuck all."

A silence fell between them. Cameron took a swig of the warm beer. "What 'bout you?"

Michael looked at him, his eyebrows raised. "What 'bout me?"

Cameron returned his gaze; his eyes glistened with alcohol, his face pale in the warm glow of the sun. He looked tired. "You should get him back. I don't know what he did to you, but I know it fucks with you. I know you don't wanna talk 'bout it. That's cool. But give me the word. I'll fuckin' do him too. That's what mates do."

"Thanks." He took a swig of the beer. "You're my best mate," he said quietly.

Cameron laughed. "Gay," he joked.

Michael felt his face burn. He took another gulp of beer to hide his face behind the can.

"I know," Cameron said finally, "you're my best mate too."

It was the alcohol talking he told himself but something in Cameron's eyes told him that he had revenge burning inside him and someone was going to pay. "We could fuck off eventually, mate. We could get a flat somewhere," he said. "Get you out of there."

"Yeah. Sounds good." Cameron smiled ruefully, watching the sun burning to an orange behind the tower blocks. Michael didn't believe him.

10

"It is not that I am scared to learn just why I am empty inside. Just hold my hand and show some concern if I live or die."

The music dripped from the speaker of the small black hi-fi system sitting on his desk. He closed his eyes and pressed the back of his head against the wall, begging to empty his mind. He felt suffocated as his brain stood over him shovelling dirt into his mouth. He focused on trying to breathe *in out in out,* in through his nose and out of his mouth, trying to ignore the crushing feeling on his chest. He pulled his legs up and rested his forehead on his knees, with his arms pulled tight around his shins. *Come on, Steven, it will pass. It will pass. But how long will last? How many years would he have to live like this?* He didn't know the answer and he had no one he could ask. He loved his dad dearly but since his wife had died, he had become withdrawn and sullen. He was now stuck in a life without his life partner looking after a teenage son, working as many hours as he could down at the post office. That wasn't fair. That wasn't the life that he asked for, but life rarely went the way it should. Steven felt a pang of guilt rotate his stomach a whole turn and another spade full of dirt fell somewhere in the back of his mind.

He pulled himself from the bed, standing in front of the full-length mirror attached to the door of his wardrobe. The music continued to chime. He tried to focus on the words as he stared at his own reflection. He stepped forward and pressed both palms either side of the mirror. He stared into his blue eyes and watched the black of his pupil contract. He stared at the boy looking back at him, a chubby loser with an ugly face. Anger coursed through him like a bolt of lightning and he smashed his fist into the mirror sending silver lines bleeding from the point of impact, leaving a distorted star and his face, looking back at him. The anger fell away as quickly as it had come. He looked at his broken reflection. *What will I tell dad?* he thought to himself and then quietly a thought whispered in his ear. *It won't matter.*

A small part of his unclouded mind screamed at him to stop, its voice subdued under a pile of dirt. He opened the door to his bedroom and went into the bathroom, a small cubicle with a bath and a sink. Above the sink was a white medicine cabinet, the mirror reflecting the single bulb that hung from the ceiling. Pulling it open, he stared at the white bottles pushed to the back of the cabinets, the instructions on the lid standing out against the grey of the dust now gathering. The label was starting to fade but he could still make out the name of his mother printed in black; *Mrs Wells Moira.* His dad struggled to throw anything away belonging to his mum including the wigs that lined the chest of drawers on top of faceless polystyrene heads and, of course, her morphine that she had to take more frequently in the final days before being admitted to the hospital. Their bedroom had stayed the same since she had been removed from the house for the final time in the back of an ambulance. Her jewellery littered the nightstand and her *Mills & Boon* romance novel lay next to the lamp, untouched, the pages browning with age and the bookmark leaving a gap two thirds through the book; never to be finished.

Steven had his own way of keeping her close. Under his pillow he kept an photograph; taken before the cancer had pulled out all her hair and stole the meat from her bones, leaving her a frail yellow skeleton. They were sat together on the sofa that still lined the living-room, though the dark lighting and yellow tint in the photograph made him believe that it was another place. Their hips were touching, her arm was draped around his neck and their faces turned towards one another; his chubby face looked up at hers and their noses almost touched. They were laughing as they stared into each other's eyes. They were happy.

He picked the white medicine bottle from the shelf. *Just one to help me sleep.* He shut the cabinet and caught his own gaze. He turned away feeling a sensation of guilt, that he had betrayed that boy in the mirror somehow. He stopped at the kitchen, filling a glass of water before returning to his bedroom, carefully placing the glass on the nightstand next to his bed. Propping the pillows up against the wall, he sat himself down with his legs straight in front of him, crossed at the ankles. He took the bottle out of his pocket and pushed down hard on the lid, rotating at the same time to release the lid. The pills were small circular, white and chalky. He poured four into his palm. *Just like paracetamol.* He stared sadly at the four circles with the numbers engraved into one side. *Thirty.* He thought of his mum's face on the last day she had been in the house; her skin looked ill-fitting and yellow against her gaunt cheeks, her eyes squeezed closed, her mouth opening and closing as she gasped for air in the plastic mask that covered the lower part of her face. He closed his eyes and try to recall her face years before, when he was younger. He imagined her eyes and her smile, but the memories had already started to fade. Photos like these were the only real memories he had left. A single tear rolled down his cheek. He put the first pill into his mouth, washing it down with water, tasting the chalky bitterness in the back of his throat as the lump worked its way into his stomach. He put the second in before he could change his mind and swallowed. Then the third and the fourth.

It was 7:30 when Gary Wells turned the key in the door of the small apartment. He kicked off his work shoes and walked through the narrow corridor, passing the door to the living room and taking the doorway into the kitchen. The house was strangely quiet. He shrugged off his jacket and hung it over the back of a chair that accompanied a small table. Opening a cupboard, he started to remove a pan. It was later than they would usually have dinner and, if he was home this late, the boy would often have a pan on the stove with beans in it or at least the hot water to make some potatoes. Tonight, the apartment was empty. With the pan in his hand, he looked down the hallway at the bedroom doors. He could see the door of Steven's room was shut, which often meant he was home. "Bloody computer games," he muttered softly under his breath as he filled the pan with water. He set it on the stove and ignited the gas.

"Steven," he shouted down the hall. He plucked a potato from the paper sack as he waited, his hand coming back covered in dirt and potato dust. Washing it under the tap, he listened for a response. Nothing. "Steve," he called again, irritation rising in his voice. He started to peel the potato with a small black-handled knife. It took him no more than forty seconds, his expert hands wrinkled and with the early stages of arthritis, rotating and cutting at the potato. He stopped. The apartment remained silent. He placed the finished potato into the now lukewarm water and put the knife onto the chopping board. Pulling the towel from the hook, he walked into the hallway drying his hands. "Steven?" he repeated. "You deaf, son?" He reached the door and slung the towel over his shoulder, turning his ear towards the door. *Maybe asleep.* His hand hovered, knuckles poised at the door, waiting to hear movement. Nothing. He rapped his knuckles on the door. "Steven, you awake?" He pushed the door open, revealing the small room with the single bed pushed up against the wall.

"Steven! Wake up. I got dinner on." He stood in the doorway looking at his son. The pillows were propped up against the wall, making his body lie at an angle. His eyes were closed, and he was unmoving. "Steven?" he repeated. The stillness in the room sent a shiver up his spine. The stillness in his son sent his blood cold. His eyes moved to the nightstand where a small bottle of medicine stood, the cap discarded next to it. He recognised the bottle. He had opened them enough times to feed the contents into his wife's mouth. He looked again at his son's face, only now noticing that his lips were a purple blue.

"STEVEN," he screamed, quickly he was by his side, pulling him from the bed to the floor. His body was heavy and stiff "No, no, no, no, no, no." The words falling from his mouth as he felt the dead weight of his son slide from the bed and thump to the floor, his head cradled in his father's arms. "STEVEN, PLEASE, STEVEN, JESUS. STEVEN, what have you done? PLEASE WAKE UP, PLEASE, NO."

He slumped back against the wall; the boys head lifeless in his lap. Closing his eyes tight, he looked to the ceiling, pleading to the god above it. "Please don't take him too," he whispered. "Please." He opened his eyes and let out a blood curdling scream in the quiet room.

11

He sat on a chair on the edge of the dancefloor watching them awkwardly swing their arms and shuffle their feet as Backstreet Boys bellowed out the speakers. Chris, Cameron and Mark were all dressed in pressed shirts, smelling of aftershave and their hair heavy with gel. Cameron had ditched the Adidas tracksuit bottoms and it was the first time that Michael had seen him in a pair of jeans. A disco was the last place he wanted to be, but he had suffered their goading and pleading for almost an hour before he had caved. The plastic cup in his hand felt warm, the bubbles had long stopped popping on the surface. Steven's face floated at the centre of his mind, his voice playing in his ears like a recording. The sound drowned out the droning of the next boyband. Instead, Mark Knopfler's voice surfaced singing *ah Steven, I used to have a scene with him* in his head, and he felt his face burn with shame. Since the funeral, he had toyed with the feelings of guilt like a cat with a mouse's corpse, batting them back and forward. The feelings of deep shameful responsibility fought with his anger at Steven. *What could I have done?* a voice asked. *Stayed with him*, another answered quietly.

He spent most of the evening to the side of the dancefloor scanning the hall. The hands on the clock ticked along so slowly, it was difficult to tell if they were moving at all. It was late, the dancefloor was mostly empty; small groups gathered at the sides of the hall conscious to avoid the spinning disco lights. As the night wore on the spaces became fewer, groups of girls pushed into the middle of the hall and were now dancing around a circle of handbags that lay discarded on the floor. The boys populated the edges casting glances across at each other as if sizing up the competition in an animalistic courting ritual. Through the groups of girls displaying their fertility and the boys marking their territory, Cameron had caught the gaze of a blue-eyed brown-haired girl, short but slim. Her breasts were large for her small frame and pressed against her slim-fitting pink jumper, making them seem mountainous. She glanced across at him, her eyes peering over the straw as she sucked at the cola in her glass. Michael watched as their eyes made and broke contact. He watched quietly as Cameron took a deep breath and walked towards her, his beak-like smile spread across his face and his arms swinging with fake-confidence at his sides. They talked and finally they danced like two scarecrows in a strong wind. Michael watched, sipping again on his warm cola.

Later that evening, he watched them sat together on a bench outside the hall overlooking a park, the trees on the far side casting dark shapes across the grass in the light of the lamps. Her name was Sharon. Up close, he could see her eyes were a deep blue, her skin was sprinkled with freckles across her nose and the makeup on her face was covering up an outbreak of spots just beneath the jawline. He watched the branches in the trees wave in the soft evening breeze, the leaves wiggling like fingers on their stalks. The sound of Cameron's voice bubbled softly in his ear. He tuned out the words, so all that was left was a sound. He could see their faces moving closer together and their hands intertwined. She giggled, he smiled and stroked her face. Michael had been waiting patiently. He stood and coughed loud enough for them both to turn to him.

"I'm gonna go, mate."

"Yes, bruv." Cameron held out a hand, Michael slapped it.

"See you, Sharon. It was nice meeting you."

"You too." She wiggled her finger, her eyes darting from Michael and settling back onto Cameron's face.

He walked away, pushing his headphones into his ear and pressing play on his portable CD player. He closed his eyes as he walked and imagined Steven by his side, his slumped shoulders and his feet that scraped the floor as he walked. It annoyed him then, but he would give anything to hear the shuffling of his feet now.

The CD changed track, the guitar gave way to the sandpaper sound of Cobain's voice singing *come as you are, as a friend, as a friend, as a known enemy. That's about right*, he thought to himself. He walked with his head down and his hands buried deep into his pockets. The air felt cool and fresh on his face. He wasn't ready to go home. He walked towards Clapham Junction, not looking up as he crossed the main crossroad surrounded by closed shopfronts. Somewhere behind him a car horn blared, and someone shouted something. His earphones muffled the noise. The road continued south. Cars swept quickly down the road, their tyres rumbling across the tarmac. He didn't cross this time. Instead, he turned right and walked until he reached a small cemetery. The black iron gate was shut; green signs hung from the bars with opening times and warnings about dogs on the grounds. The fence was no more than a meter tall but set upon a small brick wall, green with moss. The spikes on top allowed enough space to plant a foot and climb in. He knew where he was going, he had been here only a few days before. He stood at Steven's grave, looking at the fresh mound of dirt and the pristine marble headstone that his dad had bought with the inheritance planned for his only son. He slumped down to the grass lining the grave and lay his head against the cold stone.

CAMERON

12

The anger bubbled up inside of him, lifting through his stomach and making his vision go fuzzy. It was within that second that he was swinging his hand and connecting his palm with her cheek. The sound was terrific in the small flat; it crashed against the walls and seemed to reverberate all over, followed by complete silence. Her head jerked back violently, her hair spiralling through the air and falling over her face. She stumbled backwards, her heel connected with the sofa and she was falling onto her backside into a sitting position on the soft cushions. She pushed her hair away and met his stare. She raised her hand to her reddening cheek, her mouth open and eyes wide. He stared back, his blue eyes locked on hers. He was searching for the words to say. He wanted to apologise but couldn't. He had started down the road and he would continue.

"Watch your mouth," he said. His voice was calmly, a finger pointed at her but his mind and heart were racing.

They had argued all morning. He had listened as she had given an opinion on his friends, his family and their relationship. They had been seeing each other for close to nine months and as he looked into her glistening eyes, he was swept back to their first date on Wandsworth Common. The feel of her hand, small and slightly clammy as they wrapped their fingers into one another. The grass was lit with the flashing lights of the Ferris wheel, blinking in colourful patterns. They walked through the fairground and its smells of grilled meats and sweet candyfloss spinning endless clouds. The grass was covered with plastic grids acting as a makeshift pavement, littered with discarded beer cans and cigarette ends. They walked, wordlessly, between the stalls, watching kids run past clutching sweets, screaming with delight as they bounced from ride to ride. Cameron enjoyed the feeling of her beside him. He felt comfortable in the silent bubble they had created as they looked at the rows of colourful toys, staring blankly out at the crowds.

He had twenty pounds in his pocket. He held the note between his forefinger and thumb, ruffling it in his pocket, checking every couple of minutes to ensure it was still there. He stopped at the stand with an inflatable goal, paying the man with his worn note, shooting a football through the holes to win a small teddy bear holding onto an oversized red heart. Her face lit up as she clasped it to her chest. She leant in and kissed him firmly on the mouth. He smiled the small turtle-like smile and his face burned. Later that evening they sat on a bench again, this time overlooking the dark expanse of park before them. The pathways that shot across the park were visible only by the soft glow of the park lamps. People walking underneath them appeared from the shadows and disappeared on the other side of the spotlight.

They talked about their families and friends, school and estates, only stopping to take a sip from the cola bottle or a bite from the hamburgers he had bought with the remainder his money. She talked a lot, her hands moving with every word, swinging in front of her face. When her words eventually ran dry, they stayed on the bench holding hands with their faces so close together that he could feel her breath on his cheeks.

For three months, they saw each other almost every evening. She took a bus to Clapham Junction and he would be waiting for her outside of the station. The evenings bloomed into hours spent curled into each other on his little brother's bed when the house was empty. It was in the single bed they first had sex; a short breathless exchange. He felt clumsy, sat on the end of the bed, pulling his trousers over his feet and pulling his socks into long tubes before snapping them free and leaving them to tumble to the floor in crumpled piles. He collapsed naked next to her, held onto her, one arm looped around her neck, caressing her face with his thumb. He had seen sex scenes in the movies, bright sunlight streaming through the windows as the curtains billowed into the room, two people romantically holding each other and rolling between white linen sheets. It was nothing like that. The sheets were a faded blue and worn thin in the middle and she cried out in pain the first time. He awkwardly mumbled an apology, unsure whether to continue but she shushed him with a smile and a finger across his lips. It lasted minutes before they slumped against each other, covered in a layer of sweat, his head resting on her breast. Her heart beat fast at first before slowing to a steady pulse in his ear as he drifted to a hazy sleep. He awoke with pins and needles darting through his arm and her eyes watching over him. He was happy, happy and falling in love.

The arguments started like small holes in a sheet of tissue paper, spreading wide into chiasmic rows. The shouting intensified, filling the quiet sleepy afternoons with wide-eyed screaming. Doors slammed, shaking their frames before the storm would eventually subside to a deathly calm. The reconciliation was frantic and violent, tugging aggressively at each other's clothes, thumping around the room like drunk lovers. Other times, the arguments would end in impenetrable silence, their arms folded neatly against their chests, bodies forming a V shape as they leaned away from each other. She would usually send him a message on the bus home, and they would argue for a while through text messages before they both became exhausted. Time and sleep would heal the rift for a little while longer.

Now here she was looking at him, the red handprint starting to form on her cheek, the tears welling in her eyes. He had been in many fights and had been taught from an early age that problems can be solved with fists, but he had never struck a woman. He was sure that she would end it right there, leaving him alone and it would be the last time he would see her. It would be his own fault. Shame and fear boiled in the pit of his stomach. Time had stood still, his skin felt cold; his hands didn't feel like his own. He could still feel her skin on his fingers. He watched as she flicked her hair around her ear and back into place. He was in too deep; he felt it in the pit of his stomach. His body screamed for him to do something. He was too proud to apologise. Instead, he turned his back and walked towards the bedroom, collecting his jacket and flinging it over his arm. He strode with purpose towards the front door, keeping his eyes forward in case her face made him change his mind. He let it click shut behind him, the familiar sound to the end of a discussion. He was pulling the jacket on when he heard the door open again. He kept walking as a smile curled on the side of his mouth. He didn't look back. He felt her hand slip into the crook of his elbow and her weight settle against his hip. He slowed down, without saying a word and they walked side by side, with her head resting softly on his shoulder. He was sure then that he had her exactly where he wanted her.

13

They had moved on from drinking on the isolated rooftops of the tower blocks. Saturday night became an event. They started the evening in the pub his mum worked at. It was run-down, full of working men wasting away evenings sat at the bar, filling the air with smoke and exchanging words between long gulps of beer. The pub wrapped around a corner near the train station. Overhead the railway line crossed over, showering the windows in dirt and grit. It clung onto the brickwork leaving streaks down the front as if the bricks were bleeding. The windows were thin, narrow and almost black inside and out. Colourful flowers hung from rusted brackets drilled into the walls. The gold lettering above spread completely across the front of the pub; The Royal Oak.

They picked the same booth every week; the crowds jostled for position in the small area in front of the dark wood bar, leaving the booths empty. They were old with burgundy upholstery pinned to the cushions. It smelt of age-old beer, cigarettes and vomit, which was more pungent during the day when the wafts of smoke had been swept out of the bar through dirty windows and swinging doors. The first drink was always a pint glass of cola; they nursed it for an hour or two as they waited for the drunks to step up on the small wooden stage to ruin a chart hit on the old karaoke machine, laughing at the terrible ones and yelling abuse at the good ones. Sometimes taking turns to shoot balls across a rotting pool table into sagging, browning pockets. As the night wore on, the rules at the bar loosened, along with the lips of the men clinging to the edges. A lot of nodding along to old war stories got them beer and alcopops, which they lapped up willingly with no protest from the tired bar staff.

They left the pub just as the clock had turned nine. They were only two beers in but the pavement seemed to move beneath them as they walked, making them stagger from side to side. Their laughter bellowed out into the quiet streets, reaching the ears of the people that watched them from the balconies.

The bus stopped on a high street in Wandsworth and they exited into the cold March air, the sky turning purple and the clouds like shadows. As they turned from the high street, the pub stood in front of them like a beacon of light. The brick front was lit up with lanterns above each window and doorway. THE JUICE BAR sign, pencilled in gold against black, was lit by upturned lamps so the words cast shadows upwards. Outside there was a melee of people clambering to get in past the doorman as he gazed past them, snatching IDs. The queue was loosely formed up the side of the building, made up of boys and girls barely averaging twenty years of age. The boys were uniformed in white shirts, jeans and black shoes with a splattering of blue shirts amongst them. The girls huddled together against the cold in dresses and skirts that finished at the upper thighs, shoes that sparkled under the lights and added two or three inches to their height.

They joined the mass of people outside, awaiting their turn to be assessed by the broad man that filled the doorway. Inside, the room was almost in darkness except for the purple strobe lights that flicked across an empty wooden space in the centre.

"So much fanny in here," Cameron shouted in Michael's ear, once he had paid the barman. Cameron was looking at the full length of the room, weighing up the population of girls versus the boys.

"You got Sharon," Michael replied with a smile.

The small smile curled up on the side of Cameron's face as he followed Michael's gaze to the end of the room where groups of girls had gathered, watched carefully by packs of boys over the lips of beer glasses, their eyes greedy and feral. Sipping the warming beer, they stood quietly, unable to take their eyes away from the show of thighs in front of them and unable to be heard over the music pumping onto the empty dancefloor.

As the night wore on, the crowds became thinner and the girls became scarce. All that was left was the clusters of boys, chugging the beers quicker now. It was past eleven when the music cut off and the lights flicked on, leaving the bar exposed as a sad worn-down building dressed up as a club. Cameron noticed that the walls were washed white, paint peeling off in small flakes, the carpet a deep patterned green and stained with endless drinks. Bar staff were walking with large grey trays collecting empty glasses and some not quite empty ones, all the while shouting, "DRINK UP" and "MAKE YOUR WAY OUTSIDE."

They were gathered around another fruit machine as he thumbed coins into the slot, his face lit by the flickering yellow and red lights, his eyes wide. He had already lost twenty quid. He was desperately trying to win some money back. A gambler would tell you this was bad money after bad money, but he had a feeling that the fruit machine was going to pay out soon. As he expertly pushed buttons with a loud clack, his thumb holding down the large illuminous button by his hips, the lights danced and built in front of him before finally collapsing to zero again. He tutted through his teeth as another pound coin slid down the chute, rolling with a rumble before finishing with a clink into the base of the machine. He looked away from the machine, watching for disapproval.

As the ladder collapsed for the umpteenth time, Cameron scanned the empty room, watching the groups disperse. The clunking of the buttons seemed louder, followed by the sound of another pound rolling down the chute. He swore under his breath, noticing Michael steal a nervous glance at him out of the corner of his eye. The rage popped and bubbled in his stomach. It was money he could ill-afford to lose but he was in this rut and he needed something back. He knew by now that he wouldn't want to talk for some time after. He was quietly praying the fruit machine paid out soon when the young lad collecting glasses gave another reminder to start working their way outside.

"You too," he said close to Cameron's ear as he put another coin into the machine.

"Yeah, man, I'm finishing," Cameron responded, sucking the air in his teeth. Michael finished the last of his warm pint. Cameron opened his palm; two pound coins left. He slotted them in and held his breath as the familiar clink sounded from the base of the machine.

Sixty seconds later, they were pulling on their jackets. He scanned the room as Michael watched him nervously. He wanted to smack something and it couldn't be Michael. He wanted to release the knot that was clasped tight in the pit of his stomach by putting a fist through something. His blue eyes were narrow and glazed, his mouth turned down at the edges as he looked left and right, trying to make eye contact.

It was a group of at least twelve boys that gave him what he needed. One had shifted his eyes in Cameron's direction and held his gaze. It was no more than a second and he returned his eyes back to his group, but it was enough. He stood at least four inches shorter than Cameron, dressed smartly in a blue polo top with a crocodile logo on the breast. Cameron turned to him as they passed, staring directly at his face, waiting for the boy to turn his gaze back to him.

"You got a problem, bruv?" He was walking towards the small, neat boy as he drained the last of his beer. He could feel the adrenalin pumping through him, making the hairs on his arms stand up. The boy looked up, his mouth comically full of beer, his eyes wide and his eyebrows high in a look of surprise.

"You wot?" the lad responded after gulping down the beer.

"I said, you got a fucking problem, bruv? You some kinda batty man, keep starin' at me."

The adrenalin was a roar in his ears. The rest of the group turned to look at Cameron; a skinny boy with his shirt undone almost down to the centre of his breastbone, his arms held out wide and his eyes narrowed.

"I don't even no' you, mate, get the fuck aat my face."

"I'll knock you out, you fuckin' prick." Cameron stepped forward, his face close enough to the young lad that he could have kissed him.

The lad pushed him away. Cameron stepped forward, grabbing a fistful of the pristine crocodile polo shirt, pulling the lad towards him so their faces were almost touching again. The quiet flipped into chaos. A stream of insults left his mouth, he barely knew what he was saying. The rage was driving now. The polo-shirted lad had grabbed at Cameron's shirt and both were trying to lift the other off his feet. The shouting intensified as the rest of the pub came to a stop. A crowd slowly gathered around the group of boys now pushing and shoving each other. Michael had wrapped his arm into the crook of Cameron's elbow to leverage him free of hands. Like a game of tug of war, the two groups huddled together, pulling at the two boys in the centre. Somewhere a glass broke as they were bundled outside.

The faces around them looked distorted, smiles manically spread across their faces as they longed for blood. No one was interested in stopping fists from flying. A tall boy with short-cropped red hair stepped forward, pointing behind Cameron at Michael.

"We ain't got beef with you, these guys 'av got the problem, let 'em sort it out one on one." His accent was dripping South London. His meaty finger was firm, his nails bitten down to the skin. Cameron could feel Michael's anxiety, he paced around him in small steps as if trying to dance his way out of trouble. He didn't want to fight and he was scared. Cameron made the decision for him.

"A'ight," he shrugged, stepping forward.

The fight lasted less than a minute but felt like a lifetime. Cameron had seen fights at school and usually it was two boys grappling and rolling around the floor, arms swinging into fresh air and finishing when both boys were tired and red faced. This fight was nothing like that. Cameron felt fearless, he wanted to hurt this boy; he grabbed the boy on his now crumpled polo shirt and held him at arm's length. He swung the first and second punch, the sound of a closed fist slapped against the boy's face reverberated between the sounds of screaming faces. A girl shouted, "Gowan, 'it 'im." The boy clutched at Cameron's shirt, swinging helplessly. They exchanged nine or ten sickening skin-slapping punches, Cameron unflinching as the length of the boy's arm only allowed him to clip him in the chin and cheek. The tall lad stepped forward again.

"Enough, boys, enough."

The silence of the crowd made the gasps audible, there was a clink as the stub of a bottle dropped from Cameron's hand and shattered against the tarmac. The tall boy looked from the broken glass to the face of his friend. He still had his arm around his shoulder and now turned to get a better look at his face. Blood fell from long straight cuts on his forehead and cheeks, dripping down his face like rain down a glass and gathering at his chin, falling in a steady drip. The polo shirt was darkening around the neck making the blue look almost black. He raised his hand to his face, rubbing it across his cheeks and pulling it away to look at it, his palms now bright red.

"YOU FUCKIN' CUNT," the tall boy roared. The blood continued to pour as the polo-shirted boy's face went a soft shade of white then grey. He remained frozen looking at his palm. Cameron smirked, the side of mouth curling up, his eyelids half closed. *As if I give a fuck*, he thought.

"What!" he offered, opening his arms wide with his palms out.

It was the signal the gnashing boys needed. They rushed forward at Cameron and Michael; the tall boy reached Cameron first and clocked him hard on the side of the face with one big ham-like fist. He felt the pain high up on his cheekbone, reeling back but remained standing, bringing his arms to cover his face as the second punch hit him in the ear hard enough to make it ring. Michael turned to run but only got a few steps when a foot connected with his ankle. He fell forward, arms outstretched, instinctively curling into an embryonic position. A kick landed in the centre of his back and the back of his head, protected only by his hands. The crowd bayed for blood.

Cameron heard the tinkle of smashing glass near his ear, then the world disappeared. He hit the floor face first, busting his mouth on the rough surface of the road. Everything was black. Blood oozed from the wound that had opened up on the back of his head and trickled its way down to his collar, rolling round his neck. A kick landed fully into his face as he lay face down on the floor, jerking his head back at an unnatural angle and breaking his nose. Blood poured like an open tap.

Sirens rang out, filling the air and bringing the noise of the mob to a mumbling quiet as they scattered into the night, like rats.

Michael was sat alone on the curb looking at the scene in front of him. Most of the crowd had been moved on by the police and two thick-set officers were talking with the doormen. Cameron had regained consciousness and was trying to answer the paramedics' questions about his name, his address and the day of the week. His eyes still closed, the paramedic had to lean close to his face to hear his response with the oxygen mask covering his nose and mouth. The blood was now drying in rings around his neck. Cameron sat upright on the stretcher, casting his eyes towards Michael. He couldn't help but wonder what had gone through his mind. He thought of the boy's face, red streaks running across his cheeks and forehead like a Tube map, leaking lines of blood gathering at his chin. A network of scars he would see in the mirror for the rest of his life. He was just a boy like them. Couldn't be more than eighteen.

Cameron watched Michael pull his mobile phone from his jeans pocket and dialled a number. The paramedics continued to work around him, talking amongst themselves.

"Mum?" Michael started to cry.

MICHAEL

14

They never returned to the Juice Bar but every pub left him sweating and anxious, his eyes darting back and forth scouring for trouble and an exit. Raised voices left him jumping, his heart pulsating quickly in his chest. It wasn't long before he started making excuses, avoiding the pub altogether. Cameron was different. He had discharged himself quickly from hospital, against medical advice. He drank more. He drank faster and watched the bar with his cool blue eyes, scanning the corners for trouble. He wanted it. The sound of raised voices seemed to get the adrenalin pumping through his veins and his hands gripped his beer bottle tighter. His speech slurred and the words would fall from his mouth in a haze, dripping slowly from his lips as his eyes sagged to half-mast. Still they scanned the room. His mood would darken once the alcohol set in; he became trapped in his own thoughts.

At first, it was a couple of meaningless scuffles, a push and a shove in the pub before friends jumped in and pulled him away. As the months wore on, Cameron took to breaking a bottle as he was shoved out of the pub by a heavy-handed local. He would stand in the car park screaming at the closed door, with the shattered bottle held by the neck. Voyeurs from the tower blocks would come out, standing on their balconies, smoking cigarettes as they watched the young boy with the bent nose and piercing blue eyes screaming at a pub façade.

Michael sat on the small chair paired with the desk in the hotel room, his head slunk back resting on the highest point of the backrest. His eyes scanned the ceiling. *Rachel was the beginning*, he thought sadly. *He was the end.* He imagined her face, her small eyes, crowded towards the centre of her face and the smile that stretched her face into a manic grin. She wasn't beautiful but she had enough to make her attractive. He allowed his mind to swim back to the first moment he heard her voice. The music had stopped, and the herd of people stampeded across the stained carpet, large brown circles strewn over every inch like a shitty kaleidoscope, towards the door. He was still holding her hand when the lights had come on. They smiled at each other, their hands gently falling apart, her fingertips clinging on for a fraction of a second before falling away.

"Hi," she said finally, her voice high and her accent thick with south London. She had led him out onto the street, her fingers curled softly around his. He hadn't felt the cold, his skin still covered in sweat broke out in goose-bumps, but he only felt her hand and her hip gently stroking against his as they walked in silence.

They had started dating shortly after the first encounter. He had arrived at Clapham Junction station for their first date, a bunch of red roses crunched at the base in his sweaty hands. Waiting on the platform, his stomach turned, his eyes shifted left and right desperately searching through the crowds, not sure whether he wanted her to be there or not. He wanted to feel her hands again and her soft lips but if she didn't show up, the boiling vomit in his stomach would have no choice but to settle. He took the opportunity of pauses between arriving trains emptying the platform for a precious few minutes before the chaos started all over again, to lift his arm and sniff at his armpits. He smelt of Ralph Lauren Polo aftershave. He had sprayed his neck and arms in long thick pumps. *Gordon Bennett!* his mum had exclaimed as he passed her in the corridor, before bursting into a fake coughing fit. Now he was paranoid he smelt like a department store.

When the train pulled in, he watched her get off and look up and down the platform before they locked eyes. He watched her move effortlessly towards him, his brain desperately searching her face for doubt or regret. Instead, her face broke open into that manic grin that he would come to despise, and her arms draped around his neck. They hugged first and broke away, looking at each other as if considering what they should do next. Once again, she leant in and kissed him. She was dressed in black trousers again and the same faux leather jacket.

They ate at a small Italian restaurant hidden amongst the large chain restaurants that littered Northcote Road. It was a small square place with pictures of long-dead Italian men in black and white, their unsmiling faces floating above well-made suits. Dried hams hung from the ceiling like drained corpses, the yellow skin stretched over the leg and ending at the black hoof. Their table was small enough that their knees were almost touching; the tablecloth was red-and-white-checked linen and there was a single candle burning romantically in the middle. The waiter served them water as they sat down, speaking in a strong Italian accent that sounded almost comical, an Italian caricature. Michael stifled a laugh and took the offered menus. Now that they were here, he felt the rolling sensation set into his stomach, his mouth was dry, and his palms were perspiring again. He rubbed them together and looked into her eyes, searching for the next sentence that would start a conversation that he hoped would last two hours. He worried about the awkward pauses, he worried that they would run out of things to talk about, and he felt the anxious knot in his throat.

He need not have worried; she spoke for the two of them, mostly about people he didn't know. It continued through the starter and the main. She gulped on her white wine, finishing three large glasses through dinner. By the time the dessert had arrived with two forks, her words were slurring, she was butchering them with the alcohol and accent quicker than he could piece them back together. She reached across the table, stretching her hand out to meet his. She was stroking the patch of skin above his thumb, which made his cock push against the inside of his jeans. Her hair dangled so close to the flame of the candle that he feared her head would catch fire. The thought helped him forget his erection and made him stifle a laugh for the second time that evening.

The night finished on platform twelve as her train rolled in. He pulled open the door and let her take the steps on her own. She held on to the door and they kissed, her standing on the single step, looking down at him. He pushed the door shut behind her and watched her take a seat in the carriage, waving at him as she had on the first night from the bus. He sighed heavily as he tried to deconstruct the night in his mind, rewinding to every exchange. He watched the train disappear around the bend in the track. *She's a bit dull but better than no one*, he thought to himself.

15

They had coasted through the best part of two years together and he had enjoyed parts of it. It was uneventful. They shared very little moments that he would cherish. He didn't love her. He told her many times he did and even wrote it in letters, but he always felt a distance from her. He would watch her sleep, studying every imperfection on her face, wondering who she was and how she managed to be this close to him. He watched her talk with a heavy weight pressing against his breastplate, swallowing the urge to grab her by the face to stop her. Memories of the soft glow of her face resting on the pillow, her hair spread softly around her gave way to her loud voice and vacant eyes. She talked endlessly about the mundane detail of her day; he struggled to focus on the words she was saying so grunted in response. Her accent, once common sounding and endearing, drove needles through him. Her voice was a high-pitch squeal and her laugh sounded like a braying donkey.

As they approached their two-year anniversary, he now found it difficult to focus when she spoke. He had started to feel this way about many of the people that surrounded him. His mind raced forward in conversations, struggling to slow down or to keep the pace. He was impatiently willing the words from people's mouths as if he was pulling clumps of hair from a drain, hoping for the large bulb of hair that was causing the blockage. At night, he spent the time staring at the bottom of his brother's bunk bed, each knot in the wood mapped out like sunken eyes staring at him from above. The clock would tick through the darkness of the room, booming whips of sound smashing against his face in the dark as the minute hand ticked forward and back. The night behind the curtain would waver, bleeding from black to purple and finally to red and yellow. As the light wrapped its yellow fingers around the crack in the curtain, his eyes would feel heavy and he would finally slip into a troubled sleep that would last two hours before he would rise for college. The lessons usually lasted until three in the afternoon, allowing him enough time to get home and slope up the stairs to crawl under the duvet fully dressed. He would fall into a deep sleep without dreams until he awoke for dinner.

He spent days and weeks feeling the weight of insomnia in the back of his skull, waiting for breaks in the term to be able to sleep deep into the afternoon, once the clouds of the day had left his mind. The days were spent watching scenes unfold in front of him as if he was the audience and other people the actors. Life played out as he watched desperately through a looking glass. He watched them speak. Their cold white lips pulled back over their yellow decaying teeth, he imagined them omitting gases from their mouths that would hang in the air before turning to a swarm of flies and leaving via the nearest window. He studied intensely just so he could be alone. Hours spent in the college library, an open space with glass on every wall, allowing him to watch the city pass by. He wondered where they were going, the people in the cars and on the buses. He wanted to know how and when they would die. He thought the same about himself, staring at himself in the mirror. The green eyes stared back at him, had no answers. He studied each line in his forehead and the freckles that spread themselves across the bridge of his nose. He looked at that face as if it wasn't his, longing to know when the eyes would close and the lips would rot away from the teeth, the skin breaking and peeling away from the skull like the skin on warm custard.

He desperately wanted to be on one of those buses, leaving the cloud that he created behind him. He sighed heavily as he thumbed through a thick booklet of all the universities in the United Kingdom. This wasn't the movies. He couldn't clump his belongings into a red handkerchief and tie it onto the end of a stick. He imagined walking out of his house with the stick and handkerchief slung over his shoulders. The thought was ridiculous. He would leave the only way he could. He carefully wrote *Newcastle* into the box on the application form, forming the letters with the ballpoint of the pen at a steady pace as if any mistake could take the whole thing away.

Rachel was studying to be a hairdresser, a job that would allow her to talk until someone finally told her to shut up. She was excited about working as an apprentice. *An apprentice?* he thought. *These are your dreams? Your hopes?* His downturned mouth and glazed eyes went unnoticed as she rattled through their future together.

"You can study here, in London." Her voice like a high-pitched whir of an engine, slowing building to a crescendo. He moved his gaze to his hands and squeezed, habitually, on the tip of his thumb. It had taken him almost two hours to complete the applications for university, and though Imperial College in London had been an option, he had no intention of going. He had posted the envelope, dipping his hand deep into the red post box before letting go to ensure that it fell all the way down.

"I'm…" he tried to interject.

She continued to talk, the engine building, the smile manically spread across her face. He wanted to destroy her at that moment. He wanted to tell her that he didn't love her, but he already felt his body drained of energy and the thought of more drama left him exhausted. Instead, he waited for another gap.

"Listen," he tried again.

Her hands were swinging wildly in front of her, perfectly manicured nails like bright pink talons, scratching at the air in front of her. Her mouth continued to move and still the words fell. "And it had these boootiful chairs—" The word was like one he knew but the edges rounded and the letters missing. He imagined her clawing at his face and the thought was welcoming if the alternative was to listen to any more descriptions of a hairdresser she had seen. He reached across, impulsively, and grasped her arm.

"Listen," he said carefully and slowly, looking at her square in the eyes. "I am not going to university in London. I am going away. I am going to Newcastle." He said each word deliberately and softly, emphasising the towns so she understood the meaning of the sentence.

Her mouth dropped open and her eyes were wide as if someone had kicked her in the stomach. Her eyes glazed and reddened as they always did when she was about to cry. Then she was sobbing. He stared at her as her bottom lip folded out like a child's and she put her face in her hands. Her shoulders jerked up and down as soft sobs, muffled by her hands, escaped from her mouth. He watched her, waiting for her to finish. He felt nothing. He felt like laughing. Instead, he watched this girl in front of him crying into her hands. He was thinking how strange she looked to him at that moment and how little he really knew her. This stranger was now crying for herself in front of him about a decision that would influence the rest of his life. It was no surprise to him that she was more concerned about how it would affect her.

He watched her for two or three minutes, in silence. It was the silence that made her raise her head from her hands and finally look at him. "So that's it?"

He shrugged and opened his palms out as if trying to grasp the choices in the situation. It was as if that part of his brain was in a coma, but he felt an obligation to at least try to stop her crying.

"What about us?" The makeup ran from her eyes, streaking black tyre marks down her cheeks.

"Well… we can try and make it work… you know… long distance."

The words couldn't hide the tone of what he really meant. She started to cry in deep choking sobs, no longer covering her face. He could see the saliva in her mouth creating small strings between her lips. He swallowed the urge to vomit.

"You're… you're… breaking up with MEEEE."

She wailed the last word and put her face back into her hands. He continued to stare at the top of her head, all the while pressing against the tip of his right thumb.

16

August came and went. September arrived and the leaves had started to turn yellow and orange. The wind took them from the trees and carried them through the streets like wingless birds before they floated to earth. He closed the car door behind him and sat in the dark of the back seat as the overhead light dissolved. It was early; the sun was barely breaking into the sky, a shimmering orange on the London skyline against the purple of the receding night. He sat back and watched the birds starting to swirl in the air above his head, their dark outlines and flapping wings resembling bats more than birds. The front doors opened on both sides and his mum and her new boyfriend got into the car. They had been together for the last year or so. He was a nice guy. He wasn't like Terry and in that sense, everyone was a nice guy. She turned in the seat, looking at him, really looking at him. She instinctively understood him, she always had but as she battled the guilt she carried for their childhood, that instinct had become refined and sharp.

"You ready to go?" She spoke softly, almost willing him to say no.

He nodded silently.

"Ok." She started to turn away, stopped and looked back at him. "You sure?"

"Yeah," he replied softly.

He had been to see Cameron at the pub the night before with Mark and Chris; they had spent the evening in the small grotty booth at the back, reminiscing and drinking. Cameron's mood had been sombre. In the early part of the evening he had remained by their side, laughing with them but as the night wore on, he disappeared for half an hour at a time. Michael looked over, watching Cameron's form cut out against the bright flashing lights of the fruit machine, one arm clutching the top of the machine like a crutch, the other absently pushing the buttons. He wasn't scanning the pub, Michael noticed. He only looked up to take heavy gulps of his pint of beer. He was drinking quicker than usual this evening and it was difficult to keep up most nights.

The pub closed at eleven for the non-locals. It was a tradition for the regulars to have a lock-in; the landlord would shut the doors and allow them to continue drinking for another couple of hours. It was a tradition that the boys enjoyed but the last night wasn't the night to do that. He knew he wouldn't be the one driving to Newcastle that morning, but he had to be up early. He said his goodbyes at eleven and walked out into the fresh night, pulling his jacket tighter to his body. He stood, staring at the high-rise tower opposite for a minute. He hated the place. There were no happy memories for him to cherish. He wouldn't miss it at all. The door banged shut behind him, shaking him from his thoughts. He turned to look at Cameron in the doorway. His hands tucked into the pockets of his tracksuit bottoms and he was staring at the floor. It felt like an age before he spoke.

"What time you leaving?"

"Early, I think, like five or six."

"Damn, bruv."

More minutes passed in silence. They stood side by side, looking at the looming tower block. In less than fifteen years, the pub would be closed. The small parking lot they stood in would become plush flats overlooking the monstrosity. One- or two-bedroom luxury apartments that would have bankrupted eighty percent of London, located in the shadow of the biggest cesspit of crime in Battersea.

"I'm gonna head in, bruv, it's chappin' out 'ere."

"Ok. I'll give you a shout when I get there." There was a pause before Michael spoke again.

"Cameron?"

"Yeah?" Michael was looking at his shoes, his face pensive, almost childlike.

"I'm gonna miss you, mate. Always best mates."

In the blink of an eye, Cameron was hugging him, his arms clasped around his back in a firm hold. He returned the hug and in a moment they were slapping each other's backs in meaningful thumps of affection. They stood that way in the open car park of a run-down pub in a crappy corner of Battersea until Cameron pulled away, nodded and disappeared back into the warm glow and chatter of the pub.

He turned to the glass and watched the morning markets bustling into life on Edgware Road. Shutters rolled up, sounding like machine-gun fire in the quiet of the morning, trucks parked on the side of the roads had men shouting at each other from the tail lifts as they passed fruit, fish and meat to waiting hands. The gravity of leaving hit him like a slap, a fleeting moment of panic arose in his chest and tears pricked his eyes. He stifled a sob but it was loud enough for his mum to hear.

"Hey, we don't have to go, you know? We can turn back."

"No. I have to go. I really do."

He laid on the back seat full length and quietly cried until he fell asleep. Twenty minutes later, the car was roaring up the slip road and joining the M1.

CAMERON

17

Cameron closed the door behind him and took a deep breath, pulling his jacket from his slender shoulders. He hung it on the hook beside the door and walked into the living room. His mum and stepdad were both in the pub; one working, one drinking. Sharon was sitting on the couch, looking up over her phone as he walked through the door. The swelling was already forming high up on her cheek and the small dark line had bloomed in purple petals. She had arrived the previous evening, they'd huddled on the pull-out couch, the springs creaking and pushing lumps into their backs. He had woken that morning, stretching out his spine and dressed for football as he did most Saturdays. He had pulled a clean kit from the small clotheshorse on the balcony. The faded red Manchester United kit smelt damp as if it had sat in the washing machine a few hours before someone had hung it out to dry. It was likely. Often his mum would put a washing machine on after a few drinks at the pub and pass out in bed, fully dressed. The damp clothes cowering against each other in the great cylindrical drum for the remainder of the night would be thrust onto the clotheshorse later in the afternoon of the following day if someone noticed. Sharon had looked at him as he pulled the shirt over his head, the bed covers pulled up to her chin.

"What?" he said sharply.

"Where you going?" She spoke softly, he felt something click in his jaw.

"Football, innit," he said, pulling on a long white football sock. The underneath was black, and the smell hung in the air.

"What am I going to do?" She sat up, the duvet falling to the top of her breasts.

He shrugged. "Dunno. Stay here if you want. Mum's working all day."

Her face dropped, her eyes darting between him and the back of the closed door. She opened her mouth to say something, paused and when the words came the argument ended as it often did. The rage would boil up in him like a pan of water on a stove; bubbling to the surface and making his head feel light. He had cracked her hard with an open palm on the side of the face. The ring that he wore on his ring finger had connected with the bone of her cheek, tearing the skin and leaving blood trickling down her face. She had reeled back and started to cry like she always did. He never understood why she would always try to piss him off. She knew what happened when he was pissed off.

That was the morning and the time between then and the late afternoon had done little to improve his mood. He looked at her soft childlike face, the wound not quite clotted enough, small droplets of blood forming on each corner.

"What?" he snapped at her for the second time that day.

After football, Michael had hung around for a bit. They had climbed into the block, sitting on the ledge of the roof to eat crisps and drink cans of Coke in the dusty August heat. Michael had told him that he had been accepted into Newcastle University and that he was leaving in September. He'd smiled and told Michael that he deserved it and was going to go on to great things. He believed that, he always had. Michael was a quiet boy but clever. He always seemed to know the answers and the right thing to say. He wasn't like the rest of the boys around the estate. They were all full of shit, hot air and bravado. That included him. None of them were ever going to do anything special with their lives. They always talked about being professional footballers or working in football clubs, but he knew they had no chance. They didn't work hard enough, and no one ever made it out of an estate to become a footballer. Not these ones anyway. Michael was getting out and he couldn't help feeling the embers of envy in his stomach. He could only hope that they were still friends and maybe then he could sort him out with a job or something so he could get out of this shithole. Until then he was stuck here, sleeping on a rickety pull-out bed in his mum's living room.

They had walked slowly back down the piss-smelling stairs to the street level. They had paused outside the door, both looking across the football pen to the car park. The silence between them had lasted no more than thirty seconds but it was the most comfortable silence he had experienced with anyone. They had turned and walked separate ways. He had taken the long way home, mostly because he wanted to think about the things they had done together but also because he didn't want to go home. He felt a weight anchored to his chest, making it difficult to breathe. As he walked, he took long deep breaths, sucking in the smoky London air, holding back the tears that burnt his eyes.

He slumped into the brown leather armchair next to the couch, shoving thoughts of Michael aside as he kicked off his scuffed Reebok Classics. He had a slow dull pain growing behind his eyes, working its way down his jawline and thumping in his ears. He felt her gaze still on his face. He stared directly into the white light of the television. The darkness was seeping down, and he was powerless to stop it. Sometimes the weight would be so heavy, he found himself chained to his bed, a prisoner to his own mind, unable to swing his legs around. It was something that he had carried since he could remember but had worsened in recent years, creeping into his room at night and smothering him.

The pull on his sleeve pulled him from his thoughts. She was sat on the arm of the chair holding onto his arm. He couldn't bring himself to look at her. Couldn't bring himself to stand her. He whipped his arm from her grip without making eye contact, the white glare from the TV dancing on his face.

"Why you being like that?" Her voice was high, almost a whine like the whistle of a kettle.

"Leave me alone, man."

"WHAT'D YOU WANT ME TO DO? YOU WANT ME TO LEAVE?" she screamed.

The words streamed relentlessly one after the other from her mouth. The pressing nature of the questions made him feel like he was choking. He stood up, sighing heavily and walked towards the door again.

"NO, NO, NO, NO YOU FUCKING DON'T."

The tears were streaming down her face, her makeup streaked across the mark on her cheek leaving a holy cross of blood and eye liner. She held on desperately to his arm, her other hand holding a bunch of his shirt. She was pulling him back into the room. The rage was starting deep down in his gut again. She dropped to her knees, the screaming becoming a tangle of words. Her weight was pulling him to the ground. He struggled against her grip, freeing his arm and pulling at his shirt to prise it from her fist.

"NOOOO, NOOOO," she screamed.

He raised a clenched fist above his head. "LET GO!"

Standing over her as she clenched desperately at his clothes, his blood rose in his body, filling the capillaries behind his eyes. There was a muffled silence in his ears as if they were stuffed with cotton wool. He saw her face silently screaming up at him. He swung his clenched fist down, connecting with her eye socket and the bridge of her nose.

"NOOooo…"

The scream cut off. She fell back, her hand coming loose from his shirt. Her head made a thud as it connected with the carpeted floor. As if the cotton wool had been plucked from his ears, he could hear the blood roaring in his head, and he could hear her breathless cries. The blood fell from her nose, separated at her philtrum and fell either side of her mouth.

He dropped forward, planting his knees either side of her waist. His lips pulled back revealing his clenched snarling teeth. He swung punches, each one making a sickening thump. Her head jerked back and forth violently, his knuckles breaking a premolar in her upper jaw and her front tooth through the middle. A storm of blood droplets followed the piece through the air in front of him, landing in the carpet and bouncing under the armchair that he had occupied two minutes before.

Her eyes opened, shock swam on her face. She was gasping short breaths, her mouth opening and closing like a fish. He wrapped his fingers around her neck and squeezed tight, leaning forward to apply the pressure on her trachea.

"DIE, YOU CUNT; YOU FUCKIN CUNT!" he screamed.

His face was barely four inches from hers. Spittle sprayed her bruised and bloody face. Her eyes were bulging out and her lips were turning purple. She gagged, wheezing, sucking in air. Her nails clawed at his face and hands still wrapped tightly around her throat. The wheezing slowed; the movement of her hands went from a frenzy to a laboured sluggish slapping. He watched her eyes fade, the eyelids sinking shut as she fought to keep them open. Just as she looked like she would fade away forever, he let go. She sucked the air in huge gasps, grasping her throat as if to pull it into her mouth. The coughing was throaty and saliva sprayed her lips in great white droplets. He stood up, looking over her. For the first time he noticed he had a raging erection. He thought about fucking her whilst she writhed on the floor with her hands at her throat.

"Na, you're not even fuckin worth it," he whispered.

He stepped back and swung a foot hard into her midsection. The air she had been gulping in exploded out of her body. She let out a muffled scream and gasped as she pulled herself into an embryonic position, rolling onto her side and vomiting a yellow foam onto the carpet. He watched over her as the vomiting subsided and the gasps came slower and more controlled. She lay there, like an adult baby, eyes closed, breathing heavily.

"You better clean this fucking mess up before I get back." He pointed at her with shaking hands.

He needed a drink.

18

His Nokia lit up, the dark text against the green background came into view on the small digital screen, casting a glow on his face. He sat up on the fold-out bed. *Sharon again,* he thought as he saw the name appear on the screen. A look of disgust flashed across his face, he threw the phone onto the floor letting it hit the soft carpet below, settling next to three dark droplets of blood that had left their mark indefinitely. The tooth was gone but the blood didn't come out, no matter how hard she had scrubbed. He felt the duvet move next to him and the soft rustle made him turn in Rachel's direction. He hadn't broken up with Sharon yet. He wanted to find the right time to finish it, but he had been distracted of late.

"Who was that?" Rachel said, turning to look at him.

Her eyes narrowed against the light. Her hair, straw-like, was pushed upwards onto the pillow above her head.

"No-one. Why? You jealous?" He turned to her, propping himself up on his elbow and resting his face on his fist.

"Nooo," she cooed and smiled.

He returned the smile and kissed her, enjoying the smell of sleep that surrounded her and the sour taste of her breath. There had been a shift in his life the last few weeks after Michael had left. That night outside the pub, he had felt the familiar sinking feeling that happened whenever he felt things were slipping out of his control. He had returned to the pub with Chris and Mark and continued to drink until the early hours of the morning. He had not said very much for the remainder of the night, which was likely the reason that they had left early. He didn't mind; he had sat at the bar with Gerald, an old regular with an ageing brown flat cap and cheeks flared with red veins from years of drinking, sharing long silences and superficial conversations; both staring at the remains of their glasses as they spoke.

A week later, around the same time Michael was getting ready for his first weekend as a student by drowning florescent green shots in the bright afternoon sun outside the student union bar, his phone sounded and buzzed in the pocket of his tracksuit bottoms. The screen told him it was a number that he didn't recognise

"Can we talk?"

"Who's this?"

"Rachel. I got your number from Kim."

The names collided in his mind as he tried to piece them together, connecting the dots. The vision of the small girl with short hair, pulled back away from her face. The night Michael had met Rachel, he had exchanged numbers with her friend, and they had met up once in Croydon. He had spent the night in her bed whilst her parents slept in their room two doors down, he had snuck out in the early hours of the morning to catch the first train back to Clapham Junction. He had ignored all her messages. He knew she was keen to see him again, but she didn't know about Sharon and she wasn't attractive enough to make the swap.

Rachel wanted to talk about Michael. Through an exchange of messages, he had gleaned she was still hung up on him and thought that he could talk to Michael, given that they were so close. He had barely spoken to Michael in the week, a few messages here and there but the cloud that had formed over his head in recent weeks wouldn't shake clear and he wasn't in any mood to talk. He had instead suggested they meet in a pub later that evening. He had no idea what his intentions were but in the bowels of his stomach, he felt an opportunity to avenge a wrong.

She was already there when he arrived. Her hands folded in her lap, staring out of the pub window. She wore black trousers and the same black jacket she had worn on that first night he had met her. Her sleeveless top was red with frills that followed the V shape of the neck, exposing the top of her breasts. He smiled as she turned around and caught his eye. Her smile back was nervous and unsure. In that smile he saw the doubt in her face as if she was only just realising that this was a bad idea. He looked from her face to her breasts and mentally shook away the thought of the evenings he spent with Michael.

He avoided an awkward exchange by offering her a drink immediately. He felt a sense of relief at having a few more minutes to gather his thoughts. He felt her eyes on him as he stood at the bar ordering her glass of large white wine and a beer. His ego insisted that she had the same intentions that he did, that she was probably thinking of the things she would let him do to her. The doubt interrupted his thoughts; she was wondering what the hell she was doing here with someone like him. She was noticing the stain on the seam of his jeans that he had tried to rub out with a wet cloth before he had left the house. He pushed both voices aside.

The evening passed in a blur of white wine and beer. The conversation moved from Michael to growing up in London to friends and nights out. He continued to lie about his childhood as he often did. When the bell sounded behind the bar to signal the end of the evening, they had finished up and walked into the night air, intoxicated, holding onto each other and laughing. When the laughing stopped, she was still holding onto the sleeve of his shirt and he still had one arm supporting her back. She softly sighed, tucking her hair behind her ear and meeting his gaze. When he kissed her, she didn't pull away.

They continued to see each other over the following weeks, meeting up on the station platform in the late afternoons when she had completed a morning shift at the hairdresser. Clapham Junction or Croydon train station became a symbol of their affair. They spent the afternoons between the covers of his stained duvet or between her crisp white sheets in her room that smelt of perfume. It had been easy to convince her that he intended to leave his girlfriend. He had been with Sharon for over four years. For the last two he had been looking for someone to replace her as their relationship had become a chasm in which they screamed, swore and cried. Mainly she would do the crying and he would have to shut her up; however, it meant that the sex had dried up almost completely. When it happened, it was rough and quick. He would hold her by the throat, with the other hand holding her wrist, panting in her ear in short bursts as he thumped against her with force until he climaxed. The whole time, her head would be turned to the side, tears forming in her eyes and rolling across the bridge of her nose leaving a dark circle on the sheets. Sometimes he would release her wrist and hold her face so she would have to look at him, but she would squeeze her eyes shut tight until the tears formed bubbles in the corner of her eyes. The first few times he had pulled her hair and told her to look at him. Sometimes she had but often she pulled her face away from his grip, he gave up and let her stare into the distance.

The breakup was both inevitable and painless for him. The TV was casting a soft glow on his face again but this time he was slouched on the sofa, she sat beside him with a blanket covering her knees. She had arrived an hour before and had barely spoken a word since arriving. Her eyes cut out like dark shapes against her pale face, her hair was pulled back, greasy and unwashed and her jumper hung from her, making her shapeless. As the program had finished, he turned to her, she was looking at him, her blue eyes wide and red around the edges.

"You might as well go 'ome, you know," he sighed. "I don't wanna be with you anymore, anyways."

She had nodded softly, as though she was expecting this from him. He turned back to the TV, she sat silently beside him without moving. "Can I use the bathroom?" she said finally.

He removed his hand from the band of his tracksuit bottoms where it was cradling his balls and flicked it in the air, in a gesture for her to go on ahead. She stood up, folded the blanket into a square and hung it over the arm of the sofa, stepping across his legs.

It was thirty minutes later, when he looked again at the archway, expecting her to be standing there. The flat was silent except for the gentle murmur of the TV in front of him. He called after her and waited with his ear cocked towards the door. Nothing. He pushed himself off the sofa and called again, walking towards the dark hallway. The bathroom door was closed.

"Sharon?"

The other side was silent. He listened closer for breathing or sobbing. The panic started as a tick in the back of his mind was now full on and sending adrenalin coursing through him. He banged heavily on the door with a full fist, shouting her name now. He rattled the handle; the door was locked. The lock on the other side was a small silver bolt with small screws barely buried into the wood of the door. He had put the lock on himself the last time his stepdad had kicked the door in a rage after his mum. If he busted it off, he would have to explain to his mum what had happened but none of that would matter if she was dead. He had no idea how he would explain that. He rapped hard on the door again, shouting her name and simultaneously trying the handle of the door again. The noise echoed through the empty house but not as loud as the silence on the other side. He stepped back, one hand still on the handle and pointed his shoulder towards the point he imagined the lock to be. As he took a deep breath and prepared himself to smash his shoulder though the wooden door, the sound of the latch clacking back into place pierced the silence with a deafening crack. Then nothing again. He pushed down on the door handle and the door swung open.

She sat on the edge of the bathtub; the sleeves of her grey baggy jumper pushed up to her elbow. They were stained deep red as if they had been dipped in paint. Dark red streaks cut through her skin on each arm, each tear weeping blood down to her hands that were now propping up her weight. He could make out the layers of thick white and angry red lines underneath the fresh cuts. He hadn't noticed before. Had they always been there? The scissors lay open on the white tiled floor, the blades smeared with her blood and surrounded by a child-like picture of red fingerprints, accentuated against the whiteness of the tiles. Bloody handprints smeared down the inside of the bathtub. He traced the trail of blood back to her stained jumper, up to her tired eyes. Their eyes connected momentarily before she looked down at the streaks of red on the floor, tugging at the sleeve on her left arm. It slid through the blood, gathering in the grooves of the cuff and creating a bracelet of blood around her wrist as it came to a stop. Her face was pale and patchy. The skin rough and puffy from the tears. The bright florescent tube lighting made the circles under her eyes seem almost black. She was alive but looked more dead. Pity and shame flashed over him in equal measure.

"You ok?"

She didn't respond with words, only softly nodding her head.

"You need to go to hospital?"

A soft shake of the head made her ponytail flick from side to side.

"Look," he said softly. "We better get this cleaned up before my mum gets back, she'll go mental. I'll walk with you to the bus stop after, if you want."

He knew then that the pity and shame that he felt was real. In some way, he was responsible for the mess that splattered the white porcelain of his bathroom but the overriding need to finish this relationship and move on to something else smothered that shame. If he didn't follow through with this now, he could imagine himself six months later sitting on that same couch with her wormhole eyes staring at him, crying softly so as not to disturb him but annoying him anyway. That was a possibility he could not stand. Instead he helped her wipe the blood from her arms, using the last of the bandages in the green first aid box that they had kept on top of the fridge freezer in the kitchen: no one would notice it was gone, it looked like it hadn't been opened for years. They cleaned the tiles together before he walked with her to the bus stop and watched her get on the bus. She slunk to the back and sat staring at her hands as the doors closed. He looked at her haunted face and told himself that she was better off without him and more importantly, he wasn't the right person to save her. It wasn't his responsibility to be saving people. Let the next guy do that.

19

He had been seeing Rachel for five weeks when he received a message from Michael.
"How long?"
He read the message two or three times, smiling to himself before putting the phone back in his pocket. He felt a creeping anxiety in his stomach knowing he had to face into this at some point but right now wasn't that point. He was relieved that it was in the open, also a little excited at getting back at him. It was his choice to leave, after all.

He pushed the door to the pub, breathing in the familiar smell of stale beer and body odour in the warm October afternoon. He had finished a morning shift at the supermarket on the tills. He didn't enjoy the early starts, but he enjoyed the morning shift. He worked through the chaos of the morning rush, dropping pound coins into his pockets until the weight hung comfortably on his thighs. He did this until he got nervous that the bulges would be obvious to the eyes of his employers. He planned to meet Rachel tomorrow; his evening was free, and he no longer had Sharon to coax from a ledge. He planned to lighten his pockets in exchange for beer. It was Wednesday afternoon; the pub was deserted except for three men stood at the bar. Their broad backs faced him; their hunched shoulders made only the tops of their heads visible. Cameron watched a thick forearm covered in tattoos reach out and wrap thick sausage-like fingers around the glass on the bar. Their stomachs hung over the waistline, pushing against the fabric of their polo tops. All three had their collars up, their laughter filling the empty pub. Cameron hadn't seen them before. One of the men, slightly shorter than Cameron but almost twice his width, turned as he entered and looked him up and down before turning back to his group.

Cameron stood at the bar, pulling the stool underneath him and ordered a beer. He kept his eyes fixed on the amber liquid and his ears pricked towards the group. Their voices filled the air with profanity, but the content was not of interest to him. He tried to place the accent but was never any good at distinguishing southern accents. Outside of Battersea, they all sounded the same to him. They weren't from Battersea; he was sure of that. The wide-backed man put down his pint on to the beer mat and headed towards the toilet, walking behind Cameron. The heels of his loafers clacked against the wooden floor. He caught Cameron's eye as he walked past and held his gaze until Cameron looked away. Anxiety bloomed in his gut and chest.

"You al'rite, mate?" he said, looking over his shoulder. Cameron looked up with wide eyes. The man's hair was short and formed a peak at the front of his head, heavy with gel. His brown eyes were sunk back in his head. His tone was genuine, but Cameron couldn't swallow the feeling of unease.

"Yep." He nodded, looking quickly back at his drink. He felt, suddenly, conscious about how little he had drunk. *He's gonna think I'm a pussy or summit.*

"You live rand ere?"

The question was as genuine as his tone. *If this guy was looking for a fight, he wasn't going to want a conversation about where I live*, Cameron thought to himself. He turned towards him.

"Yeah, over the road. You?" he responded.

"Na, mate. Saint Albans, innit."

The stranger introduced himself as Paul and offered his meaty hand, which Cameron shook, trying not to wince at the firmness of the grip. Cameron noticed a blue swallow tattooed on the space between his thumb and forefinger. The rest of the group gathered around Cameron. Paul showed interest in him. He wanted to know where he lived, who he was and where he was from. The others nodded along as Cameron talked through his family tree up to his mum's side in Scotland. They introduced themselves as Steve and Gaz. They had travelled from St Albans to take part in a march in the centre of London, protesting mass immigration enabled by the government. Paul's eyes had lit up as he described the counter-protesters that had met them in Trafalgar Square. The area had been swarming with policemen dressed in high-vis jackets desperate to keep the two groups apart, but Paul had managed to get to one of them and pound his head a few times with those rock-like hands. They were part of a political group called the National Front. They stood for keeping Britain white and stopping the immigration of all non-whites.

"Ya see, these fackin left-wing nut jobs, fackin desperate for some black cock. But that's not wot Britain is abaat." He pointed a fat finger towards Cameron, the nails were chewed down to leave a small dirt-encrusted sliver. "We're a fackin white race. Aa ansisters came from the North, innit, if ya think abaat it. Not these fackin wogs comin from some shit smellin' countree."

He shook his head and took a swig from his glass.

"I'm not a fuckin' African or an Arab. Are you?" He was pointing the stubby finger at Cameron's chest again. Cameron shook his head, smiling.

"It's not fackin funny, mate. Yor a jock, you should know. We need to stop those fuckers coming in. Taking everythin, they are. Get paid fuck-all. Won't be any jobs for you wen yor my age."

Almost drifting into his own thoughts, he took another long gulp from his pint, the suds on the side of the glass washing away in a swirl of amber. He finished drinking and stood looking at the last remaining mouthful of warm beer sitting in the bottom of the glass.

"You should come to ah next meeting, loads of young skinny cunts like you there", he said with a smile.

They continued to drink through the afternoon. They sat in the booth at the back of the pub that Cameron had sat in so many times before with men much younger than the ones he sat with now. Paul was in his mid-forties, Steve was approaching fifty and Gaz was in his late thirties. Cameron felt a warmth sitting amongst them. At barely twenty years old, he was getting the recognition and attention that he craved. These men were part of a political organisation with a purpose, a purpose that he could see himself believing in. London had changed a lot, even from when he was a kid. He had heard countless stories about a black kid robbing a white kid in Battersea. At his school, it happened daily. He had seen it himself; the black boys would take a white boy to the end of the platform at Balham station and threaten to throw him on the tracks if he didn't empty out his pockets. He was drawn in by the stories of organised fights on a Saturday afternoon and queer bashing on a Friday night. They laughed through stories of "fags" pulled into dark alleyways outside the Vauxhall tavern, they would feel those meaty hands pounding against their faces until they lost consciousness. Steve pulled a golden knuckle duster from his jacket pocket and tapped it against the wooden table.

"Samtiomes they get a piece of dis." he said, sniggering.

It was almost ten, Paul downed the remainder of his pint and ushered for the others to do the same. It was time to catch the last train back to St. Albans. Shaking hands, they all walked out into the car park and with a nod of the head, they went in separate directions. Cameron turned to see the three large men stumble towards the station. He felt a warmth in his stomach and a spinning in his head. He removed the phone from his pocket that he had been ignoring most of the afternoon. Seven messages from Rachel. He would respond to those later. He had something he wanted to take care of, the drink in him was warm and comforting. He hit dial, the phone beeped, dialling each number before finally ringing. It answered on the fourth ring.

"Alrite Mike…"

20

The tram rattled past as he turned onto the main street, his last opportunity to avoid walking but he was fine with walking; he had time before he had to meet Paul. They had agreed to meet at the train station and walk to the church hall together. He was apprehensive about going to the meeting. He didn't know anything about politics and feared being out of his depth. He instinctively lied to Rachel. He wanted her to believe he was as clever as Michael. He omitted the fights and queerbashing. He was desperate to impress her, he seemed to be failing. They had only been together for a short period, but her mood seemed to have shifted. He would catch her texting on her phone. *It's a friend* she would whine, her eyes rolling and the phone disappearing into the bottom of her cluttered handbag amongst tissues and lip-gloss tubes. Every now and then, she would make some comparison between him and Michael that would make the rage boil inside. He would snap at her, but she wouldn't recoil at the sound of his voice like Sharon had. Instead, she would look at him as if he was a piece of shit, roll her eyes and be back on her phone again. She seemed more and more distant from him and he suspected Michael was the reason. He fought every ounce of his being not to swing an open hand across her face and revel in her fear.

Underneath the aging glass canopy that sheltered the entrances, Paul had already arrived. "Cam, my boy, ow are ya?"

They shook hands warmly, Cameron marvelling again at the intensity of the grip.

"Listen, son, you fancy a line?" Paul was looking at him intently; it felt like a test. "You ain't done it before, ave ya? Come wiv me to the bogs," he said with a smile, putting a meaty hand on the back of Cameron's neck.

They jumped over the small turnstile that separated the concourse from the toilets, ignoring the signs asking for a twenty-pence coin. Paul looked over his shoulder as he entered, checking no one had followed them and selected one of the cubicles at the end. He pushed the door open and pulled at Cameron's wrist, pushing him in first. He followed him and locked the door behind them. The cubicle was small and claustrophobic even without having to share it with someone of Paul's size. His stomach rubbed against Cameron's arm as he pushed his way forward to stand in front of the toilet. He removed a small plastic bag from the small pocket of his jeans full of bright white powder, the clouds of dust clinging to the sides.

"Just watch me."

He emptied a pinch of the powder onto the toilet cistern where it seemed to disappear against the white of the porcelain. He removed his wallet from his back pocket, taking out a bankcard and a twenty-pound note. He held the twenty-pound note in his mouth as he returned the wallet to his back pocket and started chopping the white powder into two lines with the edge of his card, one slightly bigger than the other. His face a picture of concentration, his lips curling around the note and his eyebrows furrowed. Cameron observed the fastidious preparation and then watched in fascination as the powder disappeared up his nose as if his face was a vacuum. Standing bolt upright, he sniffed, cleaning bits of powder from the sides of his nostrils whilst passing the note to Cameron.

"Your turn."

Cameron took the note, looking at the smaller line on the porcelain. He leant over as he had seen Paul do and inhaled hard. At first, there was nothing, and then there was a shot of powder and a bitter taste at the back of his throat that made him want to gag. He stood upright, sniffing hard and pinching the end of his nose. He looked at the line. He had only taken half of it.

Paul smiled. "Come on, son, you ain't finished."

Cameron sniffed deeply, clearing the remnants of the cocaine from his nose and leaned over the toilet. He rerolled the note and finished the second half with a long pull. Paul was rubbing his finger across the remains and rubbing them on his gum.

"Good?" he asked.

"Yeah," he felt nothing, just the sick bitter phlegm at the back of his throat that made him desperate for a drink.

The door clicked open and Paul was gone. Cameron heard him unbuckle his belt and urinate. He sniffed again to clear his nose, both nostrils felt full. Leaving the cubicle, he stood in front of the sink to watch his eyes contract and expand in the dim lighting. His nose was clean, but he couldn't stop touching it.

"Stop that," Paul said, joining him at the sink. "Let's go." He left the toilet without washing his hands.

There was a man in his fifties on stage, dressed in a grey suit that was too big for him. It was buttoned at the waist, making him look like a triangle. He stood on a small wooden stage that barely reached the waistline of the audience in front of him. They were a scattering of forty or fifty people; mostly men the same age as Paul, perhaps older, arms folded in front of them, nodding along as the thin man talked them through his view on why British people were no longer able to get British jobs. He was explaining low-skilled immigrants, coming from the likes of Poland and Africa, were undercutting British workers; the EU and the government had allowed this to happen in order to line their own pockets. Cameron found himself clapping along with the crowd when the thin man said "enough," slamming a thin wiry hand down on the wooden podium. He shouted, "FUCK, YES!" Others around turned to look at him, laughing and clapping harder at Cameron's outburst. His face was distorted, his pupils' large black circles sunken in his eyes with a sliver of blue around the edges, his jaw jutted out, his lips pulled back exposing his teeth in an artificial grin. He was breathing hard through his nose and mouth.

Paul put a hand on his arm. "Calm down, son," he said quietly.

"Sorry, Paul. He makes…sense…This guy."

His speech came out in quick fire rapid bursts. He felt energy in his veins, he felt confident. The muscles in his legs were pulsating and his hands moved involuntarily. He wanted to talk, he had a lot to say but putting the words that flooded his mind into sentences was difficult, his mind was racing, and his lips were failing him. The thin man was talking about racism against white people that didn't get as much media coverage as when a black kid was stabbed.

"Usually they're stabbing their own!" he roared, the slim fist thumping against the lectern. The numbers seemed compelling, they spoke to his own experience. He clapped his hand together in powerful slaps that echoed throughout the small community hall when the thin man said "enough!" again, slamming that thin hand down on the podium. Cameron felt a sense of belonging.

When the thin man had finished talking, they left the small room via the aging wooden double doors. The hallway walls were littered with cork boards with community event posters tacked to them; a circus, a fete, a boot fair. Steve and Gaz had met them at the back of the hall, joining them for a break in the toilet cubicle to top up. The second line was easier on the back of Cameron's throat but now the air was barely getting through his nostrils. It seemed blocked, encrusted with grains of cocaine. He sniffed incessantly, trying to unblock the passage. He was sniffing and pulling at his nostrils as he left the toilet, leading to that hand on his arm from Paul again. The evening was slowly descending onto the sky as they left the church, purple clouds stretched out across the moody blue skyline. They laughed as they walked, huddled in large jackets against the autumn wind. Cameron's eyes darted nervously in his head, scanning the streets, watching the faces of his friends. In the back of his mind, he felt paranoia. *They're laughing at me.* He knew how he must look to them.

He followed them into a pub that was painted a urine yellow with flaking green paint on the window sills, breathing in the familiar smell of beer through his closing nostrils and warming to the noise of one hundred voices talking at the same time over the sound of a mundane pop tune. He was pleased to be in the warm and relieved to be able to drink, still tasting the bitter powder of cocaine at the back of his throat. Paul shouldered his way through the crowd, nodding and coaxing his hand across the backs of strangers as he passed, before placing one of those meaty hands onto the bar. Standing on the thick copper rail that ran around the foot of the bar, he leant forward and shouted his order into the ear of a young spotty bar tender, the twenty-pound note he shoved into his hand was slightly curled at the ends and covered in white powder. The kid didn't seem to notice.

They pushed their way through to the back; the space was small with darkly varnished tables and matching chairs. In the middle was a pool table, littered with yellow and red balls. The green was faded but intact. The sound of balls clacking together made Cameron feel at home. They found an unoccupied table and gathered to watch the game started between young lads in tracksuit bottoms, their hair slicked up in greasy spikes and caps balancing high on the crown of their heads. One of the boys stood with his elbow propped on the point of the cue stared at Cameron as he walked in but averted his gaze when he saw his company. Cameron smirked. They drank through eight pints, only stopping to visit the cubicle. The effect of the cocaine seemed to fade but he still could still feel relentless jerky energy snapping through his arms and legs. His heart seemed to have sped up, making his breath short and sharp. The alcohol had mellowed his mood enough for him not to care if he was having a heart attack. He hadn't bought a drink all night. They didn't seem to mind so Cameron didn't push.

It was almost ten thirty when they left the pub in search of something to eat. The fresh cold air made his head spin; his skin broke into goose bumps and the sweat that lined his body ran cold. *I'm gonna pass out.* He steadied himself on the wall of the pub to the sound of more laughter. He looked at the group through blurry eyes, making out their shapes in the dim street light, sure they were laughing at him. Rage boiled up inside him, sending blood rushing to his head.

"Wot you guys laughing at?"

Paul's meaty hand fell on his back in a friendly clap. "You, ya silly twat. Cam on, let's get some food dan ya."

He put his arm around his neck and pulled Cameron in close to his stomach. The gesture was enough to make Cameron smile and the rage simmered down, leaving him feeling stupid and warm against the large man's frame. They had been laughing at him, but they would look after him. He felt safe in that moment. They staggered that way towards the train station walking side to side like crabs holding hands, except the beach was a pavement in Croydon littered with old gum.

The light of the kebab shop shone out onto dark streets like a beacon, the white front featuring large panes of glass like a late-night show. One; a large rotating slab of meat browning under the fire of the grill as a man dressed in white skimmed chunks of meat from the corpse, the second; a young couple propping themselves up against the glass counter, heads bowed in a semi-sleep, holding a ten-pound note towards the preoccupied man behind the counter. They joined the strange haggle of drunks nearer the back end of the mess that seemed to resemble a queue. Watched the Asian man dressed in white work his way through the orders, slicing meat into dry looking bread, topping with aging salads and dousing in red and white sauces.

As another drunk sloped out of view of window two and into the night, the queue continued to fill behind them, crackling with slurred speech and laughter. Cameron watched intently as Paul's eyes flicked between server and customer.

"Alright mate," he said as he reached the counter and the tall lad in front of them with his backside hanging out of his trousers had wandered into the night air. "Can I get four kebabs with everythin'?" He looked at Cameron. "You want summit else?"

Cameron shook his head with a shrug. "Na, I'm good."

The man in white nodded silently and turned, picking the long knife from the side of the sweating meat and slicing the first chunks off.

"Cheer up mate," Paul said to his back. "Might never 'appen."

His face was smiling but his eyes were not. The man in white didn't respond. He continued to take chunks of meat from the rotating corpse.

"I'm fuckin talkin to you, ya cunt, you should show some respect when you're in my cuntry." His eyes, with large black pupils courtesy of the cocaine, were dark like a shark. Cameron felt the adrenalin course through his body, the instinct of trouble drumming in his ears.

The man turned and pointed the steel blade towards Paul. "What did you say? You get out!" His voice was measured but shaking. His accent was thick, foreign sounding. *Turkish probably*, Cameron thought quietly to himself. It wasn't important now.

Paul's eyes narrowed. "You 'erd. Now give me my fuckin' food and take yor money, you paki cunt. You shouldn't be 'andling food anyway wiv your derty shit pickin' 'ands."

The crowd had stopped talking and were now watching the momentary standoff between the thin Turkish man dressed in a white jacket pointing a blade into the face of a short stocky man with clubs for hands curled into fists and resting on the glass countertop. The silence was broken when the calm in the man's face turned from shock into anger. He walked around the counter, shouting incomprehensibly a concoction of English and Turkish swear words, the blade still in his hand. Gaz and Steve had stepped aside with their hands tucked into their jacket pockets and now stood in the doorway blocking the entrance. Cameron stood at Paul's side, eyes wide and alert, the large pupils flicking between the angry brown face with grey stubble and the gloved hand holding the long kebab-cutting blade, flecked with grease and shards of meat. The man stopped two or three metres away from Paul once again with the blade pointed at his face.

"You get da fuck out OR I CALL POLICE," he shouted, his heavy accent making the words difficult to understand above the shaking in his voice.

The striped drapes that covered the archway to a hidden kitchen behind the counter opened and two Turkish men appeared. One looked older than the man in white and the other, wiping his hand on his white apron, looked in his mid-twenties with broad shoulders and thick biceps. They said nothing and watched the shaking hand with the blade pointed at the smiling face of Paul. Paul turned to look at Steve and Gaz, the smile never leaving his face, as if to check that they were still there. Steve looked at him with cold dead eyes and no smile.

"Alright," Paul said finally.

He looked again at the three men that stood beside him.

"Let's go somewhere else then."

He moved towards the door keeping his eyes firmly on the man in white, the blade slowly descending to his side. Cameron stood watching the scene like a bystander; his hands curled into fists by his side. Paul brushed by him as he made his way to the door. "Let's go," he repeated in Cameron's ear, his eyes still fixed on the Turks.

Cameron's world turned over in the space of a minute. As he turned to leave, he saw a can of Pepsi that the tall drunk before them must have forgotten to take with him. The red rage boiled up and hissed in his eyes making his vision blur. He picked up the can and, spinning around, threw it like a cricketer, staggering forward as the can left his hand, towards the man in white. The throw was good. It arched in the air and connected full force with the bridge of his ample nose; blood exploded from his nostrils like a burst water balloon. He momentarily lost consciousness and collapsed, cracking his head on the glass counter as he sunk to the floor. Paul didn't hesitate at the opportunity. Lurching forward, he stamped on the man's face. His head ricocheted off the glass counter again at the force of Paul's boot. "PAKI CUNT," he screamed.

The veins stood out on his neck as he stamped down a second and third time on the man's face. His head wobbled on his neck as it bounced between the floor and the boot, his cheek bone caved in and his nose was now bent over to one side of his face. The thickset Turkish man was now running around the counter whilst the smaller older man ran back behind the curtain, probably for another knife Cameron thought. Steve's hands were out of his pockets and his fist was wrapped up in a golden flower-like object. The punch was quick and connected with the young Turk's face. He dropped to the floor immediately, a gash opened on his cheek, the blood fell in gushes.

Paul stopped as the young man crashed to the floor and then they were all running out of the kebab shop, their laughs echoing behind them. Cameron ahead of the other three, easily able to keep ahead with a fast jog. They were still laughing when the train arrived on the platform and their sides still ached as they slumped into the stained blue seats facing each other.

21

The pub was familiar to him, but he felt like a stranger. Weeks had passed since they had kicked a Turkish man unconscious in a kebab shop. Cameron had been leaving the house when he had seen the grainy CCTV footage over his mum's shoulder. He had stood in the doorway staring at the TV in disbelief as he saw the four of them running away from the doorway of the kebab shop. It was possible to make out the corner of the first window, bright white frame against the stony grey of the pavement. Four men were running away from the camera, three of them large, arms in the air and waddling side to side, as they ran full of a mixture of drink and drugs. In front of them, there was a skinny boy, sprinting hard at first and turning around as he started to leave the shot of the camera, his face a brilliant white. It was impossible to make out his features, but Cameron was able to recognise himself. When he had phoned Paul, his tone had changed.

"Keep your mauf shut and don't say a thing to anyone." Cameron had obediently heeded the advice.

They had met up almost every weekend since; sometimes attending meetings, being careful to skip any that were in the Croydon, but mostly drinking the weekend away in a pub watching the football. It was Saturday afternoon and he was sat alone in the Royal Oak, elbows resting on the bar and looking through old text messages on his phone. He was waiting for Rachel to arrive; she was already half an hour late. They had continued to see each other with less and less frequency over the last few weeks. Her schedule seemed to get busier on the weekends and sometimes, when they had planned to meet, she would cancel. She had now sent him a message asking to meet on a Saturday afternoon. He knew what was coming. he made a point of ensuring that she came to Battersea to do it. If she was going to break up with him, he wasn't going to spend the money and time going to Croydon, besides there was more than one reason why he didn't want to be there. His attention had been flitting between Rachel and Sharon for some weeks. He was texting Sharon again and the messages were reminding him of the first time they had met. She was less pathetic than he remembered and the thought of fucking her wasn't as repulsive as it used to be. If today was going to go how he thought it would, he would meet Sharon later.

Rachel walked into the pub, her hair billowing behind her. She was wearing jeans, tight enough to show off her oversized backside. Her breasts bounced up and down in her long-sleeve V-neck jumper, enough for him to see the line of her cleavage lead down into her chest. He felt aroused and a pang of regret that he had probably fucked her for the last time. He thought of following her home and getting one last go once she was done, but he dismissed it quickly.

"Hey," she swung her bag on the bar and pulled the stool out next to his and sat down.

"You wan a drink?" he asked. She refused.

They talked for almost ten minutes, initially small talk filling in missing details on the week and the latest gossip at work, then she said the words that he had been expecting. "Listen, Cameron—"

He sat quietly looking at his beer. She explained that she wasn't looking for a relationship, he lived too far, and they had drifted apart. He nodded and agreed. He looked at her with tired eyes as she went through her script. When she finished, he looked at her for a long time before turning back to his drink and taking a gulp.

"Well?" she was almost pleading. "What do you think? You don't wanna say anythin'?"

He shrugged, his eyes not leaving the amber liquid in his glass. "What's there to say?"

"You could disagree, say you want us to be together, say anythin'!" She was exasperated and he felt a small victory. He paused for a long time before shrugging again.

"I'm not gonna cry over it. If you don't wanna be with me, what can I do?"

"Well, that's nice; I guess I was just a fuck to you then? Is that it?"

Her voice raised enough for an elderly couple to look up from the booth in the corner. He knew her ego was dented. She expected to turn up here with her speech and have him in tears, pining over her, begging her to come back. The high-pitched squeal in her voice felt like someone was filing the ends of his nerves. He pushed his tongue into his cheek, so he could physically and metaphorically bite his tongue. He turned from his pint of beer and returned her gaze.

"Well?!" she squealed again, her voice getting higher in the quiet of the pub.

When he spoke, it was calm and slow. His voice flat, not quite loud enough for the old couple in the booth to hear. "Listen, you cunt. Get. The. Fuck out of my face before you end up pickin' your teeth off the floor."

He took a swig from the beer glass and took his phone out of his pocket, scrolling again through the messages. She stood, looked at him, her mouth open but the words having fallen quiet. She finally closed her mouth, picked up her bag and jacket, and left the pub, letting the door slam behind her.

He finished his pint and stepped out of the pub, leaving enough distance between himself and her backside. He headed into the estate opposite the pub, navigating his way around the alleyways worming their way underneath the towers. He didn't know exactly where he was heading but he had a rough idea. He had approached one of the younger lads in the pub one evening, a scruffy looking man with teeth missing from the front and his cap pushed back on his head so the peak pointed. The lad had told Cameron about Thomas Walsh. It seemed he had a monopoly in this quarter of Battersea. Cameron had heard about him before; the pub gossipers painted him as a violent psychopath. He had heard a chancer had wandered onto the estate and tried to sell drugs to the kids. He had stayed on the estate for almost a week before he was wheeled away in an ambulance, his teeth knocked out and his jaw broken.

Cameron walked towards the last tower in the cluster. He heard their voices before he saw them. A group of men sat on the railings of the disabled ramp. As Cameron approached, he saw that they were boys. No more than fifteen or sixteen, immersed in a conversation with a man in his thirties. The boys had their hoods up, Cameron could only just make out their faces; four black, one white. The older man was broad across the shoulders, his hair trimmed short and his stomach, underneath his broad chest, poking slightly over the waistband of his jeans. It was February and the winter was still frosting the windows of the cars, but he sat in a t-shirt, his arms prickling against the evening air.

They all stopped talking as they saw Cameron approach. Thomas turned to look at him as the boys fell silent.

"Alrite, Thomas."

"Do I know you?"

The response was cold. Cameron felt his balls retract. He was at risk of taking a hiding here and he had walked into this bear trap all by himself.

"I'm Cameron… I…"

"I know your name. I know every fucker's name rand ere. Wot you want?"

He looked from Thomas to the five boys looking at him, their faces sporting twisted grins. *How do you ask for coke? Do they call it coke?* He sniffed nervously, touching at the red sores forming under his nose, unsure how to answer.

"Walk with me," Thomas said, jumping from the railing before sparing Cameron from an answer.

They walked through the underbelly of the towers in silence, stopping outside one of the tower blocks, hidden by the shadows and the underground carpark. Thomas shoved three grams of coke into his hand, refusing the crumpled wad of notes Cameron had offered. He wasn't sure it was enough. Thomas insisted it was part of his own personal stash and, like karma, these things had a habit of coming around.

"I see you hangin' rand with Paul," he said finally once the coke had been safely stored into the small pocket of Cameron's jeans.

"Yeah," Cameron responded. "He's been taking me to these talks."

"I know," Thomas said. "I used to go. Watch your back, Cam. See you around."

He turned and disappeared into the glow of light hanging over the entrance of the tower. Cameron watched him leave, the words playing over in his head. *Watch your back.*

At home, he sat on his bed dressed in only his pants and a t-shirt. He had a beer pressed between his legs, which was leaving a cold wet feeling on his balls, and a mirror in front of him that had two lines of white powder chopped out with the edge of his bankcard. He inhaled the lines and wiped the remains of the powder from the surface of the mirror with his finger and across his gums. Replaying the conversation with Thomas in his head, he couldn't escape the feeling he had made a mistake, he just couldn't decide if it was with Thomas or Paul. He checked his phone. It was almost time for Sharon to arrive. He jumped from the bed and put the small plastic bag back in his jeans pocket.

22

He looked across at the empty space Sharon had left before rolling over to pick his phone up from the floor to check the time. 8:45. He swung his legs from the bed, rubbing his temple to stem the throbbing pain as the knock sounded again. He pulled on the tracksuit bottoms lying, crumpled, on the floor. *Better not be the fucking postman*, he thought solemnly. The knock came again, he could almost see the door shaking. He pulled it open, swallowing to lubricate his dry mouth. The man at the door stood taller than Cameron; his hair smartly parted at the side and swept back away from his pale face. His long jacket covered his smart grey suit, and, in his hand, he was already extending an ID, his face replicated in miniature alongside his police credentials. Either side of him stood a police officer. Their hats made them seem taller than the doorway, the look on their faces was stern and unforgiving.

"Cameron Milton?" The question felt rhetoric. He felt exposed, bare chested in the doorway in just a pair of tracksuit bottoms and his stomach turning over and over.

"Yeah?"

The two police officers stepped forward, moving around the thin detective with ease. One had unclipped the handcuffs from his belt and was now opening them.

"Cameron Milton, I am arresting you on suspicion of grievous bodily harm. You don't have to say anythin' but anythin' you do say…"

The words drifted into a sea of nothingness.

Once in the car Cameron, shoved his feet into the trainers and stared out the back window at the small crowd that was now gathering outside the stairwell and on the corridor of his flat. The blue lights of the police car spun a reflection across the house, faint in the daylight. He leant his forehead on the cold glass; the cool feeling was helping the headache that thumped in his temple caused by a mixture of stress and cocaine. *Had he found the coke?* The doors opened and the policemen got in, removing their hats almost simultaneously. He felt the car rumble into life, pull away from the curb, the siren whopped once, and then fell silent as it made its way out of the estate.

He sat on the single bed. It was a simple blue plastic-coated mattress on a concrete shelf. In the corner was a small steel toilet. His shoes had been removed by one of the policemen when he had been booked in at the instruction of the woman on the counter. He wore an old t-shirt that had been peeled from his floor before they left the flat. He rubbed absently at his black stained hands, the ink was buried in the creases, making the lines prominent. *I can read my own fortune and it ain't looking good.* His head spun and the light beaming through the small window made his eyes ache.

The interview had come and gone. He had been in cell for almost three hours when he was summoned by a heavy-set policeman, who jangled as he walked from the mass of keys that hung at his hip. He had followed him to a small room via a wooden door that looked fitting for a building made in the seventies. Inside there was a small grey table, circled by four wooden chairs. On the table was a contraption that looked like it belonged in a sci-fi movie, the tape decks on the front had made his stomach flip over again.

"Water?" the officer had offered.

He had nodded silently, and the police officer had turned and left the room, shutting and locking the door behind him. He returned five minutes later with a plastic cup full of cold water. The solicitor arrived twenty minutes later looking flustered and sweaty, pulling a scarf from his neck. He sat on the chair next to Cameron, his knees were almost touching his thigh, and started scribbling notes down as Cameron talked him through the day in Croydon. The fear in him compelled him to tell the truth but he wasn't a grass. Instead, he told the young lawyer in the oversized suit that he had met the three men at the meeting and didn't know their names or where they were from.

He recounted the evening slowly, working through the events in the kebab shop, side stepping names and keeping descriptions vague. After almost half an hour, the detective that he had met at his front door arrived with a woman dressed in a simple black suit buttoned up at the waist, covering the white shirt underneath. She held the same cold look and half smile that the detective had when Cameron had opened the door that morning, which now seemed like days ago. The detective stood with one hand sunk in the pocket of his grey suit. Cameron half expected him to pull the small bag of cocaine out.

"I'm DI Shaw, this is DS Davidson," he said, pulling one of the empty chairs away from the table.

The interview had lasted almost an hour. Cameron had stuck at the story, recounting the night in the same way as he had previously, the solicitor jumping in to redirect the conversation when the detectives pressed too hard. They had shown CCTV footage that he had seen on his mum's TV of the four of them; he recognised himself once again on the small screen. He could tell his own face.

"Is that you?"

Cameron nodded quietly, lowering his head in shame.

"For the record, could you answer verbally?"

"Yes," he croaked.

Now he waited on the edge of this bed, waiting to go home. He had no idea how they had found him from some grainy footage, but it wasn't important now. They knew everything and he was in the shit. He needed a drink and maybe something stronger. The headache had disappeared, but he was left with an empty stomach and a dry taste in his mouth that needed satisfying. It was likely the charge would be lessened to actual bodily harm, a small consolation, but he wouldn't avoid a court date. He wanted to get his phone so he could speak to Paul. If they knew about him, he was sure that they must have been able to identify the other three as well. The questions spun around his mind, creating a typhoon of doubt but the one thing he was sure of was that he had done the right thing. He wasn't a grass. The door clanged as the bolt slid back into its holder for the last time, he hoped. He was led to the front desk, he signed some paperwork, retrieved his belongings and slipped on the shoes. After shaking hands with the solicitor, he exited into the cold night air. It was cold enough that he longed for the bus but with no money and no parent to pick him up, he would have to endure the walk home. Once he was far enough away from the police station, he pulled his Nokia out of his pocket and dialled Paul's number. The phone didn't ring, instead it went to an electronic voice message telling him the service provider. He cancelled the call.

He arrived at his front door; a hand pushed against his spine to relieve the ache from shaking so hard in the cold. He knocked, listening to the patter of footsteps from behind the door. They were light. Good, it was his brother. The warmth of the flat was welcome. Shapes moved in the light of the kitchen signalling that his mum was home. He heard the gruff voice of his stepdad asking about an empty refrigerator in the same aggressive tone that turned every question into a threat. He quietly slipped into his brother's room and pulled a fresh pair of jeans, t-shirt and his Adidas jumper from the only drawer of clothes that he had. His brother followed him into the room, pressing him with questions. Cameron ignored him, pulling on his clothes on before slipping his trainers back on. He pulled his phone out of his pocket and sent a text to Chris.

Where you at? Fancy a beer?

He paused, before putting the phone back in his pocket, he skimmed down the last messages he had sent Paul and typed out another. *I've been arrested. Give me a call when you can.*

Putting the phone into his pocket, he slipped into his jacket and walked into the living room. The latch silenced the noise in the kitchen, and he heard his mum scream something at his back followed quickly by the thumping steps of his stepdad. He didn't wait to hear what they had to say. Pulling the door quickly behind him, he ran the length of the corridor and took the stairs two at a time. As he pushed through the door into the open courtyard, he looked up to see his stepdad glaring at him from the balcony above his head.

"Yor a fuckin' disgrace," he shouted. Cameron held his gaze for a few seconds, he snorted through his nostrils in a forced laugh before heading for the tower block and Thomas' flat.

Chris was waiting in the bar on Clapham High Street, with Mark and Andrew; a tall black boy, his muscled torso struggling to stay contained in a white t-shirt. Chris had met him at the gym he had worked at for two years, Andrew had taken him under his wing in the early days. They formed a bond; which Cameron had come to resent. He had met Andrew a couple of times but his presence at the bar made Cameron feel uncomfortable. He had pulled two lines through his nostrils in the toilet of the Royal Oak before getting on the bus towards Clapham and the twitching of his fingers and mouth had started before he had left the bus. He was accustomed to hiding these twitches when eyes were on him, but he felt like a drunk in a group of sober people and the crushing sense of paranoia swarmed his mind with every sideways glance. Chris greeted him with a warm handshake, his behaviour normal whilst Andrew seemed suspicious. Cameron focussed on making eye contact as he spoke. The bar was poorly lit; he hoped the lack of light would make it difficult to notice the size of his pupils. It took all his willpower to stop sniffing or picking away the grains that tickled against the hair in his nostrils.

He watched their faces move as they talked, their lips and the lines on their faces as they laughed, crinkling the sides of their mouths. He found their faces strange and exotic as if he had never seen them before. They spoke about work. He wasn't interested in listening, his concentration wandered. He watched the young girls walk past with short skirts that rode high enough up their legs so he could almost see their buttocks. A tall brunette walked past him, he crouched down to see if he could look under her skirt, imagining what it would feel like to grab her. She turned and caught his gaze, noticing his half-cocked head. Her face wrinkled up in disgust. She spun around, flicking her dark hair behind her, running her hand down the back of her skirt to obscure his view. The turtle-like smirk curled up on the corner of his mouth as he turned back to the group. They were all looking at him, Chris let out a hearty laugh. The realisation of what had happened dawned on Cameron; they had been talking to him and he hadn't heard anything. Instead they had caught him imagining sexually molesting a stranger, but they couldn't see inside his head. He wouldn't care if they could. Andrew was looking at him, large arms folded across his chest, his brow creased in an expression of disappointment.

"What?" Cameron said, taking a swig of his beer and averting his gaze.

He didn't trust the guy and didn't like the way he looked at him. He considered breaking the pint glass on the table and sticking the jagged remains in his throat.

"Nuthin, Bruv." Andrew's response was annoyingly calm and dismissive. The rage boiled in the pit of his stomach. He stared at the glass a little longer before downing the remainder. Slamming the glass on the table, enough to make Mark jump, he gave the bar a small tap with his fingers before stumbling to the bar to get the next round in. Their eyes watched him fumble through the crowd. He quelled the rage with two shots of tequila, enjoying the bitter taste of the lemon slice, helping curb the urge to vomit on the bar. When the barman returned with the beer, he took a long swig to steady his stomach.

They continued to drink deep into the night and when the clock told them that the day before had turned into the day after, they continued to drink for another hour. Cameron still had half of the powder left in the small bag stuffed into the miniature pocket of his jeans. He went to the toilet, locking himself in a cubicle. A man sat at a stool by the rows of sinks with a collection of perfumes and deodorants. Cameron kept his eyes down and breathed a sigh of relief as the door lock clacked into place. He opened the bag and picked a chunk out with the corner of his bankcard, sniffing hard until the bitter taste swam at the back of his throat. He dabbed a wet finger absently in the bag and sucked it clean.

The paranoia that he had felt had slowly dissolved and with it the fuzzy feeling of rage that he felt toward Andrew had disappeared. The bell rang from behind the empty bar and he heard the familiar shouts from the bar staff, pushing drunks towards the door. Staggering out into the high street, Cameron shuddered, looked up and down the street desperate for another bar they could keep drinking for at least another hour. Instead, swarms of people were leaving; most were almost falling out or hanging on to one another. They walked through the crowds, Cameron's eyes darted from one person to the next, anxiously watching their faces. The paranoia was creeping back. Andrew pushed his way through the doors of takeaway joint. They followed him. The place was crowded, heightening his anxiety. The tables littered with brown paper bags and cartons of drink half drunk. Some had heads slumped against the surfaces with the remains of a meal forming a greasy pillow.

Cameron wasn't hungry; his stomach, shrivelled and full of beer, had suppressed his appetite. He headed to the toilet whilst the boys joined the queue, pulling his wallet out of his pocket as he locked the door behind him. He snorted the powder off the corner of his bankcard again before licking off the remains, replacing it in his wallet and relieving himself in the toilet. He left the cubicle into the quiet of the toilet and looked at his pale drawn face in the graffiti-filled mirror. His pupils were full, the sliver of blue like the sun hiding behind the moon at a full eclipse. As he left the toilet, he scanned the room. He felt lost and disorientated. His head spinning, he focused on not vomiting the contents of his stomach onto the floor.

"Can we have some, mate?"

At first, he wasn't sure they were talking to him as he followed the sound of the voice to four bulky men sat around a small table. The accent was unfamiliar. They were all laughing. They barely fit on the table, their large frames almost touching at the shoulders.

"Wot?"

He felt the paranoia flare, creeping its way into the front of his brain, the rage boiling in his stomach, making his vision blur slightly at the edge but in the centre. He could see the grinning face of a blonde-haired juggernaut in front of him.

"I said, can we have some? It must be good shit, you could put your tea on those saucers."

The blonde-haired giant was grinning at him. Chris had made his way to Cameron's side and was pulling at his sleeve. Andrew and Mark were sat at a nearby table, nervously watching. His face was calm, but his fists were curled so tight that the blood formed around brilliant white knuckles. He felt a sudden surge of panic explode in his head, the feeling of guilt picked at the lining of his stomach. They had noticed his eyes, they knew everything. He could ill afford to be hauled to the police station again.

"Shut der fuck up, bruv, I'll knock your fuckin' teeth out."

The large South African laughed. "Alright mate, it was only a joke."

Cameron turned to Chris and let him lead him back to the table. He sat quietly, whilst they continued the conversation around him. He stared at the group of boys sat only six metres from his table. His elbows propped on the table; his face rested on his fists. He watched as they shoved cartons in the brown paper bags and left, without looking back at Cameron. He waited patiently for the Mark, Chris and Andrew to finish eating.

As they left the restaurant, Cameron was leading them through the doors. They were oblivious to his purposeful walk. He looked up and down the street for the second time that evening but this time he would find what he was looking for. He spotted them standing by a curb, talking as they watched the cars pass on the busy high street. Their hands tucked deep in their pockets and their bulky arms pushed against their sides protecting themselves against the chill of the night. The blonde one was leaning out, looking down the line of cars for a yellow taxi light. Cameron broke away, walking towards them, his eyes never leaving the group of men. He plucked a bottle from the top of a black rubbish bin, overflowing with crumpled brown McDonald's bags. He slammed it into blonde guy's face, the bottle shattered on impact spraying green glass over Cameron and the other three men. The blonde guy staggered into the road, narrowly missing the slow-moving cars that passed by, and fell to his knees clutching his face.

"GWAN THEN, YOU CUNT, SAY SUMMIT!"

The veins protruded from his neck, his eyes wide and the pupils blackening his eyes. The remains of the bottle in his closed fist remaining intact only by the silver foil wrapped around the neck. The first punch caught him cold and connected with the side of his face sending him sprawling backwards, he came to a stop by using the rubbish bin to steady himself. The blonde guy was still on his knees looking at his hand which was now filling with blood from the scatter of cuts on the side of his face. Cameron lunged forward at the man that had hit him, the bottle neck still in his fist, pulled back over his head. The South African was tall and twice as wide as Cameron, he grabbed at his neck, stopping him dead and delivered a rapid bout of punches to his face. His nose busted open once more, pouring blood down his shirt. The arm with the bottle neck went limp and fell by his side as he faded on the edge of consciousness. He felt the hand release his throat and he fell to the cold wet concrete below onto his knees, his palms pressed against the damp floor. A sand-brown worn loafer came into view and connected with his mouth, breaking his two front teeth and making two from the bottom jaw exit the gum entirely. The force sent him spinning onto his back and this time he did black out as he heard Chris's voice shouting and a frantic noise from the crowd that had gathered.

23

He regained consciousness a couple of minutes later. Taking a moment to clear his head, he touched his mouth. There was now an empty space where his teeth should have been. A jolt of pain like an electric current ran through his jaw when his fingertips touched the exposed nerves in his gums. He looked over at the group of South Africans. One was propping up the blonde man as he held the side of his face. It was still bleeding and the small scratches stretching from his chin to his cheekbone were now visible. The rest were angrily remonstrating with Chris. Cameron staggered to his feet, feeling a hand grab him underneath the armpit. He turned to look at Mark's face. He had a look that Cameron couldn't place at first, but the furrowed brow and wide eyes made him realise the look was sympathetic. Without a mirror, he knew that his face was a mess. His vision was clearing. He looked down at the pool of blood on the floor where he had just been lying. He could smell the blood still in his nostrils and taste of iron in the back of his throat. The sound of sirens wailing in the distance brought him to his senses. The small plastic bag of cocaine in his pocket and the amount in his system wasn't going to reflect well when he ended up back at the police station, which appeared inevitable given the carnage on this high street.

He turned to Mark. "I need to go, bruv."

Mark looked surprised. "You have to wait for the ambulance."

"Can't, bruv."

He looked around at the crowd. Some were looking at him, but most were pulling at Chris's arms to stop him lunging at the group of South Africans. Others were on their phones. He spotted Andrew standing against the wall of the pub, his arms folded across his chest and that look of contempt across his face. Cameron made a mental note to make sure he got what was coming to him.

"I got nicked already today, I need to go. Don't say anythin', ok?"

Mark nodded and released the grip that he had on his arm, leaving his hands there in case Cameron lost footing.

"Cheers, bruv." They clapped their hands together.

"Take care, Cam and get yourself to a 'ospital. Your face is a mess."

The expression on his face was one of deep sadness, as if he was watching someone he knew die in front of him. It was true; they weren't the same kids that had played football in the pen. He was growing apart from them and he knew that it was him that was different. He left, silently slipping down a dimly lit side street. He heard a gaggle of people shout "hey!" after him but, keeping his head down, he strode onwards. In his mind, he played out a series of revenge that would be coming soon. "Starting with that black cunt," he muttered to himself as he strode through the back street working his way towards the common.

Cameron retold the events of the night as Thomas sank his first bottle of lager. They sat on Thomas' small balcony overlooking the dark London skyline. He could make out the dark shapes of the tower blocks before them, flickers of lights spread across the dark surface as the estate's nocturnal residents pushed through to the early morning. His head was throbbing, the early onset of a hangover mixed with a beating starting before the night had finished. Pushing the hangover aside, he accepted the bottle Thomas offered to him, drinking it in slow sips, urging the liquid down the sides of his mouth in order to avoid touching the raw nerve endings.

"You got suttin for me?" His speech slurred as he tried to get used to the missing teeth.

"Mate, you look like you might need summit 'arder." Thomas gave him a knowing look. "You wanna get off yer tits?" His hand was held open at his side. On the tip was another small plastic bag. This time the powder inside was grey and almost sparkled in the dim light of the living room behind them.

"Wat's that?"

"Mandy."

He raised his eyebrows and a smile turned up the corners of his mouth.

MICHAEL

24

His room was a small rectangle, overlooking the courtyard of the student accommodation, filled with furniture encased in cheap materials and coloured in greens and browns. He had taken the time to fill the space with the few pictures he had and colourful tat that they had picked up from Ikea. He now sat at the desk looking out of the window. It was October and the North Sea was sending a cold chill through the entire North East, whistling down the River Tyne and rattling the windows. He had sobbed quietly in the back of his mum's car for forty-five minutes before drifting into a troubled sleep, the car rocking him gently like a small child, as he lay sprawled on the back seat of the old Vauxhall. He had woken up in the bright Sunday morning, the Tinsley viaduct towering over the skyline and, once he had stepped out of the car a couple of hours later, he had left a big part of himself behind.

He had consciously flicked a mental switch, separating the quiet, studious boy from Battersea from the man that opened the door to the student dorm that first day. Now, as he sat here watching people walk past his window, each dressed in frayed clothes poked with holes as a sign of their authenticity, he felt he was still that same boy from Battersea. He had just ended the call with his mum. She had told him all she knew about Cameron and Rachel. She had heard things and had seen them together walking hand in hand from Cameron's work. He felt his stomach lurch with jealousy and betrayal, now it prickled across his skin and stuck like a blade behind his eyes. He hadn't loved her and didn't care for her, but he knew that she was out for revenge. Cameron was a man that thought with his dick, he knew that, but he had hoped that their friendship would have meant enough to him to resist her. Now the image in his mind choked him, the two of them naked in bed together, his hands touching the places that Michael had only weeks before, him pushing himself inside her and finishing, sweaty and out of breath, and together they would laugh at him. He wanted to ignore the sick feeling in his stomach, but it was a powerful urge burning inside him, so he plucked the phone from his desk and wrote out a message. *How long?* His thumb hovered over the 'send' button. He pushed it. He let out a heavy sigh and dropped his phone back on his desk. The darkness had fallen outside. The courtyard was lit by small lights protruding from the ground. When the phone shrilled, he jumped and sat upright. He picked it up on the fourth ring.

"Alrite Cam."

"Alrite Mike." The tone in his voice was smug. He could almost feel him smiling despite the distance, that horrible turtle smile curling up at the edge of his mouth.

"Why, Cam? Did I do something to you?"

"Na man, it weren't personal, innit. Didn't think you'd care, you sacked 'er off anyway"

"But, of all the people, why her?"

"She came after me, man, women do that."

The words were coming out slightly slurred, Michael could feel the confidence that comes from alcohol and he could feel the smile still on his face as he spoke. His heart sank in his chest. He was not going to get anything that he wanted from this conversation. In his mind, he started to slowly close the door on their friendship. He couldn't trust this guy he once thought of as his closest friend and that meant an end to everything they had known until then. Cameron was still talking, his tone only slightly evolving. He was saying that they were still best friends and if Michael didn't want him to see her, he would call it off with Rachel. Michael closed his eyes and heard himself say 'no. it's ok.' He didn't believe that Cameron would end it as much as he didn't believe that he was in the least bit sorry. He closed the call, setting his phone back on the desk in the same position. He stared at the screen, willing it to light up. At that moment he wanted to be anywhere but staring out of the window like a prisoner.

The living area was built and designed with the same cheap materials that filled all the bedrooms, spread with a faded green carpet and trimmed with pale wood skirting board. It merged with the kitchen, which was a blend of blue vinyl floor and cheap white cabinets. It was almost midnight and he had come to eat something in the hope that it would take his mind from the image of his ex-girlfriend and now ex-best friend. He could see the dull glow of the television through the glass of the living room door. Peering through, so as not to be seen, he saw John sat, cross-legged, dressed in shorts and a cotton rugby shirt with the collar turned up. He had a bowl, cradled in his lap, full of popcorn that he mindlessly shovelled into his mouth. John was one of the six people that he shared the flat with; a thick set, broad-shouldered Yorkshire lad. He spoke with an accent Michael found difficult to comprehend and a voice that was loud enough to hear him from every room in the flat. Michael paused at the door, unsure if he had the energy to work through a conversation with someone who, for one reason or another, hadn't had more than five conversations within the weeks that they had been living together. He sighed and pushed his way in to the living room letting his stomach and the overwhelming feeling of not wanting to be alone led the way.

"Alrite John," he said softly as he entered the room.

It was impossible to see clearly in the dim light. John looked up briefly from the TV. "Alright Mikey."

It was a name the Northerners had given him. The room fell back into a quiet. Michael rummaged through the fridge, picking up a block of cheese, putting it back and shutting the fridge. He pulled the loaf of bread from the cupboard and put two slices in the toaster. He stood with his back to the work surface and his palms pushed against the edge.

"You really alright, pal?"

"Yeah…" It was soft and unconvincing.

"Grab us a beer from the fridge, sit and watch TV with me."

Michael smiled and opened the fridge again. The words were meaningless in isolation but the look on John's face and the tone in which he spoke gave them all the weight and meaning that they needed. It was an unspoken agreement made in an instant. Michael didn't want to spend any more of that evening alone and John was happy to share a couch with him. If Michael wanted to talk, then there would be someone there to listen. If not, they would sit in silence, watching late-night TV and drinking beer. Michael did want to talk and for the first time in his twenty years of life, he found himself telling another human being about his life in London.

25

oose lips sink ships he thought to himself, but loose lips had lifted a weight like he had never felt before and he no longer felt like he was sinking. One beer had led to two and then three and they continued that way until the early hours of the morning. They had talked and laughed until the alcohol made them giddy and light-headed. The TV had switched from night-time channels to kids' cartoons. A baboon with a colourful backside and an elegant weasel was keeping them laughing like kids.

He was now pulling on his favourite Deftones t-shirt, the white pony now a light grey, still feeling the hazy cloud behind his eyes from the previous night. The small black CD player was blasting the gravelly scream of the band emblazoned on his t-shirt. He took a gulp of the clear liquid sat on his desk from the pint glass stolen from the student union. John had divided a small bottle of vodka between two pint-glasses, filling what was left with lemonade. The smell of alcohol made him wince, the taste even worse; it burned the back of his throat and felt heavy in his stomach. He looked at his reflection in the mirror, flicking his fingers through his red hair, no longer a mop of red on a skinny face. Now short, dishevelled and spikey. He worked the front, his thumb and forefinger finding the right balance of messy and each strand perfect. He wiped the last of the gel across his dark eyebrows. The phone shrilled into life from his desk, rattling against the hard surface. He let out a small shriek as the sound startled him away from the mirror. Turning, he craned his neck to see the name scrolling on the screen. *Maybe it's Cameron.* His stomach flipped. *Don't know what there is more to say*, he thought as he picked the phone from the surface. *William* flashed across the screen in the dark text.

"Hey man, you ok?" William's voice was softer than usual. Michael pressed the phone against his ear to hear better.

"Yeah, all ok here. You?"

"Yeah... yeah," he responded, his voice monotone, almost sad. "Mum told me about Cameron. Wanted to check you're ok."

Michael couldn't help thinking back to the night in the bathroom, William had used his body as a human shield to protect Michael from the wooden stick. On the night Michael had left to university, William sat alone in the living room, staring at the black glass of the TV. The screen was off and the stretched image of the room with the boy sitting in the centre of the couch was visible from the doorway where Michael stood. He had considered leaving without saying goodbye, to avoid the awkward exchange but the guilt bloomed inside him making his face feel hot. He had said goodbye, a brief handshake, the palms of their hands barely touching. William had mumbled something; Michael had nodded without really understanding what he had said. Then he was in the car, thinking of Cameron and leaving Battersea.

"Michael?" He snapped back into the conversation at the sound of his brother's voice.

"Yeah, yeah. It's nothing. Not a big deal, right?"

He felt guilty lying to his brother but, as he swirled the clear liquid in the glass, he could only think about getting blind drunk

"Listen, William, I can't talk long. We're out tonight. Just heading out. Shall we talk later?" *Likely a couple of weeks* he thought absently.

"Sure. As long as you're ok. Talk soon."

"Ok mate."

There was a pause on the other end, he could almost feel William holding words in his mouth, deciding whether to spit or swallow them.

He looked at his reflection in the mirror, checking his hair was still in place and taking another swig of the vodka concoction.

"I miss you, mate," William said finally.

"Yeah, same." He closed the call and put the phone in his pocket, flicking the front of his hair again with his fingers as he left the room. It seemed a rare moment of emotion from William he thought as he concentrated on walking down the stairs. It concerned him for a fraction of a minute, but it was out of his mind once he met up with John in the living room.

They were in the lower floor of the student union, a small dark room with three pool tables. John was studying the table, the red and yellow balls spread across the green cloth in a star-like constellation. Michael sat at the small table watching John, cradling his eighth or ninth glass of double vodka and lemonade, he couldn't quite remember. His brain felt like it was swaying from side to side in his head on a bed of water making him dizzy. John's eyes were glazed as he crouched over to get his face to the same level as the balls. Adam stood looking at John, his cue balanced on his right foot, both hands gripping the tip. Adam was one of the other housemates. His tall frame hunched over so his chin almost touched the blue tip of cue. He turned to Michael as he stretched across to pick up his own drink, the melted ice making the Jack Daniels and Coke a warm brown.

"Taking his time, think he was a pro."

He had a thick Geordie accent that now slurred, making it difficult to pick out the words. As Michael sat looking into Adam's glazed and weary eyes, the drink made him understand even less. He smiled politely, snorting through his nose. He let his eyes wander around the dim room.

He focussed on a group of three men and three girls. They were crowded around a small circular wooden table, barely big enough to fit all six glasses. One of the men looked like Cameron, his dark hair swept to the side covering his forehead and his large blue eyes scanning the room over the top of his pint glass. Michael's mind drifted, imagining what Cameron was doing now, wondering whether he was alone or was she with him. His stomach felt the jealousy burn through the lining and squeezing on his heart. He wanted to phone her. He knew he shouldn't, but he wanted to hear her voice, wanted to hear her say she was sorry even if he knew she wasn't. He wanted to call her a cunt to see if it was enough to make her cry. Instead, he had texted her the same message he had sent Cameron. Unlike Cameron, the response had been immediate, denying everything; she went as far as to say that Cameron was lying. She hadn't realised that his mum had seen them.

"Oi, I'm fookin talkin to you, dickhead!"

The Cameron lookalike was now standing a metre in front of him, with clenched fists at the end of his skinny arms hanging at his sides. He was a local, Michael could tell by his accent, and they had been warned about the locals when they first arrived.

"I said oo you looking at?"

The knot in his stomach tightened. First, he had betrayed him; now Cameron stood in front of him invading the only space he had made for himself and was testing him in front of his new friends. He stood from his chair, clenching his fingers tight around the tumbler that was now almost empty. *Plant it square in his face.* The thought was sharp and clear in his mind. Doubt flickered in Cameron's eyes, he took a step back, his eyes falling to the glass gripped in Michael's hand. Then Michael was lifting it, swinging it towards his face. Panic spread across his face, his eyes wide and his hands unravelling from the clench fists and moving quickly to protect himself. The glass stopped six inches from the tip of his nose. Michael felt two strong arms wrap around him across his chest, his forward motion halted by their strength as his skinny frame rattled against John's forearm. Another hand pulled the glass neatly from his hand, his flailing fist hitting nothing but the air between him and the wide-eyed boy. "COME ON THEN, YOU CUNT."

Michael was screaming, still more than half a metre away. John's arms were wrapped around his chest, pinning him back. He could hear him talking in his ears, his words coming in gruff bursts, calm and almost reassuring. Cameron looked confused, took a step back, lowering his arms and turned to look at his table. None of the other men had left their seats, which gave him the answer he was looking for.

"You're not worth it." He pushed his open palms into the air between them as if shoving an invisible object, turned towards his table and walked away. As quickly as it came, the anger went. He only felt despair and shame.

"Sorry." His voice was tired, dejected.

"Nay bother, let's gan 'ome." John put on his best Geordie accent, his mouth curling into a smile showing his crooked front teeth.

Adam slapped Michael on the back with a meaty hand as he placed the glass that he had taken gently on the table. "Alright, rocky, let's gan 'ome"

He placed a hand over Michael's shoulder and moved him towards the stairs, just as a tall bouncer appeared.

"We're off," John said to him, he nodded in agreement and they pushed out into the autumn air.

Michael rushed through the doors as his stomach turned over, the contents bubbling up through his throat. He vomited against a phone box spraying yellow bile onto the dirty glass, covering his shoes and feeling the chunks stick in his nose as they passed through his throat. Wiping it with his fingers, he turned with eyes full of water to the two men that had helped him through the door; John had one hand on his back.

"Sorry," he managed.

Adam laughed. "Nay bother." He pressed a napkin from the union bar into his hand.

Michael wiped the water from his eyes and the vomit from his mouth. He looked at them, scanning their face for disappointment. He felt a deep sadness and shame overwhelm him as he saw nothing but concern and empathy in their eyes. The kindness was unexpected and something that he hadn't experienced from friends. He began to cry, small delicate sobs as he fought against the tears. John pulled him close and hugged him hard against his large chest, which drew larger sobs as he buried his face deep into his shoulder. Adam placed a hand on his head and ruffled his hair affectionately.

"Come now, no harm done," he said.

He had felt crushed and empty for so long and now with those words he felt he could finally start filling up again with something and start feeling again. He felt a release of pressure from his chest as cried, the tears soaking the cotton jumper and taking with them the devils that had kept him company for so long. In that moment, he thought of Steven. He slept well that night. Steven came to him in his dreams and cried into his shoulder. He could feel the water soak through his t-shirt as Steven wailed for his mum, he awoke in the morning soaked in sweat.

26

He felt her stare pierce its way through all the people in the room. Her green eyes gleamed like emeralds, her long blonde hair, pulled back into a tight single ponytail, fell over her shoulder. Her lips were a bright red, thick with lipstick. It was Wednesday evening and a Student Night. He didn't understand the concept as it felt like every night was a student night, but he was enjoying the excuse to drink, he was enjoying meeting new faces and hearing new accents. Tonight, they were crammed together in another student flat identical to their own. The furniture had been pushed up against the wall and the table littered with bottles of cheap vodka and whiskey. Bowls had been filed with a mixture of crisps and tortillas. The room was full of almost fifty other students, more were coming through the doors, clutching bottles and beer cans. An American punk rock band blasted from a small set of speakers, powered by a dated looking HiFi system, the volume so high that the speakers crackled with the sound of the bass. The lights had been dimmed and there was a colourful projector in the corner of the kitchen, flinging illuminous colours of pinks, greens and blues onto the ceiling.

They stood in a circle together, Michael, John and Adam, with the other three flatmates. John was shouting above the noise of the music, reliving a rugby tour he had in Wales. His stories were always entertaining and full of the kind of pranks that made Michael's face wince with disgust. Michael was struggling to stay focussed. He watched her laugh, throwing her head back, her arm pressed across her stomach underneath her breasts. Her laughter was sweet and chaotic. John finished his story, the group laughed in unison and they settled into a conversational murmur. Michael barely heard the words. He felt comfortable watching her, as if she had consented to his gaze without saying a word. John leant towards him as the conversation continued in the background and whispered in his ear.

"Her name is Helena."

Michael turned sharply to look at him, almost touching noses as he turned. "Huh?"

"One of my merts is in her class." The word 'mates' distorted by the gruff accent. "I met him iner pub and she wa there. You should talk to her."

"Na." Michael shrugged, taking a sip from his drink.

"Gwan. What you got ta lose? She's lookin' at you too, yer know?"

"You think?" He watched John's eyes, guarding himself against a ribbing.

"Yeah, man. Gwan!" He clinked his glass against Michael's, sending a slosh of beer over the top and down his fingers. He looked over at her and watched her talk, her lips moved in slow motion, but her eyes flicked towards him, holding his gaze. He held her stare as long as he dared before turning back to John's grinning face.

He was drunk again but the cool air felt good against his face. His mind felt clearer than it had in previous nights. He was sat on the cold metal stairs that led from the flat down to the courtyard. The rain had fallen, leaving the stairs and courtyard below covered in a thin layer of water that he could now feel working its way through the seat of his trousers. He saw her legs appear beside him and then she was sitting next to him. He looked at those eyes and felt the alcohol start to melt away, replaced with a cold sensation that shook his frame.

"Hey," he said.

"Hey," she offered back, pulling a cigarette from her small black bag hanging at her hip and lighting it.

He felt the flicker of heat from the lighter and watched as she inhaled deeply, making the tip glow brightly against the dark night. She returned the lighter to the purse as she blew out a cloud of smoke. The smell of burning tobacco was pleasurable, mixed with the smell of whiskey and perfume; he was drawn in by her. She was looking at him now, her gaze scanning every piece of him, seemingly taking him all in with her eyes, working him out and reading his mind. He felt the intensity; he felt she was seeing through him.

"So…" she let the words sit in the air, as she squinted at him through the smoke and took another drag. He waited, meeting her eyes.

Her name *was* Helena and he found her addictive. They spent that night together curled up in the single bed pushed up against the wall. The smell of cigarettes and whiskey consumed all the oxygen in the room and left him struggling to breathe. He stayed awake after she had fallen asleep. They'd talked until the clock had turned four in the morning and her eyelids had won the battle, sending her off to a deep sleep, her mouth ajar and a small rattle escaping in a soft rhythm. Their conversation flicked through his mind like an old movie reel. Her mum had died in a traffic accident when she was barely five years old, which had started a series of events that resulted in her moving in with foster parents as her father recovered from a nervous breakdown. She had spoken as if it was a matter of fact but behind her green eyes, he saw a sadness. As she spoke, he began to understand her beautifully kept exterior was as fragile as the cigarette that stayed cocked between her fingers. As she elegantly recited her family history, he carefully placed his in a box and locked it away. He side stepped her questions about his family. If he told her the truth, she would hate him or use it to kill him and he wasn't prepared to take that risk. He had to be strong, she needed him, and she needed someone strong, not a weak crying boy who was bullied by an old man. He put it all into that box and closed the lid, the darkness consuming the memories. He locked it shut and watched her mouth move as the words spilled out between pulls of the cigarette.

27

The academic year ended and the days since he met her ticked by quicker than he could have imagined. The realisation that they would be returning home for the summer left him sick to the stomach. The evenings spent drinking had become more than an escape, it had become a pleasure and he began to feel like he was becoming the person he wanted to be. Helena was like another world; he was hopelessly addicted to her. Every night they spent waking up in the single bed, his back ached from being cramped against the wall and his arm numb from using it as a pillow, but he would have slept this way forever to wake up next to her every morning. He would wake up to her face only inches from his, the smell of cigarettes and whiskey blowing softly from her mouth. He would watch her until she finally woke, and they would lay that way for another hour, talking and laughing. Her laugh was gentle and echoed through his chest, pressing against his heart. It was a sound that he loved and a sound that had become his home.

The steely feeling of dread had crept over him as he thought of facing his old life again. Nine months had passed since the call with Cameron and their friendship felt like a weight that he had vomited against the phone box outside the student union. They had exchanged a handful of meaningless messages, devoid of care and emotion. A process to maintain a status quo. Rachel had continued to message him, prying and poking into his life, trying to understand what he was doing and who he was seeing. The messages had continued through to the spring and finally ran dry when he stopped replying at Helena's insistence. *You don't owe her anything*, she had said, and he knew she was right.

He watched the scenery change from green countryside to the gritty blackness that he associated with London as the train rumbled its way towards Kings Cross. He was still thinking of Helena when his phone vibrated in his pocket. Rachel.

When you home for the summer?

He smiled to himself as he thought of Helena again. He didn't owe her anything, she had been right about that and sometimes it was good to close the door on relationships that brought out the worst in you. He hit reply.

I'm here but not for long. I'm going to see my girlfriend in Brighton for a while.

This was true but it wouldn't be for a few more weeks. She wasn't aware of Helena; he had not told her as he wanted to avoid the questions that would inevitably follow. She had a question for everything, and one question gave birth to a second a third especially when the topic was someone she didn't know. He looked at the text on the phone, the flicking cursor urging him to write more.

I'd appreciate if you didn't contact me again.

He looked at the message, smiled and added *Kind regards*.

He let out a laugh in the quiet carriage and drew a look from the elderly couple opposite him on the table. He slid the phone back into his jeans and left it there as the sign for Kings Cross finally flew past the window in a blue and white haze, he didn't take it out again even when it vibrated over and over again.

Battersea hadn't changed like he imagined it would. He imagined himself like a hero returning home but instead the playground and football pen were empty as he turned into the street and he was just another boy returning home for the summer. As he had exited the car, he could make out the familiar clang of the heavy gate opening, and crashing shut in the summer breeze. He had turned towards the sound, ears keenly tuned to hear a familiar voice. A part of him wanted to see them all again and show them how much he had changed, and another part feared that they would see through him and turn him back into a shadow again. The creeping sense of shame surprised him. He decided he didn't want to face into that just yet. Facing Cameron would be difficult enough.

Ben came sprinting through the old iron gate as he stared at the football pen, wrapping his small arms around Michael's legs, his blonde hair had grown long and looped around his ears, almost touching his shoulders. His face beamed with an innocence that can only come from a child. Michael smiled, enjoying the feel of the little boy's grip on his legs. He crouched in front of him, gently moving a lock of a blonde hair out of his face.

"Benny boy. How are we?" he cooed. Ben laughed at the sound of his pet name.

"I made you a picture, wanna see?"

"Of course." He really did want to see. Ben had a talent, his pictures beautifully worked lines and full of colour. "but first, I have something for you." He reached into his backpack, pulling out a small chocolate bar that he had remembered to buy at the station. The little face in front of him exploded with joy, and his sweaty thin hands grasped quickly the treat.

Michael opened the door to his room that he shared with his brother. His bed was still tucked into the corner, one side running across the wall that they had once threw toys against. On William's single bed to his left, the covers formed a bulge around his brother's body. He swung his bag through the doorway and let it rest inside the doorway. He slipped his phone out of his pocket and pressed cancel on the messages and missed calls. It was half past eight in the evening.

"Hey," he shouted into the quiet room.

The bulge in the bed changed shape under the duvet.

"Why you sleeping at this time?"

The head finally emerged and rotated towards him from underneath the covers. The dark hair, now long enough to reach the back of his t-shirt, was at all angles and the blue eyes half closed looked clouded and full of sleep.

"Hey," he croaked. "You're back." William swung his legs from the bed, pushing his hair away from his face. He stared at Michael as if he were a stranger. In a way, Michael felt a stranger in this room. Clothes that weren't his were piled on his bed, folded and waiting to be put in a wardrobe. The frame of the bed was piled with unfolded clothes, slumped over like bodies.

"You ok?" Michael asked.

"Yeah, man, just been asleep."

"It's early to be sleeping?"

He had noticed the cloud that hung over the house almost immediately. It left the rooms feeling empty and cold. He remembered the positivity that had followed them into this house and now it had evaporated. What was left was white walls instead of wood panels, but the eyes still seem to peer out of every hole, staring at them and capturing all their secrets. The hollowed expressions on William and Sarah made it difficult to look them in the eye. He tried to spend as much time as possible outside of the house, sometimes he would spend time with William kicking a football across the grass outside the house. The hour would tick by silently with only the sound of the boots clipping the side of the football and the whistle as it soared through the air, travelling fifty metres before starting its descent. After three days, he purchased a ticket to Brighton to see Helena to relieve himself from them for a weekend before he would, inevitably have to return before the end of the summer. He began counting the number of weeks before he could head back up North.

28

He heard him between songs, the familiar South London accent drifted across the street and said his name in a way that he hadn't heard in almost a year. *Mike.* Even at home he was Michael. He turned to the sound, pulling at the earphones. Cameron was only a few metres away from him by the time he was able to pick him out against the busy high street. He was almost unrecognisable. He was wearing faded blue denim jeans and a red polo shirt. On his head, he wore a white Nike cap with the distinguishable tick across the front. It sat at a backward angle on his head, looking at the sky. His hair, still unkempt, was stuck to his spotty forehead in greasy streaks making small triangles across his forehead. His nose was flatter, pushed slightly to one side and bulbous at the bridge as if he had shoved something up there. His eyes seemed vacant, dark crescents formed underneath, and his mouth was no longer a slither of turtle lips, now formed two large swollen lips, cracked and peeling. He was smiling but his smile was rotten. Missing teeth at the front were replaced with brown rotten stumps and the remaining teeth were yellow with a textured surface. He stuck out a hand and Michael shook it. He still hadn't said anything in response to his name, wincing at the wet feeling of Cameron's palms and the strong smell of body odour that drifted towards him even after Cameron had stopped moving. He finally broke the silence as he let go of the sweaty hand.

"Alrite Cam."

"Yes bruv, what you up to?"

His breath was rancid. A mix of alcohol and something rotten. Michael began to wonder if Cameron had died and this was the zombie version of him. He was looking at his old friend in silence when he realised that he hadn't responded.

"Nothing much, just home for the summer. You?"

"Nuffin much, mate, normal, you know. Doing a bit of politics and stuff."

"Oh yeah?"

"Yeah."

There was a long silence, only broken by Cameron sniffing hard to unblock his distorted nose. "Let's go for a drink, you got time?"

Michael looked around uneasily, his eyes shifting down the high street looking for an excuse to decline the offer. There were only strange faces, drifting up and down the street.

They settled at a small dark wood table in a pub on the corner of the high street. The place smelt of stale beer and the tables felt sticky to the touch.

"So?" Cameron began.

The pub was quiet. There was a distinct chatter in the background but the silence between them was palpable. Michael nodded his head slowly without offering a response as if it was posed as a statement rather than a question.

"Look, man, sorry 'bout the ting with Rachel."

It was the first time he had heard Cameron apologise for anything. "What happened with that? You still seeing her?"

He acted disinterested and conversational, but he wanted to know. He wanted to know if the pendulum had swung back his way and now Cameron's new girlfriend was chasing him.

"We broke up, bruv. She still had eyes for you."

He smiled as he said this and paused looking for a reaction. Michael met his gaze for a fraction of a second before looking down at the bubbles forming on the side of his glass.

Cameron continued, "I didn't think you gave a shit, 'bout her or me."

He paused again looking for a response and rather than continue, he picked up his beer and took a long gulp.

"Come on, man, you know that ain't true. We were best friends."

"Were?" Cameron asked, putting his beer down.

"You know what I mean."

He picked up his own beer and enjoyed the bitter taste, annoyed with himself for allowing Cameron the small victory. He didn't respond and sat, smiling, across the table. The painful silence came crashing down once again. Michael was looking across the room at the pictures mounted on the wall, desperately thinking of another topic to move on to. Cameron sat slumped back on the chair, arms folded across his chest.

"Tell me about the politics thing." Michael asked. A curiosity nagged at him and he was sure Cameron was keen to let him know.

Cameron sat up straight and leant forward, propping his elbows on the sticky table. He talked, excitedly about meeting Paul and attending a meeting. Cameron had gone to a school, which was predominantly black and as a result, he had many black friends that he had known since he was young. This version of him, with missing teeth and the cap tipped back on his head, was starting to resemble the drunk white boys that they had seen in the pub when they had been too young to drink. Their conversations so loud it could be heard across the bar as they denounced the government for letting them down and the foreigners for ruining their way of life. As Cameron talked, his mind drifted to the imbalance he had always felt growing up in London, the divisions between the rich and the poor. He always felt on the wrong side of everything. Looking at the boy he once knew, now a grotesque shadow of his former self, laying the blame at the feet of people that had grown alongside him, he realised that the division would never heal. There were always more fissures underneath the surface. The poor divided into black and white or natives and foreigners. Whatever the split, the lack of union would always keep them out of the light and their heads submerged in the shadows.

"It's true, dow, innit?" The question shook him out of his thoughts.

"Waddya mean?" Trying to sound as if he had followed the conversation but not understood the question.

"The fuckin' blacks, 'specially those fuckin' Somalis. They always robbing and raping."

Michael froze. He was suddenly aware of the emphasis Cameron put into the word 'Black', his voice rising enough to be heard in all the corners of the pub. A group of men turned in the direction of Cameron's voice, shaking their heads and returning to their drinks.

"The Somalis?" Michael repeated. His face now serious.

"Yeah, man. Feltam's full of 'em"

He looked at Michael as if the point was obvious. Feltham was a young male offenders institute located in West London. It had a reputation for housing the toughest boys from council estates across most of London. Michael had grown up in fear of meeting someone who had spent time there.

"They come 'ere, bruv, off their fuckin' boats and start livin' like they still in fuckin' Somalia. You can rape women there an' no one cares." Cameron cocked his head to one side to get a better look at his face. "You ok, bruv?"

He thought of Sarah. He had often imagined the face of the man that had raped her, his shape shimmering in the darkness, his features hidden in the dim light, walking towards her. As he neared, in Michael's mind, he could make out the dark puffer jacket she had described, his hands buried deep into the pockets. His face warm, his large white teeth standing out against the black of his face, a smile manically wide. His eyes were big and white, small black pupils trained on her as he sat down beside her. He watched her, his eyes tracing their way from her feet up to her pale, tired face. She was cold, scared and alone. She sat with her legs tucked tight to her backside and her arms hugging her shins. She had trusted the man when he had offered her a warm place to phone home. She had trusted him as he had slung that jacket over her shoulders and walked side by side with her to his small council flat filled with Ikea furniture. He felt sick imagining the fear that rose up in her stomach as the man had tugged at his belt buckle with one hand, the other pointing a kitchen knife at her. "Take off your trousers." His thick African accent clicking between words. Michael spoke of that night to no-one, even the night he had spent with John on the couch drinking beer he had omitted Sarah's rape. He felt ashamed that he hadn't done more. He had always thought of it as something that had happened to them as well as her, but he had never considered that someone was responsible for the way he felt. The case against Mohamed Khalif was over so quickly that he hadn't considered that this man was culpable for his sister's changes and collapse of his family home. He felt an anger in the pit of his stomach.

"What's up, bruv? You're not ok."

He looked up into Cameron's blue eyes, he had been quietly staring at his beer. The silence hadn't been awkward as he hadn't really been in the room. He didn't know how he could explain away the reaction to Cameron's words. His mind was still looking through the window at that night in July 1995. Inspired by the anger burning inside him, he told the truth. The words burst through his mouth like vomit. *Loose lips sink ships.*

"My sister was raped by a Somali, mate."

He picked up the pint glass and took a gulp to hide the tears that were forming in his eyes.

"What?!" Cameron was leaning forward now, only a few centimetres from the top of his pint glass. "Why din't you tell me before?"

Michael shrugged. "Dunno."

"What happened?"

"His name was Mohamed Khalif."

He didn't know why he started there but it seemed a good place as any. The name was ringing in his ears as he stared at the corner of the table, which was now his looking glass into the past. He spilled it all out from the trip to the hospital to the conviction. He didn't cover up any of the details of the night. Cameron was well versed in flying fists in a home so there was no shame between them. Cameron sat quietly shaking his head as he spoke.

"Fuckin' bastards," he said finally when Michael had stopped speaking. "You should come wiv me to the next meetin.'"

Michael let out a small laugh. "No thanks, I don't think it will be for me."

Cameron smiled and nodded as if understood exactly what was implied and he was comfortable with it. Sarah's story had broken through the stiff awkwardness that had been stuck between them making the conversation seem like it was moving through treacle. It now flowed and they sat talking for another hour, reminiscing, laughing and updating.

Michael finished the last of his third pint and started pulling on his jacket. The summer in London had offered rain most evenings and the days seem to alternate between summer and autumn. Cameron took the cue and chased down the last of his beer. As they pushed through the aging wooden pub door, they stood in the street looking at the pavement for a few seconds. *Awkward again*, he thought, before finally sticking out a hand, in a desperate attempt to end the afternoon. Cameron took it and shook hard and then, surprised him by moving to a hug. As they broke apart, Cameron looked at him. "Still best mates?" he said.

"Yeah, defo," Michael nodded.

"Cool."

They separated at the corner of the high street. Michael reflected on the chance meeting. His fears of seeing Cameron now waylaid. *It wasn't that bad* he thought to himself as he entered under the shadow of a railway bridge overhead. *In fact, I would go as far as to say I had a good time.* It had been an unexpected way to end the summer. Soon he would take the train North again and back to Helena. She had been all he thought about all summer. Smiling to himself, he put his earphones back in and pushed play on his Mini Disc. Chop Suey by System of a Down screamed *Wake Up* into his ears.

CAMERON

29

The Magistrates Court was set back from the street, a large rectangular building with huge windows framed in white. The stairs were lined with a blue rail, the only colour other than the deeply depressing grey concrete that loomed over him as he made his way up to the front doors. As he looked up at the large overhang with the words *Magistrates Court* in silver lettering, the image of a prison crossed his mind as it had most of the morning. His solicitor had reassured him that it was unlikely given the evidence but the small fear that niggled his lower intestine had been difficult to shake. As he approached the doors towards the whitewashed foyer, with its high ceilings, he heard his name. The accent was unmistakable, barked in that Southern gruffness making his name sound like two sounds forced together. *"Camran."* He turned to see Paul striding up the stairs; he looked odd dressed in a grey suit, his white shirt was pressed well and finished with a purple tie. His fists were clenched, and his face screwed up, the brows furrowed creating deep creases in the space between his eyebrows.

"You fuckin' grass," he said as he approached.

Cameron flinched at the words, taking a step back, so his back was touching the court doors.

"Wh-wh -what?" he stammered.

"You 'erd me, you're a fuckin' grass."

Paul was close enough Cameron could smell the alcohol on his breath mixed with the chewing gum that was still rotating around his mouth. *It's not even ten yet*, he thought but dare not say.

"You fuckin' told them, you fuckin' cuntin' grass."

Cameron felt fear in the pit of his stomach; he thought Paul might lay him out on the court steps. His eyes were wide, and his mouth pulled into a grimace. Cameron could feel the droplets of saliva flick against his face.

"Paul" He held up his hands, showing his palms to calm him down. "I di'nt say nuttin', they tried, mate, but I di'nt say nuffin'.'"

Paul reached across and grabbed the lapel of his suit jacket, shoving a pudgy finger close to his face. "You better not. You keep your fuckin' maff shut or I'll fuckin' end you."

He shoved Cameron back as he released the jacket; he thudded against the doors. The security guards were now peering through the glass at the two of them. Paul glanced at them and stared back at Cameron, wagging a finger at him but saying nothing as he pushed past and entered the court doors. Cameron followed him in and watched him throw his keys, phone and a handful of coins in a small grey tray before going through the white gateway. He glared up at Cameron once again as he emptied the contents of the bowl into his palm before turning his back and talking to a young guy in a suit that greeted him in the foyer. Cameron looked past the security and could make out his own solicitor, sat alone, shuffling paperwork into his briefcase.

The courtroom was a bright, long room headed by a tall desk. The panelled walls gave it an air of seriousness that made Cameron uncomfortable. Rows of empty seats lined up in front of the desk and chairs to the sides were filled by a spattering of secretaries and a few young men wearing suits, scribbling in notepads. He stood to the right side of a small fierce man looking down at him from his tall desk, his bald head gleaming in the strip lights overhead, his glasses balanced delicately on the tip of his nose. He didn't make eye contact with Cameron, thumbing his way through the paperwork in front of him, he spoke with his mouth hidden by his large red nose. On one side of him sat a small slender woman in her fifties, her hair grey and short, her eyes dark like two small dots. She leaned across and mumbled intermittently into the judge's ear. The small booth in which Cameron stood gave him a view of the whole room. His solicitor sat at a desk, looking up at him from his briefcase, his legs pumping up and down, nervously, underneath the table.

"Name?" The judge's voice bellowed out into the empty room, his eyes flicking over the paper spread across the desk.

Cameron shuffled nervously from one foot to the other, the eyes in the room bore on him, making his body feel hot and his face glow a deep red.

"Cameron," he mumbled.

"Your full name," the judge said, putting down the pen that he had been flicking between his middle and fore fingers.

"Cameron Milton," he said finally.

The judge read through the charges, his dull tone pulsing in a steady beat that made Cameron's spine twitch.

The whole process was over quickly. He pleaded guilty to a lesser charge and was sentenced to community service. Six months of picking litter from the banks of the motorway and a fine that he would have to pay out of his dole money. He felt relief sweep over him as he left the panelled room. The young man in the large suit looked at Cameron and shrugged. His large suit barely moved.

"It's the best we could have hoped for," he spoke dismissively, his eyes wandering down the hall, scoping out the exit.

"Yeah, cheers." The lips curled up into a turtle smile. The young man looked up at him, taking in the smile and looking at Cameron's outstretched hand. He seemed to consider the hand a moment before taking it.

"You were lucky. In my experience, people aren't that lucky twice. Take care of yourself, Cameron, and stay out of trouble."

Cameron shrugged. "Yeah, bruv, thanks."

He walked into the bright London sunshine, loosened his tie and undid another button on his shirt. He looked back at the large intimidating building. *Wonder how Paul got on*, he thought to himself. He put his hands in the pocket of the suits trousers that he had taken from his stepdad's wardrobe that morning and skipped across the zebra crossing. He could kill for a pint.

30

The summer burnt through the small flat. It was unbearable to sleep and unbearable being awake, however, not all due to the sun. Sleep had become harder to come by, making the daytime exhausting and overwhelming. He had spent most of the night wrestling with the duvet, trying to find a position that was comfortable. Eventually he settled on tucking it between his legs and clinging onto it like a child. He woke drenched in sweat. He splashed cold water on his face and pulled on his faded denim jeans, sniffing the red polo shirt that he had worn the day before, pulling it over his head. *It'll do.* He planned to have a pint at the pub when it opened. The heat made him thirsty and a cold pint of beer was a quick way to cleanse his throat and numb his mind. He wanted to walk down to the high street for a new pair of trainers. His Reeboks were worn at the heel and the leather so worn that his toe was almost coming through. Trainers were expensive and he was skint. They also broke into drinking or drug money, so he liked to get the most out of them before changing them, but it was time.

He dialled Sharon's number as he walked through the estate, mostly to check in but also to see if she was around later. No answer, He cancelled the call. She had recently applied to the council for housing and she seemed excited about them living together, so it didn't hurt to keep on her good side. The thought of any more time spent in the flat with his mum and his stepdad left him feeling sick to his stomach. He had spent more time in the pub to spend less time with them and when he was at home, he would often sneak off to the bathroom to snort a line off the mirror just to take the edge off the mood. It was dark. His stepdad was angrier and talking more with his fists, his brother and sister seem to walk with a weight between their shoulders, slumped over like children in a coalmine and sometimes he heard his mum crying herself to sleep. He could feel his own mind betraying him, as if lead had been injected into his skull, making his head heavy and leaving him exhausted. Moving in with Sharon couldn't come sooner and he made a promise to himself that he would give up the drugs and drink when it happened. A new start. He thought of the church hall in Croydon, which felt like a lifetime ago and the tall thin man in the large suit. He had talked about council housing that day, through the cocaine blur Cameron remembered most council housing went to immigrants who come swanning into the country with a thousand kids from Somalia or some other third-world country and get given stacks of cash. The thought of staying at home whilst some foreigner came and took what was rightly his made his stomach churn with anger. He quickened his pace.

The clock had ticked past midday by the time he had arrived at the pub. He propped his elbows on the bar and peered over. No one.

"Hello," he called out into the empty space.

The sun was pulsing through the window, heating up the room to uncomfortable levels; the smell of stale beer and vomit was almost overwhelming. He placed his hand over his nose to block out the smell. He took another look around the bar and slowly walked to the section of the bar that gave access to the staff. The hinge stood open and he could see the fridges, fully stacked with cold beers.

"Hello," he called again but this time quietly, looking again around the pub.

With no response for a second time, he swooped into the bar, pulling open the fridge and plucked a cold Stella Artois bottle from the rows of green bottles. He put it into the front pocket of his jeans and covered the exposed top with his polo shirt. He walked briskly out of the pub, congratulating himself for his quick thinking and walked towards Clapham Junction, stopping only to knock the cap of the beer bottle on the side of a brick wall.

The high street was crowded, the weather brought people out of their homes and now they filled the streets, flowing in and out of shops with bags hooked over their wrists. He skipped nimbly through, brushing shoulders with shoppers and ignoring the gazes that followed him. He could make out the black front of the shoe shop through the crowd; he hooked between an elderly couple, brushing past the shoulder of the husband. He looked back, staring the old man in the eyes, daring him to say something. He glanced back down the high street and saw a familiar shape looking through the glass of a store, his hair, though still red, was shorter and he wore a thin jacket over a black t-shirt with what looked like a band on it that he didn't know but he was sure that he was looking at Michael's back.

"Mike," he called. No response. *Deaf cunt* he muttered to himself.

"MIKE" he called again as he crossed the road.

The figure pulled an earphone out and started looking around, searching for the direction of the voice.

"Mike," he called for a third time, waving to get his attention, finally making eye contact.

As he approached, he offered his hand and Michael shook it. They took a few moments to look over each other, silently making their own judgements. He looked the same apart from the short hair and the grungy clothes. His face still thin and pale. The conversation was slow. He felt the subject of Rachel hanging between them like cow on a butcher's hook. It was almost difficult to see past it.

"You?" Michael said, repeating Cameron's own question back to him.

He felt a sudden burst of coldness fall over him as he thought that he hadn't actually been up to anything except drinking too much, snorting too much cocaine and trying to finish his community service. He had lost his job because he was convicted, now his days were spent between the dole office, the pub and picking shit off the side of a motorway. Those green eyes bore into him, waiting an answer.

"Nuffin much, mate, normal, you know. Doing a bit of politics and stuff."

He hadn't spoken to Paul since he had almost got a beating from him outside of the court and he hadn't been to any of the meetings since, but he wanted Michael to believe that he was doing more than drink and drugs. There was another long pause. *Arrogant prick is not even going to ask me about it.* He hadn't spoken to Michael since that call in October, nine months had passed but he was disappointed to learn that he still cared about his opinion. He didn't know why he should care what this scrawny kid would think of him, but he did.

They sat in a small dingy pub on the corner of the high street. Cameron knew some of the guys that drank in here and they were soft, he wouldn't get any trouble especially being a local at the Oak. He felt superior sitting in the small, badly lit space as the old guys behind him watched on. He looked at Michael's face. He had a look of contempt that made Cameron want to put his pint glass through his eyes. He reminded himself that they had been mates, though that felt like an age ago and were different people now.

"Look, man, sorry 'bout the ting with Rachel."

"What happened with that? You still seeing her?"

Cameron felt the sense of victory tingle in stomach. He was bothered by it and now he was trying to act as if it didn't care. He considered toying with him but decided against it, he wanted to get that beer and he wanted to drink it with someone. Besides, he didn't have many people that he called friends. Paul's friendship was short-lived, and he looked like he would rather Cameron was dead. He had seen Thomas a couple of times, but the man was psychotic, and he felt anxious if he spent too long in his company. He was bad news, Cameron knew that, but he was his drug dealer. Cameron needed him more than he dared admit.

"We broke up, bruv. She still had eyes for you."

He started to recite some of the information that he had heard from Paul and the meetings that they had had in Croydon. He kept quiet about the drugs, the kebab shop incident and the resulting conviction. He didn't want Michael to think of him as a scumbag. He had got to the part about the Somalis when that pale face went a deeper shade of white, tinged with grey. His eyes went cold as if they were still in his head but looking at another time and place.

"You ok, bruv?"

He spoke a name. Mohamed Khalif. Then the rest had fallen from him as if he had been holding it back for ten years. Cameron sat quietly, listening to the story unfold, nodding and shaking his head at the right points until Michael was done. He looked exhausted but relieved, like a weight had fallen away. Cameron felt an urge to reach out and make contact in some way. In that moment, they were two boys again, feet hanging absently from their ledge, watching the world stream through the narrow streets below as they showed each other secrets that they would never share with anyone. At that moment, he felt they were friends again. He felt vindicated, the old man in the suit slamming his hand on the podium in Croydon had been right. The Somalis were no good, they couldn't adapt to the English life. They were barbaric. The conversation moved on, but the image stuck in the back of Cameron's mind. He had questions he wanted to ask but knew that Michael wouldn't answer. Ideas were forming in somewhere in his mind and he wanted time to piece them together.

As they left the pub, a silence fell between them, but it wasn't an awkward silence. It was the silence of two friends trying to summon the words that escaped them when they knew they wouldn't see each other again for a while. It was as close as he would come again to the silence, they shared outside the pub almost one year previously. It had been comfortable, and they had hugged. Michael stuck out a hand. Cameron took it and shook hard and then succumbed to that feeling by dragging Michael forward into his body and hugging him. The beer had left him feeling a warm glow and nostalgic for the past. They broke apart and he looked at him

"Still best mates?" he said.

As they parted, he smiled to himself. It had been a good afternoon and now was the time to add to that warm feeling with more beer. He had spent the money he had reserved for the new trainers so they would have to wait until the next cheque came in. He figured he might as well spend the rest on having a good night.

Mohamed Khalif, he thought to himself. *Reckon I know someone who probably knows where a fuckin' nonce like that lives. Fuckin' Somalis.*

31

The pub was full by the time he arrived. The sun was dropping out of the sky, but the evening was still bright, and the longer daylight hours had dragged people from their homes to gather in the sweltering beer-smelling pub. The front door was littered with overweight men with red noses holding pint glasses. The condensation creeping down the side made Cameron's mouth water. He pushed through the crowd, muttering curses under his breath at having to fight his way through to get to the bar. Crowds made him nervous, he avoided getting on tubes, mostly sticking to buses and routes that he knew well. He sometimes felt a crushing feeling in his chest when packed in too close to people, it would ignite a small fire in the back of his brain. He would feel a rage swamping his head like a red mist. It was better to get out before he hurt someone but at this point the heat made him desperate for a drink and that was overriding his fear of tight spaces.

Finally, he felt the comforting feeling of sticky wood underneath his palm. Using this as a pivot he pushed his way through a group of lads, standing with their backs to the bar, smelling of aftershave and gel. He met the gaze from one of them and waited for him to turn away. *No trouble tonight, boy, I just wanna drink.* He ordered his pint of lager and gave the barman five pounds of his trainer budget.

He moved towards the back. It was a larger space lined with the circular booths he used to sit in with his mates. The times of sipping

Cokes and laughing at the punters on the karaoke had long disappeared but the desolate back part of the pub remained. It was often less crowded and filled with the locals, those that had shared the pub for many years, the ones that had faces worn with red veins and deep sunk eyes. He spotted his mum standing at the corner of the bar, fingers in glasses smeared with beer foam. She was piling them into tall column for the young lad behind the bar to load, clumsily, into the dishwasher. He nodded at her as he passed, she gave a small nod back. Their relationship had disintegrated to almost nothing of late.

He pushed through the final edges of the crowd, breathing a sigh of relief as he entered open space. He scanned the room, finding a place to nestle for the evening.

"Cam!"

His name bellowed across the space, making some of the old men turn their heads. Cameron, too, followed the voice. Thomas sat in one of the booths at the back of the pub. A white t-shirt clung to his broad back and chest, Cameron could see the patches of sweat underneath the armpits and forming a V-shape near his neck. His beard looked rough and uneven and his eyes were glazed, his eyelids heavy. He was sat next to two other men that Cameron had not seen before; one had a distinct scar that ran from his right eye down to the very tip of his smile, his head shaved down to the skin. The other looked at Cameron now with sunken brown eyes and smiled through yellow teeth. Cameron could make out the gold fillings in the back of his mouth. Thomas beckoned at him with a swing of his hand. Cameron took another gulp of his pint, mostly to hide the fear on his face and the knot he felt in the pit of his stomach.

"Alrite Thomas, you ok?"

He placed his glass on their table, which drew a look from the bald man sitting on Thomas' right. Cameron picked it up again, immediately, taking another gulp.

"All good, bruv," Thomas said, nodding slowly, looking Cameron up and down as if he was scanning for some information.

"This is Eric." He pointed to the bald man, who now extended a scarred and broken looking hand in Cameron's direction. His shake was as tough as his hand looked. "This is Derek," Thomas said, pointing to the other man.

They laughed as the man offered Cameron his hand. It was a shallow laugh that made Cameron nervous. "Name's Darren. This prick thinks it's funny to call us Eric and Derek."

His voice was gravelly and he spoke out of the side of his mouth, cutting off the end of the words as they fell over each other. Cameron let out a nervous laugh before Darren moved over to let him slide into the booth.

"What you up to, son?" Thomas asked. He stared through him, making Cameron squirm in the upholstered chair.

"Not much, just getting a drink."

"You still hanging out wiv that cunt, Paul?"

"Nah," he said quietly.

"Good," Thomas said. "Eez a cunt."

They laughed again. Cameron looked up and grinned. He started to feel like they were laughing with him rather than at him and he was starting to suspect that Paul was a cunt. He relaxed as the conversation moved from Paul to the three other men's childhood. They laughed through stories of police chases and playground fighting that made Cameron feel his own childhood was tame by comparison. They sunk the beers as if they were pints of water. Two hours later Cameron felt that glow had become an inferno in his head. The men continued to throw back pints of lager and whiskey chasers. It was almost ten when Thomas looked at him and said his name for the second time that night, only this time it was a question.

"Cameron?"

Not Cam. Cameron suddenly felt a little more sober as a silence fell over the table. The other two men seemed to have taken the cue to stop talking. Cameron felt that nervous churn in his stomach. His intestines wrapping themselves in a knot and tightening.

"Yeah?"

He spoke quietly. *This is it. He is gonna kick the fuck out of me.* Thomas looked at him with his glazed sunken blue eyes, staring at him and through him in way that made him feel uncomfortable in his own skin.

"Cameron, I gotta problem. And yor the man, I think, can help me." He scratched his neck as he spoke, his face screwing up as he gazed at a spot above Cameron's head.

"Ok, I'll see what I can do," Cameron grinned.

Thomas stopped scratching his neck, looking deep into Cameron's eyes, his face emotionless and almost still.

"Don't fuckin laff, Cam. You still owe me, remember? I told ya you'd pay me back someday. Dat time has come."

Cameron felt his skin run cold, breaking out in goose bumps. He swallowed hard and tried to maintain eye contact. His head was no longer spinning. He remained quiet, Thomas' cue to continue.

"I got dis problem. Some paki cunt has sold some shit to one of der kids, ere on this estate. *My* estate, Cam. I can't av that. Ya get me?"

Cameron nodded in agreement. He didn't like where this was heading but he was caught like a fox down a hole as the snarling dogs stared down at him. He wanted to run but he couldn't escape the estate. Thomas would get him eventually and he would pay that debt in blood.

"I need you to find the guy and teach him a fuckin' lesson."

"Kill him?" Cameron whimpered, his face a pale grey.

A smile spread across Thomas' face and he let out a snigger and turned to the other men. They returned the smile. He could feel their stares boring into his cheek. "No, ya silly cunt, just teach 'im a lesson. I don wan 'im dead. Just smack 'im about a bit."

Cameron let out a sigh of relief that made Thomas bellow out with laughter. "You thought I want'd you to kill someone for three grams, ya silly bastard?"

He laughed again, the other men joined in and finally Cameron joined in, nervously laughing along with them.

They left the pub together just before the doors closed for the night. The warm comfortable feeling of drunkenness had engulfed his mind once again. He had taken the time in the bathroom to snort a couple of lines and talk to himself in the grubby mirror. *It's no different from any other fight, I just need to jump this cunt and smack him in the face a few times. Tell him to stay away from the estate. No big deal. Besides, the alternative isn't any better.* He had decided to get it done as soon as possible and to do it sober so he could have his senses about him. The cocaine had his mind feeling alert and ready, almost itching to do it tonight but Thomas had told him to wait. Now they walked through the darkness of the estate, heading to the tall block that held Thomas' council flat.

They heard the chatter of young voices as they turned the corner and almost walked into a group of young kids no older than twelve or thirteen. They fell silent as the men turned the corner. Cameron watched as Thomas looked them up and down. All five boys turned away, looking at the ground, their faces pale and fresh without the flicker of a beard or facial hair. Thomas stopped in the middle. The kids shuffled from one foot to the other.

"Wat you boys doing out this late?" Thomas asked.

"Nuttin much," the tallest boy responded, still staring at the ground.

Thomas' movement was explosive and quicker than Cameron imagined. He lunged forward, grabbing the boy by his t-shirt and thumping him against the wooden door of the block hard enough to knock the cap from his head. His face looked like a bowling ball, his eyes and mouth forming perfect circles and his complexion almost a perfect marbled white. Cameron jerked upright at the sound of the thump. He felt a sense of panic rise up his spine; he looked from Thomas to the two men stood either side of him, hoping they would stop him. They stood with their hands in their pockets, their lips pulled back in a thin grin. Cameron felt frozen and powerless, his face a mirror of the boy held almost two inches from the ground.

"Empty your fuckin' pockets," Thomas whispered two centimetres from the boy's face.

The boy reached down and pulled out a small red Nokia phone and a handful of pound coins. Darren stepped forward and roughly grabbed them from his hand as Thomas set him back down on his feet. He reached forward and snapped a silver chain from the boy's neck, stuffing it into his jeans pocket. The boy's eyes filled with tears and his grey tracksuit trousers turned darker as a stain spread around his groin. Thomas took a step back and watched the young boy piss himself, bellowing with laughter, pointing a grubby thick finger towards his chest.

The rest of the boys seemed frozen in a circle, unable to move and unable to run. Cameron could sympathise, he felt the same. He watched the scene play out as if he was floating outside his body, urging it to do something or say something. Instead, it floated there as Thomas emptied the pockets of all the other boys stripping them of coins, phones and jewellery before they all ran off into the darkness of the estate, the taller boy waddling slightly with the extra weight of urine in his tracksuit bottoms. They stood outside the block a while longer, Cameron remained silent and listened to the men continue talking as if they hadn't just robbed a group of kids. Finally, he stretched out his arms in a fake yawn and wished the men goodnight. Thomas looked at him silently as he made his excuses to leave. His eyes bore into his head, digging around, reading his thoughts.

"Night guys and thanks for tonight." Cameron turned to leave.

"Cameron?" said Thomas.

He turned to meet his gaze.

"I'll be in touch." Cameron nodded and disappeared into the dark underbelly of the estate.

Before he had reached his front door, his phone buzzed in his pocket. He knew what was written before he pulled out the phone and opened the screen. Written in thick digital text was a single name and an address.

32

He stood outside his door staring at the name on the screen, his mind replaying the face of the boy, his eyes and mouth like holes in snow. He reread the message before pushing the phone back into his pocket and tugging out his door keys. He let out a deep breath, putting his ear to the door. Inside, he could hear the loud booming voice of his stepfather shouting above the wailing of his little sister and the crashing sound of something hitting the far wall and shattering. *A plate? A lamp?* He stood up straight and rubbed his weary eyes. The alcohol had worn away, leaving him a slight throb in the front of his skull and the only remnant of cocaine was the stuffed feeling he had in the bridge of his nose. He considered getting the train to Gatwick and taking the first flight, except he was shit scared of flying and he had no money. He stood looking at the flat door, listening to the mumble of chaos from within. Its panels seem to throb as if the flat was breathing, sucking at him and pulling him in to its dark encompassing cloud. *You can check out anytime you like but you can never leave. But this isn't Hotel California.* He twirled the key between his thumb and forefinger solemnly watching it rotate over and over, noticing each groove and each edge. *This is my life.* He felt a bubble of grief rise in him and stick in his throat. Another muffled crash from within the flat followed by the sharp slap of a hand on skin. His brother's wail pierced the closed door, clear and full of pain. A tear rolled down his cheek, dropped from his face and landed on his hand, exploding on impact. *Enough.*

He pushed the key into the silver lock and quietly rotated it until he heard the latch fall away from the door and it became loose. He slowly pushed the door open. His brother was curled on the couch in an embryonic pose, holding his hand to his face, which was now turning bright red. Cameron could almost see the finger marks like burns working their way up his cheek. A lamp lay shattered in the angle between the floor and the wall, fragments sprinkled across the carpet like snow. He could hear more shouting coming from the archway leading to the kitchen. Cushions and toys were strewn across the room as if a tornado had ripped through the space. His sister was crying in the distance. *She's in her room. That's good.* His brother looked up as he felt the burst of fresh air fill the hot room. His eyes filled with hope over the floods of tears. Cameron put his finger to his lips in a hushing motion and beckoned him to come towards him. The boy got up quickly from the couch and ran to Cameron, burying his head into his stomach and wrapping his arms tight around his waist. Cameron stoked his hair and kissed the top of his head, breathing in deeply. He held his head tight to his chest and felt the second tear fall, getting lost in the tangle of his brother's hair. He pulled away and held him at arm's length, looking deep into his swollen face.

"Go to yor room. Don't come out. Stay with yor sister, ya hear?"

The boy didn't respond. Cameron shook him lightly. "Ya hear?" he repeated. The boy nodded, running towards the bedroom with his hand pressed against his face. Cameron watched him quietly shut the door behind him. Cameron closed the front door, ensuring to turn the latch so it wouldn't make a noise. The mass of coats hooked to the wall concealed a handful of umbrellas. He reached in and pulled out the golf club kept hidden there in case of intruders. He walked quietly to the kitchen archway, where he stood with the club dangling loosely by his side.

His mum was cowering in the corner, leaning back so her head was almost touching the cupboard behind her and her back arched over the work surface. Her husband had a meaty hand gripped around her throat, his lips thin and pulled back in a violent grimace exposing his teeth in a snarl. Plates, cups and cutlery lay strewn in pieces across the plastic lino floor. *It was a plate and a lamp*, Cameron thought calmly to himself.

"Alrite," he said to his stepdad's back.

He watched him slowly rotate to face him. The noise stopped. The apartment fell silent for a long moment as his stepdad looked at Cameron standing in the doorway, eyes half closed and slightly glazed, a golf club held loosely by his side.

"Wat der fuck you gonna do wiv' that?" he said, pointing at the club.

Cameron had enough time to smile and think to himself *hello rage, my old friend*. His vision blurred, then sharpened, a red buzzing starting to hum loudly in the back of his skull. He hoisted the club over his shoulder as if he was ready to drive a ball and in one motion, swung it at the grimacing face. His movement was quick and his shot true. The number five iron collided with his stepdad's jaw on the left side, shattering it and knocking him immediately unconscious. He collapsed under his own weight, his shoulder striking the work surface as he fell. He slid down the kitchen cabinets where he lay motionless. His mum started screaming, high pitched and constant. Cameron dropped the club and stepped forward, so he was standing over the motionless body of his stepfather. He grabbed a handful of his t-shirt, pulling hard to lift his head.

"LEAVE THEM THE FUCK ALONE, YOU CUNT," he screamed at the unconscious body.

He punched again and again, screaming with every closed fist slamming against the now floppy bleeding head of his stepfather. Blood streamed from wounds that opened on his cheeks and trickled onto the kitchen floor in perfect circles. Cameron stepped back, panting. The buzzing had stopped, and he felt completely and painfully sober. The headache had worsened, thumping dully in his head like a hammer. Adrenalin roared through him. He had never felt so alert. He looked at his mum; her hands held her cheeks and her mouth was a gaping hole. She stopped screaming when their eyes met but stood in the same pose, shocked, her skin now a pasty white making the red veins stand out on her nose and cheeks.

"I'll come back if he lays one fuckin' finger on them. You make sure you tell 'im." He pointed a finger at her face. "And you," he shook the finger at her, looking at her over his brow, "be a better mother."

She stared at him; no words escaped her even though her mouth was open. He turned and left the kitchen, walking towards the bedroom, wiping blood from his knuckles absently on his trousers. His brother and sister were sat on the bed, whispering quietly to each other.

They jumped up at the sight of him, both burying their heads in his stomach and wrapping their arms around his waist tightly. Their grip felt warm and honest. The adrenalin still coursed through him. They stayed that way for more than a minute; he enjoyed their embrace and feared it may be the last time.

"I love you, both," he muttered into the tops of their heads. "I have to go."

Their grip tightened.

"Stay in 'ere for a while, it'll be ok now. Some men will come but stay in 'ere. OK? You're safe in 'ere."

He pulled at their arms, prying their fingers from his waist and held them away from him.

"OK?" he said again.

This time they both nodded silently. He nodded back in agreement. He left the room and the flat, letting the door click behind him with his keys still stuck in the lock. Pulling his phone from his pocket, he dialled Sharon's number.

33

He woke up early with an echo of the alcohol and cocaine headache still ringing around his head. He looked over at Sharon, her bare back faced him, he traced the moles gently with his finger before softly pulling back the covers and letting his feet fall out of the bed before his body could follow. He felt tired, his whole body felt tired, but he had been unable to sleep. He had stared at the ceiling with his hands tucked behind his head for almost three hours after Sharon had fallen asleep and had finally drifted into a troubled sleep at four a.m. He felt no remorse or regret, only peace. For now, his brother and sister would be safe. As he woke, his body ached in his bones, his shoulder ached, his fists raw to the touch and his chest felt tightly pulled together making it hard to breath. His phone buzzed from the bedside table, shaking him from his thoughts.

A message. Thomas: *where you at?*

His heart sank. It was a reminder of what he still had to do, though it seemed less daunting after breaking his stepdad's jaw. The thought of him waking up in hospital this morning gave him a moment's reprieve from the anxiety of having to do it all again.

Tooting. You?

Lets meet. Be in Battersea for 11.

He looked at the clock, blinking on the bedside table. 9:37

The pub was desolate when he arrived. Thomas was sat in one of the far booths, his elbows propped on the table as his thumbs working expertly over the phone propped in his fingers. He was staring intently at the screen, not noticing when Cameron walked in. The clink of bottles rang out into the open space as the barman filled the fridges with warm beer. He stood and turned to Cameron as the door closed behind him. Cameron nodded and raised one finger, without breaking his stride. He got a nod in return, before that familiar sound of a pint glass being pulled from racks above the bar.

"Alrite Thomas," Cameron said as he slid into the booth.

Thomas looked at him briefly before returning his gaze to his phone.

"One minute, mate." His thumbs worked quickly across the buttons, soft clicks emanating from the small Nokia in his hand. The clicks made Cameron's fingertips and skin tingle with irritation. He briefly imagined picking up Thomas' pint glass and smashing his head in with it. Instead, he stared into the empty bar, reflecting on how different the pub was during the day without the drunk regulars filling all the corners. The soft clink of his own pint hitting the wood of the table brought him from his daydream. The barman slid his drink to him, nodding wordlessly. Cameron took a long gulp as Thomas put the phone into his pocket.

"How's it goin' mate?"

"Not bad." Cameron wiped the white froth from his top lip.

"You thought about when ya gonna do it?"

Cameron's skin went cold. Thomas wasn't one for small talk, but the reminder made his stomach sink down to his balls.

"Today," he said abruptly, looking back into his glass. He had decided on the bus that he wanted it over and done with. As a rule, it wasn't good to owe Thomas anything.

Thomas nodded approvingly. "You still talk to Paul?"

The question made Cameron pause midway through drinking. He looked Thomas in the eye. "You as'ed this last night. I ain't speakin' to him. Why?"

Thomas looked at him over his own glass, pausing before taking a swig himself. Cameron waited patiently, resisting the urge to smash his own glass into Thomas' face.

"Listen, I wanted to tell you summit last night. I 'eard summit about Paul an' I'm not sure you're gonna like it."

"Go on." His interest was piqued, and they were finally getting to the point of the meeting.

"When he saw you in court, he was pissed coz he knew he was gaing dan proper for the ting in Croydon."

The colour drained from Cameron's face. "You fink I di'nt know?" He snorted through his nose in a fake laugh and took another swig.

"How long?"

"Six years, mate, it wer'nt his first. GBH. Game over."

"Jesus." Cameron blew out the breath that he had been holding.

He felt sympathy for Paul. He had been a dick at the court, but he must have been under some stress. Six years was a long time. He had a ten-year-old kid that he wouldn't see grow up to be a man.

"That ain't the kicker," Thomas continued. "You wanna know the best bit."

"Go on?"

Cameron looked at him solemnly. Thomas was enjoying this, he could see the pain on Cameron's face and was enjoying it. For the third time in less than twenty minutes, Cameron fantasised about smashing his skull in.

"He said it was you." Thomas was smirking at him. "He tried to cut a deal by saying it was you that battered the guy's face in. How'd ya fink they found you? You ain't done nuttin before."

Cameron stared into Thomas' small beady eyes for a hint of a lie. "They found 'im easy wiv the CCTV, so he threw you under the bus. That's why they knocked on your door." Cameron's brain was running quickly, playing out the steps leading to his arrest.

"He tried to make a deal, but the witnesses said it was 'im. Cops fuck'd 'im for lying."

"How do you know all this?" Cameron finally managed to talk.

Thomas snorted another fake laugh. "Mate, I know people. Nuffin' gets past me."

Cameron shook his head. Anger was boiling at the back of his head. He was angry with Paul, but he was also angry with Thomas. He had known this information and held it over him; Cameron understood why he was asking him to kick someone's head in. He had dodged a bullet already and Thomas was ensuring that if the cops got involved, he wouldn't dodge another. If Thomas decided to turn on him, there wouldn't be any witnesses to protect him. He would be lucky to wake up again.

He needed to be out of there before he vomited his pint all over the table.

34

He left the pub car park and headed into the estate. His headache had returned and was tearing into his frontal lobe, making his eyes throb. He walked through the underground passages, keeping his head low and his eyes focused on the ground. The burning red rage was sitting at the base of his skull waiting to jump through his head and course through his body but this time it had a halo of sadness. He felt lost and rejected. *Who gives a fuck about me? They all just want to fuck me over; Thomas, Paul, my mum. Fuck them. Fuck them. Fuck them.* He exited out onto the main road, stopping to watch the buses pass by in red blurs. His eyes were blank, tired, darting back and forth following the flow of traffic. He stuffed his hands deep in his pockets as goose bumps broke out over his bare arms. He closed his eyes as the soft breeze stroked his cheeks. It was soothing, he thought of that night on Mandy. His skin had prickled like the back of a cat and the night air had felt so good on his skin. He couldn't remember a time that he felt so happy. He was enjoying the wind in the same way but instead he had never felt so sad. The sadness sank through him like a weight holding him to the pavement. He opened his eyes as a thought exploded into his head. He imagined stepping in front of the next bus and feeling the darkness consume him as his head connected with the windscreen. The thought of nothingness brought a sense of relief. He stepped forward towards the curb, looking up the road for the next passing bus. It approached at speed, the carriage rocking as the wheels sunk into potholes and bounced back out. He closed his eyes and stepped forward. Somewhere he heard a horn blast rip through the busy street, peace smothered him and then a hand pulled hard at his arm from the elbow. He jerked back before he had the chance to leave the pavement. He opened his eyes in time to see the bus whistle past. The driver with a gloved hand holding out his middle finger. He turned to his left to look at the owner of the hand.

"You ok, mate? That was a close one."

A stocky man in his fifties, his hair cropped short, just about reaching Cameron's shoulder.

"Yeah mate, thanks."

Stuffing his hands back into his jeans pocket, he turned and walked back to his mum's house. If he was going to do what Thomas had asked, he would need a tool of some kind and the club served him well last time. If he was lucky, only his brother and sister would be home.

He had walked to the off license after stashing the club in the bushes in the park. He had thought that he wanted to do it sober but instead his body ached to drink. He bought a five hundred-millilitre bottle of whiskey, mixing it with a bottle of Coke and sat on a park bench swigging through the afternoon waiting for the sun to fall behind the treeline. He felt anonymous amongst the heavy traffic of the park. People swayed through the grass pushing buggies or kicking footballs, enjoying the warm Sunday afternoon in their perfect lives and their perfect children with their perfect faces. He resented them all, wanted to kill them all. Envisaged taking a gun to their pretty faces. He drank slowly from the oversized Coca Cola bottle, watching as a football passed its way through the thick green grass past his foot and into the bushes behind his bench. He followed it with his eyes and his mind fell into another time in his life when a football was all that he lived for. To pull on those knee-length socks and pull tight the laces of his football boots until he felt the familiar tug and warmth around his toes was what he woke up on a Saturday and Sunday morning for. The first kick of the ball onto the pitch to start the warm up was a feeling of serenity and bliss, the first crack of his boot connecting to the leather of the ball, hoping the shot would cannon in off the crossbar and hoping even more so that someone was watching.

Now his body ached when he didn't drink and his mind ached when he was sober. He longed to get high, whether it was with cocaine or anything else he could get his hands on. His once thin frame was now expanding at the waist, mostly due to the takeout food and beer that he lived on. A consequence of being a nomad. His legs were still thin, but the muscle definition had disappeared with his youth and his small potbelly hung over the belt of his jeans. He once had a youthful cheeky face that could be considered good looking. Now, a crooked nose and dark circles surrounding his eyes made him look ten years older. He never smiled. Smiling showed the world the shit-show his teeth had become, and he had just turned twenty.

The light had started fading from the sky, he felt bleak and mourned what he had become. He felt shame and anger but most of all he felt alone. A lump rose up and stuck in his throat as he forced back the tears. *I'm a fucking waste of space. There is no point in even being here.* He couldn't stop the tears this time, they rolled down his cheeks and he sobbed gently into the palm of his hand. A couple walking hand in hand looked over at the young man, cuddling up to a large bottle of Coke and a small whiskey bottle propped between his battered trainers, with his head down sobbing. They looked at each other and walked a little faster past him.

The sun finally starting dipping behind the trees and purple streaks burst through the sky. The whiskey bottle was empty, and the cola bottle had a few more swigs left in it. He finished in two big gulps, threw it towards the bushes and kicked the whiskey bottle hard enough for it to strike the underside of the bench and shatter into pieces. The world moved and swayed with him and the headache had subsided. He pulled his phone from his pocket and checked the address again. It was a short bus ride from the park up the main road, passing the place Michael and Steven had been to school many years prior. He stopped on the way out of the park to recover the golf club and slide the handle down his jean leg. The metal was cold as it brushed against his thigh. He covered the top of the club with his polo shirt and walked towards the bus stop, limping from the straight bar now pushing against the inside of his jeans.

He exited the bus, looking at the tower that blocked out the last remnants of the light in the evening sky. It was a flat slab of concrete; it stretched the width of the estate painted in stripes of white and brown brick that made it look like several tower blocks stuck together. The buildings were fenced in by a red metal gate that wound its way around the estate, the playgrounds and parks. He pushed through the gate and walked past the playground. There were a handful of kids, no more than ten years old, screaming as they ran after each other, weaving between the pillars of the old wooden climbing frame. Underneath the screaming, he could make out the sound of laughing. He saw a group of men standing beneath one of the tower blocks, huddled in the doorway. The sign above the door read *Brightwell Court*. He dug his hand in his pocket, pulling out his phone to check the block he was looking for. He knew it was the right one before he opened the message as much as he knew that one of these men was who he was looking for. He limped down the path keeping himself obscured from their view by the line of trees and bushes that surrounded the playground. A tall Asian man stood in-between a group of teenage boys, his beard perfectly squared on is jawline and his hair gelled up in deep dark spikes on his head. Cameron reflected on the last time he had seen a grown man hanging around with teenagers. It had been the start of this mess that had him standing in an estate he didn't know with a golf club uncomfortably pressed against his inner thigh. *This is my guy* he thought to himself. He pulled the club from his trousers and put it under a nearby bench, scouring the area to ensure that he had no eyes on him. He sat down and waited patiently for the group of five to get smaller.

He shivered in the chilly August air as the wind brushed against his naked arms. His eyelids felt heavy as the alcohol started to wear off, his body ached for another drink. His brain felt like a weight in his head, pleading with him to put his head down on the cold wooden bench and close his eyes. *Maybe this time I won't wake up.* He scratched absently at his arms, watching the group through the gaps in the trees. It was almost an hour before three of the boys starting shaking hands with the other two and walking away. He could make out the dull glow of a cigarette in the hand of the tall Asian man. He guessed he had a few minutes before he finished and went back inside. He crouched down and picked up the golf club, walking with it concealed behind his leg, the head almost dragging on the floor. He walked around the blur of the trees and bushes, now in view of the two men talking in the doorway.

"Amir," he said as he approached. The Asian man turned at the sound of his name.

"Yeah?"

He looked Cameron up and down as he spoke and that made a spark of anger flare in his tired mind. *Thinks I'm a piece of shit. I'll show him.*

"You know Thomas? He wants you to stay away from his estate."

The other boy had now turned to look at Cameron and was the first to see the club come out from behind Cameron's shape.

"FUCK," he shouted, stumbling away, fleeing from the young man with the tired grey face. Cameron swung the club from his hip, aiming for Amir's face. He felt his shoulders and arms throb as the energy that he had the night before let him down. It felt like the club moved slowly, not able to get any higher than his shoulder. Amir raised his arm to protect his face, the club head missed him, but the shaft connected with his armpit. Amir quickly wrapped his arm over the club, pinning it to his body. Cameron tugged at the handle, meaning to swing again but he was slow, tired and hungover. His energy had evaporated, and Amir easily hung onto the end of the club.

"Wat der fuck you doin' bruv?!"

He looked Cameron in the eye, but Cameron was desperately looking at the club as if it was broken, he tugged desperately at the handle again as his arms screamed in pain. His heartbeat accelerated as he felt the panic wash over his body. Amir was pulling at club with the head still tucked into his armpit and fumbling into his jacket pocket with the other hand.

Cameron gave up pulling at the club. In desperation, he let go and swung a fist at the man's head. The club clattered to the ground with a hollow *ping* as it dropped, and Amir moved his head to avoid Cameron's lunge. His fist swung pathetically through the air, making no connection. He stumbled forward, his mind racing, his ears screaming with the raging water of panic. The soft *schinkt* coming from Amir's hand made the world fall silent. He felt a fist hit him in the stomach, the air left his lungs and blew out of his mouth making an *umpff* sound.

"Fuck you and tell dat to Thomas." He heard the sound close to his ear, his whole weight was now resting on Amir's shoulder, he slumped to the floor onto his knees as the man took a step back away from him.

He looked up at the figure standing over him, dressed in black and noticing the sliver of red and silver for the first time in his fist. He held his stomach and felt the warm pulse of liquid in his fingers, a red stain spread slowly turning his red polo shirt into a deep black. He felt the last of his energy leave and he fell, face down, his cheek connecting with the dirty paving slab beneath. Amir's white trainers were turning away, and he could make out the texture of the sole as the legs belonging to those shoes broke into long strides.

He felt so tired now, his eyes felt so heavy. He blew hard through his nostrils, feeling the dirt fly up from the pavement and flicker against his cheeks. He closed his eyes and let the sleep start to engulf his tired mind. *Sleep. I can sleep. Why are they screaming? Who's screaming?* In his dream-like state, he felt his body roughly pulled over, pushing him onto his back. A hand pushed hard and flat into his stomach. The screaming of sirens rang in his ear and a man was shouting at him to stay awake, but he was so tired. All he wanted to do was to sleep and shut his mind up for a while.

"Stay with me," the man was shouting close enough to his face that he could feel his breath. "Keep the pressure on the wound."

Cameron didn't know if he was speaking to him or himself, he didn't care.

"No," his mouth was dry, and the words sounded like a croak. "Let me die."

The man fell silent, his hand still pressed firmly against Cameron's stomach.

"Not tonight, mate. Not on my watch," he said softly.

MICHAEL

35

He lay in his bed, looking at the ceiling, with his arms tucked under the pillow behind his head, listening to her thump against the wall in the corridor as she tried to pull her boots off. There was a second thud as she slumped against the opposite side of the corridor followed by the familiar *click-click* as her heels struggled to get purchase on the plastic lino floor. *Thud,* one boot hits the wall and slides to the floor. Another thump as she swings to the opposing wall. *Thud,* the second boot is finally free. She stumbles into the bedroom, almost falling through the door as she swings it open.

"You awake?"

The street lamp cast a soft yellow glow through the crack in the curtain, making her face appear to be floating in the dark. He could see her eyes, heavy and clouded in the dull light. Summer had past and winter was already turning to spring. Another year almost gone. They had gathered together in the flat earlier that evening to party before the exams kicked in, twenty or so people, drinking vodka and whiskey mixers until they had a stream of empty glass bottles gathered like skittles on the table. Someone had offered a joint, which they had smoked together on the balcony, overlooking the courtyard below. The music and laughter echoed down, causing eyes to shift in their direction from passers-by. The smoke burned the back of his throat and sent a shiver up to his brain, his whole head felt light and empty like a balloon. For a second if felt like it would detach itself from his shoulders and drift away down the Tyne river. She was beautiful. Her blonde hair fell over her shoulders, her eyes sparkled with the first few drinks. She stood in the middle of a group of men; they seemed mesmerised by her. He wasn't jealous. He stood only a few metres away talking with John, passing a glance in her direction every now and then, pleased when he would catch her eye. Her smile would creep across her face, a curl of the edge of the lips at first before beaming into a smile that would light up her face and make her eyes shine with mischievousness. Her power to pull at him with just a look was as powerful as his ability to pull at her and after almost a year he still felt the spark that had been there when they had first met. She was a shapeshifter, able to form her personality to the people around her so people became enthralled with her.

Underneath her beauty was a horrific, unforgiving and cruel monster. Once the alcohol was finished, they all staggered into the night to continue the party in the city. They walked hand in hand. Her eyes had become dull, the sparkle had stayed behind at the flat. *You're into depression because it matches your eyes*, he thought to himself, looking at her green eyes. They had been here many nights over the last year. The whiskey was like a slow release that would tug at the padlock of whatever it was she was keeping caged inside. As they walked, she glanced at him. He was looking the other way, talking with Adam as they walked through the cobbled street of the riverside. The silhouette of the Tyne bridge hovered above them, its arch almost alien against the night sky. He felt her gaze.

"Were you jealous when I was with all those guys?" She studied his face, narrowing her cloudy eyes.

They had talked about this before. He wasn't jealous. He had felt jealousy when he had learnt of Cameron and Rachel, it had boiled inside him like a rotten egg cooking in his stomach acid. It had been a destructive force that had left him feeling weak and pathetic, so he had buried it, letting it drown there in his stomach before vomiting it against a wall outside the student union. The result was a promise that he had made to himself to never feel that way again. Her ego wanted him to feel jealous. His ego wouldn't let him be.

"No," he said with a smile, trying to defuse the situation before that venom in her eye worked its way to her words, "but it just means I trust you."

"I don't know why, I fucked someone else." She emphasised 'fucked', spitting it out of her cracked lips, the smell of whiskey drifted towards him. She turned away, her eyes trying to focus on the path ahead. He looked at her in the glow of the streetlight. The furrowed brow and distant eyes gave her away. She was pining for a fight and telling lies to make it happen.

"Ok," he said absently.

She looked at him again, anger spreading across her face. Stopping suddenly and tugging firmly at his hand to turn him around. They stood outside a bar facing the river. The disco lights pulsed across the pavement and the dark surface of the river. They could hear the thump of music grow and shrink as the door opened and closed; students staggered out into the street, balancing a cigarette in their shaking hands trying to light it in the northern wind whilst keeping their feet. She let go of his hand and turned to him now, staring past him as her eyes struggled to focus.

"You're fuckin' dead inside." She prodded a finger into his chest, her words already starting to fall away at the end. "Hardly a surprise your dad wants nothing to do with you."

She turned away, her blonde hair flicking by his face and following her bobbing up and down on her spine towards the door of the bar. He hung his head and put his hands on his hips, letting out a long sigh. He had been in contact with his dad to try and build a relationship, but it was proving difficult especially as promises would be made after a few drinks and forgotten as easily as the face that served them. He stood outside the bar, listening to the thump of the music and the sloshing of the river against the bank before turning towards the bar. He nodded at the doorman as he pushed the door open. Less than two hours later he was hailing a cab home, he had watched Helena stumble from one strange man to another. His face grew hot as he watched their faces turn away in disgust, oblivious, she continued to attempt the seduction. The first time he had pulled her away by the arm, she had almost fallen against his chest, sending him staggering back into the bar stools.

"Jealous now?" she asked.

"No, you're embarrassing."

She had spat in his face. He didn't attempt to stop her a second time. He left the bar.

She staggered through the dark, her palms out in front of her. Her shin hit against the bed. She cried out. He looked up at her, now towering over him as he lay in bed. She crouched down, planting a hand on his chest. "You're here," she whispered. "Why did you leave?"

He stayed silent. He knew she would have forgotten everything that happened. She started pulling at her jacket, making her stagger back.

She whispered again. "You awake?"

"Am now," he responded.

She pulled at the bottom of her turtleneck jumper and, in a moment of sobriety, pulled it over her head alongside the t-shirt underneath in one smooth motion. She stood looking at him, dressed in a knee-length skirt and a black bra.

"Why did you leave?" she repeated.

"You don't remember?"

"No." She stepped out of the skirt and started working the back of the bra.

"You fucked someone else."

He watched her struggle with the bra before it sprang open, letting her breasts fall out and stop with a bounce. She laughed and staggered forward, swinging a leg over him, straddling his waist.

"Fuck me," she said.

"Not a chance." He tried feigning disinterest.

"Fuck me," she repeated, kissing his face. He didn't resist a second time.

36

His head felt like it was carrying extra weight but overall, he felt ok. He filled a glass of water from the tap and downed it in three large gulps. He looked over at her on the couch and smiled. Her legs were tucked underneath her, and a blanket pulled tight over her body. Her head was resting on a cushion, but her eyes were open. She gave a small tired smile back. The hangover was worse for her, it was almost two in the afternoon and it showed no signs of subsiding just yet. The apologies had come in the morning like they usually did, the intoxicated words forgotten in the morning but each one taking its toll.

Her phone shrilled from the floor where it sat near her head. She winced, squeezing her eyes shut before looking at the glowing screen. She picked it up, looking intently before she shifting to a seated position, the blanket falling to cover only her legs.

He watched her as she spoke. Her face lacked the usual blusher that gave her a glow in the evenings, making her seem pale in the afternoon light. Her hand came up and covered her mouth, tears building up in her eyes and spilling onto her cheeks. He watched her leave the room with the phone still pressed to her ear.

He waited patiently, his palms pressed against the surface of the kitchen, watching the courtyard outside the window, basking in the winter sun. He was guessing, silently, what it could be that had upset her. *Maybe her brother got into a fight or got arrested?* She would use it as an excuse to drink more and get more obnoxious. It was five minutes after she left the room that the sound of the door slowly opening nudged him from his daydream. He turned and saw her, head down, the black mascara from the night before now leaving black streaks down her cheeks.

"Dad's dead," she wailed and fell into his arms.

Shit. Wasn't expecting that.

37

As he stood in the Newcastle train station concourse, watching the trains wail into the station, screeches ringing up to the tall ceiling, he was imagining what it would be like to lose both parents and be orphaned before twenty-one. He watched yellow numbers and letters change on the boards as the trains pulled away from the station, waiting for the train from Kings Cross to come pulling in. The funeral had been pulled together with the help of an aunt, who would also help manage the will if there was anything to divide. Relieved when she insisted that he shouldn't come, he had watched her leave a few days ago, stood in a similar spot as her train pulled out of the station and disappeared around the curve for the weekend. Now he watched the tracks, waiting for the train to pull back in. Anxiety fluttered around him, making his palms sweat. He wanted normality when she returned, he wanted desperately for them to be together again like it was the beginning, but with Helena, nothing was predictable.

It was eight minutes past midnight. They had been back at the student halls for barely five hours and she had consumed almost two bottles of wine. She swallowed each glass quicker than the last, leaving lipstick smears over the lip of her large wine glass. Her fingerprints littered the sides, like small ghosts stuck forever in a globe. Now the glass lay shattered on the concrete floor, the ghosts finally free. She was stood in the courtyard dressed in just her underwear. Her skin was covered in goose bumps as she clutched her elbows against the cold. Her hair fell over her shoulders partially covering her breasts but offering little warmth. Tears were streaming down her face leaving those familiar black streaks and her shaking hand held a knife that she had taken from their kitchen. The blade was smeared with blood as were her arms, fresh marks scratched out on her forearms against the older white scars that had been there for years. She was screaming at him as he stood in the doorway, he spread his hands out, his palms facing her, trying to calm her down. The lights flicked on in the apartment opposite and he could see the balcony door open and someone looking down at them.

"No," she screamed. "You don't know what it's like! I don't give a fuck what people think!"

"Just come in, it's cold," he pleaded.

He grabbed the coat that she had tossed to the floor on her way out and ran to her, draping it over her shoulders. She started to fight but he pulled it tighter around her. She struggled against his body, her clenched fist thumping against his chest. She finally conceded, sobbing quietly, her head slunk and coming to a rest below his chin. She held the edges of the coat over her naked body, the knife falling from her hand and clattering to the floor with a metallic ting. He held onto her and she didn't resist. He buried his face into her hair, tucked an arm underneath her armpit over the jacket and gently tugged her to her feet, stopping to stoop down and pick up the knife. *Better wash it before John sees it.* He led her inside, looking back at the balcony above to see if they still had an audience. The figure above turned away and went inside. *Show's over, pal.* He shut the door and led her to bed.

38

The summer heat poured through his bedroom window. July had arrived and with it the sun blistered into the room and turned it into a greenhouse. This summer felt different from the last. He felt an air of optimism. He spent the time working alongside William in Kings Road in a small clothes store and they had started to rebuild their relationship as adults. It felt good. They walked across Battersea Bridge, the sun often still high in the sky until the late evening, talking about university, football and Helena. Michael talked mostly and William listened, but he nodded in the right places and asked the right questions. Michael enjoyed spending the time together, outside the shadow of the house, just the pair of them and the comforting chaos of rush-hour traffic lining up beside them in the roads as the currents swirled in the Thames below. He would take the train to Brighton soon to visit Helena but having some time apart left him feeling a weight had been lifted. Her mood was dark much of the time, he had tried handholding and coaxing as often as he could, but it was becoming tiresome and emotionally draining. The drinking had accelerated and so had the self-harming; it was become difficult to hide or explain to his housemates, who often woke up on a to find bloody cutlery in the sink. He shoved this thought to the back of his mind; it drove a sadness through his head that he found difficult to shake for days. He thought back to the previous summer, how he longed to be near her, to hold her hand and stroke her face. Now her presence weighed on him, choking him.

He had to shield his eyes from the sun as he left the house, but relieved to be in the fresh air. He continued to mentally plan the weeks ahead as he walked towards the main road, slipping his earphones in letting Adam Lazzara ask him *will you tell all your friends you've got your gun to my head?* He looked across at the football pen. Noise from the caged pit was swirling up into the air; a football crashed against the heavy door sounding like a thunderclap. He slowed down to watch the kids' heads bob up and down, darting back and forth through the black cage; the wall hiding their bodies from the chest down. A shape caught his attention on the far side of the pen. A figure stood with his back to him, but he recognised the slightly curved shoulders and mop of dark hair. Cameron was talking to someone in front of him who was considerable shorter and smaller. He crossed the street and walked through the car park, smiling to himself at the thought of seeing his old friend again. Thoughts of Rachel long been put away. As he approached Cameron, he started to pick out chunks of the conversation; he could hear Cameron's raised voice, heated and angry. He slowed his walk to listen, shuffling around the side of the pen so he was able to make out Cameron's side profile through the fence and the boy standing in front of him.

The boy was no more than twelve years old, dressed in grey tracksuit bottoms and a Chelsea football shirt. His face was distorted with fear, his eyebrows pulled at angles and his eyes wide, wrinkling the skin above his nose. Cameron had a handful of the Chelsea shirt and was pulling it upwards into the boy's chin. He had him pushed against the wall. The one eye that Michael could see looked clouded, the eyelids drooping and his mouth twisted into a sneer, showing his rotting teeth. Spit was gathered in white pearls on the side of his mouth and as he spoke, he sprayed small droplets into the boy's face.

"I said empty out your fuckin' pockets, ya mug."

The young boy had both hands stuck firmly into his tracksuit pockets. Michael could see his small fist was clenched around something in there.

His face wobbled and his bottom lip started protruding from his mouth before the tears started to fall. The boy was pulling his small fist out of the tracksuit pocket. Clenched in it was a small grey Nokia phone with silver keys. He held his fist towards Cameron without opening it.

"And the other one." Cameron gave him a shake, rattling his chin with his fist.

The hand slowly emerged holding a folded ten-pound note. Michael watched the scene with a sense of dismay and powerlessness. He knew he should step in but lacked the courage. The boy suddenly looked over at him, his hands hovering in the air, catching Michael's eye. His eyes pleaded for help, making Michael feel sick to his stomach as he took a step back, so he was covered from view by the large football pen doors. Cameron took the phone and note from the boy's hand.

"Now fuck off," he said, shaking the shirt one last time and shoving the boy away, making him stumble forward. Michael took another step backward, so he was completely out of view and almost back at the car park, his mind danced with indecision. The boy ran, crying, glancing at Michael before finally disappearing over the grass and into one of the doorways of the block of flats. The choice had been made; the deed done. Michael turned and walked back through the car park, with his head down and his earphones reinserted into his ears. Lazzara lamenting *well I can't regret it, can't we just forget it?* He looked up briefly to see Cameron's shape enter the football pen. He couldn't forget it. He would likely regret it. *What happened to you?* he thought. *What happened to me? Why am I such a fucking coward?* The shame made him feel sick.

He sat staring out of the window as the bus trundled through the traffic on Battersea Bridge. The view from the bridge was spectacular and one of his favourite parts of London. The river was dark and peaceful; the sun cast an orange ripple on the surface. Across the stretch of the river, Albert Bridge ran parallel, with two white triangles pointing at the sky. Beyond the bridge, the river continued to wind its way through to the centre of London as the buildings built up at its banks like an audience scrambling to watch its majestic flow through the city. Today he couldn't appreciate that view like he had before; in his mind was the face of a small boy crying, who would likely live in fear of playing near the football pen. Shame in his stomach had been accompanied by anger towards Cameron, wrapped in a blanket of helplessness.

He felt his phone vibrate in his pocket. He stayed still, waiting for it to stop. *Could be William.* He took it out at this thought and looked at the screen. *John.*

"Allo, mate." He tried to sound cheery as he answered the call.

"Alright, mate." John's voice was low and had lost the booming energy.

He listened to John talk, his open palm cradling his chin as he watched the final part of Albert Bridge slip from view and the window became filled with the tops of a hundred cars inching their way towards Kings Road. John's girlfriend had called time on their relationship. They had been together for almost four years and John was clearly more in love with her than she was with him. Michael felt that this phone call had an air of inevitability, but it didn't make it any less painful for John. He was sobbing through confused words; he couldn't get the closure he needed as he didn't know what he had done wrong. The answer was a simple one for Michael; nothing. John was loveable and funny, but she was out of his league, most people saw it immediately. He felt a headache gather pace in the front of his skull.

The energy that he had left the house this morning had slowly ebbed its way from his core and left him feeling empty. He would have to spend some time with John when he went up North. It would result in nights sat in the corners of the bars in Yorkshire, revisiting the same stories, nodding, agreeing and listening. The rest of the group would stand at the bar downing colourful shots until they curdled with the beer and were finally fired onto a pavement somewhere in the early hours of the morning. Meanwhile, Michael was sure John would slowly get drunk, the tears would come, and they would end the night hugging, as Michael watched the bar over his shoulder, jovial and lit with colours and music. Thoughts of Helena slipped back. The weekend in Brighton would be similar but without the background of his friends dancing and drinking until they threw up in the streets.

A feeling, as if his body was filling with sand, came over him. He felt short of breath as if it had worked its way into his lungs. Breathing became a task, heavy and slow. He closed his eyes and tried to block out the sound of John's voice, leaning his head against the warm window of the bus. He was already an emotional crutch for Helena. It felt like she was dependent on him to stay alive. Left to her own devices, she would probably cut too deep one night whilst inebriated, and slowly bleed to death in her bed or on the street. He wasn't sure if he had the capacity to hold John's hand this time. He had felt like he was slipping many times in his life but as he focused on regulating his breathing, he realised that this was the first time that he was completely conscious of the process.

39

The train rolled into Brighton station, squealing and coming to a stop with a hiss. He stood up as the doors opened and passengers flooded out, herded towards the exits by the narrow platform and people in illuminous yellow jackets. She was waiting when he exited, her eyes round and lost with dark patches underneath. They embraced on the concourse of the train station. It was passionless and habitual, making him feel like they were strangers saying goodbye; in a way, this did feel like the beginning of a goodbye. She smelt of wine and cigarettes, a smell that was now familiar to him but one that he wasn't accustomed to smelling at two in the afternoon. He held her away from him and looked at her at arm's length. Her face looked tired and thin, her smile was strained and her eyes hollow.

"You ok?" he asked.

They walked silently hand in hand to her house; he let the silence sit between them. The house was now almost desolate, all her father's things packed into large boxes and stacked up against a wall in each room, almost reaching the low ceilings. The curtains were half drawn, making the room feel like it was stuck somewhere between night and day. The windows closed and, in the stifling heat, the house smelt like an attic, dusty and a distinct aging smell. She led him through the boxes to the small kitchen at the back of the house. There was a small circular table against the wall with a bottle of white wine and an empty glass, the sides a blur of fingerprints and red lipstick piercing the edge at various points. She picked up the bottle and poured until the glass was half-full. She paused as she brought the glass to her lips. "You want some?"

He knew it meant *'join in or fuck off, just don't judge me'*. He shook his head but pulled out one of the chairs that accompanied the table and sat down anyway, placing his bag on the floor next to the seat. He looked around the kitchen as she stood next to the table sipping from the glass. It was small with wooden cupboards surrounding a small white stove and a small kitchen sink, doors on the far side led out to a small grass garden that had a black metallic table with one singular chair and a white ashtray that looked like it was ready to be emptied. On the kitchen surface he noted the block of knives, one missing. He got up, brushing past her as he walked towards the sink. She grabbed him by the hand.

"Don't," she whispered.

They stood that way in the kitchen like a couple frozen in a dance. She had one hand out holding the wine glass and the other gripped around his fingers, her gaze locked on his face whilst his eyes stared at their interlocked hands. He broke away, picking up the knife from the sink.

"I thought you were going to stop this," he said, holding the knife towards her.

He couldn't disguise the disappointment or the anger in his voice. She turned away, sitting on the chair that he vacated. She finished the glass in two large gulps.

"What do you care?"

She sat with her arms crossed at her chest, one hand still holding the glass and her eyes blank, uncaring. He threw the knife back in the sink, shaking his head. The glass made a clink as she set it down on the table; she stood and took his hand.

"Let's go to bed," she said, trying her best to be seductive, but her speech was already slurring.

He followed her without resistance. She let her dress fall to the floor whilst she peeled the t-shirt from her body as she entered her bedroom. It was the first time that he had been here alone with her. It struck him that it was a room stuck in time. George Clooney adorned the wall in a range of poses, five or six soft toys sat on a nearby wicker chair, watching the bed patiently; the pink bed covers lay in a heap at the foot of the small single bed. She caught him looking and followed his eyes to the collection of bears. She let out a small embarrassed laugh.

"I should probably get rid of those."

She took his hands and placed them on her hips. They kissed as they fell onto the bed. The kissing became frantic as he unclipped her bra and ran his hands across the smooth skin of her rib cage. He moved down, gently kissing her neck and chest. She let out small gasps that slowly became sobs. He stopped and looked at her heaving chest. Her hands were now covering her face as she cried in small bursts, turning onto her side to shield herself from his gaze. He slumped beside her, struggling to find room in the small space between her back and the edge of the bed, and slid an arm around her neck pulling her into his chest. She rested her head in the grooves of his body. He could feel the tears seeping through his t-shirt. They stayed that way until he heard her gentle snoring. He watched her sleep a few minutes before slowly removing his arm and rolling off the bed, planting his feet on the warm wooden floor. He left the room, heading for the kitchen to put water in the kettle. He let out a deep sigh. He knew that he would not be breaking up with her this weekend. He stared out into the garden, trying to plot the next move as the noise from the kettle came to a crescendo.

40

The first few weeks of term, John would come to Michael's bedroom door. Michael would hear the latch of the door release. Without looking up, he would hear the soft rustle of the carpet as the bottom of the door slid over the surface and John's head would appear.

"Can you talk?" he would say.

But they wouldn't talk in the traditional sense. John would talk, sometimes for hours, whilst Michael would nod and offer the right response to the right moments. John had no idea of the destructive force that was destabilising his own relationship with Helena; Michael didn't want to create a bond between them based solely on their sadness.

After almost three weeks, he stopped nodding along, waiting for John to finish until the silence became so heavy that John would leave. He would sit at the desk, with John sat in the lounge chair to his left as if he was with a counsellor, continuing to type while John regaled the breakup and his feelings of abandonment. Michael would grunt and nod his head. This continued for another two weeks before he started locking the door altogether and turning the volume up on the music when he heard the gentle knock. The handle would rock as John tried the door; he would knock a couple more times before giving up and sloping back up to his own room to sit in his own isolation. Eventually he stopped knocking at all, which suited Michael fine.

December had whistled into Newcastle on brittle wind from the Northern Sea. He sat alone in his room looking at the bright screen of his computer. He had spent many evenings in this position, staring at the same computer screen and watching people move like cockroaches outside his window, sinking shots of alcohol until he felt a warm numbness in the centre of his forehead and his head felt light. The phone buzzed on his desk. *Helena* flashed on the screen. There was a time when that name would excite him, and he would eagerly grab at the phone but now there was a sinking feeling in his stomach that he could only call dread.

Shall I come over tonight?

He looked at the message for a long time before clicking 'Reply'. *If you want...*

The reply came back almost instantly. *I'm outside.*

He looked out the window to see her shape looking up at him, her blonde hair tucked under a grey woolly hat. She waved a small wave with her hand barley extended from her hip. He motioned for her to come up. Her face broke into a smile as she headed to the door; it was a smile he remembered from the first days. He had to remind himself how far they had fallen since then, or he would risk falling for her all over again.

It wasn't painless but it went better than he thought it would and suddenly, he was finishing the bottle. The hardest part would be the days that would follow when she began to drink; however, it was a bridge he would cross later. For now, he had a date with the rest of the bottle and a gentle, yet comforting, feeling of complete drunkenness that would be his gateway into forgetful oblivion. She had shed tears as he expected her to. She had asked if he still loved her and he had told her the truth; he did but they were destructive together and he could no longer help her. He had to help himself. She had promised to change as he had expected. He sat quietly and watched her sob into her hands; he had no words to say that would make her feel better, so he chose to say none. He didn't answer all her questions. The ones he didn't want to answer, he sat silently pressing the tip of his thumb, which infuriated her.

"So that's it then? It's over?"

He sat quietly for some seconds; the click of the clock seem to echo in the quiet room.

She was looking at him, waiting for a response. "Yes," he said, firmly and quietly.

She had stood up and walked out the room. He didn't try to stop her. A part of him felt that what he was doing was best for her too. Instead, he poured another shot in the short tumbler and sank it without the lemonade.

MICHAEL (CONTINUED)

41

He walked into the brightly lit office; the sun streamed through the tall glass windows casting a ray of light on the receptionist despite the early hour. His suit jacket held at the waist with one button and tugged gently at his rib cage, fitting perfectly to his slim body. He beamed at the receptionist as he approached the desk.

"I have an appointment with Mark Shipper," he said nervously, still smiling. "It's my first day."

As soon as he said it, he felt his face start to warm up and his cheeks blush.

"Name?"

"Michael." There was a pause. She looked at him over the top of her glasses, waiting for him to continue. "Oh… sorry…" he mumbled. "Michael Turner."

"No problem. Fill in this in and take a seat," she said.

He filled his name quickly and sat on the soft sofa that stretched its way across the reception.

He sat looking around the clean, clinical reception; windows filled every wall. The building was a tall rectangular structure in the heart of Canary Wharf, dwarfed only by the identical buildings that surrounded it, all standing proud and grey against the London skyline. The sense of achievement rose up in his chest like a blooming rose, leaving a small smile forming on the edge of his lips. Streams of people were now pulsing into the building, badges bleeping as they passed through the glass barriers.

The elevator doors slid open and Mark came striding towards him with a hand held out before him. Michael rose and shook his hand briskly. He had a strong grip and a natural smile filled with perfectly straight white teeth. His grey hair parted on the side in rough strokes, his navy pin-striped suit neatly folded over his body and the jacket pinched together at the waist. Michael was drawn in by him; his hazel eyes set in his head and warm smile made him instantly likeable. He walked towards the elevator with a hand gently placed on Michael's back, guiding him forward; all the while, he talked about the building and Michael's travel to the office as Michael nodded along to the melody of his East London accent. The lift took them up to the twenty fifth floor; Michael looked out on the sun-drenched horizon of the London skyline. They strode into a wide-open space filled with banks of desks like islands in a sea made of bland carpets. Young bankers were shuffling through the thin spaces between the islands, setting up for the morning, hair and suits perfectly in time with one another. The desks each had three monitors looming over them and phones that shrilled only once before being answered. The early morning hustle in the office felt like it was building. Michael felt the adrenalin in his body pulsate as he looked around the room. Mark watched him carefully, letting him enjoy the moment before finally gently placing a hand on his elbow and leading him to one of the desks. It was bare in comparison to the others; the screens were black; he could make out his thin pale face in the reflection. The phone had a small screen with his name already written in black block letters.

"Your desk," Mark said, pointing at the empty chair. "The rest of the guys will be along shortly, and they'll show you the ropes." His accent was warm and reassuring. "This is Sofia," he dragged out the 'o' making her name sound like 'Soofeeya', "she started with us six months ago."

Sofia's face peeked at him across the barrier between the desks. Her dark hair was pulled back in a smart ponytail, and her eyes sparkled against her tanned face. She smiled at him; a nervous look gleamed in her eyes making her shift her gaze away almost immediately. He lifted a hand in a gesture of hello; she returned it, quickly turning back to her keyboard and the screens that hung over her. He watched her type for a little longer as Mark pointed at parts of the office, directing him towards the toilets and the exit. Her face was perfect. Her wide brown eyes focussed on the screen and the way she nervously bit her lip as she typed was beautiful. He settled into his chair and leaned across to turn the screen on. He heard Mark laugh behind him.

"Keen? You'll do great, ere. I'll give IT a bell."

Mark disappeared from his shoulder. Michael sat quietly, watching the side of Sofia's face, her brown eyes moving left to right, scanning the screen in front of her before finally meeting his gaze. That soft smile appeared briefly before they both looked away. He skimmed the cursor over the screen, waiting for his log-in screen to appear.

The day went in a blur of meetings and coaching sessions. He scribbled furiously in an A4 notepad until his fist throbbed with the effort. The noise in the office started to simmer down to a murmur as the markets started to close. He peered over the top of his screen and watched a handful of suited men head towards the elevator. One broke away from the group. He was tall, his hair perfectly combed away from his forehead and his eyes behind small round glasses with deep black rims. He tapped Sofia on the shoulder with a slim well-manicured finger, making her jolt upright and turn around quickly.

"We're going for a drink, you wanna come?"

The man looked over; he was no more than two or three years older than him. Michael averted his eyes, focusing on his computer screen.

"Sure," he heard Sofia say.

"How 'bout you, fella?"

He had hoped for an invite, now he looked up, meeting the man's gaze. His smile was warm.

"Sure," Michael replied, quickly shutting off the computer monitor, catching the small smile that broke out on Sofia's face. A warm feeling burst to life in his stomach.

The sun was still bright as they left despite the evening hour, the sound of their laughter boomed through the tall buildings. Sofia saddled up next to him as they worked their way towards the riverbank. The pubs were over-flowing with pin stripe suits and white shirts, unbuttoned down to the chest and women in smart blouses and knee-length skirts, flicking their heels on the end of their toes whilst swirling wine in tall glasses.

"Where you from?" she asked, looking at the floor as she spoke.

"London." he said. "Actual London." he followed up quickly.

She looked at him, her face screwed up into a frown.

"Lots of people say they're from London but they're really not," he muttered as an explanation. She smiled a smile that made him relax. "You?"

"Madrid. Actual Madrid." He laughed aloud.

"Sounds warmer than here. Why did you move to London?"

"Work. Obviously, duh," she said with a smile.

He looked at the pavement slightly ashamed that she was able to ridicule him so easily but enjoying the sound of her voice and the smile that turned up one side of her face. They walked side by side until they reached the riverside pub. The water was awash with yellows and oranges, glimmering as it shuffled side to side slopping against the bank. The chatter and cackles of laughter of the beer-fuelled punters made it impossible to hear each other talking but they persevered. The group of guys had found a small table and they huddled around with their beer glasses perched on the beer-logged surface. Together they joined the noise with their own chatter, swigging cold beer in the warm evening until the night turned chilly and the bar bell rang out. He walked with Sofia to the tube station, his jacket slung over her shoulders and his own shirt now unbuttoned revealing the top of his naked, hairless chest. He hands tucked into the pockets of his trousers, pulling his elbows tight into his rib cage in order to preserve his heat. She had offered to return his jacket, but he refused each time. When they parted at London Bridge station, she stood on her toes and pecked him neatly on his cheek. The alcohol had formed a glow around his head that cleared with the contact of her lips. It had been a good first day.

42

Four weeks later, they shared their first kiss. He had immersed himself into the group, joining them on the warm riverbank in the evening hours. He started to feel like one of them; he watched carefully when they spoke, the hand gestures, the small twitches in the face and words that seemed reserved for bankers. Everyone was a 'geezer' or a 'guy'. His accent, which had developed a northern edge, started to mellow back into his familiar London patter, though making sure he kept pace with the East London swagger. South London was no longer a place he felt connected to, phone calls from his mum made him wince, a painful reminder of the boy from a South London council estate. Time had moved on and so had he. He rejected the calls more than he took them. He was busy, work had consumed his life and the rest of his time was made of drinking with beautiful men and women in affluent bars, bars that he would never have dreamed of spending time in when he was a teenager, bars with no fruit machines and neckless bouncers.

The first weeks were the most difficult as the nights drinking beer were followed by expensive gin and tonics in expensive glasses. His body felt worn by the weekend, he would stay in bed until deep into the afternoon. It was one of these nights when he first felt her lips on his. They stood in a circle; Michael had spent much of the time stood opposite Sofia. He felt her eyes on him as he talked. The crowd laughed at his jokes, but she smiled, putting her beer bottle to her lips and taking a small swig. Excusing himself, he pushed himself through the crowded bar looking upwards for signs towards the toilet. As he reached the stairs, a hand reached out and he felt the soft skin touch the tips of his fingers. His stomach did a full flip and he gripped the fingers without turning, embracing the small smooth hand in his own. He was stood on the stairs, when he turned to look at her, their faces almost at the same level. She leant in and kissed him, her tongue slipping smoothly between his lips. He stroked her face with his empty hand, enjoying the feeling of her thumb, which was now stoking his jawline. They broke apart. She let out a small awkward smile before releasing his hand and walking past him towards the bar toilets. He stood for a few seconds alone, a smile spread across his face and her saliva fresh on his lips before turning and following her. He next time he visited the toilet that night, he shared a cubicle with Scott, and snorted his first line of cocaine.

He waited for her outside the tube station in Covent Garden. The night was starting to crack across the sky, people scurried across his path pulling children and bags laden with shopping. The lights of the shops lit the streets from below, creating an eerie darkness above his head as the streetlamps seemed dampened against the sky. She came bounding out of the tube station, her bag hooked over her shoulder and her face lit with a smile. She skipped through the crowd with ease and slung her arms around his neck, kissing him on the lips. He pressed his arms tight around her lower back, almost pulling her from the floor. It was their first time that they had ventured out as a couple without the group, but he already felt a comfortable closeness to her. He enjoyed the feeling of her body pressed against his.

They weaved through the streets, entering an old grand pub that arched up three floors, sunken back from the main street. The bouncer gave him a nod as he walked past, almost approving of his company or it could have been the way she made him feel. The bar was a labyrinth of stairs and copper railings that spiralled up and down. He climbed up, his hand still carefully clutching hers, enjoying the soft palm in his own.

Pushing his way through the crowd, his hand in front of him and one behind, pulling Sofia through the wall of people. He found his way to the bar and ordered a drink. They found a corner with a small ledge to balance their glasses.

He gazed at her like a lovesick fool as she spoke and enjoyed watching her face and stroking her hand, touching her hair. He felt a soft comfort hold him from the inside; a peace floods his veins just to be near her. He watched her lips move as she spoke as if the world had slowed down to the beat of Newton's cradle. He wasn't listening to words anymore. All the while, something dark ticked in the depths of his mind that he couldn't extinguish. In there, he was thinking of all the things he could say that would make her cry, maybe storm out of the pub, leaving him standing alone with his beer. The desire to destroy everything good was an impulse. His mind picking at the surface until the cracks showed, waiting for the foundations to come caving in. *Why am I thinking of this?* Panic swept over him as the temptation to blurt something out rose up in him. He felt like a man standing on a ledge resisting the urge to jump, all the while she continued to talk. He pushed it down and tried to shake his head clear of the thought, instead his mind spoke to him in a soft whisper: *you might as well say what you want as you will fuck this up anyway or she will find out who you really are.* His skin went cold and sweat broke out on his forehead. *It's true. I fuck everything up eventually. I can save her the trouble.* A mouthful of vomit rose up from his stomach and wedged itself in his throat before he forced it back down, wincing.

"You ok?" she said, looking at him carefully.

"Yeah, it's warm in here. I'll just pop to the bathroom and we can head out after these." He pointed at the drink she was cradling in her hands.

He rushed away before she had a chance to answer, crashing through the bathroom door and into an empty cubicle. He retched once and twice. Nothing came. A thin sliver of drool hung from his mouth before falling and hitting the water with a small plink. He steadied himself on the sides of the cubicle opening the unlatched door.

"You ok, mate?" the black man sitting on a small three-legged stool asked him in a thick African accent.

"All good, mate. I'll take a dash of aftershave, please."

He splashed his face in the sink before spraying Hugo Boss on his neck. The subtle sting on his neck felt good as he started to recover his composure. He threw two pound coins in the small silver tray next to one of the sinks as the man handed him a paper towel.

She downed the remainder of her G&T as he sank the last of his beer. He hoped the restaurant would impress her; he had spent two hours that afternoon searching through endless reviews. *She will probably hate it*, he thought as they left the Victorian pub. *Probably thinks I'm a fucking loser.* He pushed the thoughts back again and focused on stroking the soft fingers that entangled with his. They walked in a comfortable silence. She didn't hate it. He woke up the next morning with her head still resting on his chest and his arm swimming with pins and needles. Her breath softly tickled his chest and her hand felt sweaty, planted flat on his chest. He watched her sleep, her chest heaving up and down softly, her nostrils flaring with each breath. He wanted to stay in that moment for the rest of the day; he wanted to feel her weight on him until his whole body ached.

43

He stood in the bedroom that they sometimes slept in together, staring at the full-length mirror. He wore a navy suit. His black shoes were polished to a high shine. The knot of his navy-blue silk tie was a perfect triangle and set against the background of his white shirt. The jacket fit perfectly, the shoulders broad and flat. The sleeves perfectly stopping before the bone of his wrist, revealing the white cuff of his shirt that hung two inches longer. His red hair was combed away from his face with the parting to the right. He stared through his own reflection, staring intently at his own green eyes almost waiting for them to blink. The clock on the bedside table hung on 7:04 before shifting slowly to 7:05. The sun was streaming over the horizon, breaking the morning through his window. It was coming again. He could feel it, seeping through his pores and clinging to his bones. It always started with a tiredness behind the eyes, which would spread like a cancer through his arms and legs. Joints would scream at him; his head would feel full of cotton and the eyes would burn. He stared at his reflection willing it away. A hero of nothing, a shell of a human. Staring and collapsing slowly in the mind. His brain had betrayed him again. It was urging him to bed. It was urging him to give up and go back to bed. Wait for the time to pass before his death. Just wait. Do nothing but wait. It was all he could do.

He broke the staring competition with himself and as always, he was the first to blink. He pulled on his rain jacket and picked up the briefcase that waited patiently for him at the door. He slunk down the stairs of the apartment building. As he opened the door, he pulled his jacket tight to his body to protect himself against the cold. He stood still, feeling the wind ruffle his hair. The cars roared past. When it came, it descended quickly. The smallest decisions became a task, the biggest ones became overwhelming and every one of them was emotionally difficult to make without feeling a pitch-black hole open in his heart. The pit of his stomach churned; a similar feeling to nerves before a job interview but without the anticipation of good news. He had been working at the company for almost a year, he had achieved everything that he had hoped but the sacrifices that he had made had consequences on his physical and mental health.

The bitter smell and taste of cocaine was stuck at the back of his throat and flooding his nostrils, making him feel sick. The rule was always the same when they spent the evening in the glow of East London bars and strip joints. You could be hungover in the office but never be absent. Today he wished he was absent. The cocaine left him feeling paranoid and isolated. He had made a promise to himself to reduce the amount he was doing. Last night had been a heavy session with Mark and he had felt the pull of obligation to impress the boss. He had laughed at all his jokes, thrown shots of alcohol down his throat and joined him behind the curtains whilst a tattooed girl danced in front of them in nothing more than a pair of knickers and a frilly bra before removing both. They had hugged as Mark told him that he loved him before he disappeared in a black cab hurtling towards Kent. Michael had hailed the next cab and watched London past by in a blur of yellow lights, solemnly watching the crowds getting kicked out of bars across Shoreditch high street. He had fallen into the flat that he shared with a French student. Being careful to creep past his door, falling onto his bed, he had finally shed the tears that had been bubbling inside him since he had got into the cab.

He arrived in the office, slumping down on the chair and reaching across to flick the monitor on. He stared blankly as the screen lit up and a

Microsoft logo floated into view. Sofia walked in and sat in her chair opposite, looking over at him, with the smile that made her eyes sparkle.

"How was last night?" she whispered.

He looked at her wearily, his eyes burned in the bright lights of the office. She didn't know about the cocaine and he planned to quit before she found out.

"That good, huh?" she said with a smile curling the side of her mouth.

Her eyes suddenly darted from his face to the screen, concentrating at the blank monitor that he knew she had yet to switch on. It was a sign that someone was behind him. They had been seeing each other for eight months but they had yet to make their relationship official beyond the small group of friends. He felt a hand land on his shoulder, firmly, almost shaking him out of his skin. He turned to look Mark in his weary face. Dark circles surrounded his eyes and his skin looked grey.

"You look like I feel," he said.

Michael managed a smile, but he felt like vomiting.

"A word?" He signalled towards his office.

Michael's blood ran cold, his face drained of colour and he could feel Sofia's gaze burning a hole in his skull. Mark looked at him and let out a short laugh.

"Dan't warry, you're not getting fired. You look like you seen a ghost."

He laughed again and turned towards his office. Michael followed him, shuffling his feet across the carpeted floor. He was convinced he had been found out. Mark was going to pull him into his office and lay out everything he knew. He was a fraud and now the game was up. He closed the door behind him as Mark settled into the leather chair behind his desk. Mark pointed at the sofa that ran along the glass opposite his desk. Michael sat, his hands clasped together and tucked between his knees. Mark slunk back in his chair; his own hands clasped across his stomach and looked at Michael, upright and pale. His mind was racing, thrashing through scenario after scenario. *I said something last night or he found out about Sofia and it's against company policy or last night was a trap to see if I take drugs or I made an error in the report. A big fucking error and cost someone millions.*

"Michael? You ok?"

Mark was smiling. He was enjoying this, and the thought sent a ball of rage burning in Michael's stomach. He was the mouse and Mark was the cat, playing with his corpse as he took his last short breaths, pulling air through lungs that lay beside him on the pavement.

"Fine. A bit hungover and nervous."

"Nervous? Why?"

"You never call me in to your office."

"Well, I'll keep it short." He leant forward, placing his hands on his desk. "I'm promoting you, Michael, I'm makin' you 'ssociate."

His smile widened. Michael felt cold sweat break out on his head. His brow furrowed as he tried to make sense of the conversation.

"I wanted to tell you yesterday but thought it better not to do when I was off my tits."

He leant back again and crossed his legs. "You've done a good job and I need someone good."

"Wow," Michael whispered, "thanks."

"Don't thank me. You deserve it. HR will sort out the contract and put a meeting in with us. Now get the fuck back to work and let me die in peace."

Michael laughed aloud. He felt good and the laugh felt good coming out of his mouth. Relief and joy swept through him. He got up sharply and opened the door.

"Thanks, Mark," he said as he left the office.

Mark waved a hand in the air to usher him out the door but there was a smile on his face. Michael closed the door behind him and slunk back to his chair, winking at Sofia as her eyes pleaded with him for news.

"OK?" she mouthed.

He nodded and flicked his mouse to pull up the log-in screen on his desktop.

44

The day had absorbed the last of the energy that his body could muster and he felt his mind fighting away all the positivity of the day and demanding he go home to bed. He wanted that more than anything, to slip out of his suit and climb under the duvet. He could close his eyes and sleep, sleep for hours or days.

After hearing his news, Sofia screamed so loud he thought the sound might pierce his eardrums. She squealed in delight and threw her arms around his neck. Her touch felt alien and uncomfortable, when it should have been what he most needed.

"We have to celebrate! Can we tell the guys?"

"I guess so." He rubbed the back of his neck absently where her arms and hung only minutes before. "I dunno, maybe I'll have a quiet night?"

"Nooo," she cooed, pulling at his sleeve and resting her head on his arm.

They sat in a small coffee shop overlooking a line of cars that slowly edged through the traffic. His sandwich left abandoned on his plate, uneaten, and would stay that way.

"I fly home tomorrow and I want to celebrate before I go."

"Ok," he conceded.

It was Friday evening and the bar was a scene of London workers shedding the weight of the week and poisoning themselves slowly with alcohol. He thought to himself that it must be one of the most accepted and painful ways to kill yourself. For the first time in a year, he thought of Steven. He looked around the bar, staring at the faces of strangers, watching them bellow with laughter and clink glasses together. He felt alone in a room full of people. He swirled the remainder of beer in his pint glass and tried to reattach himself to the conversation. After the initial excitement of his news, the clinking of glasses and shouting close enough to his face that he felt droplets of spit on his cheek, they had begun talking about London house prices. Scott was passionately declaring the time to invest was now – the bubble would continue to grow for at least ten years. He felt Sofia reach across and squeeze his free hand. He offered her a pensive smile and closed his eyes, cocking his head to one side in a gesture to say that he was tired.

He endured another hour of the chatter that had started to feel like white noise. He drained the last of his pint and put it down sharply on the table, so it made a hollow thud to signal it was his last.

"I'm off, guys." He pulled on his jacket, ignoring the cries and whines for him to carry on drinking. It was early in comparison to the early-morning finish times that they were used to but the pull of his bed and a night alone in the darkness was what he needed, to be encased away from the outside world. He said his goodbyes, shaking hands and planting fake kisses on cheeks caked in makeup. As he left, Sofia followed him to the street. She stood in front of him in silence, waiting for him to speak. Instead, he watched the taxis pull up and leave one by one.

"So?"

He pulled her close and held tight. He felt a sadness that came over him quickly. He choked back tears and hoped she didn't notice. She pulled away and looked at him, looked through him.

"You ok?" she said finally.

He couldn't tell her the truth. She would see him for who he was. He risked losing her and he wasn't ready to do that. He knew he was falling for her and that could only mean a disaster somewhere in the future but now was not the time to let the disaster unfold.

"Just tired, darlin'."

She nodded and kissed him.

"Have a safe flight." He stoked the side of her face, seeing every curve on her lips as if for the last time. He left her to the chaotic bar and walked to the tube station, his hands pushed deep in his pockets and his head hanging low, his chin almost stroked his chest. His phone buzzed in his pocket, startling him from his zombie walk. He looked at the screen, pausing before hitting the answer button.

"Mum?"

"Allo, darlin', you ok?"

"Yeah all good, what's up?"

"Nothin'." He could almost see her physically reeling away at the curtness of the question. "I was jus' checkin' if yor ok. I warry 'bout ya."

He didn't know why she had decided to use those words, but they drilled through him and the tears that he choked back moments before breached the barrier and came flooding down his face. He hadn't spoken to her in a couple of months. He felt ashamed when surrounded by the perfect, suit-wearing colleagues that he had just left at the bar and, deep down, he felt ashamed of the shame. His mum still managed to read him better than anyone else he knew.

He heard her saying, "Michael? Michael? What's wrong?"

He ducked out of view of the street into an alleyway, trying not to inhale the smell of urine that caked the walls.

"Dunno, Mum. Just feel shit."

"Where are you? I'll come get you."

"No, it's ok. I'm on my way home. Just about to get the tube."

"Don't go 'ome, come 'ere and 'av a cup of tea."

The idea filled him with warmth. Even the accent that he had worked so hard to change was comforting.

"Ok mum. I will. I'll see you shortly."

He hung up and left the alleyway, putting his earphones in and slipped through the tube barriers and down the escalator.

He exited out of the station. The sky had darkened and the estate that towered over the station seemed sinister. He tugged his jacket tightly around him and walked through the parade of shops towards the main street. There was a small church overlooking the shops, a sign stretched across its length in white text standing out against the black background. *Jesus said I am the way. If only* he thought to himself as the familiar and overpowering smell of African Kenkey Shop filled the air. He pinched his nose, mostly out of habit, to keep the smell finding its way down his throat. The smell subsided as the small dark path wormed its way towards the main road. To his left there was a small wooden bench, which looked out of place against the dark backdrop of aged brown brick buildings and dilapidated shops. A figure sat alone, his head slumped down, and his hands hung loosely between his legs and beside his feet was a small carrier bag. Michael could make out the shape of an alcohol bottle and a large bottle of cola. *Fuckin' drunks* he thought as he passed the figure, glancing at the tired and pale face. His head lifted and caught Michael's eye. He slowed down, staring at those blue eyes. They were familiar to him, but he couldn't place them in the distorted pale face and bloated body.

"Michael?"

The man spoke his name, making him stop, squinting in the dark to get a good look at the face that was now smiling up at him. The teeth were all missing from the front and the teeth that were left in his mouth were brown. His face was swollen; the cheeks round and pasty, his face looked like it had a thin layer of oil and his hair lay limp against his forehead. Dark circles hung under his eyes.

"Michael, bruv, how are ya?"

"Cameron!" he said incredulously.

Michael thought back to the last time he had seen Cameron; he had a child by the shirt and was forcing him to empty his pockets. For the second time in the space of an hour, he felt shame creep up in him and make his cheeks burn.

"Yeah, man, it's me. I know, I look a fuckin' mess." He laughed at this. Michael said nothing. "I am tryin' to get off this shit." He gestured at the bag that still lay at his feet.

"Good on you, man," Michael replied. "Anyway, good to see you. I gotta go."

He pointed at the lit main street and the safety of the bus stop that he could see from where he was. He started to turn away, desperate to be away from this conversation.

"Wait, mate. Wait, wait."

Cameron was getting up from the bench and moving towards him. He staggered, his shoulders slopping forward as he walked as if he was going to fall on his face.

"Let's get a beer."

"I ain't got time, mate."

"Come on, mate, we used to be best friends."

"Yeah," Michael replied, checking him over once again and glancing briefly at his watch. "Sorry, I need to go."

He turned and started to walk briskly away. When Cameron spoke again, it turned his blood cold and froze him where he stood; he turned slowly to meet his gaze. He listened to Cameron speak, without saying a word.

CAMERON

45

"Come on, mate, we used to be friends."

He was aware that he was pleading. He felt desperate. He had sat alone on a bench for two hours staring blankly at the row of shops in front of him and the concrete floor at his feet. The pub no longer wanted to serve him, so he had staggered into the night looking for an off license. He knew that he should have gone home; he had promised Sharon that he would be home in time for dinner, but he had let her down again. He had been letting her down so often now that it was a habit, he found hard to break. The night was cold, he felt the chill spread across his arms, but the warm glow of the alcohol crept up from his stomach.

He heard the clack of the footsteps on the concrete before he looked at the face. A tall figure emerged from the gloom, dressed in a crisp dark suit that seem to gleam in the dull light of the streetlamps. He wore a blue raincoat with the collar coolly flipped up, his white shirt was open at the neck and his hair perfectly parted at the side and brushed away from his face, making him seem as if he was fresh from a movie set. As their eyes met, Cameron recognised the eyes of his old friend. He was a symbol of a lifelong lost and forgotten. A life when he had hope. In that moment, as he watched the figure watching him but not recognising him, he understood that this friendship would be the only thing that could save his life. Only Michael wasn't interested in talking to him.

"Yeah," Michael replied with that look of disgust curling down the sides of his mouth. "Sorry. I need to go."

A light burst into life somewhere in his mind. "Mohamed Khalif," Cameron shouted after him, desperately.

Michael stopped, his back facing Cameron, unmoving. He turned slowly to face him, silently and wordlessly, he met Cameron's desperate eyes. Cameron looked away, needing to hide the lie that he was about to tell.

"I found him. I know 'oo he is. I can get him sort'd for you."

Michael stayed silent.

"Look, mate, I've had a rough time. I got stabbed, man. I nearly died."

He lifted his t-shirt to expose his pale, bloated stomach; below the rib cage was a deep angry purple line with pinpricks either side.

"See, some paki stabbed me."

Michael winced at the word.

"Sharon's fuckin' preggers as well and I don't know what der fuck I'm gonna do." His words were slurring, and tears brimmed in the corner of his eyes. "Just one fuckin' beer, man, for ol' times sake. We were fuckin' best mates."

Michael stayed quiet, holding the edges of his jacket. The silence between them hung heavy in the air.

"I have to go," he repeated finally and with that he was walking away, his back disappearing onto the main road.

Cameron slumped back onto the bench, his head fell into his hands and his chest heaved big heavy sobs. A croaky wail escaped his mouth; he hitched and started again, wailing into his palms. A steady stream of passengers exited the train station and walked by, making sure to give him a wide enough berth, eyes down focused on their footsteps.

He staggered from the bench after discarding the half-drank bottle of Coke behind the church wall. He took a swig of the small whiskey bottle, wincing as the liquid burned down his throat and settled into his stomach like lava. He retched, swallowing hard to resist the urge to vomit as his mouth filled with saliva. He stumbled down the small residential street leading to the estate where he used to live. He felt his phone vibrating in his pocket. *Sharon.* He left it to go unanswered. It was almost eleven and the sky had turned into a deep purple, only broken by the sparkle stars. It was late and he had missed his curfew by a few hours, but there was only one place that he wanted to be right now. He slugged the last of the whiskey bottle and let it crash against the wall of the tower block, glass sprayed against his shoes and the sound echoed upwards seeming to circle above his head. He pressed the buzzer to Thomas' flat and waited for an answer, shuffling from foot to foot to keep warm.

The intercom opened and he heard Thomas' gruff voice.

"Thomas, it's me. Cam."

The door buzzed open; the foyer smelt of piss, he covered his face with his hand as he thumped the button to call the rickety old lift. The bell chimed and the door shuffled slowly open on its runners. He took the lift to the thirteenth floor, lightly shaking side to side as the old lift trundled upwards on its wires. It opened onto a small concrete space with a view that overlooked the city. He walked to the barrier, gripping the thick bar that followed the small ledge around the building. He watched the headlights dart over the surface of London's horizon like pulses of electricity, the night air felt good on his face. He looked down, his head swam, and his eyes jittered in his head. He closed them, sucking in deep mouthfuls of air and breathing firmly out into the empty space before him. He rocked forward, standing on the toes of his dirty trainers, letting the top half of his body lean over the black painted barrier. His hands gripped, and his palms broke out in a cold sweat as he felt his weight shift from his bottom half to the top half. His body started to inch forward into the abyss, his eyes opened, and he was staring at the concrete thirteen floors below. He jerked back, staggering away from the ledge so quickly that he almost collided with the wall behind him. His body was covered in a thin layer of cold sweat; he shook his head, trying to discard what had almost happened.

It felt ok. It felt peaceful.
That ain't me. I ain't doing that.

He walked down the small corridor, making sure he was walking close to the flats to avoid looking over the barrier. He knocked once on Thomas' door. He heard the footsteps shuffling across the carpet, the door flung open and Thomas stood topless, his broad chest and rounded stomach covered in black coarse hair. He pulled at the band of his tracksuit bottoms and stared at Cameron.

"What took you so long? What der fuck do you want?"

"Anything Thomas, I feel shit. I want something to feel good."

He was surprised that he was close to tears.

"Fuckin' pathetic. You got money?"

"Na man, but I'm good for it. I'll sort you out next week."

Thomas shut the door. Cameron stared at the closed door, considering whether he should leave or wait but he didn't have the energy to do either. He stood that way observing the silver knocker on the white plastic door, it swung back open, startling him. Thomas pushed a small plastic bag into his palm. Inside were two small circular slightly pink pills.

"It's all I got."

"What is it?" Cameron asked.

"What do you care?" He pushed the door to close it in Cameron's face once again.

"Thomas?"

"What?"

Thomas pulled the door back open, his face full of disgust.

"Do you know a Mohamed Khalif from Tooting? He might've done some time for bein' a nonce?"

Thomas raised his eyebrows, looking at Cameron's face as if he was looking for the joke. There was no joke; Cameron's eyes remained heavy but serious.

Cameron sat on the same bench outside the Church of the Nazarene. He stared, open mouth at the words that wrapped around the front of the church. *Jesus said I am the way.* He had swallowed one of the pills almost immediately after leaving Thomas' doorstep and now he was coming up hard. The saliva was gathering in his mouth, almost more than he could control and his back teeth were grinding together. He barely noticed that he was folding and unfolding his fingers, extending them so hard that the knuckles were going white. Goose bumps broke out on his skin, his thin dark hairs raising and standing to attention. The world swam in front of him as if it was immersed under water; colours exploded from the sky in deep blues and brilliant yellows from the streetlamps. A pigeon flew past him so slowly he felt it would fall from the sky. He watched it go, a smile broke out on his face, it was a distant, unforced smile that made him look goofy. The soft breeze tickled the skin on his arms, feeling almost orgasmic. He was thirsty. He felt the clicking in his throat as he swallowed. He stood slowly, wobbling on his feet before steading himself on the bench. Staggering to the church, he retrieved the half bottle of cola he had discarded and drank in large gulps.

He watched the last travellers leave the station and walk through the small path towards him, appearing to glide like ghosts. Their eyes were wide and staring, making him feel paranoid. He started to walk, aimlessly, staggering into the high street, closing his eyes and breathing deeply when a gust of wind stroked his skin like an invisible stranger. *Home*, he thought. *I'll go to home.* He touched his groin at the thought of slipping into a warm bed with Sharon and slowly edged towards the bus stop, carefully putting one foot in front of the other with precision and effort. The world still swam slowly around him and he marvelled at the sky, the feel of the breeze and the sound of humming cars as they passed. It took him almost thirty minutes to walk the half mile to the bus stop.

He sat on the bus with his head leant against the glass, feeling the rattle of the ground as the bus trundled on the way to Tooting. He closed his eyes, but his mind danced and sang inside his skull. His body felt tired, his eyes darted energetically beneath his eyelids. He exited the bus and turned towards home, slowly pacing the street, stopping every few yards to enjoy the feel of the wind of his skin and admire the shop fronts. They seemed beautiful to him, the darkness behind the glass a complete mystery with the ghostly version of his reflection staring back at him.

Khalif he thought as he stood staring at the front of a charity shop. *He lives here too. I can talk to him. Make him see what he did was wrong. What did Thomas say they call him? Leon?* He pulled the yellow Post-It note with the address scrawled in Thomas' handwriting; with the other hand he fingered the switch blade that Thomas had pressed into his palm as he had left his flat. *I'll talk to him.* "Just talk," he muttered to himself. He buried the Post-It back into his pocket, his fingers brushed the small plastic bag with the last remaining pill. He pulled it out, stopping to stare at it in the middle of his palm as if it was completely alien to him. He marvelled at its roundness; the soft looking surface coated in fine powder. He opened the bag, pushing his grubby fingers between the plastic sides and plucked the last pill. He rolled it in his fingers a moment longer, marvelling at it before slipping it onto his eagerly waiting tongue.

46

He walked the length of the high street, not knowing Sarah had walked the same sheet before meeting Khalif. He barely noticed that the streetlamps were dimmer, and the darkness smothered the end of road. Dreamlike, he wandered the street, looking upwards at the clear night sky. To his right, a cemetery stretched out, its end disappearing into the dark. Headstones emerging, from the ground, left long shadows stretched across the uneven grass in the dull lights. He ran his fingers across the black fencing, listening to the *plink plink* sound of his fingers strumming the iron and enjoying the vibration that shivered its way up his arm. A small side road led to a council estate. The blocks were three stories high of deep brown brick, only broken by white pillars that supported the overhang. Underneath were doors all coloured in reds and blues. Cars were parked against the railings; he ran his fingers across the condensation on the windows as he passed them, leaving a thick line that bled gruesome drops like blood from a wound.

He walked into a gated area, there was a small patch of grass and two or three trees that were starting to get their bloom back after a cold winter. He pulled the Post-It note from his pocket once more, looking at the scruffy curled six that Thomas had scrawled with a biro. He looked up at the row of doors in front of him and checked the name of the building. Satisfied that they matched, he followed the rows of door, stopping outside number six. It was past midnight, but he wasn't aware of time. He felt good. The ecstasy pulsed through him though now, he could feel the anxious twitching and scratching claustrophobia working its way through. He listened intently to the door, his ear cocked, his mouth ajar. He heard the distant chatter of a small child and an adult talking. He stepped back and rapped the door with his knuckles, laughing quietly as he noticed the knocker for the first time.

He heard shuffling of feet on the carpet before the door swung open and a tall black man stood in front of him, naked except for a pair of white Calvin Klein briefs. His face was thin with high cheekbones and a long forehead, his skin blemished with spots and scars. He looked confused, his eyebrows furrowed and his mouth slightly ajar, pulled open by his large bottom lip. He eyes flicked up and down at Cameron, taking in the white man with pasty skin standing at his door, with pupils so large it was almost impossible to see the blue that sparkled behind. Cameron spoke first, pointing at the man's groin.

"Ha, I can see your dick."

The man's eyes widened, he let go of the door and took a step forward. "Oo der fuck are you?" He pointed a finger in Cameron's direction, his eyes fierce and narrowing.

"Mohamed, right?" Cameron continued.

"Oo der fuck is Mohamed?"

The man looked around behind Cameron as if expecting a camera crew of a prank show to be behind him.

"Mohamed. Mo. Listen, I like you, but you can't rape people."

His lips made a slapping sound as he spoke. He talked in quick, jerky bursts and the saliva built up in the corners of his mouth. His speech felt frantic, his heart pumped quickly in his chest. The man turned and closed the door gently behind him, enough to block Cameron's view of the living room and the small child that had been staring at him through the doorway.

"Listen, mate. Yor fuckin' buzzin'. You want some shit or summit?" he said quietly.

Cameron shook his head, almost dramatically side to side, holding up an open palm. "No. I have had enough. I'm here to tell you to not rape." It sounded ridiculous to him to say it out loud, but his mind struggled to form the right words.

He looked into the man's face. A brief moment of silence fell between them as they stared into each other's eyes.

"Get da fuck outta here," the man said, finally, shoving Cameron in the chest.

He stumbled backwards, just managing to steady himself. The man turned to go back inside. Cameron removed the knife that he had been fingering in his pocket and released the short blade. The click was enough for the man to turn around; panic had spread across his face, his eyes wide and his mouth forming a circle. He started to raise a hand, but Cameron had stepped forward quickly and plunged the small blade into his stomach. There was no anger descending over his mind, just an anxious itch that made his legs twitch. He imagined Michael's face in that moment; he imagined telling him what he had done and the delight that would spread across his face. He pulled the knife out, blood burst form the wound, pouring quickly down the man's stomach before hitting the band of his underwear and spreading down the front. The white pants slowly bore a pink rose in the font. The man placed his hand over the wound, the blood still pouring from his fingers and slumped against the frame of his door, sliding to the floor. His eyes never left Cameron. He looked shocked, his eyes asking *why have you done this?*

"I told you," Cameron said calmly as if the man had spoken aloud. "You shouldn't do it."

The man muttered something quietly that Cameron couldn't make out. He didn't bother asking. He turned and walked away from the flat, striding through the gate with more purpose than when he had arrived. The euphoria was gone. He dropped the blade into a large black steel bin, the top flipped back revealing a week's worth of rubbish bags. The smell was nauseating. He forced his hand deep into his tracksuit pockets, rubbing the blood on the cloth to remove it. With his hands still buried deep in his pockets and his head low, he walked back past the cemetery towards the high street and home.

47

He rolled over onto his side and opened his eyes. The light streamed through the window; the curtains pulled open. He groaned. His mouth was so dry his tongue was sticking to the side of his mouth and his head throbbed. He still felt his back teeth grinding together and a sharp pinch in his jaw. He heard the shuffle of slippers on the carpeted floor and turned towards the door. Sharon came in, dragging her slippered feet as she walked. Her stomach swelled in front of her underneath her loose blouse; her hands gently cradled the bump.

"You up?"

Her tone was cold, she didn't look at him as she picked up a used cup from the bedside table. He didn't remember what time he had gotten home in the end; he didn't remember a lot of yesterday. The face of Mohamed as he slid down the doorframe was burnt into the front of his memory. *Evidence.* The word was sharp in his mind and made his headache worse. He remembered wiping his hand in the pocket of his tracksuit bottoms, he knew he would have to burn them. Throwing them out wouldn't be enough. He swung his legs out of the bed and started searching the floor for his clothes.

"Where are my clothes?"

"In the wash, they stunk, and they were disgustin'."

He slumped back into the bed, putting the pillow over his face. He mentally retraced his steps back to Mohamed's front door, trying to remember everything he touched, every moment in which he could have transferred his DNA. He had dropped the knife in the bin, there was small chance they wouldn't find it. His tracksuit bottoms were the least of his worries. The urge to cry built up like a bubble in a glass of water and burst its way to the surface. He waited for her to leave the room before sobbing quietly into the pillow. He heard plates clinking together in the kitchen. He had a few minutes alone, he climbed from the bed, using the frame to support him as he staggered towards the bathroom. He closed the door behind him and slung the bolt into place. He stared at his reflection in the mirror, watching closely as his pupils retracted, large and shining in the overhead light. The whites were soaked with red veins that spread across his eyes like cracks in porcelain. His skin looked drained, almost grey. *Death is coming*, he thought. *What have I become? Nothing. A useless fucking drunk. A waster of space. A burden.* He opened the medicine cabinet, shifting through the collection of sanitary towels and cans of deodorant until he found what he was looking for. He took his simple plastic-handled razor, rotating it slowly in front of his face. Small clumps of hair still hung between the blades. He pressed the blade into his forearm, pushing a crater into the skin, tensing his arm, he closed his eyes, drumming the courage from within. *Do it. Do it. Do it.* His heart quickened and his teeth clenched together.

Sharon screamed. He eyes shot open, expecting her to be standing at the door. The plastic handle snapped with a loud *crack*, the blade falling into the sink. A small line of blood appeared from the mark and trickled down his arm, rounding the curve and disappearing from his view. The scream came again, only muffled by the closed bathroom door. *Where is she?* His heart was beating so fast and loud, he suddenly became aware of the sound. He sprung the latch open and yanked the bathroom door so hard it crashed against the rubber stopper and swung back, almost hitting him in the face. He was running, using his hands to guide him and stop him falling. That scream ripped through the house again. He steadied himself and concentrated on where the sound was coming from. *The kitchen*, he thought.

She was on the floor, her legs sprawled out in front of her, her back pressed against the glass door of the oven. She was looking intently at her stomach, her arms cradling it, her palms pressed evenly on the bottom of her bump. A dark patch spread over her groin. Her face was flustered and pained.

"What happened?"

He almost shouted, checking himself at the last moment. He could hear the blood pumping in his ears, and he was desperately trying to stop himself from panicking. She looked at him, tears filling her eyes, her face consumed with pain but smiling. *Jesus, why is she smiling?*

"She's coming!"

She laughed a forced painful laugh, followed by a deep groan, leaning over and pressing firmly onto her stomach as she did so. He stood staring at her, his brain slowing gathering the scene and putting the pieces together.

"AMBULANCE," she screamed, finally breaking his catatonic state.

He ran towards the bedroom, losing his footing and falling onto his hands and knees at the doorway. He scrabbled across the carpet to the bedside table, snatching his phone. His hands seemed to vibrate as he tried to focus his mind to prepare for the call. Finally, he dialled 999.

48

He was slumped in light-blue long back chair in the hospital ward. Nurses were moving swiftly around the room with a sense of purpose but calm on the exterior. Sharon's screaming had finally stopped, she lay back on the bed, her hair plastered to her forehead with sweat. Her face had softened from bright red to a soft glow in the cheeks, shining from the layer of sweat, funnels of water making lines down her chests. The baby in her arms looked up at her from her cocoon of towels and blankets. Cameron felt empty as he watched that small smooth face. He didn't feel the love that he hoped he would feel immediately; his body and mind were exhausted. He watched the mother of his child watch the small face of his child with the love and admiration that he had wished and dreamt for. He felt a flower of jealousy bloom in his stomach. He would never feel love in that way and, at a time when he should feel happy, he felt empty and numb. He watched the nurses instead, robotic and efficient but tentative and caring towards Sharon and the baby. *They must have seen thousands of babies. How can they still act like each one is so fucking brilliant? I should feel something if they can. What kind of monster am I?* He felt the urge to run and never see either of them again.

He turned to Sharon and met her tired eyes, they both managed a small smile.

"You want to hold her?"

He wanted to want to, but he didn't want to. He didn't want to hold his only child, confirming that he felt nothing, and he was, as he suspected, completely dead inside.

"Sure."

A midwife, who was flicking through buttons on the monitor and scribbling notes on a pad, turned and walked to the side of the bed closest to where he sat. Her face was stern, deep lines formed down her cheeks, but her eyes were kind and when she smiled her face was ten years younger. She picked the bundle from Sharon's arms, little arms and fingers reached out grasping at the air. She walked towards him, her face lit with a wide smile. Cameron wondered again at the number of babies she must have seen and wondered how she could keep that plastic smile on her face for so long as she put each sack of skin into the arms of its parents. He sat upright on the chair and held out his arms. The chair groaned under his weight as if complaining of its burden. She rotated the child expertly, placing the head into the crook of arm.

"Here," she said as she moved his hand to cover the backside of the child.

He smiled nervously. She seemed almost weightless in his arms; he pushed aside the blanket from her face to allow her to breathe and to make sure that she was still there. A small hand stretched out from beneath the whiteness and clutched the tip of his finger with surprising strength; the eyes pulled themselves open and looked at his face. Her eyes were dark; a deep blue ring circled the pupil, and her mouth pulled open in a perfect circle. Her hair, deep black and thick, swept away from her forehead in a long quiff. It felt as though his heart had dropped from his chest and plummeted into his stomach. Speechless, he looked from the small smooth face with the shark-like eyes to Sharon's expectant face. His throat closed, he choked back tears, helplessly trying to prevent himself from crying. It felt as if his mind was a tower made of blocks, precariously balanced and wobbling under the softest breeze. It had stood through the drinking and the beatings, through the drugs and the abandonment and it took a small delicate girl with a gently formed fist to send the whole building tumbling down. The surge felt like a weight collapsing and releasing at the same moment. He cried hard with the small human looking at his face, deep pulls that burnt up from his stomach to his chest, his throat contracting and releasing. The relief was palpable, it felt like ecstasy. Better. It felt better than any drug he had ever taken. He curled his arm comfortably around the child and placed a palm over his face. He didn't notice Sharon, gingerly, get out of the bed and put an arm over his shoulder as the midwife crouched next to him and stroked his upper arm. He was lost, wave after wave of tears shuddering through his body and taking away the weight he carried.

The sobs subsided. He wiped at his face with the back of his hand, being careful not to disturb the baby, who had closed her eyes during the commotion and slipped back into a sleep.

"Sorry... sorry," he was repeating almost to himself, desperately trying to regain his composure.

"Don't be," Sharon said softly. Her head rested on his now and he felt her breath brush past his ear.

"It's been an emotional day."

You don't know the half of it, he thought.

He stroked the small face that was now making a sucking sound. He was mesmerised by her, she was the most beautiful thing he had ever seen.

"So, what's her name?" the midwife asked.

They turned towards each other. Sharon had talked about names and he had grunted at each one with disinterest, staring blankly at the TV screen.

"Well, I like Katie?" she said.

She gazed at him, the statement posed as a question. He smiled a natural smile that felt good on his face.

"Me too," he said and returned to staring at her face.

Katie. Katie. Katie. You might have just saved my life, Katie. It all changes from here.

49

Her cry was shrill, piercing the quiet of the room and waking him from his sleep abruptly. He stayed with his head buried in the pillow, eyes looking at the crack in the curtain that was streaming the morning sunlight onto his face. He heard Sharon talking softly, the crying continued to bellow through the flat until it became muffled and finally stopped, replaced with a delicate sucking noise. He had slept less than four hours, the clock on the bedside table said 7:42 and his mouth was already crying out for a drink. Instead he rolled out of bed, pulled on a pair of tracksuit bottoms that were folded over a chair and walked into the living room. Sharon was sat in the small tatty armchair, the t-shirt that she wore to bed was pulled up and Katie's mouth was wrapped around her nipple. He approached her, placing a hand on her shoulder and kissing the top of her head. She looked at him, smiling. The bruise underneath her eye from the last time they had argued was now turning a faint yellow but her eyes glowed and made her beautiful in the morning light. He felt a twinge of shame nibble at his insides.

"Wanna tea?" he offered.

"Yeah, that'd be lovely."

"I'm going job centre after," he said as he stood in the doorway towards the small kitchenette.

She looked up at him, surprise dangled in her eyes. She said nothing but a smile lingered.

He left the room before she could respond, flicking the switch on the kettle and pulling his phone from his pocket. He thumbed through his contacts, THOMAS rolled into view making his jaw clench and his tongue long for something more than alcohol. The thought of Mohamed had left him until he saw that name. He convinced himself that they wouldn't find the blade and unlikely spend a lot of time investigating the stabbing of a convicted rapist. His thumb hovered over the buttons of the phone, the kettle boiled in the distance and clicked to a stop. The name offered him an out. It was a name that gave him real freedom. He closed his eyes and pressed *delete.* His phone put doubt in his mind; *are you sure?* it seemed to shout at him. He looked up at the ceiling, tracing the small cracks and cobwebs that had made homes in the corners. It was proving to be harder than he had imagined. He thought once he decided enough was enough he would be able to close that chapter in his life. Now as he stood with his hand hovering over *continue*, he felt the indecision swarm his body as he remembered how good it felt to be high. His body yearned for more. He let out a long breath, blowing deeply through pursed lips. He hit *yes*; the number disappeared from his contacts with a small bleep. He tipped the phone back into the pocket of his tracksuit bottoms and pulled two cups from the cupboard, flung in a teabag and carefully poured the steaming water in the top. The teabag swelled and rose to the top.

The job centre was a tired looking building on the high street, the windows single glazed and fixed in a white frame, standing out against a brick front. The front door was littered with men and women, chatting idly and smoking. The gutter was awash with the gold boxes and cigarette ends. It was a collection of tracksuits with the bottoms stuffed into socks, the faces drawn and aged. Even the young men looked ten years older. Their fingers were yellow, their eyes dark and tired. He walked past them. *Like ghosts*, he thought. *Lost ghosts.* He took a ticket at the reception and sat in one of the many plastic uncomfortable chairs that were lined up in the small waiting room. More ghosts sat staring blankly at the walls. He absently read each of the posters that surrounded them; a mixture of colours advertising forums and events where jobs were plentiful and there were people on hand to help write resumes. His eyes settled on green and black poster advertising for people to work in the local supermarket. *Good benefits. Competitive package.*

The screen buzzed and thirty-four lit up on the board. He looked at the small triangular paper in his hand. *Thirty-four.* He walked to the desk and sat in the chair facing a plastic screen, littered with scratches, lines drawn into the hard plastic like scars. Behind it sat a large black woman. She seemed to have sunk into her chair and started to melt. Her face has hidden behind large glasses, her lips glowed with a deep red lipstick. He couldn't make out her eyes from the reflection in her glasses, he smiled anyway as he sat down.

"Help you?" she barked.

He swallowed the urge to call her something that would likely get him escorted from the building.

"I need a job. I've been looking but not found anything," he lied.

"What you looking for?" Her arms were stretched out in front of her, wrapped around her stomach, fingers interlocked. She hadn't made any movement since he had arrived except for her mouth moving like a red glazed doughnut.

"I dunno, anything. There is a job at the supermarket, I saw. That looks good."

"Name?"

He spelled out his name, she began slowly tapping on the grey keyboard in front of her as he spoke. Each letter a painful slow clack that made the hair on his neck stand up on end. Cameron watched her black fingers move over the dirty keys. He imagined breaking her fingers one by one, stifled a laugh as he imagined that arsehole of a mouth screaming in agony. The printer by her leg whirred into life, humming at the silence between them. He watched her face as she continued to tap slowly on the keyboard. Paper slipped onto the out tray. She plucked it up and slid it through the gap under the screen.

"You can apply on those computers over there," she said, pointing to a row of large screened computers over his shoulder. "Anything else?"

"Is there any other jobs I can apply for?"

"If you look on the computer you can find some. Just remember to put the reference number in," she said, pointing to the digits on top of the paper that he was now clutching. He thanked her begrudgingly and left the desk. He wiggled the mouse as he sat down on the chair. His backside pressed against the hard plastic. The screen came to life, a blue background with an animated window appeared briefly before giving way to the dark desktop screen bearing the job centre logo. He scrolled through endless jobs, each looking exactly like the last. He punched in his information into the formulaic template, fighting the urge to surrender to the boredom and find the nearest pub. His blood ran cold when the last few questions appeared on the screen. *Criminal convictions?* He looked over his shoulder to ensure no one was watching him, the desks were full again with other jobless ghosts. With a flick of the wrist, he selected *NO*.

An hour later he was leaving the waiting room with a few more papers rolled up and shoved into his back pocket. He looked at the clock mounted on the wall above the row of plastic screens. Twelve thirty. *Applications done. Reckon I deserve a drink.*

50

He sat nervously on an uncomfortable bright green plastic chair in a thin corridor. The sweat was forming on his palms and in the folds of skin on his stomach. He was distracting himself with the white board that filled the wall in front of him. There was a grid of some sort, days were written vertically down the board and numbers stretching into the hundreds of thousands were scribbled in bad handwriting beside them. He anxiously rolled his printed resume in his hands, pulling it tight before letting it unfold into a loose cylinder. The tie felt like a noose around his neck and his armpits were moist and hot under his shirt. He checked to make sure he wasn't developing a sweat stain, subtly sniffing his armpit. His body ached for a line to help calm him down. He looked up the corridor, he could make out the reception desk in the distance. He figured he could cover the length of the corridor in less than thirty seconds and be out in the fresh air in thirty-two seconds. He looked back in the opposite direction. There was a noise coming from one of the open doors, people talked loudly but he was alone. He stood up, anxiously looking left and right. He was sweating hard now; the thought of escape had encompassed him, and he was focused on getting to the exit. His legs gently shook under the cheap black trousers that he had bought the day before. Behind him a door clicked open and a small fat man wearing a green polo shirt and black trousers appeared. His head was bald except for a small grey fluff that lined the back of his skull and above the ears. He shuffled nervously, adjusting his thick glasses up his small pig-like nose.

"Cameron?"

Too late. Cameron felt the rising panic. He couldn't run now, but this man looked more nervous than him.

"Yep, that's me," he said with a smile, covering his mouth with his hand to hide the gaps.

"Derek Flint. This way, Cam, can I call you Cam?" the man asked.

"No problem."

He shook the man's hand firmly and let him lead the way into the small office. There was a computer on a wooden desk, the back of the large grey monitor filled most of the space. A leather chair faced him and two smaller cushioned chairs with their backs to him. The office was small, the grey filing cabinets and piles of products on every surface gave it the appearance of being smaller than it was.

"Sorry about the mess," the man said as he held open the office door as if he had been following Cameron's gaze. "Please, take a seat. I've read your CV and, honestly, you got a lot more experience than some of the others they send from the job centre."

He had a squeaky London accent that made Cameron feel comfortable. He sat on one of the cushioned chairs and unrolled his resume on the desk.

"Yeah, I was working for a while. Had a baby a couple of weeks ago so looking for a job again."

"Well, that's good because we're looking for someone."

The day was warm. By the time he finally got out into the fresh air, the sweat had developed patches down the back of his shirt, and under each armpit but he didn't care. He felt adulation; he felt a swelling of pride in his chest. He opened a couple of the buttons on his shirt and ran his hand across his sweaty chest, enjoying the cooling of the breeze on his bare skin. *The job is yours if you want it* Derek had told him as they had shaken hands in that narrow corridor. He did want it. They had arranged for him to return the following week to start his induction and to sign the contract. He almost skipped down the street towards the bus stop, flinging the roll of paper, which was now damp with his sweat, into a bin.

He sat on the top deck overlooking the street below from the large scratched windows. He rested his feet on the small ledge below the window, sitting back and watching the lunchtime traffic of cars and people shuffle on the streets below him. He closed his eyes, leant his head on the window and allowed his mind to daydream of his first pay slip. He wanted to buy a new pram for the baby, they had loaned one from Sharon's sister. The wheels were sticking, and the cloth was stained and jaded. It looked every bit as old as it was. He wanted to shower Sharon and Katie in gifts, only to start making up for the way he had been these last few years. The drinking and the drugs had left him in bad shape, mentally and physically and now was the time to turn that corner. He ran his fingers gently on the window, feeling the warmth of the sun against the glass. The bus rumbled, hitting potholes and finally juddering to a stop on Tooting High Street. He leapt down the curved stairs, swinging his weight on the rail and jumping out into the bright sunshine. He dragged his keys from his pocket, swinging them a full rotation on his finger before clasping them in his hand. He smiled, the corner of his mouth curling up as he began the short run home.

He turned the key in the door and immediately heard voices that ceased as soon as the door latch clunked back. He stopped in the doorway, holding the door slightly ajar. The silence filled the flat as he stood motionless, he waited quietly for someone to make the first move. He felt the rage burn up inside him, he was sure he would catch her with another man, he imagined her trying to hide him as he stood here with his face inches from the front door. He flung the door wide, letting it bounce with a bang against the wall and stormed into the living room, desperate to catch her in the act. The jealousy burned in him, uncontrolled, making his skin feel like fire. The words rose in his throat, ready for a feral scream but stopped cold before they left his lips. Sharon sat on the armchair that he had left her in that morning; her hands were curled around a cup;

steam rose in gentle swirls into the air above. Her eyes were red, and a tissue lay scrunched on her lap. Katie slept peacefully in the rocker by her feet. On the sofa sat a tall man, his white shirt was crisp and buttoned to his neck even though it was twenty-five degrees outside and the flat felt warmer. His blue silk tie was long enough to cover his crotch. He put his cup down on the small coffee table and rose to his feet as Cameron appeared in the doorway. The policeman sat next to him did the same, reaching behind his back and withdrawing a pair of handcuffs from his belt. There was a pause and a soft silence as the detective looked at him, his eyes seemed to be filled with pity. Cameron looked from the two men to Sharon, to the open front door.

The detective had moved across, putting a hand on Sharon's shoulder. "Now son, let's not make this more difficult than it already is." The police officer stepped forward, he was tall and stood above Cameron by at least half a foot, but he moved smoothly and with agility, side stepping the coffee table and taking hold of Cameron's wrist. "Cameron Milton. I'm arresting you on suspicion of grievous bodily harm, you do not have to say anything, but it may harm your defence if you do not mention when questioned…"

It was a stream of words, each seemed to be connected to the last. Sharon was standing now, screaming at him. "WHAT DID YOU DO?"

The cup of tea now lay on its side, a brown stain spreading from the cup like it had fallen over and vomited. He didn't remember seeing her put the cup down, but he thought she must have kicked it over when she stood up. Katie started to cry. He let himself be rotated so he was looking at the open front door. It was easier than looking into her eyes. The handcuffs clicked around his wrist. The world swam in greys. Words were caught in his throat like fish bones. The metal didn't press against the bone like he remembered from the first time. The officer held Cameron gently on the shoulder to lead him out the door. Quietly, Cameron allowed himself to be led.

MICHAEL

51

The crowds swarmed into the festival, tramping through the dry grass dragging suitcases behind them, the wheels bouncing and bowing against the rough terrain. He watched them from the front seat of the Mercedes, the air conditioning was on full blast, the cold air making his skin break out in goose bumps. He looked on with disdain as the car drove close enough to almost clip passers-by with the wing mirrors, people turned and gave them fingers as they went. Their clothes were dusty, their bare legs caked in dirt. Scott was driving, he barely seemed to notice they were there. If they didn't move, Michael was sure he would drive over them. They had been propping up the bar two weeks ago in London, Scott was dabbing the red sores that were appearing under his nose and bragging about his new Mercedes that he had bought two weeks prior. Michael had heard the story before and was looking absently over his head at the crowd of young girls packed into the back. Like the girls, they had been drinking since the late afternoon and his vision was making the room unfold into two before coming back into focus. They were celebrating Michael's second promotion since being at the firm; same job, more money is how he saw it. They had been chugging beers in the riverside bars before jumping on the tube to Liverpool Street and now stood in a bar where the girls seemed tall and barely dressed. The music blasted from the stands above the DJ stand, the lights flicked between red, blue and purple making Michael feel sick. The cocaine burned at the back of his throat, and he could smell it in his nostrils.

"Listen," Scott had said between the sniffing, "let's do summit mental. I got a mate in a band; he plays at a festival in a capple ov weeks. 'E'll get us in VIP."

Michael had nodded along, distracted and not listening. "Great idea, Scott, yeah sounds great."

As he watched the travellers drag their belongings through the dusty track leading to a row of tents, the dirt kicking off the surface giving the air a warm brown textured look, he regretted not paying attention. He wished he was at home, his mind wandered to Sofia. His eyes ached from a lack of sleep and a cocaine hangover. They had set off early that morning for Suffolk after Scott had snorted a line off the marble counter that stretched around Michael's new kitchen. Once he had bought the new flat in Angel, it made sense for Sofia to move in but this weekend she was back in Spain, which was just as well as she wouldn't have liked to see Scott ploughing his nostrils with class A drugs in her kitchen. He watched the back of his head with a prick of disgust for them both. He had made a pact with himself that he would stop and, though, unlike Scott, he didn't take any during the week, Saturday nights out would often involve two of them huddled in a toilet cubicle snorting powder from a flat surface or the edge of a credit card.

The crowds thinned as the Mercedes swung into the luxury camping area. The tents stood in a line, their peaks a series of triangles pointing at the sky. The name 'tent' was the only thing they shared with the cheap canvas structures that littered the grass. Inside they would be kitted out with showers powered by a generator and the bed were comfortable and large. Michael looked across the field beyond the VIP area, the canvas tents stretched far into the distance, pots of smoke already rising as the barbeques were fired up. The car bobbled over the grass, coming to a stop in a dusty field.

It was another bar they stood at in the late evening sun. This one was private, designated for those that stayed in the white pointed tepee tents. The bar was dim, lit with low-level colourful lighting and made almost entirely of wood. It was a welcome relief from the warm summer sun. The bar was filled with young girls in high shorts that finished just above the line of their backside and wellington boots that covered their calves despite the heat. Michael imagined their feet must be sweating in the warm rubber. Their faces were covered with large dark glasses and thin t-shirts with midriffs exposed. Michael had opted for a pair of chino shorts and boat shoes, disappointed to learn that many of the men had the same look. Scott was scouting the wooden hut, watching the girls jig up and down to the music that pumped throughout the venue from the large central stage.

"You wanna go dance?"

He was fidgeting, shuffling from one leg to the other. His eyes were wide, and his jaw was tense, his teeth were grinding with a soft crunch that made Michael's skin crawl. Michael looked at him with a touch of envy, he longed for that level of escapism.

"Not yet, Scott, it's a little early."

He looked at the Rolex on his wrist, a short glance that was not long enough to comprehend the time. *Just a habit, he has no idea what time it is.*

"You want somethin'?"

"Na, I'm gonna lay off the coke."

It had become an accepted part of his work life. Scott wasn't the only one that would spend weekday evenings with wide eyes and a jawline like a bulldog. He was grateful that he took part in these occasions ever less frequently. It brought out the worst in him. Worse than that, it brought out the kid that he had kept submerged for so long. He became paranoid and nervous, he talked coherently but quickly, he knew people noticed and this made him even more paranoid.

"This is summit else."

He pulled a small plastic bag from the pocket of his green shorts. The powder was grey and unrefined, Michael could make out the chunks, like glass, glittering through the plastic. He held it in his palm, covered mostly with his thumb to keep it out of view of the bar, but they were alone, the rest of the bar had crowded into an open stretch of grass and were bouncing up and down in time with the music. Beer foamed in their glasses, spilling out onto each other and the floor.

"What's that?"

"Mandy. It's pure. It's the fuckin' best. It turns everything beautiful, you'll see"

The dark nagging in his mind had been put to sleep for several months. The distractions of buying a house and spending every waking moment with Sofia had left him feeling bright and energised. He looked thoughtfully at the small packet in Scott's hand. The thought of escaping for one weekend and getting lost amongst the bodies that surrounded him was beckoning. A strong part of him strove to be better than his upbringing, to earn more, to be more and to get everything that he never had as a child. This part of him shared a room with a young reckless kid, who wanted to spend life in a state of inebriation and to tear away at the things that worked. This part saw beauty in destruction.

"What do we do?"

Scott smiled a wide, mischievous smile. He took the napkin that had been the mat for his beer glass and ripped two small little squares from the corner. Michael blocked the view of the bar with his back as he poured a little of the grey gritty powder into the pieces of tissues, his face tense with concentration, sweat breaking out on his forehead. He put away the plastic bag, safely into the pocket of his chinos, twisting the end of the tissue, he held it up to Michael's face. It reminded him of a very small fig. That smile was back on his face.

"Now we get fucked up."

He had told him that it wouldn't be subtle when it happened. They had ventured out of the private bar into the main venue and were walking through the crowds. He watched the sun start to set over the large arch that filled the skyline, the main stage. On the stage he could make out people setting up equipment, pulling leads from under the stage and connecting them to various microphones. He walked slowly, his hands sunk deep into his pockets enjoying the warm evening and feeling his skin starting to bristle slightly. Scott was right. It wasn't subtle. The temperature seemed to drop immediately, he felt something sweep over his body, he could almost feel his pupils dilate as the drug swept through his system. The hairs on his arms stood at an angle and his brain took a euphoric leap inside his head, colours exploded behind his eyes and the scene in front of him heightened with colour, each element florescent and sharp. He stopped sharply and closed his eyes, enjoying the warm joy rise from his stomach to the tip of his head.

"Woah," he whispered quietly to himself.

Scott turned to look at him. Standing silently beside him, he nodded with a dopey smile on his face. Michael wrapped his arms around himself despite the warm summer evening, Scott moved behind him and wrapped his arms around his waist, resting his head on his back.

"I love you, man," he mumbled into the back of Michael's shirt.

His speech was rapid. Michael could feel his heart beating fast in his chest. He felt wonderful and the evening was bursting to life when he opened his eyes. "I love you too, man, we're, like, best friends."

He knew he was speaking like a machine gun rattling off rounds, but he didn't care. He was enjoying the warm embrace of Scott's arms wrapped around him and his head resting on his back. He felt home. Everything was beautiful. Scott let go and put an arm over his shoulder as Michael gripped his ribs, and they walked through the crowds holding closely onto one another, stopping to watch the sun dip further and further into the skyline, their eyes wide, their pupils eclipsing the iris and their faces staring in amazement at the sky as if they had never seen a sunset before.

"Listen, man," Michael started. He looked around suspiciously, checking no one was listening. "I need to tell you something."

"What?" Scott's face was drawn and intrigued. He looked at Michael as if studying his eyes would tell him the secret.

"I'm fucked."

There was a pause and then Scott burst into a braying laugh. They drew close to one another and embraced, a strong firm hold, slapping each other's backs. Michael broke off and held him at arm's length, gazing deep into his face as if they were lovers.

"I'm gonna ask Sofia to marry me. I love her, man. I have to do it."

"No way!" Scott spoke quickly. *No way* came out of his mouth in two small exclamations, he was shuffling from one foot to the other again.

"That's so great, mate. I love you guys. I so 'appy for you."

Tears welled in his eyes, he leant forward, and they embraced again, standing in the middle of a crowded area with people dancing around them in wellington boots. They stayed in each other's arms, holding tight to one another, enjoying the touch of another human being. The sun was finally setting behind the line of trees in the distance, their night was only getting started.

52

He was happy. He thought he was sure of that, but he really didn't understand how he could feel this way. Empty. The flat was empty. The silence echoed off the walls and surrounded him in an invisible cocoon. It was Monday. They had returned from the festival the day before, arriving in the early hours of the morning. Scott's face had been drawn and haggard from a weekend on drink and drugs as he left him outside the front to his apartment building. He had dropped his bag at the door to the bedroom, stripping off his jeans as he walked. They trailed behind him like a snake shedding its skin and he tumbled into bed, pulling the duvet over his face to cover his eyes from the first light from the sun that burned deep on the horizon. He had slept a long but troubled sleep, rotating from one side to the next under the duvet.

He sat alone on the couch, the TV played in the background, but he didn't hear or see it. His eyes open, blankly staring as the shapes changed on the giant screen that was mounted on the wall. The volume was off, the characters talked in mime. A soft drum was thumping in the back of his mind, he shifted his attention to his hands, wriggling his fingers in front of his face, slow and steady until they no longer felt like his hands or his fingers. He felt like a stranger in his own body, a being taking the body and home of another man, sitting on his couch and watching his television. His mind was dejected and lonely, it cursed his lungs for breathing. His heart was a weight pinning his lightweight skeleton to the sofa, sinking down in his body. He thought it might eventually break his spine and maybe he would just dissolve into the cushion underneath his backside. All that would be left would be his eyes, sat in a puddle of tears and a brain that screamed relentlessly inside.

He looked around the room, not wanting to be part of this life. He had to remember he was one of the lucky ones even if right now he was a worthless empty vessel staring at a TV screen. To cry would have been a release but he held the tears firmly locked in his throat, bubbling there before he swallowed them. He really didn't deserve to feel that relief so, instead, he kept them inside. The nights had been good but the come down was crippling.

53

August in Italy and the sun scorched the pavement under his feet. He felt it burn his shoulders and the back of his neck, making him thankful for factor fifty sun cream. They walked hand in hand through the cobbled streets of Catania, licking greedily at a cone of gelato. Many of the shops had pulled the shutters down, the streets desolate with only a spattering of pasty tourists hovering around, taking pictures with oversized cameras. Sofia stood on his left, in his right pocket of his shorts the small square parcel uncomfortably pressed against his thigh. The sun exhausted him, but the evening ahead was making him anxious. As she shielded her eyes against the windows of the closed shops, he took the relief of shade by standing in doorways, always keeping his right side out of view in fear of her noticing the square bulge on his thigh. It felt like it weighed twenty kilos.

The afternoon was starting to cool when they finally left the small city. The rental car was parked mostly in the shade of an old Sycamore tree, yet the heat made the steering wheel impossible to hold and the chairs burnt the back of his legs. He put the air conditioning on full blast and the car drifted through the narrow country lanes, passing through acres of green either side and olive trees that leant over so far into the road he could almost reach out and touch them.

"Where we going?" She looked over him, breaking him away from his thoughts and the burning square in his pocket.

"It's a surprise."

She smiled. She wasn't hoping for an answer. He watched her close her eyes behind the dark sunglasses and let her head roll over and face the window. The breeze was a relief.

A little over an hour later they rolled into a gravelled car park, he parked the car and switched off the engine. She opened her eyes and turned towards him; a sleepy smile crept on her lips.

"Where are we?"

He leant across and kissed her before pushing the door open into the warm evening. The sun was still bright, but the clouds were now acting as cover against its heat. She joined him at his side, and they walked, fingers interlocked, towards the country house, its frame alone on the skyline surrounded by an expanse of green, only broken up with lines of lime trees that led them down the path to main reception. The walls looked freshly painted and the doorways stood under huge arches. The trees cast shadows across their path in perfect lines and in the distance, they could see the sun reflecting off the surface of the blue pool. Small wooden tables were scattered across the grass and around the pool like discarded toys. He watched her face beam, her mouth open as she absorbed the beauty of the rustic Italian landscape.

They checked in and headed to the room without getting the suitcases from the car. The sun streamed into the room through the large arched windows that overlooked the endless horizon of green. He stood at the door, throwing the keys onto the bedside table, as she went from the sleeping area into the large bathroom. He heard her gasp.

"Have you seen the bathroom? It has a jacuzzi."

"I know."

She walked to him and put her arms around his neck and pushed herself up against him. "Maybe we should try out this bed."

Holding her tight around the waist, he lifted her from the floor, she wrapped her legs around his waist. He stepped forward and they fell onto the bed together, laughing. As the laughter stopped, she kissed him. He held tight to her so he could enjoy the feeling of her tongue on his lips.

The dark of the evening came late, the heat hung in the air, touching their skin like a warm blanket. She wore a knee-length linen dress that seemed to float around her shape, her eyes glittering in contrast to her olive skin. They walked barefoot across the beach, shoes dangling loosely in their hands. The moon reflected on the ocean, casting a pale glare across the water. He held her hand tightly, hoping she wouldn't notice his palms sweating. The waves softly whispered against the shore peaceful and calming as if they sung a lullaby from his childhood. He watched the deserted beach, looking for the perfect spot. The darkness hid all the contours and anything in the distance was impossible to see. He finally stopped her in a dimly lit stretch of the beach.

"Sofia?"

He looked at her face, beautiful in the soft glow of the moon. Her eyes met his, concern spreading on her face. He let go of her hand and reached into his pocket. Her eyes watched him suspiciously, realisation dawning on her. Dropping down to one knee, he held the open box in front of him.

"Will you marry me?"

He waited. The seconds felt like hours. He was a boy again, begging for something they couldn't afford, and he was about to be told *no* for the umpteenth time. She was the ultimate prize. The fear swept through him as he started to believe the decision was a mistake. She burst into tears, covering her face with one delicate hand. A bubble burst in his chest at the sight of her tears, he shed his own, his vulnerability put to one side.

"Is that a yes?" he whispered, pushing the fear that was building inside him down. To his relief, between her tears, she nodded, hugging him fiercely before he had the chance to fully get to his feet.

CAMERON

54

It wasn't as dramatic as he had seen in movies, though the front gate of the prison now towered behind him like he imagined it would. The stone brick structure looked almost medieval, the large wooden double gates nestled under an arch and surrounded by two large turrets. He hitched up the trousers that he had put into the locker almost three and a half years previously. The weight that he carried then, had now fallen away. His frame was thin, his face gaunt, the cheekbones protruding like hillsides on his face falling away into his large blue eyes. His hair was shaved short. He rubbed a hand over it; the day was warm for a November, but he could still feel the breeze flick the top of his ears as it whistled past. He pulled his jacket tight around his withered frame and walked away from the prison, towards the bus stop. He felt the saliva build up in his mouth as the urge to head to the nearest pub swamped his taste buds and tried to lead him. He swallowed hard and made a choice to ignore the temptation. There was no one to greet him at the gates, no Cadillac with a stranger leaning against the door coming into view as a bus full of prisoners rattled past. There was no desert landscape. Instead, there was a line of trees hiding the terraced London houses and a grey tarmac road. Cars made a crisp whirring as they shot past. He had barely spoken to his mum since he had moved out of home and she seemed even less concerned with him now that he was a convicted thug. The weekly visits from Sharon had dried up quickly after the first six months and he came t to resent visitor time. He stayed behind with the other inmates that had no loved ones to check in on them, no hands to hold and no children to bounce on their knees. It dawned on Cameron that he was no different from the others; lost and loathed. Scorned by society and finally abandoned by their families and friends, they were a plague just by association as if their wicked minds and wrongdoings could spread like a virus.

In the early days, he had thought himself different. They had a look in their eyes that straddled the seams of madness. Their eyes burned with hate, they always looked like men that had nothing to lose. He was different in those early days. He had everything to fight for and people that loved him. When the visitors stopped coming, he sat alone on a plastic chair, watching the television screwed high up on the wall, thinking he was no different at all.

The streets seemed empty as he looked down on them from the top tier of the bus as it made its way past the common, but they looked the same. *Three and a half years.* He repeated it over again in his mind just to check it was as long as it sounded. He imagined that in that time, things would have changed beyond recognition, but the truth was that London still had that grey tinge around the edges and the people that filled its streets during the day were the same people that hid in its underbelly throughout the night. All the good people were hard at work, they weren't leaving prison and hoping to restart their life where they had left it as if it was a movie on pause. This was no movie. He knew that, and he knew that he had a lot of making up to do if he was going to get Sharon to trust him again. He had been dry since the day he had left her screaming at him as they led him away from his home. The first nights had been difficult, his whole body ached, and he cried in the night as the pain tore through his arms and legs. As time had gone on the pain had subsided and was replaced with a deep longing that hung on his chest like a weight for all the things he had left behind and the things that he would never see. He tried to imagine what Katie's face would look like now, but he could only imagine the small delicate embryonic face he had seen in the hospital. Sharon never wanted her to see the inside of the prison. He understood but a picture would have seen him through some of the darkest times. She had denied him even this.

As he jumped from the bus, he turned into Tooting High Street, hitching his trousers up again and watching the familiar faces swim around him. The high street was alive with people as the smell of the fish stalls from the markets wafted through the air. The streets were littered with decaying vegetables and men shifting crates of fruit from underneath large tables covered in plastic grass and replacing the empty crates. People lined up, hugging bowls of fruits and carrying the rest in battered old shopping baskets that looked like they had been lifted from a supermarket some time ago. He turned into her street, his heart pounding so loudly in his chest that he could feel it in his ears.

She lived in an old terraced house that had been divided into two flats. He peered through the bottom floor window, not wanting to get too close in case she saw him. He looked for movement through the netted curtains, but the living room was still. Disappointment spread through him with the realisation that this may have been a wasted journey. Three and a half years was plenty of time to change address. He pressed the bell, listening out for the shrill in the house. He held his breath patiently, waiting to hear anything from the other side of the door. Time seemed to almost stop; seconds ticked by achingly slowly before he heard the shuffle of her slippers on the carpet beyond the door. He heard the latch fall back from the internal door and he let out a long sigh of relief.

Her face fell as she opened the door and it was almost impossible to miss the disappointment in her eyes. She was prettier than he remembered, her face had lost the rough skin of her youth and her eyes were free of bruises. She wore less makeup making her seem paler, but her skin looked smoother and her eyes sparkled brightly in her face. She had lost the weight that she had carried after Katie's birth, she had the same small frame that he remembered when they first met. She looked at him from head to toe without speaking.

"Hey," he finally broke the silence.

"What do you want, Cameron?"

"To talk."

"I can't."

She stepped outside, pulling the door almost to a close behind her. She allowed herself a short guilty glance into the hallway before it disappeared from his view.

"Why? Is someone 'ere?" His voice raised slightly; the jealous green burned behind his blue eyes.

"Cameron" she looked at him, almost exasperated. "It's been more than three years. I've moved on. So should you."

Pity. He was searching for the word to describe the look on her face. She pitied him and he didn't need a mirror to understand why.

"I'm clean," he said finally and desperately.

"I'm sorry."

She stepped back inside the house and started to close the door. He stuck out a hand to stop it closing. The door gave a disapproving judder.

"Can I see Katie at least?"

"I don't think that's a good idea."

"Why?!"

"She doesn't know who you are, Cameron."

He felt the rage burn inside him and turn his stomach over.

"And oo's fault is that?" he almost screamed.

"Yours." Her tone was cold and calm. "You stabbed someone, remember? And went to prison."

He stared at her, his mouth open, the words kicked out of him like air escaping his lungs. His stomach tightened. He wanted to reach over and grab her by the throat and shake her. Her eyes burned with fury and confidence.

"Look, you can't just keep 'er from me."

"I can and I will. You're a convicted criminal and a drunk. It won't be hard to prove you're a danger."

The look never left her eyes. She was unforgiving.

"Listen, you fuckin' bitch…."

"What's the problem, love?" The door opened fully, pulled by a hand above Sharon's head. Standing behind her was a tall man wearing shorts and a thin white t-shirt. His hair was pushed to one side like he had just got out of bed, his skin was olive and he stood at least four inches taller than Cameron.

"No problem," Sharon said. "Cameron was just leaving."

She looked at him almost pleading. The anger rotated and burned in his stomach collecting mass and working its way through his veins.

"You just got out, av ya?" the man asked.

"Yeah, what ov it?" Cameron's fists clenched.

"Well, you really don't want trouble then, otherwise you know where you'll end up."

Cameron had an appointment with the parole officer that afternoon, he was warned not to miss his time slot as the consequences would be severe. He imagined caving the skull of a man on his doorstep might be worse.

"Ok," he finally conceded. "I'll go but this ain't over. I wanna see her." He pointed a finger at them both.

"Bye Cameron."

The door slammed shut unceremoniously.

"It ain't over" he muttered to himself before turning away and retracing his steps to the bus stop.

55

The room was a small rectangle with bunkbeds lining the walls. He sat on one of the bottom bunks staring at the metal springs of the bed above him. All around, gentle snoring echoed. He picked absently at the lime green paint that covered the wall as he let the rhythm of their breathing try to send him off to sleep. He longed desperately to sleep, longed desperately to drink and then to sleep but he had done neither for the last few hours and his body ticked and twitched. He replayed the meeting with Sharon in his head repeatedly, imagining planting a brick into the face of her boyfriend the moment he spoke. He wanted to focus on how to get his life back, but he could only plan revenge. It was almost two in the morning before he finally drifted off to a shallow sleep.

He woke before nine, the sun streamed through the thin curtains and washed over the black lino floor. The sound of the beds creaking, and moaning filled the room as men woke up and staggered like zombies to the communal bathrooms. The familiar sound of a bottle top unscrewing made him sit upright. A middle-aged man sat with his legs hanging over the edge of his top bunk, topless and swigging from a small vodka bottle. His eyebrows were large and furrowed, making his eyes almost impossible to see and his hair stuck out at different angles from his head. Something in the man's sad face made Cameron think of his own future. He pushed away the thought and joined the trickle of bodies limping to the toilets.

He washed himself in the basin, pulling on the jaded tracksuit bottoms that was one of the last items of clothing that he had left in this world. He made a mental note to treat himself to some new clothes when he got his first payslip.

He walked out of the squalid looking reception. Outside the door, drunks gathered with plastic carrier bags full of bottles of cider. They spoke in slurring dialect through mouths that were missing teeth, as they teetered from side to side. He pushed through ignoring the incoherent shouts. He pitched up at the bus stop in time to jump on the first bus heading towards Clapham Junction. The bus was empty, which suited him. He walked to the back and slumped into rotten looking seat and watched the daytime traffic meander past.

Her back was turned to him when he walked into the pub, but he recognised her small plump shape as she wiped a table down with a damp cloth. "Hi Mum."

She jolted upright at the sound of his voice, turning quickly to look at him. For the second time in two days, someone was looking at him up and down, registering the changes he had made since he had been away.

"Cameron," she was surprised, and did he detect a twang of disappointment? "What you doin' ere? You escaped?"

"Na, I got out yesterday."

They stood in silence, their eyes wandered around the pub as if searching for a topic to talk about. Cameron observed his old haunting ground, noticing how old it looked now that he could look with fresh eyes.

"Come 'ere," she said finally, leaving the cloth on the table and reaching over to embrace him. It was tense; he returned her hug with a gentle pat on the back before quickly releasing himself from her grip.

"So wat's new?"

"Nuttin' much, all the same really."

"You didn't visit, Mum."

As she looked down at her shoes, the expression on her face changed to shame.

"You know how I feel about that place, love…" She trailed off, as if that was enough to answer the question.

"You mean, he wouldn't let you go."

He looked away, not needing to see her face to know that he had spoken the truth. She didn't answer. Her eyes darted from the door to the bar.

"You still with him then?" Cameron continued.

She coughed an acknowledgement. He nodded slowly into the silence between them.

"How's the little ones?"

"They're good, Cameron." She was wringing her hands the way she did when his stepdad started getting angry.

"They're doing good at school?"

"Yeah, they are."

Her eyes locked on his, her head tilted to one side, looking at him as if he were a puppy or a new-born baby. It was the face she used when she didn't want a smack in the mouth. He knew that she feared him. He made her nervous.

"Listen, Mum, can I stay with you for a bit, just 'til I get myself sorted?"

"Oh luv." Her hands were turning white she was squeezing so hard. "I can't."

"Mum. I stayed in a hostel last night. Sharon won't talk to me, she 'as a new fella."

"I know."

He looked at her, fire burned in his eyes. "You know?"

"Yeah, I went over to see little Katie not long back."

He turned away, rubbing his shaven head. He counted to ten quietly in his head to calm the rage that was starting to fire up in his stomach, as he was taught by the prison therapist. *Take your time and focus on your breathing* she had told him. It was easy to say in an office with windows and battered furniture but difficult to do when his mum was telling him she would happily see his kid, but not him.

"Look, mum. I got nowhere to go, just gimme a few days, please." His voice was pleading.

"I can't, luv, he won't let me."

"Where do I go then?"

"I dunno, luv." She looked away, studying the beer taps.

"Can I come and grabs some clothes at least, I got nuffin'?"

She shifted uneasily, still studying the bar and the beer taps.

"Mum?"

"It's all gone, we threw it out."

The silence in the pub echoed around them with only the thumping of the second hand rotating on a clock behind the bar.

"What's goin' on 'ere?" He held his arms out from his sides, hands spread out. "Are you disownin' me or summit? You gettin' rid of me? You want me dead? Is that it?"

She stayed silent as his voice slowly raised in volume. He looked at her as her eyes refused to meet his.

"TELL ME!" he shouted into the empty pub.

She looked at him with her eyes filled with tears and looked down at her pale hands, a tear dropped onto her thumb and she absently wiped at her face.

"I'm so sorry, Cameron, I shoulda bin a better mam."

"Fuck your sorry," he said quietly.

It was the second time in the space of two days he had heard "sorry Cameron". Both times it had been an empty gesture to precede more nothingness, more empty words. The silence was once more filling the space between them, thick and palpable.

"Listen, luv." She suddenly came to life, unclasping her hands. "Take this." She reached for her purse sat on the bar, unzipping her wallet to remove a twenty-pound note. He looked from her face to her outstretched hand, studying the purple note and her small squat fingers, the nails bitten down to the skin. She traced his gaze back and forth, unsure of what to do next. She waivered, her hand shaking before pulling it back.

"Here," she said finally. "Take this." She dipped back into her wallet, keeping the note pinched between her fingers, and pulled out another twenty. "Tip money," she said awkwardly with a shrug of the shoulders, shoving both notes towards him. He snatched the money from her hand, folding it and pushing it into his pocket. She said nothing as he looked around the pub for the last time.

"Ok. I guess that's it," he conceded. He hitched his old jaded tracksuit bottoms over his hip and walked out of the pub. His mum quietly watched his back as he left.

56

He stormed across the car park, arms pumping and legs making long lung-busting strides. His mind raced; images of his past flashed in brief moments, moments with Sharon, moments with his family and moments when he was happy. He physically swallowed the anger down to stop it exploding out of him and blinding him. He conjured Katie's face in his mind, shoving aside all other thoughts.

The station approached on his right-hand side and he could make out the white walls of the job centre stretched around the base of a block of flats. Its windows looked small and dark from the outside. His last visit had been three and a half years before and he had almost skipped out of the building, his resume rolled up and shoved into his back pocket. That hope had gone. His shoulders slumped as the anger that had fired him up was now replaced with a sadness as he mourned his loss. He kicked absently at discarded papers that fluttered across the surface of the pavement like birds learning to fly, scrapping and bouncing, only to crash land at his feet.

The waiting room was almost empty. He took a ticket and sat on the hard, plastic seat, looking at the posters filled with smiling employees dressed smartly in uniforms for various companies, their eyes bright and promising a better future. He looked down at his scuffed trainers and tattered tracksuits bottoms, now fraying and thinning at the knees. He was a stark contrast to the smiling man in the poster, whose shirt was perfectly ironed and tucked into ruler-straight trousers. The buzzer shrilled; his number blinked at him in the board above the rows of glass booths. He walked forward and sat in another hard seat. The woman behind the glass sat, squatting deep into the chair. Small round glasses perched on the tip of her nose and were lost on her large round face. She looked at him, her finger poised over the keyboard in front of her.

"I... er... I just got out of prison. I need to sign on."

He stumbled through the sentence, not enjoying how the words sounded coming out of his mouth but knowing he would have to get used to it. She didn't respond except to ask his name. The keys clacked loudly in the empty office.

"Ok," she said finally. "You can come back in six weeks to pick up your cheque."

She stopped typing and looked at him through the glass.

"But... but what do I do until then? I got twenty quid left an' I 'av to pay for a room tonight."

Her face didn't change as she shrugged, folding her hands across her lap to signal that she was done. "Sorry," she offered.

Another apology. They were all sorry. Sorry for fucking you over. Sorry your life is a shit heap. She wasn't sorry at all. The only person that was sorry was him. He rubbed his forehead, running his fingers through the creases that seemed to deepen every day since he had left prison. *It was easier to stay in there*, he thought.

"Is there some jobs that I can apply for?"

She huffed loudly and started tapping at the keyboard again. He pretended not to notice her irritation; it was the only way he could suppress the growing sense of panic working its way through him. She looked at the screen for a long time before answering.

"Not anything there." She looked at him blankly.

"Not even in a supermarket? I got a job there before."

She shook her head and tutted through her pursed lips. "Criminal record," she said as if that told him everything he needed to know. He cursed himself for mentioning prison.

"Nothing?" he repeated quietly.

"Try again next week, stuff comes in all the time." She was starting to sound almost sympathetic.

He stood and walked towards the exit, stopping at the row of computers, their blank screens reflecting the empty waiting room. He knew he should look himself; he was sure she wasn't interested, but those two words had taken much of the fight out of him. *Criminal record.* It was his life now, declaring that he had served time, telling the world that he was a bad person. Untrustworthy, rotten and a liability. Society's worst. He shuddered once and walked out of the door. He stopped outside and looked left and right. The roads were busy, but the shops seemed empty. He looked across the road at the bus stop; it seemed to be surrounded with aging women pulling tartan trolleys. In the distance he could make out the old pub arching around the corner. His mind flashed back to the afternoon spent with Michael in that very pub. His mouth watered; he could almost taste the bitterness of the first swig of beer. He walked across the road and past the bus stop, stopping outside the pub to look through the window at the old fellas sat slumped in corners, cradling tall glasses of beer. He dug into his pocket and pulled the remainder of the cash out. Sixty-two pounds with the money that his mum had given him. He looked past the pub, spotting an off license, the door wide open almost beckoning him to enter. His hand clenched around the notes and coins, instinctively.

Do this and there's no coming back.

I'm a fuckin' waste of space anyway, what's the point? Might as well get cunted.

Never see her again if you do.

You can have one. Just one night. Stop again tomorrow.

He walked fast, keeping the notes wrapped tightly in his fist before he could change his mind. The off license was warm but the cold air blasting from the fridges was a relief. He stalked to the counter and slapped a twenty down on the counter, exchanging almost half of it for three hundred and seventy-five millilitres of cheap whiskey.

57

He had found an illuminous yellow jacket belonging to a builder, left over the handle of a spade at a work site. The place was empty. He clambered through a gap in the wire fence and whipped it over his shoulders, pulling it tight to shield himself from the bitter evening that was descending on the November day. He tucked the whiskey bottle into the large pocket. The last third of liquid swilled and sploshed against the sides as he walked. His head buzzed and his skin glowed as the alcohol took hold of him. He swayed gently from side to side as he walked. The feeling of loss still sat with him but now its edges were blurred, soft, and no longer stuck in him like the needles. He had sat quietly on a bench for the remainder of the afternoon, enjoying the smooth feeling of the bottleneck on his lips and the warm burn of the whiskey down his throat and stomach. As the dark descended, he staggered back towards his old estate, more out of habit than purpose. He had nowhere to go. The last of the money he had in his pocket would have to last him six weeks, so the hostel was not an option for tonight.

As the tower block loomed up on his right, he stopped underneath its shadow staring up at the thousands of small balconies, clothes fluttering in the wind, shaking like flags. He softly stroked the bottleneck in his pocket with the tips of his fingers, lost in thought; he looked like mannequin, badly dressed and left in the street. Finally, he started moving, changing direction and walking deeper into the estate. The underpass was as dark as he remembered but the fear was gone. The distant chatter of voices danced on the wind and swept past his ears and as he turned the corner, he found the owners. There were five men. Boys, really. They sat on the rails surrounding the doorway of the tower block. Their dark jackets were zipped up and their hoods pulled over their heads, making their faces seem like shadows only visible from the whites in their eyes and the white of their teeth. He didn't break his stride, he walked through the middle of them, listening to the conversation and laughter die on their lips as he appeared. Their eyes followed him as he walked and stayed on him as he punched the number of Thomas' flat into the intercom system. The wind whistled through the silence, rustling the leaves in the trees overhead. He kept his eyes trained on the red numbers, ignoring the silence and the eyes that bore into the back of his head. He hit call, the intercom wailed into life.

"Bruv, oo you lookin' for?"

He turned at the sound of the voice, pressing the cancel button on the intercom to cut short the next scream. He looked into the dark face of the boy. His teeth were brilliant white, and his skin looked almost black, his brown eyes uninterested.

"Thomas," Cameron said pathetically, pointing at the tower above him.

"Thomas Walsh?" the hooded man responded.

"Yeah."

The man looked around at his friends. Cameron noticed they all were smiling. The man turned to Cameron again.

"Dead, bruv. He ran his mowff off to some yardie an' he got popped."

He put his fingers together in a gun shape and made a *pow* noise so quietly it was almost a whisper. The other boys burst into laughter, the man smiled, still looking Cameron in the eyes. Cameron scanned his face. The man's eyes were serious. He opened his mouth, but nothing came out, so he shut it again. He turned and pressed the number on the intercom again.

"Bruv, I'm serious. He's dead."

The intercom screamed its high-pitched wail again. He imagined the empty flat on the other side with nothing but unwanted furniture and cobwebs. He let the intercom scream, ignoring the eyes trained on him, focussed on the red digital numbers.

"Bruv. You dumb. He's dead."

More laughter. Cameron turned and ran, leaving the intercom screaming and the boys laughing.

58

He had spent weeks stalking the streets, drifting from off license to park bench. The wind rattled his oversized jacket and his trainers had finally been breached. A hole appeared in the toe and the sole was disintegrating. He spent every night and day with the damp set in his socks and squelching between his toes, but he could barely feel it. He sipped from the whiskey bottle that he kept safe in the jacket pocket, keeping the warmth in and reality out. The pain that drove through his head in the mornings was quickly numbed with a sip from that bottle. He ate when his body cried out in hunger and only when necessary, picking through the waxy papers discarded in the bin outside McDonalds, hoping for the remains of a half-eaten burger. Saturday and Sunday mornings, he would scour the streets outside of the kebab shops as the debris from the nights before would leave Styrofoam boxes of chips and kebab meat, freezing cold and caked in hardening sauce but a welcome treat for his desperate stomach. The front of his jacket was smeared with week-old ketchup, mayonnaise and vomit, when his body finally rejected the alcohol before being forced to consume more.

He had walked the length of Battersea. He now stood quietly under the shade of a tree in the entrance to a park, watching families meander into the park, pushing strollers in front of them with small children trailing behind. Oversized helmets protected their heads as their bikes wobbled over the uneven surface. He stayed in the shadows out of sight;

his eyes drooping, his hand planted on the trunk of the tree, watching the perfect lives of the others that surrounded him. He felt a burp of anger and resentment in the pit of his stomach but, like him, it was soaked in alcohol and struggling to move. Mostly he felt apathy and a need to urinate. He thought about slinking further back into the bushes to be out of sight from the passing crowds. His mind wanted him to move but his body refused to listen. Instead, he fumbled at the band of his tracksuit bottoms so he could at least get his penis outside of his trousers. He realised he was too late when he felt the warm trickle down his leg, spreading a dark shadow over his greying trousers. He let his hand fall to his side and enjoyed the slow release, letting out a small sigh that would be heard by no one but him. Before he could apply the cut off, a warm grainy liquid exploded out of him at the back of his pants. He groaned a little louder as the shit filled his underpants and fell through following the urine down to his shoes.

He waddled from his hiding spot, shaking bits of shit down his leg, and wandered into the street, away from the park. He slowly edged along the side of the park; one hand stretched out with his fingers flicking the painted iron railings whilst the other hand softly rubbed the top of the bottle in his pocket. He was becoming accustomed to the cold, wet feeling in his trousers and, gradually, the waddling reduced, and his normal laboured shuffle resumed. He walked the length of the park and stopped outside an old Victorian pub, looking longingly through the large arched windows. Flowers bloomed from pots that hung over his head in pretty pinks and purples and the wooden benches outside stood abandoned as the punters gathered inside against the cold of the day. He watched the tables inside heaving with fresh beer and hot food; he could hear the chatter and laughter from within; the tickling of resentment fluttered in his stomach again. He watched the faces, smiling, hands touching on the table surface and cutlery clinked against porcelain plates. There was a larger table on one side of the pub, a large family sat in two long lines. He scanned food laid out in front of them, the drinks that lay scattered between the plates and, finally, their laughing faces. They were faces that seemed strangely familiar to him but the buzzing in his head made it difficult to focus. Then he saw him. He was sat in the middle of the family; his arm was slung around the shoulder of a pretty girl with a deep tan. Her hair was pulled away from her face in a neat ponytail and in her arms; she was cradling a pink faced baby wrapped in blankets, sporting a small white hat that reminded him of the first day he held Katie.

His hair still perfectly cropped and parted like the last time he had seen him, but his face seemed older. He watched the baby with adoration on his face. He looked happy. Cameron had been friends with this man once. They had been best friends and now he stood outside a pub watching his friend enjoy his life without him. He had sacrificed his life to revenge the bad thing that had happened to *this* man's family and now he was smiling, oblivious of the consequences of those actions. The consequence was staring at him through the tinted window of the Victorian pub. The resentment burned and boiled inside him and worked its way through his veins, coursing through his blood and finally firing up in his blue eyes. He slammed an open hand on the window. The *thud* made most of the tables in view turn to look at the scruffy pale man, swamped by an illuminous workman's jacket standing in the window, staring intensely at the long table. The moment seemed to last an eternity, the whole pub staring at him, waiting for his next move before they all turned back to their dinners and Sunday drinks. He saw Michael look at him, their eyes met briefly and now he was back to ogling over the baby as if Cameron hadn't existed. Cameron took his palm away, leaving a greasy hand mark on the window, spread out like a flat spider. He walked to the door, yanking hard at the handle so it flew back, connecting with the rubber stopper with a *crack*. The man behind the bar was already walking around the long black top bar, his eyes never leaving Cameron. He had seconds before he was thrown out so staggered towards the head of the table.

"Michael!"

His voice raised and now the table turned to look at him, confusion spread on all their faces. They didn't recognise him, and he knew why. His face was distorted from the number of fists that had reshuffled his face, the drinking had left him pale, dehydrated and he was skinnier than when he was a teenager. The whole pub had turned to look at him and the barman was saying something, but he could barely hear what he was saying over the thumping of adrenalin in his ears. He was angry and he was feeling more than he had in weeks.

"Ya don't recognise me, do ya, ya cunt? I almost fuckin' killed someone for you."

It was Michael's turn to stand, his face turned from confusion to recognition to anger.

"Don't speak like that in front of my family, I don't care who you are."

He pointed a finger at Cameron; it was firm and confident in comparison to Cameron's pale shaking hands.

"You did this to me."

He sounded pathetic but he couldn't stop himself. The tears were welling up in his eyes.

Michael spread his arms out as the pub looked on. "What are you talking about?" he said finally.

"You fuckin' abandoned me, you did that to ME. We were on that ledge together, remember?"

Michael shook his head and went to return to his seat. The barman was at Cameron's side and gripped his arm firmly, leading him back through the door.

"This man," Cameron shouted, pointing at Michael, "had me kill someone."

He was desperate for the watching crowd to believe his lie. His speech was slurred but the pub understood him perfectly. Michael stood quickly and followed the barman, crossing him in the doorway as he let go of Cameron's arm with a shove.

"You ok, mate?" he asked Michael, touching his elbow as Michael passed. Michael nodded, leaving the barman to turn back into the pub.

"What you fuckin' talkin' 'bout?" he asked Cameron as they stepped out into the brisk afternoon. "Yor talkin' shit. I did no such thing."

Cameron turned to him; Michael was perfectly dressed for a Sunday afternoon in chinos and a navy cardigan. "Mohamed Khalif. You remember? I found 'im. Fuckin' stabbed der cunt. Done three years for you and now I can't see my little girl. Look at me!"

Michael's face scrunched in an expression mixed with disgust and confusion.

"What?" He brought his hand to his forehead.

"Khalif. Mohamed fuckin' Khalif. You 'member him?"

Michael shook head, slowly. His hands were now held out at his sides, palms facing Cameron. "Khalif was deported after his sentence," he said. "That was the kicker, mate. That was the part I didn't tell ya. He was illegal, he shouldn't even bin 'ere." His words were measured and calm, his face exasperated. He watched Cameron's face, letting the words sink in.

"You didn't stab him, mate," he continued.

Cameron's mouth dropped open. He eyes flicked back and forward in his skull as he absorbed the information.

"Yeah. I did. I got 'im. I stabbed 'im." He stammered but he was no longer sure.

"No. You didn't. I spoke to Chris. You went away for stabbing a drug dealer in Tooting." Michael's arms were held out again, the exasperation back on his face.

"Thomas." Cameron whispered. "Thomas. You bastard."

"What?" Michael was leaning forward trying to hear the words.

"He told me where he lived. He gave me the blade."

"Who's Thomas?"

"My… a… drug dealer," he said pathetically, almost whispering to himself.

Michael snorted, turning to the door of the pub. "Well, there you have it."

Cameron's mind swam, pieces seemed to click into place. He felt betrayal but, most of all, he felt embarrassed. His eyes watched the pavement, studying the cracks, desperately clawing through his mind to bring back the memories of that night. It was empty, he barely remembered what Thomas had said to him but the more he thought of Thomas, the more he knew Michael was right. He looked up at Michael, he was turning away, one hand on the gold decorated handle of the pub door. Cameron ran towards him, tears streaked down his face. He lunged for his arm, clutching his elbow and feeling the soft fabric of his cardigan.

"Michael, man, help me. I need help. Please. I 'av a dawt'ah. I 'av a baby too," he wailed, his eyes clenched shut, feeling and smelling the man in front of him but lacking the courage to meet his gaze.

Michael shoved him back, making him trip over his own feet and land on his backside on the hard pavement.

"Get the fuck off me, you stink of shit." He looked down at Cameron, crumpled up on the floor. "I can't fuckin' 'elp you. You fuckin' stabbed a guy for nothin'. What'd you want from me?"

Cameron looked down at his own hands; they were still shaking. He felt sick with shame. He didn't know what he expected from his old friend.

"What do I do?" he said desperately.

"I dunno, mate but it ain't my fuckin' problem. Stay away from me." Michael pulled open the door of the pub and disappeared inside.

59

He slumped down between the bins, the empty bottle tumbled from his hands and the familiar echo of the glass clinking against the cold concrete echoed up into the small space. He could barely smell the odor emanating from the bins over the smell of his trousers, which had now hardened and scratched against the back of his thighs. The night had darkened, and the wind had picked up, rattling the large metal doors that housed the estate bins. He let his head fall into his palms as a soft helplessness grew in the pit of his stomach. He scanned the small concrete space that had now become his home, no more than two hundred metres from Thomas' old apartment block. The desperation of his life stuck in his throat like a bone. He couldn't shake the restlessness that followed his thoughts. He didn't care what happened to him now. He only wanted to be rid of the torment that screamed at him from the depths of his brain.

Instinctively he reached down and caressed the neck of the empty bottle, feeling its smooth contour up to the ribs of the screwcap. He picked the bottle from the floor and held it in his palm; he stared at the brown label as if looking for solutions in the gold script. *Who am I?* he thought. *I have no fuckin' idea anymore. I thought I knew once. Thought I made a difference. Thought people would care if I was gone.* He caught the reflection of his reddened eyes in the glare of the bottle from the cold strip-light overhead. Disgust swept over him. He raised the bottle up and slammed it against the concrete. Glass exploded around him, flicking against his hands and face, the sound rattling against the small room and booming out onto the estate. A shard of glass dug into his palm. He watched the fleck of blood bubble and then draw a red line down his palm, curling over the back of his hand and resting there. He picked a curved triangle of glass next to his leg and twirled it in his fingers, looking at the empty room in front of him through the small window.

He lifted the sleeve of the large workman's jacket and traced the veins on his arm with the sharp point of glass. His weight loss had left his arm like a map of veins and tunnels that ran from his wrist to his elbow. He had heard somewhere that when people cut across their wrists it was a sign that they didn't really want to kill themselves. The trick was to cut down the vein to open it up. The thought of forever being in darkness brought a flutter of peace to his tormented skull. He imagined sleeping, peacefully forever, with no hangover and no one to kick him awake in the morning to move him on. He wouldn't miss Katie as they would all be gone. He wouldn't hate his mum as she wouldn't exist. The weight that he carried on his chest would lift and he would breath easily as he slept. Alone and in peace. There would be no consequences as no one would even know he was gone. He would carry on being as invisible as he was now but without the pain.

He buried the sharp point of the glass into his arm, dragging downwards through his skin. It sliced through easily, opening a thin red line that stretched six inches down the length of his forearm. There was a moment of a hot sharp pain that eased as his heartbeat quickened and his breath ran short. The seal broke and the line became a gush as the deep red blood fell in splashes around him. A feeling of cold swept through him. He felt a churn of nausea in his stomach and his head swooned between sleep and awake as he became aware, he was about to pass out. The glass tumbled from his fingers, splashing in the blood that now soaked into his jacket and trousers. He grasped the wound with his free hand to try to stem the bleeding, but the blood poured through his fingers and around his palm. *Fuck. Fuck. What have I done?* He tried to scream but his throat was dry, and the energy leaked out of him. It was cold and he was suddenly so tired. His skin crawled with goose bumps, his face a deathly grey as his eyes rolled upwards. His movements had become slow and the world was swimming, dreamlike in front of him. Colours burst like fireworks behind his eyes and it was almost impossible to see the shifting room in front of him with the vertigo spinning in his head. He softly leant over with his head on the bin and let his eyes close. A dreamlike peace warmed him. He drifted into unconsciousness as his hand fell away from the wound on his arm.

Theresa walked in flip-flops, tip toeing on the wet pavement to avoid getting the rainwater between her toes. In her hand hung a black plastic bag that she held away from her body. She pulled at the steel door that housed the large waste bins. She lived a couple of floors above the bin and on a warm summer day the smell would drift through open windows, but it was the mid-December and the air was frosted. A thin white layer covered the rubbish that scattered the floor inside and outside of the room. The door wailed as she pulled it open. The first thing she noticed was the battered Reebok sticking out from the space between two of the bins and the leg that was attached to it. She had seen a homeless man wandering through the estate some nights and heard the door beneath her flat open and close. He must have made a home, but she wasn't interested in getting into a fight with a crazy guy about where he slept. She intended to open the bin quietly and deposit her bag before leaving. She felt her flip-flop stick to the floor and looked down at the pool of sticky red liquid. It crawled from under the bin like a shadow. She slowly edged closer. Her body screamed for her to turn and run but her mind had no interest in leaving without seeing the face that belonged to the leg. She peered around the bin; the figure lay with his head slumped, his mouth wide open and his skin a deathly white that made his hair seem jet black. The sleeve of his illuminous jacket was rolled up, exposing a long cut caked with dried blood. The bag dropped from her hand and this time she did run. Her flip-flop stuck in the puddle and lifted easily from her foot, but she didn't stop, planting her feet in the blood and then every puddle as she ran the short distance back to her flat. With shaking hands, she dialed 999.

MICHAEL

60

She screamed in agony, holding onto her stomach as the pain surged through her like a current. Her swollen stomach was exposed, straps ran across its diameter attached to a screen that hovered near her head. He watched the lines pulse across the screen in peaks. They had some time before the next contraction, so she lay back, and closed her eyes as if she was falling asleep. When they opened again, they met with his.

"You ok?" he offered.

He felt powerless watching her in so much pain and not being able to stop it or offer any words that would take it away.

She nodded, wearily. "Tell me when the next one's coming."

"You should feel it," he said with a smile.

The next one came quickly. She groaned and held onto her rounded stomach, squeezing his hand at the same time, hard enough that he felt his fingers click together. He watched her face intently; the uselessness came flooding over him again as he sat silently waiting for this round of contractions to be over. He turned at the sound of the door opening as the doctor entered the small hospital room, relieved to be able to share the tension with someone other than his wife. The doctor seemed young; her brown hair hung loosely at her shoulders, held into place with an Alice band. Her figure was hidden underneath her baggy scrubs and knee length white jacket, a stethoscope hung loosely around her neck. She waited patiently for the contraction to stop before speaking. He welcomed her gentle tone in the silence of the room.

"How's it going?" she asked, looking at Michael.

He managed to nod and let out a sigh. He felt tired, he wanted it all to end as soon as possible. Her suffering had somehow become his suffering, which filled him with guilt as he sat, uselessly, by her side offering a kind word and a gentle squeeze of her hand. The doctor nodded as if she understood how he felt, looking at Sofia, her eyes closed, and head slumped to one side.

"Ok, I spoke with the midwife." The empathy slowly evaporated from her words and was replaced with a seriousness that made him sit upright. "We haven't dilated much more than a couple of hours ago and his heart rate is dropping."

He tried to absorb her words, looking frantically from Sophia's exhausted eyes to the face of the young doctor as she explained their options. There were few; continue to wait for something to happen or an emergency caesarean. He felt a sense of relief that it was coming to an end, followed by a bout of shame as he saw the tears form in Sofia's eyes. She was scared. He could feel it pulsating from her and it made him uncomfortable to watch. He stroked her cheek, watching every curve and imperfection in her face, rubbing his thumb across the tear tracks that had formed lines through droplets of sweat covering her face.

"What do you want to do?" he whispered quietly.

His had pulled his face close enough to hers so that he could feel her breath on his face, like the first night they had spent together and every night they had spent together since. Fear had welled up inside him and now punched at the walls of his stomach as his brain did a slideshow of his life after her death, broken and alone with their child. She shook her head, her eyes never leaving his.

"I don't know. I'm scared."

"I know. It's gonna be alright." Despite what his brain was telling him, he knew this dishonesty was needed.

"We don't have many choices."

She shook her head and mouthed 'ok'. He kissed her fully on the lips as the next contraction kicked in, making her pull away and grimace with the pain. He looked at the doctor, standing with the clipboard held across her breasts and her arms folded across it as she watched them.

"Ok," he said finally.

Thirty minutes later room was busy with midwives. Sofia was crudely bent over, her hospital gown unfastened at the back and she was bent over a pillow on her lap. Michael turned away, his hand still clasped around hers, as they applied the anesthetic to the skin before plunging the needle into her spine and numbing her below the waist. The epidural started its work as she was wheeled into a theatre under the glow of white lights. Michael felt like a bystander as the world inside the operating theatre moved around him, oblivious to his presence. He took a moment to consider that they both might be ghosts, unseen and unheard, until one of the midwives approached him, asking how Sofia was doing. He looked over at her, her face still stretched out in fear, tears swelling in her eyes and rolling down her cheeks. She nodded as a tear touch her lip and her tongue met it, sucking it in. The fear boiled inside him like a kettle, gently simmering, never allowing him to relax. It intensified as a blue screen was pulled up, covering her lower half and leaving them both alone in the busy operating theatre. He leaned over, their faces close again, and softly stroked the loose hairs plastered to her forehead that had escaped the cap.

He watched her eyes open and close, each time the blink getting heavier and longer. It had been almost thirty hours since they had made the short journey to the hospital and neither of them had slept since they had pushed their way through the rotating doors.

"What do you feel?" he whispered in her ear.

"Nothing, just someone pulling. Can you see anything?"

"No. I don't want to." He answered honestly

He leant forward and placed his forehead against her, enjoying the feel of her warm clammy skin. The room was filled with chatter and the clinking of instruments moving between hands and dishes. The wail of a child broke through the mild noise, bringing everyone to a silent standstill. It was Michael who spoke first.

"Is that him?"

"Well, it isn't me," the surgeon replied smartly.

The curtain dropped for ten seconds, as a bright pink and purple human stretched out in his hands, his gloved fingers firmly gripping the armpits. Michael watched the small thing wriggle against his hold before the curtains were returned and the baby disappeared along with the surgeon's hands and face. A small gasp escaped him as he looked at Sofia. The tears streamed down her face; her bottom lip curled outwards as she cried with one hand covering her face.

"It's ok," he managed. They seemed to be the only words he could say. He felt pathetic repeating them to her with no idea if they were true.

He comforted her, running his sweaty hand over hers being careful to avoid the tube embedded into her skin. The midwife appeared by his side, getting his attention with a soft tap to his elbow. She beckoned at him and led him to a small table. The baby lay on his back, pink legs thrashed in the air and his arms were straight and erect above his head. He screamed a small shrill wail, making his face a fierce red in contrast to his purple extremities. A long black slug like thing hung out of his stomach, sealed near his skin with a white clip that reminded Michael of the clips they had brought from Ikea. The midwife handed him small curved scissors.

"You want to cut it?"

He looked at the doll-like human wailing in front of him, looking back at the midwife with disbelief. She nodded reassuringly at him, pushing forward the scissors. He felt overwhelmed but nodded back slowly, taking the scissors. His heart raced as he put them over the black tube and cut through the gooey meat. It fell away easily, leaving a small piece protruding from his stomach and the clip still hanging from what remained. The midwife leaned over and pulled the towel tight around the baby, pushing his arms down so they were tightly wrapped.

"Sit down," she directed, signaling towards the chair near Sofia's head

He sat, wordlessly, not taking his eyes from the red face of the thing that he had somehow managed to create. He was engrossed, the small spots that covered his face, the swirl of hair that was plastered to his head and the thick substance that was clumped in the creases of his face and body. The nurse placed him in Michael's arms, gently guiding his hands into the right position to support his backside and neck. The baby stopped crying and the chatter continued from the surgeons behind him as they stitched Sofia's stomach back together. The baby's small eyes tried to open, pulling against the sticky residue that caked his face. It took two or three attempts before they finally peeled open and he blinked in the bright lights of the operating theatre, seeming to study the ceiling intently before resting his gaze on Michael's face.

Michael's world stopped. The chatter in the background became a murmur and the operating theatre swept away, leaving him alone with the bundle in his arms. He felt an ache in his chest as if his heart was expanding to make room for the alien-looking thing that he clutched in his arms. He stared in wonder again at its face and, as the seconds passed, its small eyelids blinked against the harsh light, a part of his mind opened and swept his body with adrenalin and serotonin. As he ran a finger across the arch of the baby's nose, he thought he understood what it was like to love, but in the moment, he realized there were different types of love and he had never felt one like this. *I know that God exists. I held him in my arms,* he thought absently without realizing he was thinking at all.

61

The scream pierced the quiet of the house, jerking him from sleep. He sat up in bed, looking around the darkness of the room, expecting someone to be standing at their bed. He felt the duvet move as Sofia turned in her sleep. *Waaaaaah.* The sound crashed through the house once more. He spun his hips out of the bed and planted his bare feet on the cold wooden floor; he was up in a fraction of a second and running for the door. He didn't know why he was running but panic coursed through his body, adrenalin surged through him. He swung the door open with a crash, waking Sofia with a start. He reached the side of the cot, Alex wailed from within the tightly wound blanket, his eyes squeezed closed, his fists clenched in the air and his mouth formed a small toothless circle. *Hungry. He's hungry.* He ran a hand over his face, feeling a thin layer of sweat had formed on his forehead. He picked the baby up and held half the small body over his shoulder, softly tapping his back as he walked towards the kitchen to put the milk bottle in the microwave. It hummed to life and the small glow from the door created a bubble of light on his face. He waited for the ping, before taking the bottle and rubbing the nib into the baby's mouth. He sucked greedily at the rubber nipple, falling quiet as his hand came up in a fist and rested on the side of his face. Michael watched him, a small smile curling the corner of his mouth, he ran a finger softly across the cheek and let it stroke the arch of the Alex's small button nose.

He walked back towards the bedroom, pausing at the large mirror that hung in the hallway. His face was drawn and pale, his eyes shadowed by dark circles and his hair stood on end. He listened to the small sucking coming from the crook in his arm, watching the lines that had grown in his face. He had never felt so tired, his body ached, pain climbed its way up his thighs as he rocked back and forward on his heels soothing the feeding child. A feeling at the back of his mind was circling him as if he were prey. He willed it away, but it leapt forward taking chunks out of him to weaken him. It would only be a matter of time before it stepped forward and devoured him whole. He looked at the small face, quietly, peacefully falling back into a sleep. It wasn't important now. Alex was what was important now. He had to keep him safe. He walked back to the small nursery, laid him down in his bed and tip-toed gently back into the bedroom, slipping underneath the covers.

"You got up in a rush. All ok?" Sofia asked. Her voice was croaky from sleep and her eyes stayed closed.

"Yeah, all ok."

He curled his hands underneath the pillow as he lay his head down. The clock told him it was four in the morning and his brain had no intention of going back to sleep. He lay awake for two more hours, staring at the dim glow of the clock on the wall before finally rising from bed to shower. It was Sunday. He mourned the lie in as it escaped him for another weekend. His mind drifted to the family lunch that afternoon. He began to daydream of a quiet afternoon with a couple of beers and a *siesta* afterwards.

He sat in his office, overlooking the maze of buildings that swarmed Canary Wharf, watching the subtle movement of the people and cars below. He was a voyeur in his own life, he was back behind the looking glass on the outside looking in, unable to talk or touch anything, doomed to watch as people went about their lives oblivious of his existence. His tired mind stalked their every movement; he wondered what they were thinking and what they were doing. The human behavior felt alien to him and pointless. They woke up in the morning and donned suits and wrapped ties around their necks like leashes, they led themselves through the streets into glass, manmade structures and watched monitors all day. They did nothing important or worthwhile. He did nothing important or worthwhile. He moved numbers from one screen to another and someone became very rich, but they were just numbers on a spreadsheet. *We were on that ledge together, remember?* His exchange with Cameron weighed heavy on him from the weekend. He replayed the conversation over, scolding himself for being so heartless and then instantly justifying his words. *He ain't my problem no more. I can't save everyone.*

Cameron was right. They were both on a ledge and it was thinning. He thought of Alex's face as he had left that morning, his eyes closed and his face serene. He had no idea of the life that lay before him, a life of disappointment and sadness that followed people around as they forced themselves to follow the routines set out by the men and women before them. It was a pointless, insipid life that they all had to endure before they finally had a heart attack or a stroke or collapsed in a puddle of their own shit and piss on a pavement somewhere. *He is the only thing that matters* Michael thought, rubbing his hand absently across his chest as if the thought of him had made his heart ache. *I must protect him from all of this.* The thought felt irrational but absolutely normal as he stared out at the street below.

There was a thin knock, lightly rapping on the glass surround. He pulled himself away from the window, beckoning for the associate at the door to come in. The apprehension in his face made Michael feel a taste of disgust for them both. He didn't consider himself a hard boss, he socialized with the team when he could, but it was a business that was founded on hierarchy and the kid feared him because he sat in an office staring out of a window several floors up from the shit-show below. He was disgusted that he played his part in the façade. The associate handed him a wad of papers. He looked expectantly at Michael, awaiting a response.

"Thanks," he said, lifting the paper up to show that he had taken responsibility for it.

"It's… the… erm…" the associate stammered.

Michael felt pity for him and an urge to push him back through the door, onto his backside to be rid of him from the office. He wanted to be alone and the bumbling associate was making him feel uncomfortable. All human contact was making him feel uncomfortable, except for Alex. The thought of his weight in his arms, and his breath on his neck, made Michael feel serene.

"I know," he said, forcing himself to smile.

It felt foreign on his face. The kid nodded in return and backed out of the office as if he was worried Michael would sink his teeth into his back. As the door closed, Michael flung the paper down on his desk, letting it smack against the surface and spread like a deck of cards. *Pick a card, any card.* He slumped back on his chair and watched the clouds drift slowly through the sky.

62

The weeks drifted past. He would stare at the soft glow of the streetlight on the wall for hours before drifting into a light troubled sleep that would inevitably be broken by a baby's scream. Sometimes Sofia would wander, zombie like, down the hall to feed Alex. Some nights he would do the run himself but every night he was woken up with a start and sleep would then evade him for the final few hours before he rose to get in the shower. His eyes were sunken holes in his face, focusing became a chore as he found himself staring aimlessly out of windows trying to work out the very fabric that kept human existence together. The looking glass had become thicker and the view obscured by the fogging in the glass. He felt further away from reality.

The meeting room was cold, the air conditioning blasted through the grates sunk into the ceiling. The white walls were a welcome distraction. The room was windowless, otherwise he would watch the clouds meander across the sky. Mark stood at the front of the room, behind him a white backdrop was filled with the colours streaming from the overhead projector, casting a rainbow across his face. He was talking and pointing at something on the screen. Michael wasn't interested, instead his focus was a small chip in the paint on the wall opposite him. A man swung to and fro in one of the leather chairs that surrounded the large table in the centre of the room. His grey suit was buttoned at his stomach and his hands lay on his lap; his fingers clasped together. His face looked pensive as he studied

Mark. He was no older than fifty, his face lined with wrinkles and his brown eyes lit against his dark greying hair. Michael watched his face as he watched Mark, trying to know his story just by looking at him. He imagined he was still behind his looking glass; the man could not see him. The woman sat next to him was around the same age, her blonde hair fell over her shoulders and the top of her back in perfectly straight line. Her legs were crossed, on her lap was a small notebook that she scribbled in with quick flicks of her slim wrists. She carried an air of authority, her face was concentrated, her eyes peered through her large black framed glasses with an intensity that made Michael uncomfortable.

The room fell silent and all three turned to him. He looked at them one by one. A horror sank into him. He had been asked a question and he had been preoccupied. He stuttered, looking for a clue to the subject from the screen that lit Mark's face. Mark stepped in, breaking the silence.

"Well, growth rates across South America have been unpredictable."

His eyes fixed on Michael's, the fierce anger in his eyes. Michael felt the heat rise in his face and he returned his attention to the chip. It calmed him and allowed him to climb back into his looking glass. There was serenity in that chip, a quiet comfort that allowed his tired mind to sit back into his skull and melt away. He knew he should listen, but his mind struggled to fixate on anything more than the small circle that watched him from the white walls. A cloud swarmed over him, insulating his head from the outside world. His job was a memory of something that he used to do and do well but now it felt like it was something that someone else did. Someone that he used to know. He suppressed the urge to scream out in the white room, to throw his notepad in Mark's face and put his foot through that chip until it became a hole that he could escape through. The occupants of the meeting room were now talking; their noise was a muffled sound like a small tapping at the window. The shuffling of furniture broke him from his thoughts; they stood and offered him a hand. Michael got to his feet, taking a hand and shaking firmly, forcing his face to smile to keep up the pretense that he was somehow still with them in this room.

As they left, Mark turned to him. "What der fack are you playin' at?" His accent had dropped back into the comfortable East London twang. His finger was pointing at Michael's chest.

"Sorry, Mark, I'm not feeling so good."

"You ain't been feeling good for weeks, then. Pull your shit together or get der fack out!" His face was ablaze with fur, swinging his arms as he spoke. He turned and left before Michael could respond.

Michael sat for a while looking at the open door before grabbing his jacket hanging on the back of the chair. He walked to the small collection of desks; some of the associates were picking up their bags and pulling on jackets as he approached. They turned to look at him and looked undecided whether to remove their jackets and continue to work or continue to head for the exit.

"You guys heading to the pub tonight?"

He watched their confused expressions with amusement as they looked at each other, waiting for one of them to be brave enough to speak.

"Yeah." One of them finally spoke.

It was almost midnight and he sat alone at the table as the last of the associates had picked up her things and staggered towards the door. She had been tall, attractive and seemly interested in him. He had allowed her to steadily match him drink for drink until she was stroking the top of his arm and talking with her face close enough to his to be able to kiss him. She had asked if they could get a hotel room together and, though he enjoyed her attention, he wanted to be alone. The alcohol swilled around him, making him lightheaded and longing to sleep. He had looked her in the eyes, quietly shaking his head before returning to his drink. She had taken the hint and shuffled out of the booth with a pained expression on her face. He watched her let the door close behind her and raise an arm towards the passing cars. Seconds later the shape of a black cab pulled up at the curb and she disappeared. He watched the door, silently, as the music blasted through the speakers and crowds gathered around the bar behind him. He finished his drink and stood up, pulling on his jacket.

A weight pulled on his chest; he feared he could drown in the middle of the bar amongst all these people. He wasn't ready to go home. The house would be dark and quiet, but it would be full of responsibility and he had no energy for any of it. *Be reckless. Destroy the fuck out of all of it.* It was a voice he once knew well, one he tried to ignore but couldn't resist. He walked into the street, pulling his jacket tight around his waist to keep out the cold.

"Michael."

His name, It came from somewhere behind him. He turned, trying to focus the image in the centre of his vision, it felt like he was looking through water. Chris's face appeared in front of him, the same face he knew but slightly older. His hair was no longer spiked in tall towers on his head; instead it parted at the side desperately covering the receding hairline.

"Chris? How are you mate?"

They shook hands warmly.

"Not bad, mate, what you up to?"

"Heading home actually, just about to get a cab."

"You got time for a drink?"

The thought of having to spend time in the company of anyone made his stomach turn. For the second time that day, he resisted the urge to run.

"Need to get back mate, baby at 'ome. Next time? We'll arrange something soon."

He said it almost before Chris had finished his sentence, the look in Chris' eye suggested he knew. As they said they said their goodbyes, Chris's face lit up as if something had occurred to him.

"Hey, before you go, you hear about Cameron?"

The name made his blood run cold. He didn't want to share with Chris that he had seen Cameron a few weeks before and pushed him onto his backside. He hadn't looked in great shape and Michael imagined that he hadn't got any better in the weeks that had passed. *He's going to tell me what a loser he is now, but I already know.* It was old news, as far as he was concerned, and he struggled to find the compassion to care. He took a glance at the road as another taxi slowed down, its yellow light lit showing it to be available. He sighed, looking at Chris, thinking how quickly he could wrap the conversation up.

"No, what's up with him?"

"He's dead, mate. They found him in some bins, wrists slit."

The blood drained from his face; his mouth dropped open. His veins felt heavy in his body, he could almost feel the blood trying to force their way through. Chris's mouth was downturned but the slight glimpse of a smile on the edge of his lips said he was pleased to have news that Michael didn't know. He was pleased at Michael's reaction. It was what he was looking for. They had both been good friends with Cameron, but Chris had always been second best once Michael had appeared on the scene. Michael suspected he had carried that resentment until the point that Cameron's life had fallen apart, as had their relationship with him.

"When?" Michael managed.

"A couple of weeks back."

"That's… terrible."

It was terrible. The time between their meeting and his death must have been a matter of days. *We were on that ledge together, remember?* He looked away from Chris, unable to maintain eye contact through fear that he would see the guilt in his eyes. He was right, they had been there together, and he had watched as his old friend had plummeted to his death. Worse, he had pushed him.

"I'm sorry to hear that."

He turned back to Chris. His expression hadn't changed.

"Yeah, terrible," he repeated.

"Listen mate, I need to go," He said abruptly, pointing towards the row of taxis now waiting at the traffic lights, to finish the conversation. Chris opened his mouth to speak and closed it again quickly.

Michael stuck out a hand and a black cab burst away from the line leaving the traffic lights and pulled up at the curb in front of him. He gave Chris a wave before opening the door and disappearing into the dark space, relieved to be alone in the dimly lit cab.

"Where to?" The cab driver's eyes were looking at him in the small rear-view mirror.

"Start the meter, fella, I'll get the address"

He pulled his phone out of his pocket and scrolled through until he found a number he hadn't used in a few years. The name read *X* on his screen to keep the identity secret in case Sofia were to pick up his phone and be inquisitive enough to look through his contacts. He didn't need to know the name as the relationship was a transactional one. He provided the money and *X* provided the cocaine.

63

He woke up with the taste of bitter powder in the back of his throat; he was slumped across the bed in the spare room, his legs hanging idly over the edge and dressed in his suit from the previous night. He rose from the bed slowly, rubbing his head. The pain behind his eyes intensified as his body came up straight. He leant forward so his head was almost touching his knees and groaned. Regret washed through him as he swallowed heavily in his dry mouth, working to stop the contents of his stomach making their way over his shoes and the carpet. He heard Sofia's soft accent from the hallway; the sun streaming through the curtain and burning through his head told him it was late. He took a glance at the watch on his wrist to confirm. It was almost eleven. He stood slowly, steadying himself on the post of the bed and stripped off his jacket, tugging at the knot of the tie to loosen it before whipping it over his head and leaving them both strewn over the bed.

She stood in the hallway, gently talking in Spanish to Alex in her arms. She looked at him as he came out of the bedroom, one hand pressed against the wall to keep himself upright and the other hand pressed against his eyes to shield them from the light. The clack on the wooden floor made him look down at his feet. His shoes were still on. Sofia followed his gaze, shaking her head in disappointment. He slipped off his shoes and walked past her. His head pounded for some medication and his mouth desired something liquid. She watched him walk past, wordlessly, before following him into the kitchen.

"Where were you last night?"

He grunted as a response and pulled open the fridge open, pulling a carton of orange juice from the shelf.

She continued. "You're not going to tell me where you were? You came in at four in the morning and woke Alex up."

He grunted again, looking at his watch. Mentally he was calculating the difference in time between seeing Chris and getting home. It had been almost midnight when he had jumped into the taxi. Four hours had disappeared. Pockets of memory blinked in his mind like a beacon, but it was mostly black.

"HEY!" she shouted, pulling at his arm. "Do you want to explain this?" She flung the plastic packet on to the countertop. It was almost empty, the last of it lingered on the sides of the bag, giving it a cloudy look. *Jacket pocket?* he thought uselessly.

"Not mine." It was the only response he could think. "Probably Mark's" He didn't sound convincing. Her face was disbelieving and furious. He turned away from her, looking out towards the garden to avoid looking her in the eyes. He felt a mixture of guilt, shame and anger at being caught.

"You really expect me to believe that?" She reached across and grasped his arm again to turn him towards her.

"Fuck off." He pushed at her arms, forcing her to stumble backwards. She adjusted her feet, managing to keep her balance, and shifted the baby in her arms. She looked from Alex to Michael, her mouth stood ajar.

"What's wrong with you?" Her voice was almost a whisper.

"Just give me space," he responded.

"Why don't you fuck off back out then, snort some shit and you can have all the space you want? You have a fucking baby." She lifted Alex's head slightly as if may have forgotten he was there. "You have a family. You're not a fucking kid anymore."

Her voice elevated, her Spanish accent thickened, over pronouncing the words. Alex began to wail in her arms, disturbed by the commotion, He felt a bubble of rage burn inside, starting in his stomach and working its way up through his throat until his vision became hazy. It cleared quickly, leaving a burning red anger in the centre of his head. He threw the glass towards the cupboards. It crashed against the door exploding into a shower of glass, orange smeared the cupboard in a grotesque hand shape. He stepped towards her, his eyes wide, the pupils large and black.

"You fuckin' ungrateful bitch. This is my house. I paid for it. I gave you everything you have. You have everything you want and now you try and kick me out of MY house?!"

She looked at him for a couple of seconds, her mouth open in shock before her bottom lip came out and she started to cry. The anger left him as quickly as it had risen.

"Sofia," he said softly, lowering his pointed hand to his side.

She turned and ran from the room, clutching Alex's head to her breast. *Too late. Damage done.* He didn't follow her. Instead, he opened the small cupboard that was home to a collection of mops and brooms and gathered the dustpan and brush, all the while resisting the urge to vomit.

64

He pushed the off button and watched the screen go black in front of him, looking up at the wall clock in his office. The night was descending on the world outside. He had a sense of dread of going home as he did most nights now. Sofia had spent most of the weekend only talking to him when she needed to. A sadness hung on her face like a mask and it felt as if Alex sensed it. He seemed to cry most of the day, making Michael's headache throb in his brain like the slow beat of a drum. It was Thursday and they were slowly getting back to talking beyond grunts and single-word answers. He knew that he should have apologised, but he didn't have the energy. He preferred the time without her and Alex around him. The isolation comforted him.

He watched the associates gather at the doorway, pulling on their jackets and chatting to one another. He pulled open the drawer immediately next to his thigh and reached to the back, his fingers feeling at the bottom of the drawer above it. He felt the small plastic bag taped there and pulled. The remains of the weekend's adventures that had created a hole in his memory. He looked at the bag a moment before opening it, making sure to keep his hands under the desk, licking his little finger and dipping it into the powder. It came up coated like a bonbon. He put the finger in his nose and snorted hard. He felt the familiar burn at the back of his throat. His finger was still coated so he sucked the remains. *Destroy it all. Destroy everything.*

He sealed the bag and shoved it in the inside pocket of his jacket. He grabbed his briefcase that sat neatly at his feet and headed for the door. He flicked the lights off and pulled on his jacket as he approached the group that had gathered by the door. They looked at him nervously as he approached.

"Going for drinks, guys?"

They looked at one another, awkwardness reflected in their glares. He was sure that the gossip around the office had already started about his heated exchange with Mark, but he didn't care. He wanted to drink and wanted an excuse to drink. He wanted to run from the cloud that followed him and one of the most effective ways was to get drunk enough to numb everything.

"Sure," one of the associates offered with a shy smile, "but it won't be a late one." Her mousy eyes darted around the group for approval.

By the end of the night he sat alone at a stool, his knees pressed against the bar, his elbows leaning on the soft cushioned edge of leather pinned along the its length. Most of the associates had finished one beer each and headed for the exit, leaving him alone with a struggle of twenty-something men all looking awkwardly at the remains of their glass, almost willing it to evaporate in front of their eyes. The conversation was patchy as they tried out different subjects like dresses. Each ill-fitting and thrown into a pile. He had finally taken the initiative, desperate to be away from people and be away from company of any kind; he had downed the last of his beer as a signal that they could continue with their night. He wished them a good evening and walked enough distance from the bar to not be seen before jumping into another one that seemed quiet enough for him to be left alone. He finished his fifth pint quickly to hurry up the drunken glow that he longed for and the moment to forget. The cocaine stayed in his pocket, he feared it now. He feared what it could make him do.

"Another?" The barman stood in front of him, a bemused look on his face.

"Sure," Michael replied. *Destroy it all.* "I'm going for a piss."

He walked the short distance to the bathroom, taking the small plastic bag out of his pocket as he locked the toilet behind him. He placed it on the cistern of the toilet. Removing his wallet, he scooped the last of the powder onto the corner of his credit card, inhaling deeply. He licked the edge of the card to clear the last remnants. He returned to the bar; his pint stood waiting for him on a fresh square napkin. He threw a ten-pound note down on the bar and took a long pull of the beer. *Another step towards oblivion*, he thought to himself. A crowd swarmed into the bar; noise filled the quiet room drowning out the background music. He looked at the group as they bundled into one of the larger booths. One of the group caught his eye and froze. He felt a small tap of panic shout something in his ear, but the apathy and alcohol drowned it out. One by one, the group turned slowly and looked at him looking at them. He wasn't surprised that all the associates had regrouped and continued drinking without him, but he imagined that they were not expecting to see him sat at a bar drinking on his own. *Well, what can you do?* He turned his attention back to his pint glass, taking another long pull on the bitter gold liquid.

65

They whispered about him in the corridors. He saw it in their eyes when he passed them or when he spoke to them, which was less and less now. He spent large parts of the day sat in his office with the door closed. He cancelled meetings regularly or blocked hours in his diary so he could pretend to be busy. Instead, he stared at the clouds as they drifted past his window. He had barely spoken to Mark since his outburst, even though their offices were connected. Mark travelled most weeks so that gave him the opportunity to close himself off. On the days Mark was in the office, he found himself wandering the streets at the time allocated to one of his many pretend meetings. They exchanged small talk when necessary and he continued to farm the work out to the associates via email to avoid having conversations with them.

He had been betrayed by his brain and he didn't know how to stop the slide into darkness. The looking glass was getting thicker and thicker and he had lost the will to care or the motivation to try to reverse the damage that he had done. Instead, he swam in his own ocean of isolation, fear and desperation and the worst part was that he enjoyed it. He could only admit this to himself. He enjoyed being alone where he didn't have to pretend to be one of those awful human beings with grins plastered on their faces, shaking hands with one another and asking, "how was your weekend?" like they gave a fuck about each other's weekends. They were suits and skins that walked around the world as if it was theirs to own.

In the end, when the world crashed and burned, they would be sent to dust like everything else. They would be no different. *It was all pointless.*

He was looking in the mirror again in the sterile office bathroom. It was something he did a lot in the last few weeks. He wanted to look through his own eyes and see what was beneath, he wanted to remember who he was, and his face was the only thing that remained unchanged. It always felt like he was looking at a stranger. He didn't know the man in the mirror, the man who had happy memories, a successful job and a family. That wasn't him. He was a shell, void of all emotion. He sighed heavily and flicked the top of the tap. The gush of water made his skin tingle and break out in goose bumps. He dried his hands and pushed through the door. Mark stood in the corridor, waiting for him.

"Mark." A shiver of panic went up his spine

"Michael, can we talk?"

"Sure."

"In my office?" he pointed down the wide corridor where the glass door of his office waited. The shiver of panic grew into a landslide.

They walked side by side in silence until they reached the office and the door was closed behind them. Mark motioned towards the seat and sat in his chair looking at Michael across his desk.

"Michael. I'll get to the point. I dan't know what is goin' on wiv you, but you 'av become increasingly disengaged. Yor missin' deadlines and yor losing the respect of yor colleagues. Is it the baby? Are you getting enuff sleep?" His accent had softened as if he were talking to clients.

Michael sighed and shrugged his shoulders. The time had finally arrived. He had been caught out as he suspected he would be at some point. He felt like a fraud and he had been doing it for so long that he forgot where the real Michael stopped, and this new person started. It was about to end. He stayed quiet as Mark gazed at him, waiting for a response.

"I spoke to Sofia," he continued.

Michael looked up, a flash of hurt and anger blew across his face. Mark must have seen it, he held up a hand and leant forward.

"She says yor the same at 'ome." Michael said nothing. Mark sighed and slumped back in his chair. "Michael. Yor my guy. I trust you and yor one of the best I've 'ad but I will 'av to let you go if it carries on like this. I need you to get back the Michael *I* know. The Michael I hired. You should be taking over in a caaple of years. The way yor going, you'll be unemployed."

Everything he said was true and the honesty of it made him want to sob in the office in front of Mark. He wanted to tell him the truth, tell him about the looking glass and the fraud that he hired all those years ago. He wasn't who Mark thought he was. He was just a kid himself and he was on the outside looking in on this freak show without being able to be a part of it. Instead, he quietly nodded and choked down the tears that built up in his throat.

"Go 'ome." Mark said. "Go 'ome and take some time. I'll cover for you 'ere. Call me when you're ready."

He stood to signal that the meeting was over. He stuck out a hand, his lips pulled tight in a sympathetic smile that made Michael feel pathetic. Michael stood and shook his hand. *It's over. I've been caught and it's over.* He left the office closing the door and walked the few metres to his own office. *She'll leave me. She'll take Alex and go.* He collected his jacket and briefcase and walked slowly to the elevators, the eyes of the associates following him.

He clenched the black leather steering wheel, almost feeling the dimples in his fingertips and palms. The road stretched out before him, a single grey line like a snake, only broken with the white line that followed it through the bends. Trees littered each side giving the sensation that the road was tunnelled, and the walls were soft leaves. Overhead the blue sky was barely visible through the treetops. He was pushing the accelerator hard as he exited corners. He felt the tug of the Mercedes' back end, as if it wanted to spin him around and send him back to the office. Instead, he tethered the brake as he worked into another corner; the tyres gripped and omitted a small screech as they held the road around the corner.

His head was in overdrive. It clouded the events in the office with every memory that he had as if it was building a case to prove that the world was a horrible place. It picked the most painful images and faces from his memory and spun them around his skull like a carousel in a gameshow. He pushed them aside, mentally willing them to go away but each one made his stomach turn. His hands and arms felt heavy on the wheel of the car, he was so tired, but the burn of tears kept him from closing his eyes. His stomach and heart ached, yearning for something, some kind of release but he wasn't sure what that was. The heavy sadness rose up through his body, turning slowly to rage. He was screaming into the empty void of the car. The car barrelled down the middle of the road, the white line now spitting out the front and back of the car as if it were a string that could control its direction. He was screaming an incoherent stream of words and guttural noises, the veins standing out on his neck. The road curved to the left in a sweeping arc, the trees still gathering at the side of the road like spectators. The car drifted slowly away from the confines of the white line, correcting itself into the right-hand lane towards oncoming traffic. The road was empty.

Steven, who he hadn't thought about in over ten years, appeared in his mind in perfect clarity. His eyes were blue and sunk into his face. His hair had grown long, lying flat, unwashed and greasy on his forehead. He wore an illuminous yellow builder's jacket. Michael felt a peace overcome him, sitting back feeling his head against the headrest, arms stretched out before him. The right-hand wheels rattled as they touched the rubble strips signalling the edge of the road. Ahead of him, a black sign came into view with white arrows pointing to the left. He pressed his foot into the accelerator, closing his eyes as the car left the road and crashed into the trees below.

When he opened his eyes, his view was obscured by the bonnet, which had flipped back shattering the windscreen, leaving a trail of cracks from top to bottom. Both windows had disintegrated either side of him and the pieces were piled in his crotch and across the passenger seat. The car had crashed through the shrubs, ploughing through mounds of dirt and rock before coming to a stop on an old Alder tree. He could hear the engine hissing as it omitted its final breaths, smoke meandered from the engine block and blew past his face. He looked back towards the road, the deep dirt marks dug out by the wheels visible against the serene forest floor. *Shit. Still alive,* he thought.

66

He stumbled out of the cabin of the tow truck and walked the short distance to the front door, past the empty driveway. He turned to watch the truck pull away with his car attached to the back. The usually shining silver no longer gleamed. The sleek elegant lines were impossible to make out against the ugly spikes and sharp curves standing out at various angles from the front and side of the car. *Looks like someone should have died in there*, he thought morosely. He hobbled up to the house, limping slightly at the throbbing from his right thigh. He took a moment to look at his reflection in the large windows that stretched across the front of the house. His hair was out of place and his face ghost-like in the tint of the window. He ran a hand through his hair to reset the side parting and looked at his suit. It was covered in streaks of mud, small holes were punctured in his trousers and shirt, and blood flecks blossomed like small flowers across his chest and arms. Mud clung to the bottom of his shoes in large clumps. He reached into his jacket pocket slung over his arm and pulled out his set of keys. He let out a heavy sign and pushed open the door.

Sofia walked down the corridor at the sound of the door closing behind him. He shook off his shoes, being careful not to kick the mud off onto the polished wooden floor.

"Michael, what happened to you?"

He had used all his energy screaming into the nothingness of his car and climbing up the slope away from the wreckage. He had managed to convince the police officer that he had swerved to avoid a fox, which had sent his car down the slope. He had passed the breath test for alcohol and had politely declined the offer from the young medic to take him to the hospital for a checkup. He would have to continue with this lie for Sofia and anyone else that asked the question but the energy to utter any words at all had left him.

"I had an accident in the car. It's all ok," he said dismissively.

"Why were you in the car? Why weren't you at work? What happened?"

He looked at her and let out another heavy sigh as he realized that he wasn't going to get away with the short version.

"I wasn't feeling well so I left. I swerved to avoid a fox and ended up going off the road. The windows broke. It looks worse than it is."

"What? Your face is bleeding. You look like shit. Sick, how?"

She stepped forward, grasping his arms and staring up at his face. He looked away and tried to brush her arms off, but she held firm.

"Sick, how?" she asked again, squeezing his arms.

"I just… felt… sick." He hadn't had the time to come up with a suitable cover story. He grabbed her hands and prized them from his arms.

"I'm ok," he said. "I just need to lie down. Where's Alex?"

He walked past her and started slowly climbing the stairs, unbuttoning his shirt. He felt a need to hold his son, to be close to him. He wanted to feel the small weight on his chest as he drifted off to sleep.

"You're not ok and you haven't been for a while. Mark called me and he thinks the same. I want to know what's going on. Are you seeing someone? Why do you hate me?"

He stopped; his head slumped. "I know you called Mark," he said softly. "You might have got me fired. Nothing is going on except you overreacting. Where's Alex?"

He turned to look at her small fragile face and was alarmed to feel absolutely no remorse or concern for her. He only felt the irritation of the noise that scraped on the inside of his skull like nails on a chalkboard.

"WHAT IS WRONG WITH YOU?" she screamed. From the living

room, he heard Alex's soft cry as the noise tugged him from his daytime nap. Michael shook his head with irritation and said nothing. He felt nothing. He wanted to find the right words to say; instead, saying nothing was a way of conserving the little energy he had.

Sofia stepped forward. Grabbing the cuff of his shirt and pulling their faces inches apart, she kissed him hard on the lips. He felt her soft wet tongue try and slip into his mouth. He pushed her away with open palms, firmly, on her shoulders. She staggered back, her feet catching the patterned rug, she landed on her backside. Her back thumped against the small cupboard hugging the wall of the hallway and the small vase above her head wobbled slightly before maintaining its balance. She looked up at him with wide eyes.

"Sorry," he said, plainly. "I'm tired, I'm going to bed."

He looked longingly towards the room. The sound of his son's crying pulled at him. He wanted to console him, hold him, but he was empty. As he looked at his beautiful wife looking up at him from the floor of their beautiful house, her eyes red and tear laden, full of fear, he knew that she didn't deserve any of this. He turned and started walking up the stairs as his one part of his brain screamed at him to go to her whilst the other half told him to go to bed and forget the world.

"I'm going to go home," Sofia said softly behind him. "I'll book a flight. I don't think we can carry on like this."

A knot tightened in his stomach. He climbed down from the stairs as Sofia looked on and walked into the living room, looking into the small Moses basket. Inside, Alex had started to settle again, his cries no more than whimpers making his small chest heave and stutter like a spluttering engine. Michael reached down and stoked the baby's head, the hair was soft and scarce, the small flakes on his scalp rippled against his fingertips. He wiped away tears forming in his eyes, leant over and softly kissed the baby's forehead.

"Goodbye" he whispered softly, stroking the soft curve of the baby's nose.

When he awoke, night had descended. The curtains were open, but the house was dark and quiet. The thumping in his head had receded but now his neck ached. He winced as he pulled himself upright. The hallway clock made a steady click that echoed through the empty house. He listened to the steady hum of traffic pass by, gently working its way into the night. He stood slowly, a pain shot through his legs and lower back making him stumble forward and prop himself against the mirrored surface of the wardrobe. One of the doors of the wardrobe hung ajar, leaving a dark void peering back at him. He swung the door open. A few dresses hung absently on an almost empty bar. Gaps were filled with empty coat hangers dangling like skeletons. *She's gone.* A sheet of paper was stuck to the mirror with tape; it dangled close to his face, close enough for him to read in the glow of the moonlight.

Goodbye, my darling. I hope we can find a way to be together again, but right now, we can't stay around you. You make me sad and Alex can feel that. I hope you call me and maybe you can come visit us there and spend some time together again. Love always, your wife. Sofia xx

67

It had been two days since she had left. The silence in the house was eerie. He sat on the couch; a tumbler of Southern Comfort pressed between his thighs. The TV was on. Someone was shouting at someone else and a large man dressed in black stood between them. He stared absently at the window. The curtains had been shut since the night that she had left. He seemed to sleep in batches of three hours and his body still ached from the base of his spine to his neck. He ate when he needed to, rummaging through the freezer to find something he could put into the oven and leave. Usually this was a handful of chips or fish fingers. Once he had finished with the case of beer that was chilling in the fridge, he started working his way through liquor cabinet. It helped him to suppress the hollow feeling of emptiness that grown in him since his family had left. They wouldn't be missing him. Alex was too young to really know who he was, and Sofia would already be enjoying the warm glow of the Spanish sun with old friends whilst her mum repeated that she had made a mistake marrying him. He had proved her right.

The phone vibrated next to his thigh. He looked down, hoping to see her name. *William* lit up the screen. *William*, he thought. *William*. They had grown up together as friends and brothers but over time, they had drifted away from one another. He was unsure when it started but it had happened, and he missed him now. He missed his face and his bright blue eyes. He missed his touch and an arm slung loosely over his shoulder. His heart ached to see him now, but he didn't want to put that burden on him. The phone stopped ringing. He had needed Michael once, but he'd run away and had been running ever since. The phone buzzed to life again. *William.* He took a sip from the glass.

    It was over, anyway. He had nothing else to give and it was better this way for his family. He had fucked it all up. He downed the last remaining mouthfuls of the warm alcohol. He leant over, grasped the sheet curled up by his feet, and stretched it out across his lap. One end of the sheet was formed into a crude noose. He ran his hands through it, feeling the strength of the cotton in his hands. Soon he would swing it over the dark wooden beams that they had paid vast amounts of refurbish in the living room. They ran the length of the room and in the alcove above the window they formed a triangular structure to the ceiling. They just had to be strong enough to support his weight.

68

Probably the postman, he thought as he stared at the dark lines between the wooden planks that covered the floor below him. He imagined the eyes hidden in those gaps staring back at him with anticipation waiting for his final act. It was the final scene and he could finally sleep. The weight that he carried would be lifted. He imagined Sofia's face as she was told the news. She would probably cry but in the end, she would have everything that they owned, and she would have a comfortable life. Alex would spend his life in Spain, he would grow up happy and he would never have to know what a fuck up his dad was. He wouldn't have to carry that burden. Everyone wins, right? The wooden chair creaked with his weight as his bare foot pushed gently onto the back. They had bought it last year at an antiques dealer in Kilburn. Sofia had loved it as it reminded her of home in some way. The aging wooden rungs and chipped wooden legs did look like something found in a rustic Spanish kitchen. The seat was straw, the centre dipped under the weight of his standing foot. He leaned further, letting the chair tip enough to take two legs off the floor.

Knuckles rapped sharply on the window, rattling the window in its frame. A dark face appeared pressed against the glass, peering in at him, its hand pressed against its forehead to block out the light of the day. He had opened the curtain to see the sun one last time and now regretted it. He was sure that they were unable to see through the netted curtain that covered the length of the window, but it would have been better if they couldn't see him at all. It was distracting. *Fucking nosey postman. Don't give a shit about a fucking Amazon delivery.* He looked away from the peering face, relieved when it finally disappeared. He rocked gently on the two legs of the chair, feeling his weight balanced on both sides of the chair.

The first thump crashed against the door just as the chair slipped from underneath his feet and hit the floor with a hollow *clack*. His feet kicked against the nothing, thrashing in the air that had now opened up beneath him. The pressure on his neck was unbearable, panic flooded through him as the ceiling above him blurred and turned from white to grey to black and the oxygen was immediately cut from his airways. The second thump roared through the house, accompanied by the sound of splintering wood.

69

The curtains were closed, and the house seemed eerily quiet. He hit cancel on the phone and walked to the window, rapping his knuckles against the glass. He pressed his face against it, with his hand shielding his eyes from the sun. He could almost make out the long couch that stretched along the wall of the empty room. His eyes strained to see more through the netting as he picked out the blurry outline of familiar items. From the corner of his eye, there came a movement. He wasn't sure but he could have sworn something moved. The netting was bunched against the curtain, making it impossible to see through or around it.

He stepped back and looked at his reflection in the window. *Was it a reflection or did I see something move?* A sense of unease flicked at the corner of his mind. The silence made him uncomfortable as if there was a dark trouble hiding behind those curtains. He made his mind up. He walked to the door and took a few steps back, lining his shoulder up with the door. Lunging forward, he planted it against above the lock. The *thump* echoed up the quiet street and the door shook in its frame. He took another step back, flinging his shoulder back at the door. The cracking of wood followed the *thump* as the lock gave way, the door sprung open and crashed against the wall as he stumbled forward into the house.

The house was deserted but he felt that unease kick up a few notches in his mind.

"Michael," he called into the empty house.

He craned his neck to look up the stairs. Immediately to his left, the living-room door stood open. He ran into the room, his hands pressed against the door frame, ready to move on if the room was empty. It wasn't empty. The chair lay on the floor on its back, the four legs pointing at the wall, accusingly. Michael hung from the beams by a stream of white cloth, his hands limp at his side. His legs twitched slowly as if he was trying to climb some imaginary stairs.

"No," he whispered. "No, Michael, no. Jesus, Michael!"

He ran to him and drove his head between his legs, lifting his body from the tension of the makeshift rope. The weight of his body flopped forward. He reached up and tugged at the sheet, sweat poured from his face, damp patches were breaking out underneath his arms. He prised his finger between the skin of his brother's neck and the cloth; he grunted and tugged to create some space. The cloth gave way a couple of inches, enough to pull the him free. He dropped to his knees and let the body drop from his shoulders, crashing to the floor with a sickening thump.

He pinched his nose and blew a blast of air into his lungs. One. Two. Three. He clasped his hands and pushed against his chest, pumping hard from his shoulders. He grasped his wrist with his fingers, feeling for a pulse as he reached into his jacket pocket and pulled out his phone.

"Michael. Please. Michael please come back. Please. Don't leave me."

Salty tears dripped into his mouth and onto Michael's chest, leaving small dark circles on his t-shirt. Sweat poured from his forehead, streaking down his cheeks. He opened the phone and dialed 999 as he felt the soft and fading pulse of his brother beat against his fingers. He threw the phone down as a woman's' voice asked him which emergency service he needed. He blew three large breaths into his brother's mouth; he could hear her small voice calling from the telephone.

"Hello, hello."

He clasped his hands together once more and placed them firmly on his brother's chest, counting one hand down from the small gap at the end of his clavicle. He spoke to the woman through grunts of effort, reverberating off the walls of the silent room and he pushed at Michael's heart through his quiet chest.

EPILOGUE

The Sao Paulo sun rose in the sky and burst through the shutters that now stood open in the hotel room. The alarm rattled his phone into life, vibrating against the glass that coated the top of the bedside table. He shook himself awake, rubbing his thumb and forefinger into his eyes to extinguish the burn of insomnia. He had finally drifted off to sleep at three with the remains of Steven and Cameron whispering softly in his mind. His mind had fought the sleeping tablet as long as it could before finally allowing him to sleep. His face unshaven but older, he swivelled his hips and, once again, planted his feet on the carpeted floor, letting his eyes follow the pattern. The alarm had been set early to allow the privilege of an additional thirty minutes sleep courtesy of the snooze button, but he wouldn't be using it this morning. The client meeting was later that morning, he needed the time to clear his head. He absently stroked the faint mark on the side of his neck, to the left of his Adam's apple. The faint angled line was a reminder of how bad it could get, barely visible to the naked eye but he knew it was there, he could almost feel its texture.

He rubbed his face, pushing away the last of his dreams, his head desperately revisiting the scene of their old house, a different version of him, standing on a chair with sheets forming a crude noose around his neck. He remembered nothing beyond tipping the chair in the barely lit living room of their old house. It had been some time before he could put the pieces together over a beer with his brother. There was no postman and no parcel. Only William with an intuition that would save his life. He had thanked him enough times for William to insist that he stopped but he didn't remember him being there. He remembered Sofia's touch in the hospital, her fingertips stroking the skin between his thumb and forefinger, softly, making the hairs stand up on his arms. It had been enough to shake him awake from his troubled sleep. The white of the ceiling started as a grey blur before coming into focus, the bright lights above his head stinging his eyes. He had swallowed and the pain had torn through his throat as if he was swallowing needles. He had raised his hand, touching the space underneath his chin and recoiled from the burning pain. He had looked around from her face to the windows that looked out onto the blue London sky, his eyes running across the curtain rail above his head to the fluorescent tube lights that hung from the ceiling. He remembered the shame that spread over him like a blanket as he looked at her face. He remembered all of that, but he didn't remember the sound of the chair hitting the floor.

He stood from the hotel bed, and walked into the bathroom, planting his hands on the edge of the basin. He let his face lean into the mirror and watched the pupils in his green eyes expand. His face was strained, the dark circles exaggerated by the light above the mirror. It had been more than eight years since he had awoken in that hospital bed, her deep brown eyes, wide and beautiful, staring down at him. His face was older, his hair was greying at the sides and throughout his sideburns, short and dishevelled. Lines stretched across his forehead and around the corner of his mouth.

Hey. That had been the first thing she had said. He smiled now at the sound of her voice in his head. Softly spoken, the Spanish accent elongating the Y. She had wiped the tears that had formed and rolled down his cheeks with her thumb, her whole palm resting gently on his face. It felt good to work his way through the memory. It should be a hurtful and terrible, but in many ways, when he started to slip again, it was a reminder. An open hand stretched from the pier that he could grasp before the water filled his lungs and his head disappeared under the foaming waters. It reminded him of what he had and what he had to lose. He needed that now, as the darkness swooned and tapped at the inside of his skull, squeezing tightly to his organs. He turned from the mirror and opened the valves to the large shower. Grabbing his toothbrush from the glass beside the basin, he watched the man in front of him squeeze toothpaste onto his electric toothbrush.

I'm sorry. That had been the first thing he had said to her. He had cried then. It was painful to do so but the pain spewed out of him in a vomit of tears. He had been sorry; he had felt a deep shame. There were days after when he had wished he had been successful and then felt a deeper shame, scolding himself for thinking in such a way. He rinsed his mouth with water, spitting the white foam into the basin and stepping into the jet of tepid water, a blessing in the Sao Paulo heat. As the water cascaded around him, he allowed it to wash away the memories that his brain wouldn't allow him to forget.

Steven.

He wasn't sure why Steven mattered so much to him. In some ways, he mattered more than Cameron. Maybe if he had been able to save Steven, he would have been able to save Cameron. He had been told many times that he shouldn't blame himself for their deaths. He did it anyway. Foam splattered in huge drops around his feet, he watched them flow and spin rapidly before disappearing down the drain. He pressed his forearms against the shower wall, his head dipped, letting the water crash around him. He watched the floor until the white soapy water became clear. He shut off the valve and stepped out of the shower, wrapping the soft hotel dressing gown over his shoulders and tying it at the waist. He opened his toiletry case, a tanned leather bag, the size of a book, pulling out the deodorant strapped carefully to one side, his eyes strayed to the small tin case tucked neatly in one of the pockets. It was the tin that he kept his daily dose of pills. There were only a couple remaining, once again a reminder. He had stopped taking the antidepressants almost five years ago. He had wanted to feel again, the pills provided stability levelling out the peaks and troughs of his mood, but he missed the highs as much as he hated the lows. Sofia and the doctor had disagreed with his decision but supported him all the same, under the condition that he would be honest when he felt he could no longer reach an outstretched hand. He had agreed and five years later, he was still here. Still fighting. Still slipping every now and then but alive.

It's ok. I'm here, she had said as he had cried on the hospital bed, resting her cheek on his, holding his head in her arms and letting him turn his face into the nook of her shoulder. He had stayed that way, safe, his forehead rested against her clavicle until the tears ran dry. She was both wrong and right. It wasn't always ok, but she was always there. He had watched over her shoulder as she read article after article over the years, desperate to understand him better or maybe just to understand his mind. He would catch her watching his face intently, trying to read his eyes when he got frustrated. Each time he would smile softly, taking her small hands in his to let her know it was ok. They were approaching their tenth wedding anniversary; they'd had a second child and seen both children go to school. Life had continued and he was happy to be a part of it for now. He had held Alex a couple hours after he had awoken and the small delicate weight of him in his arms had brought more tears. He stroked his finger across the small curve of his nose and enjoyed the feeling of rolling his fingertips across his soft skull. He was bigger now, but it didn't stop Michael throwing his arms around him when he could and enjoying the feeling of being close to him.

It had been around the time he had stopped taking the medication that he had summoned the courage to seek out Sharon. It hadn't taken much to get her address, he had picked up the phone to Chris who knew the guy that had warned Cameron off her doorstep on the day that he left prison. She had been pleasantly surprised and pleased to speak to him but less keen to talk about Cameron. He had been cremated in a small ceremony at Richmond Cemetery with only his mum and siblings present. He had asked her about Cameron's life in the lead-up to his death. She became cold, her face sullen, her eyes darting up and down the street as if searching for an excuse to cut the conversation short. She had told him briefly about the day Cameron had come to her door after leaving prison. Michael had moved the conversation on before she became upset and shut the door in his face. They had parted, making false promises to keep in touch. He had pulled away from her flat and driven the Aston Martin to the cemetery. A small plaque had been placed in the grass, no bigger than a sheet of paper. Its grey stone glimmered under the droplets of light rain that fell around him, the gold lettering shimmering a brief message: *Cameron Andrew Milton.* The date was obscured by wet sodden leaves. He didn't need to remove them to know that Cameron hadn't reached thirty by the time he was discovered lifeless between two large rubbish containers, but he removed them anyway and stared vacantly at what was left of his boyhood friend. The tears came easily, he crouched over the small plaque and placed his palm on the cold stone. His fingers spread, covering the name that had haunted him for so long. Tears streaked down his cheeks, falling from his chin and got lost in the droplets of rain kissing the back of his hand. He gathered himself, standing again to full height, his eyes trained on the gold letters.

"Sorry mate, I didn't keep you from falling," he whispered softly, mostly to himself, but he wanted Cameron and Steven to hear. He turned and walked away.

Cameron, how did we end up here? he thought to himself as he shrugged on his suit jacket. He talked to Cameron often when he felt like he was slipping back into the hole. He looked at himself in the full-length mirror, his suit perfectly hugging his frame, the crease of his trousers a thin line running the length of his leg and his shoes black and flawless. He ran a hand over his hair, parted at the side, dishevelled in a purposeful way. His eyes sparkled like Mark's had done the first day that had met. He smiled at the thought of his old boss and now friend, enjoying his early retirement. He had left the door open for Michael to replace him and Michael had done so willingly. It felt good to be back where he belonged. He smiled, once again, at his reflection; opened the door to the hotel room and picked his briefcase up from the small table. He stepped out into the cool corridor and let the door shut behind him with a click.

I need help. He had whispered those words softly into her shoulder as she had held him on that hospital bed. Though it was painfully obvious, the simple utterance and acceptance of those words had been a turning point. It was the first time that he had accepted that he didn't have all the answers and that he didn't have to find them alone. It was the moment he decided to get better, and it was the first time he had been honest. It was the start of a journey that got him this far. He pressed the button for the elevator. A soft blue glow surrounded the down arrow. He flicked his wrist, exposing his watch and checked the time. 7:30. It was almost midday in London. He pulled his phone from his pocket. The screen lit up with three faces looking back at him. It had been autumn in London the day she had taken the picture, the brown and orange leaves lay scattered around the feet of his family. He thumbed his passcode into the phone and scrolled into his most recent call list. He hit Sofia's number as an overwhelming need to hear her voice rose from his stomach. His face broke into a soft content smile as her voice greeted him on the third ring. *Hello?*

Dear reader

You've got this far, and I hope to keep your attention only a moment longer. Thank you for reading, it is for you that I write, and it makes it worthwhile. If you enjoyed reading this, I would be grateful if you could visit Amazon or Goodreads and leave a review for the next reader. It really helps encourage others to take the plunge and is the life blood of our work as writers.

If you would like to contact me directly you can contact me via Twitter @danjameswriting or via email danjameswriting@gmail.com. It would be great to hear from you.

Finally, this book explores many issues that have impacted my life in one way or the other. Sometimes life is difficult. Please remember to reach out before you drown, you are not alone. There are people that understand, there are people there to help you.